Advance praise for Joanne Skerrett and *She Who Shops*

"A classic underdog story that will leave you rooting for
Weslee as she struggles to keep her head above water in
African-American society."
—Patrick Sanchez, author of *Girlfriends* and *The Way It Is*

"*She Who Shops* is a charming novel—I laughed, I cried, I
had an overwhelming urge to shop!"
—Kalyn Johnson, co-author of *The BAP Handbook: The
Official Guide to the Black American Princess*

"Joanne Skerrett has written an engaging novel about
New England's black upper-middle class and what happens to one young woman after she's drawn into their
world. Her story will inspire readers to follow their
dreams, as well as their hearts."
—Karen V. Siplin, author of *Such A Girl*

"*She Who Shops* is an entertaining story of friendship,
love, and romance. The characters are introspective and
well drawn and it is an interesting examining of the new
race relations and social class within the Black
Community."
—Nina Foxx, author of *Going Buck Wild*

She Who Shops

Joanne Skerrett

KENSINGTON BOOKS
www.kensingtonbooks.com

KENSINGTON BOOKS are published by

Kensington Publishing Corp.
850 Third Avenue
New York, NY 10022

ISBN 0-7582-0855-3

First Kensington Trade Paperback Printing: June 2005
10   9   8   7   6   5   4   3   2   1

Printed in the United States of America

For Theresa Skerrett,
who always had the shoes and bag to match.
Thanks, Mommy.

Acknowledgments

First and foremost: Praise God from whom all blessings flow. To my family, thanks for being there: Daddy, Desry & Spencer, Been & Mark, Herman & too many to mention, Jeff & whoever it is this minute, Lucy & Brian, Curtis & Ellen, little Spencer, Jasmine, Sam and Steve, Caron, Nichelle, and all the other folks in Dominica, Guadeloupe, Paris, and beyond.

Thanks to my friends and colleagues for their support. A million thanks to my editor, John Scognamiglio, whose astuteness saved me from all those abrupt endings. And my deep gratitude to the most efficient Frank Weimann.

Chapter

1

The plane hit the ground hard, and Weslee feared she would lose her Cheez-Its and pretzel snack mix, her only meal of the day.

The woman seated next to her was obviously shaken, but elected to appear as nonchalant as possible as the aircraft roared up the runway. The woman had used the satellite phone nonstop throughout the flight, talking to a daughter whom she would be meeting for dinner.

"Well, honey, what in the world do you want me to do?" she had said, agitation in her voice. "You chose to move to Boston. No one forced you!" The woman had even yelled at one point, causing other people to turn in her direction.

Now the elegant-looking woman did her best to look composed, smoothing out her white linen pantsuit as the plane taxied to the gate.

Weslee didn't fully calm down until the engine stopped.

She absolutely hated flying.

She looked at her watch as the seat belt light darkened. Two hours and eleven minutes from Chicago to Boston. She was glad she had parted with those frequent-flier miles to get the first-class upgrade. No waiting a half hour to de-plane while everyone in front of her wrested their luggage from the overhead bins. Plus, she had had the pleasure of listening to the well-dressed, perfectly made-up middle-aged woman talk to her daughter.

Weslee stepped gingerly from the plane onto the jetway leading to the terminal, careful to thank the pilot and the stewardesses.

Good job, but make it smoother next time, she wanted to tell the very young-looking pilot.

She adjusted her overnight bag on her shoulder. The movers were bringing the furniture and most of her clothes to her new apartment tonight, so thankfully there would be no waiting in baggage claim. She started to look for signs leading to a taxi stand.

Relief swept through her. She was finally on the ground and on the way to a new chapter in her life.

Strangers stole glances at Weslee Dunster as she walked through Terminal C at Logan International Airport. Maybe they had seen her before. Maybe. They were looking at the former power forward for the Northwestern women's basketball team, and that would explain those legs. Weslee never thought of that much these days—of herself as a star athlete . . . or as a leggy goddess, for that matter. After all, she did spend most of those three years on the bench. And goddess was something she associated with other, more glamorous people—not people like her, who wore Gap jeans and button-down shirts with tan loafers.

If she ever caught people looking at her, she always assumed that it was because of her height.

And maybe it was. At 5 feet 11 and 131 pounds, she cut quite a striking figure. And, in her opinion, for a tall, skinny black woman, that wasn't always necessarily all good. Her sister, Terry, who had the same willowy build but a better sense of humor, always said people either thought that Weslee was a crackhead or a supermodel the first time they looked at her.

Thanks to her parents, both string beans themselves, there was nothing she could eat too much of that would change her physique. And, her sister's comments notwithstanding, to most observers she appeared to belong more in the supermodel camp than with the emaciated junkies, thanks to the strong cheekbones and high, naturally sculpted eyebrows she had inherited from her West Indian–born father, Milton.

She was no great beauty, but she managed to turn heads. Maybe it was her natural athletic grace, those legs finely tuned from her passion for running. Who knew? She certainly didn't. If you asked Weslee, she'd say she wanted to be shorter, prettier, with a tiny nose and smaller feet.

She walked down the escalator, following the signs to Ground Transportation and ignoring the tempting aroma of Dunkin' Donuts coffee.

And people still looked. Why did she have that half smile on her face? men wondered.

Why did she walk, not strut, women thought, as they would if they had a body like hers?

The hum and drum of the harried passengers did nothing to pierce her daydreaming.

She skipped past the more immediate task of starting business school to picture herself two years from now: a fabulous job at one of the major investment banks, an even more fabulous apartment in New York City, or perhaps here in Boston, and hopefully a fabulous new husband. She'd even settle for a fabulous boyfriend. One nothing like Michael, thank you very much.

There were plenty of cabs waiting as she exited the terminal.

Weslee knew it would not all be a bed of roses. She had done her research. The economy stunk, and everyone at her firm had told her the last thing she needed right now was an MBA. Everybody had an MBA these days, and everybody was still getting laid off. Well, it wasn't just getting the MBA, she had argued in defense of her decision. It was the whole *getting* thing. Getting away. Getting something else than what she had now. Something better.

But, yes, Boston would be a challenge, no doubt about that.

Look at all this construction, she thought, surveying through the smudged taxi window the big wreck that the Big Dig had wrought on Boston's infrastructure. *This new highway was "almost done" the last time I was here five years ago, and it's still "almost done."* She shook her head.

Despite her months and months of detailed research, it still felt new to be in the city now. In typical Weslee fashion, during her last six months in Chicago she had read almost every book, article, and newspaper story that had to do with Boston, Boston University, and her new neighborhood. She was a planner, always prepared. So she took inventory as the cab made its way through the city, making sure that everything was where the books had said it would be.

It satisfied her somehow that it was seventy-three degrees, though it was August. That was what she had expected: unpredictable weather.

The skyscrapers leaned against the grayness of the late summer day. Some of the buildings looked as if they were decaying, as if the life or lives inside of them were just not enough to keep them standing. And the colors of orange and construction yellow were omnipresent and threateningly permanent: cones blocking off lanes and heavy-duty highway building equipment. And detour signs everywhere. It was as if all the old roads now led to new, unknown destinations.

The taxi crawled through the snaking afternoon traffic. The driver turned up the talk radio station even louder as the radio host poked fun at the female former Massachusetts governor. The cab driver laughed, and Weslee unconsciously tapped her cell phone in her pocketbook, like she often did when she was uneasy.

She tuned out the sound of female-bashing and nervous laughter from the cab driver. She started to go down her mental checklist again to make sure that everything was in place. Account balances: savings, money market, 401(k), IRAs, mutual funds—a grand total of $376,935.50. A year's tuition was already paid up. The only thing she would have to worry about was rent and other living expenses. She had budgeted everything down to the last penny. If she spent no more than $1,879.00 a month over the next two years, she would come out of this with barely a dent in her treasured savings. She smiled with satisfaction again. She had saved well over the years, thanks to her father, who had instilled the value of frugality in her since childhood.

The traffic barely moved. Two months ago, when she'd come here looking for a place to live, she'd been stuck in traffic on her way to and from the airport, too. And five years ago, when she had visited Harvard with Michael, they had been stuck in traffic as well. She remembered him almost losing his mind with worry about being late for his interview at Harvard Medical School.

That seemed so long ago now. When Michael was rejected from Harvard, he had "settled" for Northwestern. She had supported him through the disappointment but was secretly happy that he would stay in Chicago. She had never thought about Boston again until she decided to get away from Chicago—and Michael and his new live-in girlfriend.

Boston had won out over New York and Philadelphia. Actually, she couldn't afford to live in Manhattan—at least not the way she wanted to live in Manhattan—even with an NYU fellowship. And the Wharton School had laughed in her face. Or at least that's the way she liked to explain their rejection letter.

Those rejections had hurt her so much. They tore at her soul for weeks. She must have read each letter hundreds of times: "We're sorry . . ." "The competition was so . . ." All that, plus Michael's "It's just not working out right now."

It would be six months exactly in two weeks. One night Michael came home to their loft from work and said that he was moving out. His explanation was that he had to get his head together. He wanted to wait a few more years before settling down and getting married. At twenty-eight, he was just too young, he said. There was still so much of the world he wanted to see. That world turned out to be some internist at the hospital, a University of Chicago graduate, he had said, proudly. After five years with Weslee, he had found the perfect woman—not Weslee. She created the picture of Michael's new love in her mind: most likely petite, light caramel skin, probably long, naturally straight hair, and light brown eyes. *Maybe she did deserve Michael more than I did*, Weslee had told herself then.

Ugh. She frowned. *I'm not even going to think about this anymore.*

She reached for her cell phone to let her parents and sister know that she had made it to Boston in one piece.

"What did you say the address was?" The cabbie peered at her through the mirror again.

"Sixty-eight Commonwealth Avenue."

"Coming right up," the cabbie said as he turned onto Storrow Drive.

Weslee could see the university's buildings in the distance. She couldn't help but feel excited. She hadn't been on a college campus in seven years. And she had never been on an urban college campus. This would be nothing like Northwestern. No idyllic settings, picturesque ponds, tranquil surroundings, and, of course, no loud, stomach-churning basketball games—and no Michael.

They had met at Northwestern. They both loved basketball. He played on the men's team; she played on the women's. She thought it was so cute the way he would always let her win when they played together. She knew she could beat him fair and square. She was a better shot.

The year they had lived together in the Chicago Loop had been a dress rehearsal for what was surely to come, she had thought. Weslee had never once thought that she would not marry Michael, not even when she found herself constantly walking on eggshells when he came home in a bad mood every other night. She had even learned to ignore the way he made her feel as though her career as a fund analyst at the top mutual fund rating firm in the country was basically as good as being a check-out girl at a grocery store. Those things didn't become clear until the day he walked out of her life and she was really honest with herself about the lie she had been living.

But that was all in the past, she thought, as the taxi pulled to a stop in front of the five-story brick apartment building. She had risen out of that fog, and the road was clear in front of her now. She would finish her MBA, make new friends, visit Cape Cod and Martha's Vineyard, and go to Cheers.

Maybe I'll even run the Boston Marathon, she thought as she rifled through her wallet to pay the cabbie.

Chapter

2

Weslee tried to concentrate as the professor droned on about globalization. No matter what those protesters said, he was saying, it was what made the world the global village it was today. Multinationals employed people in impoverished countries, created roads and infrastructure in tiny countries most Americans had never heard of, blah, blah, blah.

She wondered if everyone else shared her boredom. She wondered if everyone else was thinking *Tell me something I don't already know*. No. Some guy had his hand up and was asking a question: Why is it that multinationals ignored the African continent?

Her mind kept wandering back to the previous night at the meet-and-greet.

Weslee surveyed the classroom filled with her fellow students. She shifted in her seat and tapped on the keyboard of her laptop. *Appear involved. Interested. Present.*

Last night she had shifted her weight often, too. From one painful foot to the other, cursing her new pumps as she smiled at her new classmates. They were all dressed casually. Her calves had ached from the long run that morning. Her head also hurt because she had forced herself to drink a glass of white wine when all she wanted was a diet soda. But everyone else had wine and seemed to be enjoying it. What was she to do?

The professor's answer to the Africa question was lame.

Last night had been OK. But she wondered about the impression she had made. What did people think of her?

She was one of three black faces, she had immediately noted upon walking into the faculty dining room. *Yup. Just the three of us.* There was a very attractive woman who was most probably biracial and seemed to be sucking up all the attention, and an older-looking man. Married, to judge by his ring. There were a few Chinese and Japanese and Indians among the group, but the two other black faces stood out— at least to Weslee.

The gathering was meant to give everyone a chance to network and get to know one another. She could tell that school was going to be competitive, but she had been warned. People seemed to have no problem asking her to recite her resume. So for the fifth time, here she was proving to some white guy that she belonged.

"Nice to meet you, Charles . . . uh, Chad," she said, shaking his hand firmly after he corrected her on his name. He seemed nice enough.

"So, are you fresh out of undergrad?" he asked, beginning the inquisition. She took it all good-naturedly. Everybody did it. She told him about her short and unspectacular journey from Northwestern to fund analyst at Research Associates Inc. Of course, she left out the Michael angle when he asked her why she had decided to leave such a good company to return to school.

She recited her "elevator pitch" to several more students and professors. She couldn't wait to meet the other black girl, but she seemed so busy chatting up a storm with everybody else. She seemed to already know some of the people. Weslee could hear her laughter all the way across the room.

She decided to go introduce herself to the lone black man in the room, who was off talking with an Indian guy she had already met. She racked her brain to remember his name. Too bad it was an Anglo name—that made it even harder to remember.

"Hi guys," she said, smiling at the two men.

"Hello again," the Indian guy said as she struggled to remember his name and not look at his name tag. She didn't want to give herself away.

"It's Weslee, right?" he said, peering at her nametag.

"Yes"—she smiled back at him and quickly looked at his tag—"Brian."

"We haven't met," she said to the black man. He looked to be either in his late thirties or early forties. He wasn't terribly good-looking, but he was tall and carried himself very formally. He was the only man in the room wearing a tie. The other guys wore polo shirts and khakis.

"No, we haven't," he said in a clipped, tight voice. "I'm Harrell Sanders." He extended his hand.

"Weslee Dunster," she replied. She asked the requisite where are you from and why are you here, and somewhere in the conversation, Brian, the Indian guy, slipped away to hobnob elsewhere.

Harrell was from upstate New York and worked at Prudential Securities in Boston. He was taking a couple of years off from work, he said. He told her that his wife was a kindergarten teacher and that they had two toddler-age children. Boring, boring, boring.

"Hey, I'm Lana," a high, perky voice said on her left. She turned, and there was the only other sister in the room, smiling at her.

"Hey," she said brightly. "I'm Weslee Dunster. I've been meaning to come over and introduce myself, but you seemed to be always talking to someone else."

Lana was a couple of inches shorter than Weslee, very pretty—in an unattainable, Vanessa Williams kind of way. That was a fierce little outfit she was wearing. Weslee was no fashion expert, but she recognized quality when she saw it, and she knew that this hadn't come out of TJ Maxx.

"Yes, girl, I've been getting my networking on," Lana said in a strange accent that struck Weslee as a hybrid of New England, Valley Girl, and Ebonics. Lana flashed a perfect white smile at Harrell Sanders and guided Weslee by the elbow in the other direction.

"Some of the people in here are so bullshit," Lana said conspiratorially as she waved across the room to some guy who was smiling her way.

"Have you met them before?" Weslee asked.

"No, I've never seen any of them before," Lana replied, her big grayish eyes casing the room.

"Oh, it just seemed that you—" But before Weslee could finish, a pair of women came up to them.

"Hey, you guys," one of them said. Weslee had met her. Her name was Kwan; she was Japanese via Encino, California. The other woman was a local, white and attractive. They seemed to want to stick to Lana like glue.

As they made plans to meet later, Weslee began to feel better, more excited, less intimidated. She could see herself hanging out with this Lana girl. In no time at all she had gone from almost being the wallflower to near-center of attention. Yes, it was going to be all right.

"Where are you from?" Weslee asked Lana, trying to get to the bottom of her accent.

"New York. Rye. And Martha's Vineyard."

Weslee laughed. "Your accent is so different."

"Oh, it's not really an accent. It's just the way I talk. I've been practicing for years." Lana smiled widely and then laughed wildly at the confused look on Weslee's face.

Weslee laughed, too. She thought she had gotten Lana's joke. It didn't matter. She thought she had made a friend. Sort of.

So, this morning before class, Weslee had worried. She had wanted to look good. She remembered the way Lana had sized her up the night before. She hadn't liked the appraising look in Lana's eyes. But Weslee, a traditionalist, had nothing but khakis, skirts, lots of navy and black—nothing cute. She had settled on a khaki linen dress and red sandals. Lana had swished into class wearing a knee-length white skirt, camel-colored stiletto sandals, and a tiny black tank top. Weslee had marveled as the male members of the class gawked or quickly looked away from Lana, maybe ashamed of what they were thinking. She so wished she could put clothes together that way.

Now Lana had her hand up. The professor beamed at her like one would at a precocious and adorable child.

Her comment was a very obvious rip-off of what the professor had just said. Yet he gushed, "That is a very interesting point!"

Someone groaned behind Weslee, but she didn't look back. It was strange how she immediately felt defensive of her new friend.

Lana's beautiful condominium in the Charles River Park building was perfect for entertaining: lots of space, sparsely but tastefully furnished, with a real bar. Weslee was impressed.

"How do you keep this thing stocked all the time?" she asked as she sipped ginger ale and Lana refilled a shot glass with something strong looking. Weslee had never been much of a drinker. Matter of fact, she never quite knew what to order when the wine list came or on the few occasions she had been out to bars with her co-workers back in Chicago. Ginger ale was her mainstay.

"Oh, my dad owns this place. His assistant takes care of all that stuff," Lana chirped.

"Oh" was all Weslee could say as she mentally did the math. So in addition to a house in the New York suburbs, on the Vineyard, and in Manhattan, Lana's father also owned this apartment. Must be nice, Weslee thought.

"Lana, I just love this place!" a girl giggled as she sipped one of the apple martinis that the bartender—one of Lana's friends, a handsome guy Weslee did not recognize—had been making over the past half hour.

Lana basked in all the praise and attention. She was the perfect hostess, flirting with the guys and complimenting the women on their hair, their dress, anything that did the trick. She listened to the women talk about their boyfriends or lack of, gave advice, told funny stories, and charmed them. She flitted around the room in her tight little black dress that showed off her perfect little body, balanced on impossibly high heels. "Jimmy Choos," she had told one of the girls who marveled at them.

It had been this way for a while. Lana had anointed herself social director by scheduling dinners, drinks, or baseball game outings every other day or so. Weslee went along to all of them admiringly, half-enviously. From her point of view, it was either go along or stay home alone. Boston seemed so unfriendly. Besides school, she had yet to meet another soul. The nights that she chose not to attend one of Lana's social outings, she studied or watched TV idly, distractedly, longing for Michael or just any form of companionship. It was a strange feeling, the loneliness. At least in Chicago she could have buried herself in work, staying late at the office writing reports weeks and weeks before they were due. Or she could have spent time with her parents or with Terry and her twin children, Weslee's niece and nephew. But Weslee had no one in Boston. No one to call to say "Let's go see a movie" or "Let's grab dinner." She was totally alone.

But here, among her classmates and Lana's friends, she felt as if she belonged somewhere—that she was not just a random person in a random city doing random things. At least she was part of a group. People knew her name, knew that she was the quiet introvert who had a quick wit once she loosened up and was the only "girl" in the class who could hang with the guys when it came to statistics. Yes, she was a part of them.

Lana was becoming louder and more effusive and flirtier with the quiet Kenyan who she had said was her date— nothing serious, she had explained to Weslee—with each sip she took out of her seemingly bottomless glass.

Weslee stood back in typical fashion and took it all in: the scene, the apartment. She loved the doors that led out to the terrace. She imagined that if she lived here she would sit out there at sunset and read every single night. She was about to make her way out there when she stopped herself.

No, she wouldn't play the wallflower tonight.

She walked off to join the group of female class members who were gathered around Lana.

She was telling them another story about her travels. Lana, it seemed, had been everywhere, from Cape Horn to Oslo. It made her even more interesting. The story of how she mistakenly brought a stash of pot into the United States from the Netherlands was eliciting howls of laughter.

" 'Oh my God,' I told the guy at the airport. 'I didn't know I still had that!' "

Weslee laughed with the other women, all of them under Lana's spell, Weslee the only one to notice it was being cast but falling under it anyway.

She stayed behind after everyone had left, thinking Lana needed help cleaning up. She insisted on helping although Lana protested that the maid would come in the morning.

"Weslee, where are you from again?" Lana asked after they had finished putting away glasses, half-empty bottles of champagne, strange-colored drinks, and such. "I mean where you're really from. Not Chicago."

"I was born in Barbados, but my parents emigrated here when I was six."

"Oh, I knew it," Lana exclaimed. "Your facial features are definitely West Indian. I love the Caribbean. I spent a month in Barbados right after I finished college. My father knows the prime minister well. They're such great people."

Weslee was impressed, but that was short lived.

"My mother used to have a Bajan maid in our house on the Vineyard. But she's in medical school now. Can you believe that? She's forty-five years old and studying to become a doctor. That's what I love about Caribbean immigrants. They're not afraid to work hard, and they're not ashamed that they had to start from the bottom."

Weslee almost opened her mouth to protest what she detected as a veiled insult, but she couldn't pinpoint exactly where the insult was in that statement.

"Anyway," Lana continued, "we need to hang out more. I think we should team up on the statistics project."

Weslee nodded, although she had already agreed to team up with two other people. "Maybe you can join Koji and Haraam and me on our team," she offered.

Lana made a face. "You know, it's really not a good idea to team up with people who are still struggling with English. When you do your oral presentations at the end of the term, they're going to make you look really bad."

Weslee was shocked at Lana's ignorance and petty snobbery. "Koji and Haraam are two of the smartest students in the class," she said, laughing so as not to offend Lana.

Lana shrugged. "You want a drink?"

"Actually I think I'm going to head home," Weslee said as the handsome Kenyan reappeared. She had thought he had left with the others.

Lana shrugged again. "Hey, thanks for staying to help. I owe you."

During the cab ride home, Weslee decided that she had to do better at making new friends. While Lana certainly was an interesting and sometimes entertaining person, her shallowness and underlying meanness unnerved Weslee. Everyone seemed to like her so much, but Weslee was not sure it was a friendship that she should pursue.

She thought back to her former best friend, Ann Marie. They had been neighbors, close since childhood, though they had gone to different schools. Ann Marie was never one for books, and she always did the barest minimum when it came to academics. Weslee, on the other hand, was always pushing or being pushed to excel or at least do better than most people in school, in sports, in Sunday school—it didn't matter. Ann Marie coasted through life, bringing her troubles about boys, clothes, make-up, and bullying girls in public school to smart, dependable Weslee—who spent a miserable twelve years of primary and secondary education in Chicago's best magnet schools.

It was no surprise then that Ann Marie had married at twenty-three to a professional football player. She now lived in a huge house in the Chicago suburbs with her four lovely children. She and Weslee had grown apart but managed to talk on the phone once a month or so. But as the years went by, they had less and less to say to each other, especially after the Michael breakup. It was as if that had dealt the final blow to their friendship, seemingly forever excluding Weslee from the happily married suburb-dwelling club.

Weslee missed Ann Marie. She missed her teammates from college, too. She wished she was the kind of person who made the effort to hold on to her friends. They always just seemed to slip from her life like water through her fingers. A part of her blamed Michael. He had been her life the last five years; she had no room for anyone else. Now she regretted giving him so much of herself. She hated feeling like the new kid in school who has to jump hurdles to feel accepted, get invited to parties, feel like one of the crowd.

I am too old for this, Weslee thought as the cab drew near her building.

If only she had given Michael just a bit less of herself.

Chapter
3

Boston was preoccupied with a horrendous car crash that had killed four teenage boys in an instant. The families were on all the news channels and in the newspapers saying that they were good boys, loved sports, had girlfriends. No one had the guts to ask the question that burned in the city's collective mind: Why, then, were these four good boys fleeing the police after a night of underage binge drinking at a party in one of the city's toniest suburbs?

Weslee missed having someone to discuss the news with. She and Michael would argue for hours about politics, sports, you name it. She held the more conservative opinion, while he was the left-wing radical—according to her, anyway. She now read the *Globe* while eating Raisin Bran at the kitchen counter as Bloomberg reporters barked loudly on the TV. It was a routine she had grown used to over the years—just not solo.

An hour later she stepped out into the warm Saturday afternoon air, heading to the Charles River for her jog. The city was overrun with college students—undergrad girls wearing flip-flops and tank tops with their skirts low on their hips, young men with baggy cargo shorts and skateboard shoes. Youth was everywhere.

The city's geography was confusing. Nothing line up or made sense. Her research and endless supply of maps were not a whole lot of help. Walking, therefore, was a time-consuming and sometimes precarious proposition. Hadn't these people ever heard of a city grid? The streets sometimes stopped at a turn and started again at another angle. Printed directions never panned out. Weslee had grown used to getting lost every time she ventured out.

Sometimes she felt as if she were in a foreign country when trying to absorb Boston's culture. She was learning not to say hello or smile at people in elevators, people she bumped into on the subway, not even the operator on the Green Line trolley. No one in Boston ever said hello just to say hello. Matter of fact, if you did they eyed you suspiciously, edging away slowly and grabbing on to their purses or briefcases—their very lives, it seemed.

Her apartment had ceased to be a mess of unpacked boxes and was beginning to look more like a home. Thanks to a Bed Bath & Beyond in the Fenway, she had robin's egg-blue drapes. She had decorated the bathroom in the same color. Her living space was finally habitable. She didn't dread coming home anymore after a day of classes to the dreary, messy, one-bedroom flat.

She missed her Honda Accord desperately. She tried to walk as much as she could instead of taking the subway, but she knew that once winter rolled around that would have to change.

She had already decided that the seventeen-mile running trail around the Charles River was her own private oasis in the crowded city. She managed to get all her thinking done while she ran the trail, even when it was crowded. The first time she ran the loop she decided she would start training for a fall marathon so she could qualify for the Boston Marathon the following April. Now she ran five days a week.

So things were going well, she decided this Saturday. She took long, slow, deliberate strides on the asphalt path, letting other joggers pass her. Business school was no breeze, but that was not a surprise. Most of the courses were as challenging as she had anticipated. She felt rejuvenated now: by the coursework, by the goal of qualifying for the marathon, by the need for sustainable human companionship. She wanted those things, and she decided she would get them even if it meant getting outside of herself a bit.

She nodded at a white-haired man she had seen almost every day during her early morning runs. He made her smile because she could just see herself at seventy years old, shuffling along a running trail every day.

"Great pacing," he said as he waddled past. She yelled out a thank-you and smiled. *OK, maybe the city is not entirely unfriendly.*

There were three messages on her voice mail when Weslee got back to her apartment: one from her mother, Clara, and two from Lana.

Weslee couldn't help but smile as she listened to the messages. Her mother wanted to know why she hadn't called all week. Lana, assuming rightly that she had nothing to do this Saturday night, was inviting her to yet another party. "This one's a little fancy, so you'll need to wear something nice," she said in her postscript message.

Something nice, Weslee thought. She had packed two black dresses, a set of pearls she had bought years ago for job interviews, and one nice pair of suede Stuart Weitzman shoes that had made her feel guilty weeks and weeks after she had purchased them.

Maybe it was best that she stay home, Weslee thought. She was beginning to tire of looking like the poor cousin at glamorous Lana's side when they went to restaurants, bars, or parties. It wasn't that Weslee was jealous; she was just uncomfortable with being in the spotlight. At first it had been different and a little fun, but now she was beginning to miss being in the background as she had happily been her whole life. In school she had been a good athlete but not great enough to get a lot of time on the court; she had had friends in high school, but she definitely did not run with the cool crowd. At work she had a couple of acquaintances who were all married; she never felt that she had much in common with the nightclub-crawling scenesters at the office who were around her age. She had thought them shallow and petty, and she felt that her solid relationship with Michael gave her an edge over them. She would feel a little superior when they would relate their horrible weekend-dating experiences to one another in the office on Mondays. She was so much better off, she had thought back then. After the breakup, it had become unbearable to stay there among them, single like them. She could almost feel them laughing at her, taunting and pitying her. Ms. "I'm Dating a Doctor and We're Going to Get Married" was just like them now: alone, approaching thirty, with no prospects. They had the edge, she knew now, because they knew how to navigate their way out there.

Spending time with Lana over the past few weeks was showing her that there was a whole other world that she had unwittingly become part of but that she was horribly unprepared for. It irked Weslee to have this twenty-seven-year-old tell her what kinds of clothes she should be buying, the type of restaurants she should eat in ("Oh, sweetie, I don't care how good the food is, you should never be seen at Cheesecake, or any other chain for that matter), that her nails should always be done ("Not long; that's so 'ghetto' "), and how to style her hair ("Highlights, highlights—you want to look a little exotic"). She had reluctantly signed the three-hundred-dollar credit slip at the salon, hating the haughty stylists who gave her the same appraising look that Lana had given her the day they met.

Weslee was having trouble with all of this. She didn't see anything wrong with the way she looked, and she hadn't the foggiest idea of how to transform herself into a fashionista. Since the only magazines she ever read were *Fortune* and *Newsweek*, she really wasn't even very familiar with the term.

"Weslee, you've never heard of Roberto Cavalli?" Lana had asked incredulously one day. "You're never going to get a date with that mass-market, department-store wardrobe, sweetie."

That had stung. Weslee defended herself. "Lana, why would I spend one hundred dollars on a tiny tank top? That's such a waste!" They had been standing in the middle of Neiman Marcus, Lana in tight Seven jeans, halter top, and her customary heels. Weslee in a Banana Republic khaki skirt, slides, and a pink T-shirt from Ann Taylor. They looked like the before and after in a *Glamour* magazine makeover section.

Though Weslee would never describe herself as cheap, she had always been sensible with her money. It was what had allowed her to quit her job worry-free and head off to business school for two years with only a minor dent in her total savings. She couldn't have done that if she was the type to spend most of her eighty-seven-thousand-dollar yearly salary on designer clothes and shoes. Such things had never even been a temptation; she went to the mall in Skokie only when she was really in need of something to wear, and that was not very often. Spending two hundred dollars at Ann Taylor was her idea of a splurge.

What Lana had tried to explain to Weslee was the wisdom behind dropping huge sums of money on designer clothes. "Trust me. Men care. They say they don't. But they do. And it's not just that; they make you feel better.

Great clothes will change your attitude. You'll feel better about yourself, trust me. You'll walk taller. The right shoes will make you forget all about that old boyfriend you're always depressed about."

Weslee wasn't convinced. But she had gritted her teeth and purchased the Cavalli tank top anyway.

Now she looked at the top in her roomy closet.

Something nice, Lana's message had said.

The Cavalli top, despite its price tag, could not be considered "nice."

Weslee grabbed her trusted black cocktail dress.

I'm trying, she told that voice in her head that was making her clench her teeth because she would have to shove her feet into these high-heeled shoes after an eleven-mile run and no doubt have to stand around and smile and chat with people whom she did not know. *I'm trying.*

The phone rang. Lana was on the other end, making sure that Weslee would be ready when she picked her up.

"Why me?" Weslee wanted to ask her. Why didn't she pick one of her more glamorous friends? But Weslee knew that Lana would just laugh off such a question. It was not for Weslee to understand. Lana just did whatever she wanted—like a child.

Lana seemed to totally live in and for the moment, shrugging everything off her slender shoulders as if nothing mattered except her needs—or rather her wants, for there was very little that she actually needed.

While Weslee guarded her money—cashed-out stock options and savings—with military discipline, Lana let loose with her cash . . . or her credit cards, to be more exact. Lunch, drinks, dinner—all on her. It seemed that she was either always shopping or going somewhere that required spending a lot of cash. Knowing that she didn't work, Weslee had gone on a sleuthing campaign to find out who was footing the bill for Lana's glamorous lifestyle.

She found out that Lana's family had owned one of the few black-owned banks in the country. They had sold out to a bigger bank and made a ton of money. Her father was now an executive at the biggest bank in New York and on the boards of several other Fortune 1000 companies.

That money had seen Lana through six years at Brown, three years of traveling all over the world, and now business school. Nothing took much effort for her. Looks—she had high-society light caramel skin, light eyes, and flowing hair, thanks to her biracial mother; education—she was no genius, but she had a respectable pedigree and enough cultural exposure to make up for her not getting into Wellesley or the big H. She had almost everything, it seemed. She was generous, eternally optimistic, and except for an occasional streak of meanness, a "nice person." This was how Weslee had described her new friend to her sister, Terry.

"Hmmm. She sounds interesting," was all Terry would say.

But as different as they were, Weslee saw the beginning of a friendship. They both had the same biting sense of humor, though Lana's was toothier. Weslee hoped that once they got to know each other better, Lana would turn things down a bit, stop trying so hard to dazzle her—at least that's what Weslee thought was going on. There was potential there, she thought.

Well, she did always have that gift for seeing the good in other people.

Chapter

4

"Bad girl," Weslee giggled as she looked at her striking image in the mirror. "Bad girl."

Her black dress was snug around her slim hips and modest B-cup breasts. Her high-heeled shoes made her long legs absolutely breathtaking. She smiled at her image. Maybe Lana was onto something with her "great clothes will make you feel better" philosophy.

She reapplied her reddest La Mer lipstick as she waited for Lana to pick her up.

The great thing about going out with Lana was that you were sure to arrive in style. Lana's red convertible Mercedes CLK always set the tone for the grand entrance she tried to make everywhere she went, and Weslee couldn't help but begin to feel a hint of importance, too, every time she stepped out of the passenger side.

When Lana arrived, Weslee took one look at her and immediately felt like kicking her shoes off and spending the night in front of the TV. Lana was wearing a tiny little white dress with the teeniest straps over her bony but attractive shoulders. She wore long, skinny earrings and a silver necklace with a diamond pendant to match, of course, as well as the requisite strappy sandals.

"Girl, you look gorgeous," Weslee said to her friend. "I feel like such a cow next to you."

"Uh-uh," Lana said, grabbing her hand. "You look like the girl that every guy wants to go home with and wake up with the next day. I'm just the girl they want to go home with and send packing two hours—in some cases, two minutes—later."

They both laughed and headed for the door.

Lana was not exactly wrong. Next to her, Weslee looked nice, very nice. But Lana was the one who would turn all the heads.

A woman like Weslee had the kind of beauty that took careful study to be fully appreciated. All her facial features were in the right place, yet she didn't possess a cute button nose or long, straight hair down to her back, light-colored eyes or any of those pretty-prerequisites. There was an inner strength and grace that combined with a hard-to-describe quality to her looks that made everything about her fit beautifully. So, for those out for a quick, head-snapping look, she wouldn't do the trick.

Minutes later they walked into the crowded art gallery, and Weslee immediately felt heady from the aroma of expensive perfume and cocktails that pervaded the air. Everybody looked great, the women as well as the men. Lana grabbed a table in the center of the room near the makeshift dance floor, where they were certain to be seen.

It was a fund-raising event for a new African art gallery in the city's South End neighborhood. The crowd was young and diverse, lots of Junior Leaguers and former debutantes mixed in with upwardly mobile professionals.

It seemed that Lana knew every other person there. Weslee stopped counting after the fourth or fifth handsome, nattily dressed young man stopped by their table to say hello, and although Weslee knew she wasn't the source of it, she was starting to enjoy all the attention they were attracting. Well, that Lana was attracting.

A tall, light-skinned guy strode over, and at first Weslee thought or hoped he was going to speak to her. Wrong.

Lana immediately got up.

"Hey, Jeffrey," she chirped, giving him a hug. "Let's go dance," she said, waving good-bye to Weslee.

For some reason, the jazz band had stopped playing standards and had begun to liven things up a bit with more modern covers.

Weslee sighed. She was on her own. She decided to walk around and observe this crowd of attractive, intelligent young people. She was having so much fun just looking. She'd never done the party scene. In school it was always studying, training for basketball, and Michael. The few parties she had gone to in college were in her senior year—with him. Before that, she never socialized much. Most weekends, she would take the train down to the South Side to spend time with her family, excluding herself from the social atmosphere of college.

Now, as Weslee observed the crowd of pulsating bodies on the dance floor and the lively conversations at the bar, she couldn't help but feel that she had missed out on a lot. *Maybe this breakup with Michael was meant to teach me some new things about life*, she thought.

But then she saw a couple sitting on one of the red leather couches underneath a wall-sized painting. They were oblivious to what was going on around them and seemed so in love. Weslee looked at the woman's finger and felt a pang of jealousy at the beautiful engagement ring that she wore. She forlornly made her way to the bar. Maybe she would have one of those cocktails that Lana seemed to love so much.

She tried to wiggle her way through the bodies that had massed at the bar. As she tried to work her way in, a voice said angrily behind her head, "Will you watch it?"

She spun around. "I'm sorry," she apologized to the knot of the angry stranger's tie. She looked up into the most amazingly beautiful set of golden-brown eyes she had ever seen. Boy, was she sorry. Those narrow, honey-colored eyes showed a mix of irritation and fury that made her recoil but yet drew her in to them.

"I'm sorry," she said again, more softly. "Did I spill your drink?"

"Just watch it," he sneered and walked away.

She shook her head and ordered a whiskey sour from the bartender. It was what Lana was drinking.

Then she felt a tap on her shoulder. It was Lana.

"So, who's that cutie you went off dancing with?" Weslee asked.

"Oh, that's just Jeffrey. He's this guy I've been trying to get with since my freshman year at Brown. He had this girl-friend up at Smith, and no matter what I did, he wasn't about to cheat on her. I even tried to spread rumors that she was a lesbian."

"Lana, you didn't!" Weslee wasn't faking the shock.

"She *was* a lesbian; I know it for a fact. That's why they broke up three years later," she said.

Again, Weslee wasn't sure if she should believe Lana. She had the tendency to embellish the truth or just twist it to suit her own purposes.

"So, did you make any progress?"

"Nah, I think he thinks that I'm evil and materialistic or something."

Weslee laughed. "He's wrong, of course."

"Of course," Lana said, tossing her long hair back, and they both laughed.

Weslee wondered at how Lana dealt with such things in a totally offhand way, as if it didn't matter to her one bit what other people thought of her. Why did Lana make it look as if being bad was so much fun?

Weslee continued to survey the room as Lana chattered on and on about Jeffrey. Weslee spotted Mr. Honey-colored

Eyes across the room. He was talking with a tall, exotic-looking woman who looked like a runway model. Her hair was jet black and pulled back tightly into a fierce ponytail, and she wore a slim-fitting black pantsuit. If she weren't so beautiful, she'd look like a librarian. *Humph*, Weslee thought. *Morticia and Count Dracula. There's a perfect match if I've ever seen one.* At that moment, he suddenly looked at her. Their eyes met and she quickly looked away. A minute later she could see that he was walking toward her and Lana. She panicked. She wanted to run, but why, and to where?

"I'm going to go find the ladies' room, Lana," she blurted, but it was too late.

"Hey, Lana," he said in a deep, slightly hoarse voice as he looked at Lana.

"Duncan, what are you doing here?" Lana asked, her light mood suddenly changing.

"What are *you* doing here, Lana?" he asked, looking down at her like a concerned father. He must have been at least six feet five.

"I'm here with my friend, Wes—"

"I can see that you're here with your friend, but I thought you were going to take it easy on the parties and concentrate more on school," he said, the whole time ignoring Weslee, who was just happy he wasn't there to remind her that she had almost spilled his drink.

"Why don't you mind your own business? Aren't there some hoochies in here you should be trying to get with?" Lana snapped.

"Watch your mouth. Remember I've got your dad on speed dial," he said. He turned to look at Weslee and started to walk away.

"Get a life," Lana muttered.

"What!" he said, narrowing his eyes, which flashed again the way they had in the no-doubt ill-fated drink encounter.

"Nothing."

"That's what I thought," he said and stalked off.

"Who was that?" Weslee asked.

"My cousin, Duncan. Thinks he's my father," Lana replied, annoyed.

Weslee decided not to tell her about the drink incident.

"Sorry I didn't properly introduce you, but he likes to get in my business. It drives me crazy," she said.

"That's OK," Weslee replied. "Seems like he's just looking out for you."

"Do I look like I need looking after?"

Weslee didn't dare give her honest opinion.

Just then she felt someone nudge her elbow. She turned to her left, and there stood another tall, dark, and handsome man. *What is with this party?* she thought. *And women say there are no men out there!*

"Wanna dance?" he asked.

OK, she thought. *He's not very smooth*. But she did want to dance. The band was doing its best adaptation of James Brown's "Get Up." Not her favorite song, but a lot of people seemed to be dancing, even the uptight debs in their tightly pulled-back white-blond updos. "Sure," she said, letting him lead her to the dance floor.

He was a decent dancer. Yet you could tell he didn't spend all his Saturday nights in the clubs. *He isn't going to be in anybody's rap video*, Weslee thought, *but at least he has rhythm. Kinda like me.*

"Can I buy you a drink?" he asked when the song was over.

She almost said yes, but then remembered that she had already had two and that her low tolerance for alcohol could not endure another. "No thanks, I think I've had enough to drink tonight. You're a great dancer, though," she smiled.

"Thanks, so are you," he said, extending his hand. "I'm William."

"Weslee."

"That's a beautiful name," he said.

Cute but unoriginal, she thought.

"Are you Jamaican?" She could tell that he was by the tiny hint of accent in his voice, but she asked anyway.

"Yes, man." They both laughed at his attempt at an exaggerated lilt.

Just then Lana walked up to them.

"William," she cooed. "I see you've met my friend."

Did Lana know every single person in the city of Boston?

"Hey, Lana, isn't it past your bedtime?" he said to her, smiling and revealing the most perfect white teeth Weslee had ever seen.

Lana rolled her eyes. "Where's the after-party?" she asked.

"My after-party days ended years ago," William said, scoring big points with Weslee. "Besides, I have to work tomorrow," he added.

"On a Sunday?" Weslee asked, glad to get back into the conversation.

"Yes, young entrepreneurs don't get weekends off," he said.

"Oh, what kind of business are you in?" Weslee asked, suddenly interested. Starting her own business had always been a dream of hers. Perhaps this man could give her some advice, she thought.

"I'm an architect. I have two partners, but we're all equal owners," William answered.

"Wow, that's impressive," Weslee said, unaware that she was gushing. "I've always wanted to start a business. How did you do it?"

Lana, suddenly bored that the conversation did not revolve around her, sighed. "I'll leave you two alone," she said and walked away, no doubt to some other handsome young gullible bachelor.

"Well, it took a lot of work and sacrifice," William said, smiling.

"No, I mean, how did you do it," she said, and they both laughed.

"OK, we had the idea, we wrote up a plan, got a few investors, went to a lot of shindigs, including some like this, to meet people who could be clients or who could find us clients. Piece of cake," William said.

"Of course," she replied.

"So, what kind of work are you in?" he asked her.

"I'm a student. I left the work world and all its hassles a few months ago."

"Oh, you and Lana are at BU?"

"Yup."

"Well, I'm glad she's got someone who seems to have their head straight to look after her."

"Why is it that everyone treats her as if she's some problem child?" Weslee asked William.

"Let's just say that she is and leave it at that," he said.

"OK," she said, thinking that it was best not to push it, but at some point she'd have to try and find out just what it was that Lana had done to inspire so little trust from the people who knew her. Weslee wanted to see her new friend only as a fun-loving free spirit with a few minor flaws.

They went back to the dance floor again and stayed there for what seemed like forever. Their attempts at conversation meant shouting at each other above the music, and a couple of times he leaned in close to hear what she was saying. She almost fell over when the scent of his cologne hit her. She was too shy to ask what it was. But whatever it was, it was doing its thing with her. She just loved the fact that he was from the Islands, too. That was at least one thing they had in common—that and the fact that he had also been a miler in high school. Oh, and that royal blue was his favorite color, too. She had complimented him on his shirt.

Weslee looked at her watch.

"Wow, am I that bad?" he said, affecting a look of dismay at her gesture.

"Oh, no!" Weslee was horrified. "I really wanted to know what time it was. I'm not typically up this late unless I'm studying."

"Me, neither." He smiled that sun-splitting smile of his again.

"Listen, it was really nice to meet you," she said. "I'm going to find Lana. She's my ride home."

He stopped dancing and looked at Weslee as if to say, You have got to be kidding me. He took her by the elbow and led her off the dance floor, away from the music.

"Number one, you'd have to be crazy to let Lana drive you home the way she's been putting away those whiskey sours all night. And number two, Lana left ten minutes ago with Jeffrey Knight," William said.

Weslee looked around the room anyway, hoping that he was wrong. She looked back at him, and she thought that his eyes were laughing at her apparent panic.

"No!" she said. "How am I going to get home?" She scanned the room frantically again.

She had been so attentive to William that she hadn't noticed the party was winding down and that people were beginning to leave. Lana was nowhere to be found.

He laughed. "I would offer you a ride, but I know you'll refuse, so I'm going to call you a cab, OK?" He took his cell phone out of his inner jacket pocket.

He was calling the number before she could say anything to him. He requested the taxi and ended the call, returning the cell phone to his jacket.

"How did you know I'd say no to your giving me a ride home?" she asked, getting a strange but good feeling about him.

"Instinct," he said. "Men have intuition, too, you know. I

also know you're not going to give me your phone number because you think it's tacky, so here's my card."

She laughed and took his card and put it in her purse. "It's not just intuition, William. I think you're psychic."

It was his turn to laugh at her. "We'd better go get you in that cab," he said.

As they pressed their way out of the restaurant, she felt his arm brush against hers, and her heart flip-flopped.

Come on, girl! she scolded herself in her head. *This guy's probably the biggest player on the planet. After all, he knows Lana.*

When they finally made it out into the cool, clean night air, she felt her head and her senses clear up a bit. No more swooning over hard-bodied entrepreneurs, she told herself.

She turned to face him. And it happened again. Her heart flip-flopped. She wondered if he could tell. He looked deep into her eyes like he could tell exactly what was going on in her mind right now.

"Well, thanks again, William." Should she shake his hand? Hug him? A peck on the cheek? *Whoa, down girl.*

"My pleasure," he said.

Then he turned and walked away. She got in the cab and tried not to stare after him.

What had just happened? She didn't know when he turned from merely interesting to I-want-you-to-take-me-home. Must be that last-call thing she'd heard people talk about. Everybody looks good when the party's about to be over. And he looked darned good, she thought.

Chapter
5

The next day, Sunday, Weslee tried to concentrate in church. She didn't even know why she went. She felt guilty the minute she walked in. People had their hands up, praising God. She felt like such a hypocrite; she knew where she had been the night before and the kind of thoughts that had gone through her head before she finally nodded off to sleep at three A.M.

But here she was at New Covenant Church, singing . . . though not too enthusiastically. When the pastor finally took the pulpit to give the sermon, she was relieved. *Now we can all sit*, she thought. And at least she wouldn't be the only person in her row not lifting her hands and shouting God's praises.

That relief was short lived. The title of the sermon was "Playing Church." A term she had heard her mother use all the time to describe other members of their Pentecostal church back home. Weslee never thought that term could be used to describe her, but she was seeing herself in the preacher's words.

True, she was very busy and came to church only out of obligation. And yes, it made her feel good. Yes, she did use to lord it over other people in her office that she went to church every Sunday. But the pastor was saying that that was worse than not coming at all. She was fooling herself. Going to church was not going to change the fact that she wasn't fully committed to living a Christian life. It certainly didn't change the fact that she was out drinking the night before. And having less-than-clean thoughts about a man she had just met.

She reminded herself that at least she could tell her mother when they had their usual Sunday afternoon chat that she had gone to church.

Her mother was ecstatic at the fact that her girl had found the right place to be on a Sunday morning. "That's so good to hear. I was waiting to hear from you. I wanted to tell you about Pastor Hank's sermon today."

Weslee listened dutifully. Pastor Hank's sermons had always put her to sleep. He was nothing like the man she had heard that morning. But she would never dare disparage the man her mother had revered for the last twenty or so years.

Clara Dunster had raised her two daughters in church, Trinity Pentecostal Church, three times a week, come rain, snow, or sunshine. They had had their wild years in between, but as the Bible said, "Train up a child in the way he should go, and when he is old he will not depart from it."

And it had worked. Terry had married a boy from the church, and they were happy and prospering and multiplying in Country Club Hills. Things hadn't gone so well for Weslee, but she was still young. And Clara Dunster knew that her youngest daughter was a good girl, with solid values. The right Christian man would come along.

When Weslee got off the phone with her mother, she felt complete, happy, loved.

She missed Chicago, she realized. Not just the city itself, but what it represented: home, comfort, familiarity. The excitement of embarking on a new adventure, going to a new place where she was unknown, had been a challenge she had thought long and hard about. She knew she had needed to do it. But now she longed for the predictability of home.

That evening she sat in her apartment waiting for Lana to come over. They had planned to quiz each other for the Operations Management exam the following day. It had been Lana's idea.

"That's so undergrad!" Weslee had protested.

"Come on," Lana had said. "You're no fun." So Weslee had relented.

As she had promised Lana, Weslee cooked up a storm. Maybe it was the whole church guilt thing or the missing home, but she attacked her kitchen like a fiend. She made oven-fried chicken, potato salad—with low-fat mayo, of course—corn, rice and beans, and a salad. When she finally finished, she looked at all the food and decided that what-ever was left over she'd take to the homeless shelter on Harrison Avenue.

Lana was running late as usual. Weslee decided to begin going through the pages and pages of notes she had taken over the past few weeks. She was prepared for the test. She had a feeling that Lana wasn't and that that was the reason she wanted Weslee's help. But Weslee didn't mind.

An hour later, Lana arrived. She held up a bottle of champagne as Weslee let her in.

"Are we celebrating something?" Weslee asked.

"Oh, yes, we are," Lana said, brimming with that strange brand of happiness that she always brimmed with. "Two words: last night."

"Oh, that Jeffrey guy must have been something," Weslee said.

"He was a monster."

"What!" Weslee said, alarmed.

"No, in a good way," Lana said with a sly look on her face.

"Ohhhh," Weslee said. "It takes me a while to catch on." Then she really caught on. "You did the do with him?"

"The do, and a whole lot of other things," Lana said with no embarrassment at all.

Weslee felt herself blushing. "But I thought you said he thought you were evil."

"Apparently, that's not a huge problem for him. And speaking of huge . . ."

"OK, I get the picture," Weslee said, holding up her hand. She wasn't sure how much detail she wanted about Lana's encounter. "So, are you going to see him again?"

"I'm sure I will." Lana shrugged. "Where's your champagne-opener thingy?"

"Did you make a date?" Weslee asked her.

Lana looked at her, puzzled. "Oh, hon, I'm sure I'll run into him at something somewhere."

"Oh," Weslee said, sensing the condescension in Lana's voice. *What do I know*, she thought as she walked off to the kitchen to get the opener.

"So, you know this William guy well?" Weslee asked as she sipped her champagne slowly. She really wanted to have only one glass. Alcohol made her sleepy, and there was a lot of work to cover before bedtime.

"Well," said Lana, "he's one of Duncan's friends. Not real friends, but business associates. You know, my cousin Duncan, the one who was giving me a hard time last night?"

"Yeah," Weslee said, cringing. She hoped he had forgotten about their unfortunate meeting.

"So, did you hook up with him?" Lana asked.

"No, we talked. He's kinda nice."

"Hmmm," said Lana.

"Hmmm what?" Weslee asked. "Is he married, does he have a girlfriend, a baby mama?"

"A what?" Lana asked in her most Valley-girl voice. She did that sometimes. Weslee would finally feel at ease enough with her to resurrect some "sister-girl" slang and Lana would pretend as if she had no idea what Weslee was talking about.

At first Weslee was embarrassed when Lana would attempt to school her in how to be proper. After all, her family was not wealthy, but her parents made a good living and gave her and her sister a good life, so it wasn't that she was some kid straight from the projects. But despite the resentment she felt, she had been learning to ignore Lana's occasional class issues.

"Anyway," Lana said, dragging out the word and giving Weslee one of her really-we-don't-talk-like-that looks, "he's a total workaholic. My father and my uncle helped him start his business. Duncan was his company's attorney, I think, pro bono because they went to school together. I've never seen him with anyone. You two would make a good match; he's from Jamaica, too."

"Actually, my family is from Barbados, almost a whole world away from Jamaica. But you already know that, Lana."

"Gee. Stop being so touchy. I just meant that you both have island backgrounds."

"I wasn't being touchy." Weslee wasn't truly offended. She was beginning to see how Lana, for no apparent reason, tried to hurt other people with her words. It was almost like a test to push you to see how much you could take before you turned your back on her. Weslee was beginning to feel sorry for her.

"OK, let's get started," Weslee said, hoping to move on to another subject—the exam.

"Let me finish this champagne," Lana said. Weslee noticed that the bottle was almost empty and that Lana was draining her glass.

"Did you drink all that?"

"Can't let good champagne go to waste. That's what my mom always says," Lana giggled.

Weslee shook her head. She hoped they'd be able to get some work done. She had noticed that Lana had been falling behind in some of her classes. Word was going around the cohort that her Financial Management team members were going to complain about her lack of preparation for meetings and presentations. Weslee had warned her. But it had fallen on deaf ears. "Screw them." Lana had shrugged. "I'll catch up. Besides, it's only one class. My grades are great in the other four."

Lana switched on the television, and Weslee looked at her incredulously.

"Ooooh. I love *E!*" she said, turning up the volume.

"Lana, I thought we were going to study," Weslee said to her.

"In a few minutes," Lana said, not looking at her. "Relax. Why don't you get started?"

She didn't have to say it twice. Weslee took her books off to the bedroom and shut the door so she wouldn't have to hear the blaring television. The words on the pages stared back at her as she tried to concentrate. What was up with Lana? Was she just a scatterbrained, spoiled, selfish BAP, or was there more to it? *She's like the bad boyfriend you know you should kick to the curb but you keep hanging onto, hoping he'll change,* Weslee thought. Then she laughed. *Yup, that was it. At least we always have a good time when we go out,* she rationalized. *And who else is going to introduce me to fine, smart brothers and take me to parties like the one last night?* She could think of no one else who had Lana's connections, who got Lana's invites, who turned everyone's head when she entered a room.

So what does she want with someone like me? Weslee wondered of Lana, who was still preoccupied with celebrity worship in the next room. Lana was nothing like Weslee's old friends, mostly tomboys and average girls like her. Girls like Lana inhabited a rarefied world that Weslee had never even aspired to. In high school and in college she'd always been either annoyed by or slightly envious of those girls. They were always going out on dates, to parties, on shopping sprees, and always seemed to maintain some hulking football player on relationship retainer. Surely they had no idea what it was like to be so constantly seized with terror—about grades, parents' expectations, and reputations—that clothes and a social life were distant, distant afterthoughts. They were not uptight. *Uptight, like me*, she thought. Weslee wanted that now—to not care, to just have fun and to say to hell with it. Screw it. All her life she'd done everything right, been a good girl, and where had it gotten her? Jilted by Michael and still unsure of what shape her future would morph into. And here was Lana, who had broken all the rules, or at least most of them, and she was as happy and carefree as a three-year-old in a sandbox. So what if she was a bit annoying? You had to be when you lived life on your own terms. *It's the uptight people like me*, Weslee grimaced, *who are always worried about hurting other people's feelings, all the while sacrificing our own.*

But you can't deny who you are, scolded a voice deep inside as her eyes dutifully tried to make sense of the lines of text in front of her. *Can't screw up business school. Don't have the luxury to. No rich daddy's gonna bail you out.*

Fifteen minutes later she peeked out through the door and saw her worst fears realized. Lana was passed out on the couch with the TV on at full volume and the empty champagne bottle lying sideways on the table.

Weslee walked over and turned off the TV and went back to her room.

She drank the whole thing? Weslee shook her head in amazement, feeling a bit frightened by Lana's irresponsibility. It was one thing to slack off on studying, but to pass out on someone else's couch after downing a whole bottle of champagne . . . And on a Sunday!

She pushed away the thought that immediately entered her head—that she should end this friendship now. This woman, while she could be fun, was toxic in some ways. *I could never, ever . . .* What must her parents think of her? Weslee peered at the sleeping Lana again, her hair all over her face, her mouth slightly open. *What a waste*, she thought. *If I looked like her . . .* She turned away guiltily, fearing that she was invading Lana's privacy.

The girl had been given every opportunity in life and had treated her good fortune as something to be taken for granted.

Weslee picked up her book and lay back on her pillows. It was as if Lana valued nothing. Not the expensive clothes she wore once and never wore again, not the money her parents spent on her education and her careless lifestyle, not her God-given beauty, which she squandered on undeserving men. She valued nothing, but she got everything anyway.

She sighed and got up again. *There has to be more to her than that*, Weslee thought. *Maybe her folks are jerks. Maybe she's one of those sad little Mommie-Dearest rich girls, acting out in a misguided attempt to be loved.* She grabbed a blanket and stood over Lana thoughtfully. *Everybody deserves some kindness, right?* She covered Lana with the yards of blue flannel. *Right.*

Chapter
6

The ride down to the Woods Hole terminal inspired a new sense of resolve in Weslee. If Boston, with its icy populace and antiquated infrastructure, could be so beautiful around its edges, then maybe there was hope. For everything. She'd heard vague things about the South Shore, the Cape, and the Islands, but she'd never ventured out this far. So she only half-listened to Lana prattle on about this or that while she kept her eyes out the passenger window. Shortly before they reached Hanover, the salt in the air began to come through the vents of Lana's Mercedes. Weslee inhaled it deeply. The reedy authority of the marshes along the highway fascinated her. The color of the soil—a raw and distressed brown—was not what she was used to seeing in Chicago. And the closer they got to Cape Cod, the sandier the soil and the saltier the air.

"I can't believe you've never been down here before!" Lana said more than once. "My parents know people from the Midwest—Michigan—who come up here every year."

Weslee hadn't bothered answering. She drank in all the sights: sand, salt water, spindly vegetation. Not even Lana could spoil this for her.

Though she hadn't wanted to be here, she was glad she'd

come. She'd been trying to pull away from Lana, immersing herself in the cultures of the less flashy international students, whose only focus seemed to be Harvard Business School case studies, Blockbuster DVDs, and ethnic restaurants, which had suited her just fine the last couple of weeks. It was a change of pace she could comfortably keep up with.

It had become too exhausting and scarily expensive, this Lana lifestyle. She thought back to the weekend before, which had confirmed for her why she wanted to go back to her old boring self.

They'd been sitting outside a restaurant on Newbury Street, and as Lana people-watched—and, like a golf-tournament announcer, provided commentary on the parade of fashionistas that Saturday afternoon—Weslee had a tiny epiphany. *What am I doing here?* she'd demanded of herself. She'd been freezing in the midfifties weather, her new D&G jeans bit into her inner thigh, and those pointy Robert Clergerie sandals that Lana'd told her she "just had to get" were pinching her little toe as her feet trembled on the skinny heels.

"This is supposed to be fun?" Weslee had asked again.

"Oh, relax. Just enjoy the scenery," Lana had snapped back.

Weslee had sipped her lemonade as if to swallow the retort that was rising, not wanting an argument. She was silently, resentfully counting the money she had just spent on their all-day shopping extravaganza, and the beginnings of a headache slowly climbed from the base of her skull as she tallied the damage. The five hundred dollar leather jacket had been on sale—and Lana had turned up her nose at it for that reason. The seven hundred dollar Christian Dior boots had been on sale, too. Those had received Lana's seal of approval— "Those are sweet"—though Weslee had thought them showy and a bit too black patent leather. The only thing she'd truly loved was a three hundred fifty dollar cashmere sweater from TSE. It was royal blue and the most beautiful thing she'd ever owned. But she'd felt miserable about everything else in those stacks of bags that were piled into Lana's trunk. *My retirement money*, she'd lamented when she saw all those bags. But once she started to compare what she had bought with Lana's purchases, she began to feel better.

"Three thousand three hundred twenty-seven dollars and thirty-eight cents," the stunning saleswoman at Saks had said, her perfectly lined, wine-colored lips forming each word beautifully.

Weslee had gasped, thinking she'd heard wrong. Lana, without missing a beat, handed over her Platinum Amex.

"It's just money," she'd shrugged as they walked out of the store.

It occurred to Weslee then that she needed to run away from Lana as far and as fast as possible. Three thousand dollars was not *just money*. It was almost half a year's salary for some people. *My goodness*, Weslee had thought. *Who is this woman, and what is she doing in my life?* She immediately devised a plan to extricate herself from the situation.

"Hey, so what are we doing tonight?" Lana had asked, still scene-beholding the busy stretch teeming with tourists, townies, and Boston's conservatively fashionable set.

"I'm kinda tired. I think I've done enough today." She didn't feel physically weary. What she felt was a materialism mental overload. She needed to decompress. Maybe, Weslee had thought, she could regain her sense of responsibility and perform some fiscal penance by living in a convent, wearing sackcloth and ashes, and consuming nothing but saltines and tap water for about a month.

"Come on! It's Saturday. You can't just stay home."

Weslee had sighed. Yes, it was Saturday. And, of course, she could just stay home.

"Are you just the most boring person in the world? Or is something wrong?" Lana had asked in that seemingly offhand, smiling way of hers that was like a bee sting laced with honey.

Weslee had winced but found herself apologizing. "Lana, I'm really sorry that I can't come out tonight. But I'm just so tired. It's been a long day."

I'll never speak to her again, Weslee had vowed as she saw the red Mercedes speeding off that Saturday night. It was too much. The unpredictable moods, the constant cattiness about who was wearing what or whose shoes were cheap, the constant feeling that she, Weslee, would never meet Lana's fashion specs, and that she never knew what to expect from Lana on any given day. It was exciting, yes, but burdensome. And totally unnecessary. There were other girls out there who would make better friends. *I just have to get off my lazy butt and go find them.*

But Lana wouldn't let go that easily. Once she noticed Weslee's coolness, Lana did all she could to get back in Weslee's good graces. She brought Weslee coffee in class, called incessantly, even complimented her on a pair of shoes she'd picked out herself, and finally apologized for falling asleep on her couch. Before Weslee knew it, Lana was almost begging her to go out shopping again. The gesture was touching, Weslee thought. *This friendship is worth something to her.*

At last Weslee had decided to loosen up and give Lana another chance. She allowed herself to attend another and yet another of Lana's must-be-seen-at events: a party—hosted by the Hennessy-drinking, Hummer-driving, First Friday set, who reveled in their buppiedom with grand style—that was a fund-raiser for the Boston Public Library, which on its own was worth a million snores. But the event made her realize that Lana was as known among elderly, old-moneyed people as she was among the young up-and-comers. "Lovey" is what the white-haired society ladies called Lana as they beamingly embraced her and eyed Weslee skeptically. Lana's Junior League and Jack and Jill–type friends had said polite hellos before dismissing Weslee with disinterest. But Lana had laughed at them as she and Weslee left the fancy event that night. "What a bunch of brownnosing, up-tight idiots!" she'd hooted. Weslee had thought, relieved, *Okay, so Lana's not totally blind to the real world.* So she'd laughed along with Lana. It took away some of the sting from feeling so out of place the entire night.

This was part of the reason Weslee was doing the Vine-yard trip. She was beginning to feel something of a bond developing. It was her and Lana against all the brownnos-ing, uptight idiots of the upper class. Also, it would reveal even more about Lana, since her family was hosting the party. Of course, Weslee had never been on Martha's Vineyard be-fore, and she was more than a little curious—even though it was almost fall and the air was a little nippy. She wanted to see what all the fascination was about. She kept waiting for the color and class-lines drama from Dorothy West's books to start playing out in front of her eyes.

She didn't have to wait long.

As soon as they drove up to the parking lot at Woods Hole in Falmouth, Lana began to spot people she knew: the ticket seller, the parking lot attendant, and other passengers buying tickets to get over to the island. Lana introduced Weslee quickly—when she remembered—and apologized afterward when she didn't.

There were very few tourists on the ferry. Lana had pointed this out—triumphantly, in fact—and Weslee was starting to get it. Apparently, the people who had owned homes there for generations and generations, or even just a few years, made that fact known in the tried-and-true New England way of ignoring those who did not. Weslee was shocked and more than a little embarrassed when a young black woman boarding ahead of her had not even smiled back in response to Weslee's "How are you?"

She raised the point with Lana, who told her that it was all her imagination. Yet there was Lana chatting happily along with some other long-haired, near-white debutante and artfully ignoring her. *My imagination, all right*, Weslee sighed. She knew better than to try to join their conversation; the introduction had been frosty enough. She looked around at the ferry passengers; everyone knew everyone, it seemed, except for her. *Out of place again. I could get used to this, or I could try to play this game*, Weslee thought. *Smile a bit, glad-hand and ingratiate myself into this world, maybe.* She looked over the edge of the ferry. Jumping into the water seemed like a much better idea. She laughed to herself. *Nah. I'll stick with this outcast thing for a while. See how it plays out.* She smiled at the bobbing waves. *See, I'm making friends already!*

The pert, perky girl to whom Lana was talking also belonged to the sisterhood of the shallow and phony, or so Weslee gleaned from the conversation. The girl was brandishing a massive engagement ring in Lana's enthralled face.

"Yes, well, I just couldn't turn him down again," the girl was saying breathlessly, the ring gleaming in the sun. "Mummy would have just killed me. You know how she is. Finish having the babies by thirty, that way you can still lose the weight." She said this and erupted in a weird cackle of laughter that made heads turn. Lana joined in with her own maniacal laugh. "And of course you know I'm going to have to quit working. He just won't have any wife of his working."

Weslee turned away, marveling at the sitcom quality of this exchange, and looked at the ocean. It was such a beautiful late-summer day, just a few see-through clouds accessorizing the sky. The water looked peaceful and inviting, though she knew it must be at least twice as cold as the briny air. The last time she was out on a boat had been with Michael on Lake Michigan. The memory elicited a pang of victorious surprise. She hadn't thought about him in weeks, she realized. Her life was now full, bursting at the designer seams almost. School took up most of her time, and Lana took care of the rest. She was transforming, caterpillarlike, from a dowdy, grieving dumpee into a social butterfly. She had to admit that as annoying as Lana could be, she had brought something to her life that Weslee never could have found on her own.

Yes, it bothered her that she was using her credit cards so often to buy new clothes, for weekly trips to the beauty salon, and to the spa for facials, manicures and pedicures. But she was beginning to run out of things to wear for those endless outings—so it was all necessity buying. And it was not that she wasn't having fun. She was starting to see a change in her appearance that she liked. Now she looked more put together. She no longer frowned when she opened her closet in the mornings. In just a matter of weeks she'd amassed an inventory of clothing that would be the envy of any editorial assistant at one of those Manhattan glossies that were piling up on her living room floor. Issues of *Allure*, *Vogue*, *Essence*, and *Elle* were now filling the spaces that Jane Austen, Maryse Conde, and J. California Cooper previously occupied. Those former Saturdays spent engrossed in dusty pages of worn paperbacks were over. She now heeded the siren song of the shiny pictures in those magazine pages— all the way to Saks and Neiman's, along with Jasmine's and the other funky shops on Newbury Street. And then she'd spend hours in front of her mirror trying on those outfits, matching bags to shoes, tops to bottoms, earrings to necklaces. Yes, her life was quite full now.

How had it all happened, she wondered. When exactly did she stop wagging her finger self-righteously at Lana's sprees and begin to partake herself? She couldn't put her finger on the minute. The fever had been stealthy, creeping up on her slowly like the effect of a cocktail, deceptively innocuous in its sweetness but packing a dangerously addictive high. Just the day before, she'd found herself purchasing Ralph Lauren linens for her bed. She cocked her head to the side as the memory of that purchase sent a geyser of guilt from her belly to her throat. *But it had been the aesthetician's idea!* she tried to console herself. The woman at Rosaline's Spa had suggested—admonished, really—that "You can't sleep on just anything. You have to think of your skin!" *Yes*, Weslee had thought as she caressed the rich bedding material, *I must think about my skin. It deserves so much better than Linens 'n Things.* And she couldn't buy just one set. What would she do when the one set was at the cleaners? So she'd bought four. And as she lugged the bloated bags through the store, she'd stopped in the shoe department. And there was no arguing there. It was not often that a girl who wore a size 11 shoe found beautifully crafted, supple, sumptuous, sexy footwear that made her want to walk around wearing nothing but *those* shoes all day long. She'd tried on one pair, and they felt so right, so comfortable in the way the leather wrapped itself around her foot. And with the three-and-a-half-inch heel, they put her well over six feet. But she felt empowered, even more Amazon-like as she strutted through the shoe department. She had to own that feeling forever. *Why in the world did I never wear high heels before*, she asked herself as she took in her image in the store's full-length mirror. *These shoes make me look like a fierce, fierce sistah!* The kind, encouraging salesgirl brought another pair of Christian Louboutins; Weslee tried them on and believed she could walk on water. And another. And another. They began to pile up. "I'll take them all," she'd said to the smiling salesgirl, who was no doubt counting her commission. Afterward, Weslee had felt like Goldilocks. But she ate all three bowls and then after that went back to the kitchen, made more porridge, and ate that, too.

She'd bought and bought and felt like she'd gotten away with murder when she signed the credit card slip. Almost five thousand dollars. *Almost five grand! But I've worked hard for this*, she comforted herself. *It's not like I do this all the time. Like Lana! Besides, I deserve this after all Michael's put me through. And I look so good in these clothes. Lana's right. If I don't treat myself well, who will? Five thousand dollars! But I've saved so much over the years. I deserve this.*

Now her apartment resembled something out of a heady daydream. Her bathroom was a splash of Kiehl's, La Mer, and Chanel jars, tubes, pots, and bottles. Her closet burst with Stella McCartney, Tracy Reese, and Chloe tops and bottoms. She had her pick of Vuitton, Bottega Veneta, Dior, and more in purses. Three months before, she would have heard these brand names and thought they belonged to girls from South Side or West Side Chicago. But she cared for those names now as if they were family members. Much more than she wanted to admit. Her life had been invaded by things; her body, her skin, her very soul sometimes felt immersed in lush fabrics, soft, rich smells, and creamy textures. It felt so warm and cozy, like that Ralph Lauren comforter.

But common sense had a way of occasionally insinuating itself into her newfangled luxurious existence. It was unwelcome and unyielding. She was out of control, and she needed to perform triage on her finances. So she'd flirted with the idea of getting a part-time job to help counterbalance the steady outflow from her savings to MasterCard and Visa. The idea kept her up nights with its constant buzzing in her ear. *You're spending too much. You're spending too much. You're spending too much.* But a job? That would be deviating from her carefully crafted plan. She wanted to give school her full attention. She had budgeted business school down to the last penny. Of course, that was before knowing the cost of a friendship with Lana. She couldn't keep up the spending, she knew. But work just seemed so unpalatable an option.

Out of all the possibilities she had considered, a job as a personal trainer had sounded the least painful. She had done it for six months after college, and it had been fun. She had been running and was still in great shape; it wouldn't take a major effort to become certified in Massachusetts. She could make just enough money to start to pay off some of the debt she had been racking up.

Ugh, work, on top of all this studying. Weslee grimaced.

She could see houses on Edgartown in the distance. *I could live here,* she fantasized. *Maybe someday.*

She looked over to where Lana was talking excitedly with her friend.

"Oh my God! Yes, we were in Milan the same time. Where were you staying?" the girl was saying, her eyes wide.

Weslee sighed. *Bet the last thing on Lana's mind right now is getting a job,* she thought. It wasn't fair. Lana, who appreciated nothing, was given everything. Weslee, on the other hand, felt that she had to work so hard for every single little thing she got out of life: her academic scholarship to prep school in Chicago, her basketball scholarship to Northwestern, those grueling interviews and ridiculous tests for her job at Research Associates. She had been given nothing, though her parents always told her how lucky she was. She wasn't lucky, she realized. Lana was lucky. Weslee knew without a doubt that she was smarter than Lana, but she hadn't been accepted into Brown. When all the other teenagers in her high school went overseas for vacation to exotic countries in Europe and Africa, she either spent the entire summer in Chicago working at church camp or went back to the Caribbean for a week or two with her father while he worked on his business back there. She didn't play the piano like Lana did. She'd wanted to and had asked for lessons, but her mother had said it didn't make sense since there was no piano at home to practice on.

What was irking Weslee now was that she'd thought

those feelings were hidden, buried, silenced forever. They had always been near the surface in high school, and in college sometimes. She had always seemed to be meeting people who had so much more than she did that nothing she had done or accomplished ever seemed to measure up. Well, she got into Northwestern on an athletic scholarship; but Jenny Matheson got in on an academic, which was so much more prestigious. That had been high school. Now she was starting to feel like that insecure, angry person again. Someone she barely recognized anymore.

She hated thinking such thoughts. *Am I envious of Lana and her life?* she asked herself. It had been bugging her for weeks, but she just couldn't bring herself to think it. Lately it just seemed that everything Lana did got on her nerves big-time. The way she flaunted her expensive clothes, car, fancy friends—making Weslee feel that she just had to be a part of it and that her own life was a pitiful existence she needed to be rescued from.

Sometimes Weslee looked at the new clothes hanging in her closet as if they belonged to someone else. The brand names confused her. She didn't always like the way they looked. But Lana always was so sure. "You *have* to get it. It's Miu Miu."

Weslee sighed. She wasn't sure if she wanted this life.

"That was so awful!" Lana grabbed her shoulder.

"What?" Thoughts interrupted, Weslee was almost surprised to see Lana standing right next to her.

"Peony," Lana answered.

"Her name is Peony? I thought it was Penny."

"No, it's Peony. Her mother's a nut, and she's worse. That guy she's marrying is so gay. Everybody knows he's gay; even her mother knows."

"Really, then why . . . Never mind." The answer to that question usually was: These people are nuts.

Before Weslee could say anything else, they were interrupted again. This time by an older woman, maybe Peony's mother or some relative. Weslee tuned Lana and the woman out as they air-kissed and began their little dance of telling where they had gone, who they had seen, where they had eaten, and what they had bought.

The blue water, stirred into a frenzy by the ferry, was more interesting to look at. And listen to, Weslee decided. She hoped these people would not be at Lana's parents' barbecue.

The only reason Weslee recognized the Pratesi table-cloths was because housewares and linen were her newest obsessions. *Someday,* she thought, *someday I will only sleep on Pratesi.* She admired the spread of gourmet finger food—some of which she did not recognize—wine and more wine and imported beer that Lana's mother had laid out for her guests. This was the kind of party that she had half-dreaded having to host some day if she and Michael had ever gotten married. Now she was relieved. She could never have pulled this off.

She recognized Eleanor Brown, Lana's mother, the moment she laid eyes on her. She was the woman who had sat next to her in first-class on her flight into Boston a couple of months before. But Eleanor shook her hand, not a hint of recognition in her eyes, when Lana introduced them. Weslee decided not to ask her why she had been so angry at Lana on the satellite phone that day.

It was easy to see where Lana had picked up her skills as limelight-craver extraordinaire. Eleanor was the same. She bubbled over as she greeted guests, squealed as she complimented their appearance, asked about their jobs, their children. Weslee found it almost laughable. Mother and daughter read from the same script.

Eleanor approached her, smiling.

"Weslee, please make yourself at home here, dear. Mingle, mingle, mingle. There are some really great folks here that it may be worth your while to know." She winked and touched Weslee on the shoulder and quickly made her way to speak to an older couple.

Weslee cringed inside. Sure, it would be worth her while to know the Kensingtons of Newton, the Feinsteins of Brookline, the De Villars of Prides Crossing, the Mercers of Back Bay, the Shermans of Newport, the Bromfields of Sag Harbor, and the Tennisons of Southfield. They had intimidated her at first, and then they irritated her. They all got around to asking the same questions.

"Dunster?" Jack Sherman, philanthropist and venture capitalist, had asked her warily. "Dunster of Chicago? What does your father do?"

Another woman had said, "Dunster . . . I don't think I've heard of your people, honey. What does your father do?"

Where was Lana? Her current conquest, Jeffrey Knight, had made an appearance, and she was in hot pursuit.

Weslee stood alone near the food, sticking with the crudités. She watched the fifty or so people socialize and felt like an outcast. Again, Lana had left her alone in a room with people she did not know and with whom she had nothing in common. Their empty questions swirled in her head.

"What does your father do?" "Dunster of Chicago? I've never heard of any Dunsters in Chicago." "Oh, are you related to James Dunster, the doctor, of Lake Forest?"

No. No. No. No. Sorry, no. Great meeting you, too. Weslee wondered if it was pity or disinterest that she saw in their eyes as they studied her briefly and then moved on.

The few guests who were in her age group were just as boring and tired as their parents. They shook her hand limply. Looked uncomfortable then fled to the refuge of people they already knew. One of them had asked, "So, been anywhere interesting lately?" She had answered a bit too truthfully, "This is the most interesting place I've been in quite a while." The young woman walked away, looking confused.

Weslee had run to the bathroom and checked her under-arms, her teeth. No, she smelled fine. There was nothing stuck in her teeth. Yet she was not wowing this crowd. *Oh, well,* she thought, popping another baby carrot into her mouth. *I'll just have to wait this one out.* She felt as if she were marooned on an island, all alone.

"And who are you?" she heard a voice say from behind her.

She turned around, and there he was, Weslee's cousin Duncan. She opened her mouth to answer, but nothing came out.

God, he was beautiful. His polo shirt matched the sky and his khakis were perfectly creased. He was wearing Docksiders. He had perfected the preppy look, which Michael had carried off so well, and it drove her out of her mind with desire.

Then she smiled. "Hi."

But there was no recognition in those honey-colored eyes.

He doesn't remember me? Maybe he's had a few beers, she thought. But he didn't seem to be the beer-drinking type, if one were to judge from his athletic body.

"I'm Weslee," she said, sucking in her tummy and trying not to breathe as he very obviously took inventory of her from head to toe.

She immediately wanted to kick herself. He had been a jerk to her at that party at the art gallery. She couldn't be-lieve he didn't remember her. She certainly remembered him.

She thanked her lucky stars that she had followed Lana's advice and bought the outfit she was wearing. The way he looked at her made her worry for a quick second. At least, thanks to her Kate Spade shoes and Cynthia Rowley dress, she fit right in with the rest of the younger women at Eleanor's party.

"That's an interesting name for a girl."

"All my father's doing. He really wanted a boy." She tried to suppress a sigh. What did it matter? She knew what question was coming next.

"That's understandable, I guess," he said.

She waited, but the question didn't come. *What does your father do?*

Apparently, he wasn't going to introduce himself, and she certainly wasn't going to ask. She started to look around for Lana.

Then another handsome young man came running up to him.

"Hey, Dunc," he said. "I need your keys, man. I've gotta go get some beer. Hey you," he said to her.

Her heart skipped. "William, what a surprise!"

The Crest smile she had tried hard to forget over the last couple of weeks made her heart flip-flop again. She had called him once, but his answering service had said he was away on business. She didn't bother trying again. Now here he was, reappearing like magic.

He nodded. "You look great."

"Thanks." She smiled and blushed as their eyes met. She looked away.

"Oh, you must be the Weslee that everyone's been telling me I have to meet, then," Duncan said.

"Huh?" she said, looking at him. He frowned. "Oh," Weslee said, coming back to reality. "I didn't know people had been talking about me."

"Nah, just Lana," Duncan smirked.

She could see that William was embarrassed.

"Well, I'll see you around later, Weslee," William said as

he took Duncan's keys and ran off toward the front yard, where all the Jaguars, Mercedes, and monster SUVs were parked.

"William's a good guy," Duncan said. "He's worked hard to get to where he is." *Gee, I hope that's a good thing*, Weslee thought, getting the distinct feeling that Duncan might have worked to get to where he was—but not hard.

Weslee, for lack of anything better to say, asked him about his family's ties to Lana's family. He spoke purposefully, as if he had taken diction lessons, in a voice that was somewhat hoarse. She wondered if he smoked. He was a beautiful man, and she barely listened to what he was saying. She caught phrases here and there—his father, Lana's uncle, close families, going to the same camps together as children, taking vacations together.

She couldn't possibly be his type. Matter of fact, she could just picture him with a more toned-down version of Lana: golden skin, straight hair, Ivy-educated, Talbots-clad, and whatever else went along with that old stereotype. She, Weslee, was not those things at all. She would rather spend a Sunday afternoon going for a sixteen-mile run instead of sitting around pouring tea and serving petit fours on perfect china to prim and proper women who hated to perspire. So what did he want with her? Did he feel sorry for her because she was standing here all alone, marooned on her own little island? He made her uncomfortable. He seemed kind, but she worried that she would say the wrong thing to him.

"Oh, business school is great," she heard herself saying in reply to one of his questions. "It's challenging, but that's what I was after."

"I know what you mean. I like to be challenged, too."

Again, she had no idea what to say. "So, what kind of work do you do?"

A lawyer, of course. Corporate.

He seemed apologetic to answer "Harvard" when she

asked where he had studied law. Was he ashamed of his platinum pedigree, or was it false modesty?

"Wow, that's really impressive," Weslee said, and she meant it.

He blushed, and for some reason that made him seem less daunting.

At that moment, a part of her wanted William to come back and rescue her from this man, and another part of her wanted him to continue staring at her the way he was now: intently, curiously. *It's so rude of you to just look at me that way,* she could have said. But no such words came out of her mouth.

"So, what do you plan to do with your MBA?" he asked.

"Join a major investment bank and then cash out in ten years and start my own business. Not sure what kind yet."

"You've got it all worked out," he said. She thought she detected a bit of sarcasm in his voice.

"I'm a planner," she said defensively. "I like to know where I'm headed at all times."

He pondered that for a second. "Wharton has a much better program," he said.

Her temperature rose immediately, and she clenched her fist. "I didn't want to go to Wharton. I wanted to come to Boston," she lied. She could tell from his eyes that he didn't believe her.

"You should talk with Pearl Martin. She went to Wharton. She works for Goldman."

"Duncan, I appreciate what you're trying to do here. But I really don't need anyone telling me where I should be at the moment. I'm in a program that's the right fit for me." *And, besides, Wharton rejected me.* But she would never admit that to him.

He shrugged. "Lighten up. It's not a big deal."

She sniffed.

"I'm back," William said from behind her. She almost

hugged him. He looked at her and then looked at Duncan quizzically and then gave him back his car keys. He knew something was going on.

"Did anyone show you around the property?" Duncan asked her.

"Not really," she said, silently cursing the absent Lana.

His cell phone rang. "Pardon me, but I have to take this call. Good to meet you." He extended his hand to Weslee. He shook her hand firmly and strode away.

"I can show you around, if you'd like," William said.

A minute later they walked to the other side of Lana's parents' property. There were only a handful of people by the pool. It was an unusually warm late-summer afternoon. The pool was covered, but the Sunbrella furniture was still out.

"This place is so gorgeous," she said to William.

Lana's parents had purchased the house when Lana was born. It was one of a few homes their family owned on the island. This one was the newest and largest and most modern. The four-bedroom house looked like a French country cottage inside but was all old New England weathered clapboard—effect, not real—from the outside. Eleanor was all about silk taffeta curtains, lots of flowers, crystal chandeliers, and porcelain figurines. It was pretty but definitely not Weslee's style. The grounds, however, were stunning. The house was not near the beach, but it had a large swimming pool and splendid old trees. Plus, Eleanor's gardener had made her front yard the envy of her neighbors.

"Yeah, it's all right." William smiled back.

"Just all right? I think it's a bit more than that."

"I'm the city type," he said. "I'm more glass and concrete than flora and fauna."

"Hmm. So what does that say about you?" *OK*, she thought, *that is a pathetic way to flirt with a man, but it's all I've got.*

He didn't say anything, but she noticed that he smiled.

"Well, what does it say about you that you like all this B. Smith stuff?"

"B. Smith?" She was horrified. "I don't even like B. Smith. I like nicely decorated homes, but I'm not one of those women."

"Ahh. I see. Then you're more like Martha Stewart. You'd have someone else do all the decorating and just enjoy it," he teased.

She rolled her eyes at him playfully. *What are we talking about?* she wondered. *I should probably be trying to impress this guy by talking about art, geopolitics, and the state of the stock market.* But not talking about anything in particular didn't seem to bother him.

He only continued to rack up points. He grew up in the city, too—Roxbury, though his parents later moved to Randolph, a suburb ten miles out of Boston. They both had Caribbean parents. He was the first nerdy jock she had ever met. He talked about old buildings and architecture—and football—like they were the only things on the face of the earth. She almost laughed out loud at the way he got all excited talking about the first time he went to Rome, with an Italian-English dictionary and one hundred dollars in his pocket. One would have thought he was talking about heaven the way he described the old buildings, the culture of the place, the people, and the old-world style of living.

"Oh, you have to go, Weslee. You have to go." She noticed that the more passionate he was about something, the stronger his accent became. She liked that.

"Am I boring you?" he finally asked when he finished describing the Coliseum.

"No, not at all, I'm really enjoying hearing about all these places you've been to. Makes me wish I were better traveled."

"Well, there are beautiful spaces everywhere, even all over this country." He was back in full architect mode.

"Take Chicago, for instance. To some people it's just a jumble of skyscrapers. But when I look at it, I see the same thing I think you see when you look at all these trees and even in the way you described how you saw the water when you were coming over on the ferry. I've always loved the city. It's not that I hate nature. But I guess when I see all those buildings, I just see possibility, the power of building, of constructing, of making space work. And to me there is so much beauty in that. My father was a foreman, and I used to go to some of his construction sites after school when I was a kid. Man, it always amazed me to see those buildings go up so fast. All the steel beams, the concrete, the foundation. In a matter of months, all those things would take the form of a huge, towering, complete structure." He paused as if reliving the memories. "All those things that you can just do with your own hands and your sweat—and years and years and years later they're still standing there. People work in them and live in them, make their living in them." He stopped. "Here I go again," he said.

"No, go on. I like hearing you talk about that stuff."

She was fascinated by his ease with her. She had never met a man who was so animated about what he did. From what she knew, most men did what they did because it paid the bills or allowed them to brag to their friends and impress women. But William was like a little kid talking about a video game or baseball card collection. It made her realize how glad she was that she had quit her job. She could never feel that way about writing reports about mutual fund performances.

They talked for what seemed like hours. By the time it had started to get dark, she realized that she hadn't mingled after all, as Lana and Eleanor had advised her to. She had spent the last two hours with William. She made that observation as they walked to the backyard, which was emptying. Many of Eleanor's guests had left or were leaving.

"What are you doing later?" he asked.

"I think Lana's taking me to some nightclub."

"You really don't seem like the club-hopping type to me. How did you and Lana get hooked up?"

"It just sort of happened," Weslee said. "I really can't explain it."

"You two are so different."

"Well, we're not that different," Weslee said, racking her brain for things that she and Lana had in common.

"If you say so." William shrugged. "I guess I'll catch up with you later, Weslee Dunster."

As he walked off to his Jeep, now unblocked by the near-empty makeshift parking lot, she hoped to herself that he would catch up with her again. Something about him made her feel so relaxed and comfortable. Maybe it was his casual manner. Or the fact that he was so handsome yet didn't seem to know it or care. Or that there was just a speck of dirt under his left third finger. Or that though he was quite muscular, he did not seem to be the type to spend hours every day at the gym. He was a man's man, she decided. Only the bigger picture in his sights, not the details; thus there would be no manly manicures or personal tailors, nor would there be Kiehl's products in his bathroom, she imagined. What were the odds, she thought. Someone like him in a place like this. She felt like she had found an ally.

She noticed Lana and her mother deep in conversation off in a corner and walked toward them. As she approached, she heard Lana say, "Oh, yeah. She's from a good family. I wouldn't bring her here if she were common."

Weslee gritted her teeth. She didn't even want to know what that conversation was about. "Hey, Lana, Eleanor."

"Hi, sweetie." Eleanor's voice oozed honey. "Where've you been?"

"Just admiring the property with William."

"Oh, that William. He's an intense young man," Eleanor said.

Intense how? Weslee wanted to ask. But she knew better. "Need help cleaning up?" she asked Eleanor.

"Oh, honey, no, the caterers will do that." She looked at Weslee, horrified, as if she were from another planet.

"OK," Weslee said brightly. She was getting used to being treated like the poor cousin visiting Oak Bluffs straight from the Ozarks.

Lana and Eleanor were ignoring her, so she decided to go mingle among the few people who were still lingering.

Then there was Duncan again. "Did you enjoy your walk with William?" That smirk again, and she began to see that it was not intentional.

"Yes." She bared her teeth, but the smile never reached her eyes.

"Are you usually this rude to people you barely know?" he asked her. She couldn't read his expression now, but the smirk was gone.

All of a sudden she felt guilty and a little ashamed of herself. "I'm sorry, I had no idea I was being rude to you."

He looked right at her but said nothing. "I guess you're going out with Lana tonight."

"I guess," she said.

"You two make quite an odd pair," he said.

"Hey, who says two people have to be carbon copies of each other to become friends?"

"Oh, I'm not saying that at all. It's just different to see Lana hanging around someone so . . . sensible."

Weslee sighed. "Well, you really don't know me at all, so don't assume that I'm sensible."

He laughed. Of course his smile was as perfect as the rest of him. She couldn't deny that she was beginning to feel hypnotized by it.

"You're absolutely right, and I apologize. Maybe I could . . ."

"Duncan, would you stop trying to steal my friends!" Lana appeared again.

He gave Lana that condescending look that Weslee had seen him give her the night she met him at the party—a meeting he didn't remember.

"Are you partying with us tonight?" she asked him, faking a dance move.

"Dream on," he said.

He looked at Weslee. Long. "I'll call you," he said to her and walked away.

"What was that about?" Lana asked in a teasing voice.

"I don't know. He doesn't have my number."

"Oh, he'll find it. He's like that. But don't take him too seriously. Come on, let's go get a glass of wine. I have to introduce you to my cousin Sissy."

Weslee groaned inside. *How many times do I have to tell her I don't drink anymore because I'm training for the marathon? And how do I work up the nerve to tell her that I don't want to meet any more of these people?*

But she allowed herself to be dragged along to meet Sissy.

Chapter
7

Weslee was never happier to see her tiny apartment than when she walked in that Monday afternoon. The weekend had been exhausting—from the long drive and ferry ride to the Vineyard, to the parties at Eleanor's and then later at the nightclub. It had been all about Lana and her family and her friends and, of course, their money and their pedigrees. She had never felt so out of place. Even at the club, she had wanted to just disappear. Lana quickly sucked all the attention from the room as she climbed up on the bar, dancing in her tiny shorts and tank top. Weslee had left at that point, walking all the way back to her guest room at Eleanor's house. It had been dark, and she had feared getting lost, but it was better than staying at the nightclub, watching Lana make a spectacle of herself.

She had hoped to see William again, but he hadn't shown. The disappointment, plus the feeling of not belonging, had kept her up the whole night. She had fled early that morning before Eleanor's lavish breakfast, saying that she had forgotten her migraine medicine. She hadn't had a migraine headache since high school.

Lana didn't seem to mind that her friend was leaving before the official end of the holiday weekend. "I'll call you once I get back in town," she had said sleepily from her bedroom as Weslee waved good-bye.

The ride back on the ferry had been a little choppy, and the older couple who gave her a ride to the city talked her head off the whole way about politics. At first it was refreshing to have a grown-up conversation about poverty and education. But then the conversation had taken a turn that left her counting each mile back to Boston.

It was so like certain people to assume that she would be a Democrat, a liberal Democrat at that. But they were so wrong. "Yes, it is the government's duty to ensure that the public schools are up to par or close with the private schools," she had tried to tell the woman, Ellen MacLean. "But it should be up to parents to choose where their children go to school. Why should they be forced to send their kids to an underperforming school just because they're from a poor neighborhood? Yes, of course, I'm in full support of school vouchers."

Ellen, who was driving, had said, "Well, that's the kind of thinking that deprives our inner-city schools of the students who can help them rise to excellence."

"At their own expense?" Weslee had almost asked aloud. But instead she had bowed out of the argument. She had wanted to laugh, though. *Our* inner-city schools? Weslee herself had never stepped foot in an inner-city school, and she was positive that her captors, or drivers, had not either. *Liberals*, she had sighed.

Now she was home and glad to be away from all of them: the good, the bad, and the pretentious.

Her message light was blinking. She hit the play button.

"Hi, Weslee, it's Duncan. I got your phone number from Lana. Wondering what you're doing for lunch tomorrow. Give me a call at my office." She frowned as he recited his number.

Wow. He sure moves quickly, she thought. *What makes him*

*think that he can call today and have lunch with me tomorrow!
For all he knows, we only met yesterday.*

She dropped her weekend bag on the floor and walked to
the shower. Thank goodness she had the night all to herself.
All she wanted was a nice, slow, long run by the river and
then a bath. She was almost done with the Paul Theroux
book, which she had read on the ferry ride back to Woods
Hole. She couldn't wait to get back into it.

The phone rang. She picked it up. "Hello, this is Weslee."

It was Duncan. "Didn't you get my message?" he asked.

"I just walked in."

"It's too bad you rushed off so quickly this morning. I
heard that you didn't feel well. I hope that had nothing to
do with me."

The ego.

"Listen, Duncan, I'd really rather not have lunch tomorrow. I have a training run in the afternoon, and a big lunch is
the last thing I need before I do it."

"OK, we'll have dinner, then. I'm not taking no for an answer," he said. "Unless you already have plans."

She thought for a moment. "OK, but I can't stay out
late."

"Good. Me, neither."

Weslee looked around at the restaurant. Gosh, the place
was beautiful. It was a French restaurant in the middle of
posh Copley Square. She'd walked by it enough times as
she trailed Lana on the way to Saks and Neiman's. She had
noticed the high-brow crowd sitting at tables with white,
white tablecloths, silverware glinting in the semidark dining room. Now here she was at one of the best tables, looking out on Huntington Avenue at passersby, with a man
whose dinner invitation she still wasn't sure she should
have accepted.

"How's your salad?" Duncan asked her.

He was all charm and dash. She could see how a woman could fall easily for him. He was one of those men who never had to work hard at that sort of thing. He was the total package. The looks, money, education, class, and manners—she tried hard to remind herself that she wasn't buying it; there was no way a man like him would truly want to be with someone like her.

"It's great. This place is amazing." And it was. The wait staff was so polite and attentive; it was as if they were the only diners in the room.

Duncan was talking about Paris. Thankfully, she had been there once for a week in her junior year at Northwestern, so for the first time she felt comfortable adding something to the conversation. Funny thing was, she kept comparing his recollections with William's excitement about Paris and Rome and the architecture there. But then Duncan lost her when he began to talk about wines and all the vineyards he had visited in France. She nodded politely, mostly feeling that she was getting a lecture but liking the way he spoke with his deep, hoarse voice, the way he leaned back slightly in his chair but held her eyes with his intense brown stare. She couldn't look away.

"So, which of your parents gave you those athletic genes? You're a runner, right? You know, you didn't even have to tell me. It's obvious. I ran track, too. I know the walk." It jolted her out of her reverie when he turned the conversation back to her.

He didn't know it yet, but he had begun to score some points.

"Really? What did you run?" Her interest suddenly perked up. Maybe he wasn't so bad after all.

"You think I'm just some preppie, golf-addicted type. But I'm actually a sprinter at heart," he said.

She listened intently as he talked about playing football and running track at Exeter and then at Harvard. He was obviously a very competitive athlete. It reminded her of Michael's forever-burning desire to win at all times—and the way he displayed all his medals and trophies in their living room, where everyone could see.

"In my last year of high school I wanted to win every single race there was. I only missed one—I lost to William." He grinned. "But I ended up winning us the biggest meet of our season, so that made up for it."

She grinned back at him because she knew where he was coming from. To the average person, what Duncan was saying would have seemed like bragging, but not to Weslee. Like most athletes, she understood what went into a win: sweat, hours of training, aching knees and hamstrings, and your lungs screaming for air with the finish-line tape nowhere in sight. Duncan understood that, too.

"So, have you stopped running?" she asked.

"Just about. I ran the marathon a couple of years ago, but that was just on a dare."

"You're kidding! I'm training for it," she exclaimed.

"Really? What time are you expecting to make?"

"Hopefully three-thirty." She held up crossed fingers.

"I did it in two forty-two."

"Wow, that's amazing."

"Not really. It almost killed me."

Twenty minutes later, after dessert, they were laughing and talking about his work, sports, movies, and books. Weslee was genuinely surprised at how easygoing Duncan turned out to be. She admired his drive and competitiveness. He talked about his work as if it were a battle. He made his law firm colleagues sound like enemies and the office a battleground for clients and favors from partners. She enjoyed listening to his war stories. He made everything he did sound so exciting, so important. She would never admit it, but if she closed her eyes she could imagine she was sitting across the table from Michael.

They didn't notice that the restaurant had almost emptied and that the wait staff stood at the edge of the kitchen, glancing between the two of them and their watches.

"We'd better get going," he said finally, after finishing another of his stories about another semicriminal businessman he'd helped save from going to jail.

"Oh," she said, suddenly leaping back to her senses and looking at her watch. It was eleven-thirty. "I didn't realize it was so late."

"Guess it was the good company."

She felt her cheeks grow warm. He smiled. She blushed again.

Then he blew her mind. In what seemed like a second or less, he stood and leaned across the table and kissed her. It was short and sweet and totally unexpected.

Then he sat back and looked at her. "I couldn't help it," he said almost apologetically. "I just haven't met anyone like you before. I'm sorry. That was forward of me."

She didn't say anything. She was surprised that she wasn't angry with him and that she had wanted him to do it all night long, surprised that she told him that it was OK and that her eyes said she felt the same way he was feeling.

Later that night, her new two-hundred-dollar bed linens were not doing much in the way of lulling her into an opulent slumber. *Why can't I just stop seeing his face, feeling his lips? Aaargh!* Weslee tossed and turned and squeezed her eyes shut. Her heart flipped every time she replayed the kiss. It had sent a bolt of lightning through her, and she was surprised that she'd not shot up from the table at that very moment. She sighed. She'd already dissected the dinner conversation twenty-three times. Each time she felt more and more embarrassed about her lack of worldliness. *I must have sounded like a real hick to him.* She balled up a fist. *An inexperienced refugee from the ghetto, probably. What in the world could he possibly want with me?* she wondered. She remembered the parade of pretty girls at the Vineyard party who were certainly more suitable for a guy like him. *I'm just a recovering tomboy,* she wailed to the dark, empty room. *I can't deal with this!* She opened her eyes. But he seemed so . . . so interested. It couldn't have been her imagination. Or was it? Maybe the whole night had not even happened. And even if it had? *What happens next? Aaargh! I need to get some sleep!*

Chapter

8

Weslee had to face it. Her life was hemorraging money. She couldn't bear to take another withdrawal out of her emergency savings. Things were just not going according to her spending plan. The plan was to never, ever exceed two thousand dollars a month. But in the last week or so she had already spent fifteen hundred. She had been buying new clothes, getting her hair done, and spending on parties like crazy. When she was planning this move to Boston, she did not plan for an active social life. So something needed to be done.

The credit card bills on the coffee table were not going to go away. She was horrified when she looked at the balance on her Visa card of nearly two thousand dollars. How could she pay that all off at the end of the month? Would she have to carry a balance? That was out of the question. She had never carried a balance in her entire life. She rummaged through the rest of the bills. The new Saks Fifth Avenue card and the Nordstrom account would also need to be paid off immediately. Her savings would have to take the hit this month. Again.

Even if she cut down on the spending, the damage had already been done. She needed to replenish her savings.

What if an emergency really did happen? She needed more money in that account.

She really didn't want to have to do it, but she had to get a job. Once again, she considered working as a personal trainer. She hadn't done it in ages, since just after college. But it was easy, and she could probably make enough money to at least handle her utilities and groceries. She picked up the yellow pages and began to call health clubs.

The holiday season was in the air. Some merchants had already put up Christmas lights in their store windows. Lights sparkled through the trees near the Christian Science Monitor building. The shopping crowds were thick and focused on Boylston and Newbury streets. The cold air was beginning to be a menace.

Lana and Weslee walked quickly from the coffee shop where they had just met.

"So, do you think I even have a chance of getting a B?" Lana asked.

Weslee had read Lana's paper and had done her best to suggest changes that could save the disastrous piece of work. "If you make the changes I just suggested, you'll get an A. It's really not that bad."

Lana sighed. "I cannot imagine having to take Organizational Behavior again next semester."

Weslee set her jaw. OB was the easiest course in the curriculum so far, yet Lana was having trouble with it. "But your grades for the other classes are OK, right?" she asked.

"Yeah, I guess."

"Lana, you can't guess. They'll kick you out if your cumulative is below a B average."

"They can't kick me out. My father donated hundreds of thousands of dollars to that school," she said defiantly. Then, in one of the abrupt changes of subject that Weslee had learned to expect from her friend: "Hey, I think Neiman's is having a sale. Wanna go look-see?"

Weslee stopped. "I got a job, Lana."

"A what?"

"A job. I start next week. It's at the HealthyLife Spa. I'll be a personal trainer there."

"But why? Where are you going to find the time?"

"I'll have to find the time. I need to find the time. I've been spending way too much. And no, I don't want to go to Neiman's."

They had stopped walking.

"Wes, that's so . . ."

"So . . . what?"

"Can't you just ask your folks to lend you money?"

"Lana, I'm almost thirty years old. I'm not asking my parents for money!"

"But you're in school. They'll understand." It seemed as if she was pleading.

"What's the big deal? I don't mind working."

"But you shouldn't have to." Lana looked dismayed.

"Lana, not everybody goes through life the way you do," Weslee laughed.

"What is that supposed to mean?"

"Well, just doing whatever feels right and not taking responsibility."

Lana narrowed her eyes. "Don't criticize me, OK? Just because I have certain things doesn't mean that I don't take responsibility."

Weslee, seeing the beginning of a tantrum, decided to leave it at that.

"Well, I'm going to Neiman's," said Lana.

"Fine. I'm meeting Duncan in Kendall Square tonight for a movie. A French film."

Lana rolled her eyes and walked away in the other direction.

* * *

The clanging of weight machines and loud techno music was bad enough, and so Weslee tried not to show her irritation as the elderly woman struggled to lift fifteen pounds on the shoulder-press machine.

"Ms. Goldberg, let's try a lighter weight, OK?" This woman was testing every last bit of patience Weslee had left.

It was her first client on her first day of her second week at HealthyLife. The best thing about working the mid-morning shift was that it was slow enough so that she could actually get some studying done between clients. But then, her clients tended to be either the really overweight type who were terrified of working out at the trendy gym during peak hours or the elderly who had nothing better to do all day than putter around a health club before heading out for a big lunch that would cancel out all their efforts.

But hey, Weslee rationalized, *I'm getting eighteen dollars an hour, and some of these women know how to tip!*

"Oh, honey, I thought I could do it. It just doesn't look that heavy," Ms. Goldberg whined.

"It's no big deal. We'll start off light, and when your muscles get a little warmed up, we'll work our way up to the heavier weights."

One-on-one training was not as easy as it looked. The personal interaction could get to be a little too much. Some people wanted to deviate from her planned routine, and that made her crazy. It was a standard script for most of them: She'd take them through a weight circuit and then send them off to one of the cardio machines for twenty minutes—twenty minutes she used to catch up on reading her textbooks. She even had time to work on assignments on her laptop while her clients sweated themselves out on the treadmill or stationary bike.

For some reason she hadn't told Duncan yet about her job. She couldn't explain it, but she felt ashamed. They had only been out on a few dates, she mused, so she really had no obligation to reveal all—at least not yet.

She knew her feelings of shame were irrational. It's not that she didn't have money; she just didn't want to spend any more of it. And with Duncan asking her out more and more, she would need to spend money on hair, clothes, and makeup to impress someone like him.

It had taken her two hours last night just to get ready to meet Duncan for yet another foreign film, this one in the Coolidge Corner theater in Brookline, and coffee. She remembered that going out with Michael had only required thirty minutes of prep time: shower, put on a little foundation, lip gloss, jeans, flats, and a sweater. Now it wasn't that simple. She knew that Duncan expected her to look a certain way. He always commented on her appearance and she found herself looking forward to his compliments. Every time she grew weary of Lana's childish attitude, she checked herself. Had it not been for Lana, she could never have kept a guy like Duncan interested. Duncan required a full face of the most expensive makeup that made her look as if she was not wearing any. Her outfits had to be classy, understated, and sexy at the same time. It was a look she had seen Lana carry off sometimes, and she was learning that it was not as effortless as it seemed. So, she decided to ask Lana, who had replied: "Calvin Klein, Max Mara, and BCBG. You're tall, and thank God you barely have any curves, you're not fussy, plus you're cheap." Weslee had rolled her eyes at the last jab, but she had taken the advice and it was working well for her.

Duncan was well worth the effort. He was almost like a teacher to Weslee. They'd spent hours talking about the movement to repatriate land to black farmers in Zimbabwe and the wisdom or lack thereof in U.S. foreign policy. She was in awe of him as she saw the similarities in their political viewpoints: he was quasi-conservative, too! "And you don't have to be ashamed of it," he'd smiled. He knew everything about everything and had been everywhere. He had traveled to half the countries on the African continent and through most of Europe, all before he started law school. He was fluent in Swahili and French, and he knew German well enough to travel there without difficulty. He was so smart. *God, he is so incredibly sexy and smart,* she thought as she took her elderly client through the motions.

Since her first date with Duncan, he had called every day. She was almost dizzy from all the attention. He had even brought her a flower last night. He was so romantic, and a great kisser, too. She got weak-kneed just thinking about the hot-and-heavy twenty minutes they had spent at her apartment door last night. She couldn't let him in. She couldn't trust herself.

"One more set?" Ms. Goldberg interrupted her less-than-pure thoughts.

"Yes, just twelve more repetitions."

She couldn't wait until Saturday. He had promised to drive her up to the White Mountains in New Hampshire to see the fall foliage. She had never done that before. It was one of those New England things, he had told her, that when she did it once she would have to do it every year. She couldn't wait.

Chapter
9

An early morning rain had cleared to reveal a perfect fall day. The air was crisp and clear, and there was color everywhere. They had left early, after eating a huge breakfast Weslee had made. It was the first time she had cooked for him, and she watched him apprehensively, desperately seeking signs of pleasure on his face as he took each bite.

He cleaned off his plate, but she still asked him two or three times whether he really had enjoyed his eggs, pancakes, bacon, and hash browns. She knew that it wasn't the gourmet breakfast that he was probably used to. She had flirted with the idea of salmon and bagels with Bloody Marys, but she hadn't wanted to seem pretentious. She'd decided to stick with what she knew. Yet she still wasn't fully convinced even after he told her over and over that he had enjoyed her cooking.

She would never admit it to him, but she just loved Duncan's BMW Z3. She teased him about how impractical the two-seater sports car was, especially for the rough New England winters.

Now he was offering to let her drive it.

"Are you serious?"

"Yes, I'm serious. I think once you drive it, you're never

going to be able to go back to that Toyota or Chevy or whatever it is you drive," he laughed.

"For your information, I have a Honda Accord, America's number one choice."

"For mediocrity."

"Duncan!"

"It's true. If you had your choice, what car would you drive?"

She had to think for a minute. "Maybe an Audi A8." She loved that car.

"Now we're talking. So, get one."

"I wish I could."

"Well, once you're done with your MBA, you'll be able to."

"First I have to find a job."

"Oh, you'll find a job. You're young, smart, fine, double-minority."

"Duncan!" She smacked his knees playfully.

He looked at her and laughed as he took the car up a gear on the clear highway. "So, where do you want to live after school? Will you stay here?"

"I don't know. I've always wanted to live in New York City."

"Why not stay here? There are plenty of financial companies here."

"I know. But I might want to try New York for a while."

"Why?"

"I don't know. It's just so big, bad, and exciting."

"Boston's exciting."

They both laughed.

Weslee breathed in deeply as she gazed out the window. She had to ask Duncan twice to slow down so she could take in the beauty of the fall foliage. He had been so right. She would have to do this every single year. The myriad reds, oranges, burgundies, golds, and greens, all just fluttering on the trees against the cobalt sky went on for miles and miles. She couldn't take her eyes off it. She had never seen anything like this in Illinois.

Duncan kept his eyes on the road. She could tell he was having the time of his life playing with his car. For the first twenty or so miles of the trip up Route 93, he showed her every single function, gadget, and whiz-bang technology the car came with. He was like a little kid with a toy.

By the time the tips of the White Mountains were in view, she had learned so much about him. The pressure he felt as the youngest of four brothers was apparent to her. He talked about his strict, uncompromising father, who ran their Brookline household with an iron fist. He was much closer to his mother, who had Creole roots and was also a lawyer until she and his father had decided to start having children. He was the only one of his siblings still living in Boston. He spoke fondly of his nieces and nephews, who were scattered all over the country.

She was finding that the more she knew, the more she grew to like him as a person. He was boyish in that he gave in to his every childish whim—like the car, his pet cobra, and a horse that he kept at his parents' other home in Carver, Massachusetts. He was a bit spoiled, yet he was inquisitive about other people—her, anyway. He drilled her about her family, her niece and nephew, even about Michael. She was reluctant to talk about that relationship, but he dug deeper and deeper until she told him the whole story.

"So you moved here to get over him?"

"No, I moved here to go to business school."

"University of Chicago and Northwestern have great management schools."

"I don't think that Chicago would take me."

"Did you even apply?"

She sighed.

"OK, Weslee. I see I'm hitting a nerve."

"You're not hitting any nerves. Don't give yourself so much credit."

He cocked his head to the side, and she wondered if she had hurt his feelings.

"No, I didn't apply," she conceded.

He nodded as if to say, *I thought so.*

They stopped in Littleton, New Hampshire, a tiny town near the Vermont border. Weslee stretched as she inhaled the chilly, clean mountain air.

"Where are we going?" She looked around unconsciously for other black—or at least brown—people.

"To a diner." He pointed to a small eatery across the street.

Weslee was glad she had worn boots. There was snow on the ground, and it crunched under her feet as they walked to the diner.

"Are we going to be OK up here?" She felt uneasy. She thought that she felt a couple of stares from the occupants of a passing truck.

Duncan looked down at her and smiled. "This is not the Deep South, Weslee."

"I know. But I don't see anybody who looks like us."

"This is New England. The sooner you get used to that, the better."

They walked into the diner.

"How are you guys doing today?" a friendly waitress greeted them at the door.

"Good, and you?" Duncan replied, totally at ease.

Weslee followed his lead and smiled politely while he made small talk with the waitress as she led them to a red Formica-topped table.

Once they had ordered lunch, Weslee felt more comfortable. An interracial couple walked in, and she felt even better. Duncan laughed at her obvious relief at seeing another black face in New England's North Country.

"My, you really need to deal with your race hang-ups."

"What is that supposed to mean?" She didn't mean for it to sound as curt as it did.

"Calm down. That's all I'm saying. Just calm down."

She cocked her head to the side the way she did when she was irritated.

"Did I say the wrong thing?" He reached for her hand across the table.

"No, I'm just thinking."

"Thinking?" he asked.

"Well, we're just from different places."

"Everybody's from a different place. Everybody."

"I know." She pursed her lips.

"Hey, you're with me, it's OK." He said it softly and squeezed her hand. When she didn't reply, he nudged her feet with his under the table. She couldn't help smiling.

After they ate, they drove farther up into the mountains.

"I want to show you something," he said, pulling off an exit onto a one-lane highway. He drove for a couple of miles, then pulled onto a dirt road.

"Where is this?" she asked. He didn't answer. He just drove the little roadster over the bumpy dirt path. He stopped at a tiny stream. They got out of the car.

It was a scene straight out of an Impressionist painting. The trees in all their wild colors leaned over the stream on both sides, some branches joining to form a bridge above.

"Wow!" Weslee looked around. "This is so beautiful."

"I knew you'd like it." Duncan put his arm around her waist.

They stared at the beauty in front of them, not saying anything for minutes.

"Thanks for bringing me here, Duncan."

"Don't thank me. I brought you here for selfish reasons. I wanted to see you around all this beauty."

He held her to him and kissed her. She kissed him back

and let his hands slowly move over her body. She moved closer to him, melting into the hardness of his chest.

He pulled back after a few minutes. "We should head back."

She looked at him, dazed. "Uh. Sure."

Oh my goodness, she thought, *was I too eager? Maybe I should have at least tried to stop him.*

He held her hand as they walked back to the car. He walked her over to her side of the car and opened the door. Their eyes met, and the temptation rose again. His kiss made her weak, and she folded her arms around his neck.

"Weslee," he said. "You're driving me crazy." And kissed her deeply.

This time it was her turn to stop him. She knew that if they went even one step further, there would be no turning back.

On the ride back to Boston, Weslee felt truly happy. Duncan laughed at her rants about her clients at the health club, suggesting that she start her own personal-training business. She teased him about his obsession with his car. He dared her to drive the rest of the way home. She refused.

"I've never driven anything so small and fast," she protested.

"You're such a chicken."

"You won't be saying that when I wreck it."

"You're not going to wreck it. If you do, I have insurance for that."

She looked at him. He took his eyes off the road briefly to meet her stare.

"Come on, Dunster, show me what you got." He pulled off to the side of the road.

"OK, you got it." She got in the driver's seat and adjusted the seat. "OK, show me again what all the buttons do," she said nervously.

"Just drive the car. It's not going to bite you."

Weslee sighed and looked in the driver's side mirror for traffic. She pulled onto the highway slowly.

"Um. You might want to try to at least drive at or above the speed limit," Duncan joshed.

Weslee rolled her eyes and hit the gas. "Oh my God!" She hadn't expected the car to lurch forward so quickly and violently.

"Now we're talking," Duncan said, strapping on his seat belt.

Two hours later, Weslee pulled up in front of her apartment building. She giggled from the driver's seat. "Can I keep it?" she joked.

"Sure, go ahead, keep it." And he did it again. Without warning, he swooped across the front seat and kissed her: long, hard, and deep. She felt like she was melting. It may have lasted a few minutes or a half hour. But when she opened her eyes, it was considerably darker than it had been when she had pulled up to the curb.

She tried to think. Third real date. What to do?

"I guess I'd better go up." She wished she had it in her to be a bad girl.

"OK, I'll call you tomorrow." He caressed her face and kissed her on the lips.

I'll be waiting, I'll be waiting, I'll be so waiting, she sang to herself as she bounded into her building.

She kept replaying the day over and over in her mind. Duncan, Duncan, Duncan. Sometimes it was good to disobey your instincts, Weslee thought. Or else she would never have found out that he was so romantic, so sweet, so irresistible. She never thought herself to be the type to attract guys like him, but here he was, obviously crazy about her.

The phone rang. Wow, couldn't he wait? She answered in her sexiest, most I'm-not-waiting-for-your-call voice.

"Hey, Weslee."

It was William.

"Hey, William." She found her real voice.

"What's up?"

"Um. Nothing."

"Hey, I have two tickets for *Riff Raff,* that Lawrence Fishburne play." He sounded excited, and she hated to burst his bubble.

"Um. Tonight's kinda bad, William."

"Why, what's going on? Are you OK?"

"Um. I'm just tired. I was out all day. I went to the White Mountains today."

"You did? With Lana?"

"Um. No. Duncan took me."

A long pause ensued.

"Oh. That must have been cool. It's nice up there this time of year."

"Yes, it was," she said quietly, almost apologetically.

"OK. Well, maybe another time then. Take care." William sounded wounded.

"Sure, William. Thanks for asking me."

He said good-bye quickly and hung up.

They had been playing phone tag over the last few weeks. In the last message she had left him, she had said, "William, you're the busiest man I have ever not gotten a minute to get to know."

Lana had convinced her to let him go. "I told you, he's a total workaholic," she had said.

But Weslee felt rotten. She knew what had just happened. William knew now that she had picked Duncan. There was no going back.

Chapter

10

Weslee hurried. She quickly pulled on her spandex tights and a tank top. She grabbed her Windbreaker and her bag and headed for the door. It was the day of her first trial marathon, and she didn't want to be late. It would be a long drive out to Lowell. She walked out the door to her rental car.

She tried to ignore the cold as she pulled out the keys to the Chevy Cavalier that would take her to Lowell, Massachusetts. She switched from the hip-hop station to NPR and pulled away. She had asked Lana to cheer her on at the start and finish of the Bay State Marathon, but Lana had declined. She had a date, and Lowell was just too far. "But tell me all about it and good luck," she had said.

Weslee couldn't deny that she was disappointed, but that was the way of things. Doing this race didn't depend on having the support of Lana or anyone else. It was all about her and the ultimate goal: the Boston Marathon. If she could make a qualifying time in this race, she would be running Boston in the spring. Lana's selfishness would not get in the way of that.

Her cell phone rang. Had Lana changed her mind?

"Are you there yet?" the deep, hoarse voice said.

"Duncan," she said, her face breaking into a smile.

"I'm really sorry I can't be there for you today," he said.

"It's OK, I understand."

Weslee was actually relieved that Duncan's childhood friend, also a friend of his family, was visiting for the weekend. She wasn't sure whether she was ready for him to see her running a race where she wasn't 100 percent sure she would accomplish her goal. It was too early to fail in front of him.

"Listen, if I can get away later, I'll stop by and massage your feet," he said.

"I'd like that," she smiled.

She was glad he had called. It took her mind off the race a bit. The report on the situation in Iraq that was coming through the car speakers was not doing anything to relax her nerves.

There really was no need to worry. She tried to calm the distracting nervousness inside of her. Her training had been going well. She knew that all she had to do was finish this race in three hours and forty-five minutes and she'd qualify for Boston. *This is not hard,* she told herself. *This is not going to be hard. Mind over matter.*

Weslee thought of Duncan again. "I'll stop by and massage your feet."

She didn't understand what was happening to her. She found herself looking forward every day to his calls. And it wasn't because of the flowers and the gifts that had started a few weeks after their first couple of dates.

Two weeks ago, he sent flowers every day for the entire week. He said he was trying to guess her favorite flower and would send them every day until he guessed the right one. He hit white orchids that Thursday. The extravagance of the whole act had overwhelmed her. No man had ever paid this much attention to her. She felt as if she was the only woman in the world for Duncan.

It had only been a month, but she felt like she had known him for years. They fit so well together. She had learned to laugh at his sarcastic jokes, even when they were at her expense. He just loved to make fun of her Midwest naiveté and rosy outlook on everything. He was making her dream. He was making her feel safe: that it was OK to trust again and maybe love again. She had reached a point where she couldn't go a day without hearing from him.

She put her wrist up to her nose. That perfume he had bought her smelled so good. Ralph Lauren's Romance. She had worn it all week since he had given it to her. He had hidden it in his refrigerator the first night she went over to his duplex in the South End. He sent her to the fridge under the pretext of fetching a bottle of wine, and there it sat: a purple box with a white bow. She didn't say anything. She didn't want to assume it was for her. She handed him the bottle as he stood leaning on his kitchen counter staring at her.

"Well?"

"Well, what?"

"You don't want it?"

"What?"

He glanced at her nonchalantly. "Your present."

"It's mine?" she asked innocently.

She went back to the fridge and opened the box. He came to her as she stood in the middle of the kitchen sniffing her wrist, the bottle in her other hand.

"You're so beautiful," he said as he pulled her toward him.

She was floating on a cloud of doubt and ecstasy as his mouth traveled over her body. *This is not the time . . . I'm not ready,* her common sense protested. *Not here! Not on the kitchen floor!* But as her clothes fell around her feet, her physical desires took over her brain function. Her hands were furiously unbuttoning and unzipping as she and

Duncan sank to the floor. She stopped him as her naked skin felt the chilly tiles of the floor. "Duncan, we need to get a thing . . ."

He looked confused for a second. Then "Oh!" He grabbed his wallet out of his pants and took out a condom.

Doubts dissipated as she began to trust him with her body and explore his. *Goodness,* she thought as she ran her hands over his muscled arms and chest. *This man is the most beautiful I've ever seen.* His skin was golden brown and taut over his sinewy frame. And he was as much an athlete in his lovemaking. It hadn't been this way with Michael. Duncan was a giver all the way. He asked, "Is this good, baby? Is this good for you?" He surprised her again with his intensity, and she let herself go, unashamed to let her voice carry up to the high ceilings and echo through his apartment when she reached climax. When it was over, she'd lain back on the cold, hard floor, giggling like a teenager.

"What's so funny?" Duncan had asked, confused and turning to face her.

"I've never done it on the floor," she laughed.

It was sooner than she had wanted, but Duncan was different. He wasn't out for a quick hit. She knew that. They talked every day. He was so attentive. He listened to every word she said. He was always smoothing her hair back from her face or making other small gestures that showed her he cared. She couldn't believe that the man whom she'd thought was an arrogant, self-absorbed jerk was actually sweet, sensitive, and deeply misunderstood. He was just moody enough to keep her interested. She wanted to get to the source of his dark silences and the mystery behind his brown eyes.

Yes, she sometimes regretted that things between her and William hadn't quite worked out and that he had given up so quickly and never called anymore. She wondered if it had been something she'd said or done. *He must be dating someone else,* she thought. That had to be it. *Else why wouldn't he call after we'd spent so much time together talking. . . . I'll never understand men.*

She'd wanted to call William several times, but fear kept her away. What if a girl answered? What if he simply did not want to speak to her and was unbearably kind? She couldn't bear another rejection. Not so soon after Michael. Some things were just not meant to be, and this was one of them, she decided. Besides, according to Lana the guy was a crazed workaholic; he probably had no time for a girlfriend. *Oh, well. We'll file that one under eternally unresolved issues and unanswered questions,* she thought.

But she couldn't discount the present and what was happening with Duncan. It was fate that had led her to him. Even with William falling into the background, it was nature writing the perfect script. She felt so right, so on her way, when she was with him. She was turning into a swan, the kind of person she never imagined she could be. It had to be fate.

An hour later she stood at the starting line at the Bay State Marathon. Weslee was so excited—her heart was racing, and she hadn't even started running yet. The crowd of about five thousand runners was packed tight on the street near the town's high school. Weslee felt comfort from the few other women she noticed who were alone. She listened to people complain about the cold, the traffic, the lack of Gatorade. Couples rubbed each others' hands and arms as the wind whipped through. Weslee ignored it. She was a Chicago girl, and forty-eight degrees to her was balmy.

As the clock ticked down to the start time, Weslee stretched her calves and hamstrings again. She prayed silently. *I have to make three-forty. I have to make three-forty.* Then the starting gun went off.

She didn't start feeling the pain until mile eighteen. Her

legs began to feel like rubber, and she began gasping for air.
She looked at her watch. Eight miles to go, and she had an
hour and a half left. She wasn't discouraged. She had prepared herself for the inevitable wall. She slowed down a bit
and let some runners pass her.

"Wanna run together, sister?" said a voice next to her.

She turned, and another black woman who looked to be
about her age was running next to her. "Sure, I think I'm
about to hit the wall—I could use some support." Weslee
smiled, but it came out more like a grimace.

"You'll make it. I've been tagging you the last ten miles.
You've kept me going."

Weslee laughed this time. "Wow, thanks."

"I'm Sherry."

"Weslee."

They said nothing for a few minutes. The race had thinned
out quite a bit. There were a few runners about a quarter of
a mile ahead and a few about a hundred feet behind. The
race was at the point where the true athletes had separated
themselves from the amateurs, and the gap was quite wide.

Weslee was glad Sherry wasn't too talkative and that she
wasn't too slow, either. They were running at an eight-
minute-mile pace, which was a little slower than Weslee
wanted but really was all she could handle at this point. Her
thighs were still screaming, but for some reason having
Sherry next to her really helped.

Then Sherry started to sing. At first Weslee said nothing.
She wanted to laugh, but then she recognized the song. It
was a song that she had heard in the church she had gone to
that Sunday a few weeks ago.

The words said something about running a race and not
getting weary, and something about He didn't bring me this
far to quit on me.

She figured she could stop Sherry from singing and looking stupid by getting her talking again.

"I know that song," Weslee said. "I heard it at a church in Boston."

"Oh yeah? Which one?"

"New Covenant in Mattapan."

"No! That's my church, girl."

"What a coincidence." *At least that's stopped her singing,* Weslee thought.

"You're not a member?"

"No, I just visited once. It was really good."

"Girl, I don't know how you could just visit once and not go back. I went there one time with my sister, and I've been going ever since. That was six years ago."

OK. Worst-case scenario is that she keeps on singing. I can handle her preaching to me for the next six miles. Maybe, Weslee thought. *Or, I may just have to speed up and leave her in my dust.*

Sherry went on and on. She sang in the choir there. She apparently was involved in every youth, poverty, and prison-outreach program there was.

"Where do you find time to work?" Weslee asked her when she finally could get a word in.

"Girl, all I have is time. The *Boston Beacon* only claims about eight hours of my day; the rest of my time is mine. Sixteen hours is a lot."

Sherry was a general assignment reporter at the *Beacon*, a smaller competitor to the *Boston Globe*. Weslee had been very impressed with that. Sherry was only thirty, but she had already worked at some of the top newspapers in the country—a fact that Weslee found out only because she asked detailed questions. Sherry didn't seem to care much about her impressive resume. She was more excited about her choir singing and all the work she was doing with the church.

"You should really come out next Sunday, girl," Sherry said. "We're going to be doing a new song."

"I'll try to make it," Weslee said.

Well, I might, she thought. *Depends on what Duncan has*

planned for the day. Last Sunday he had driven her all the way down the Mohawk Trail to Western Massachusetts to see more of the fall foliage. New England was so beautiful, and Duncan had made the day perfect.

"So, do you have a boyfriend?" Sherry asked after being silent about ten minutes.

Weslee thought for a minute. *Well, OK.*

"Yes." Then yes again to herself, yes, she could finally say that she had a boyfriend. She told Sherry about him. How sweet and attentive he could be despite his moodiness.

"Why is he so moody? You say he withdraws into his shell about one day a week?"

Trust her to focus on the one negative thing I said, Weslee thought. *Maybe I should speed up.* The race was getting thick again. Runners could finally get a taste of the finish line, and the slackers were upping their pace. *Four miles left,* Weslee thought. She felt great. She had hit and passed the wall, and she didn't even know when it had happened. She glanced over at Sherry. *I'm glad I met her,* she thought, *nosy as she is.*

"I don't know why. I think he's just one of those people. Things bother him, and he doesn't want to talk about it. He fights a lot with his family. I'm sure once we get closer he'll trust me more and be more open."

"Hmmm," Sherry said. "I'm sure you're right."

"What about you?" Weslee asked. "Who's the man in your life?"

Sherry laughed out loud. "That would be Jesus."

Weslee groaned inside.

"I'm living for God. Girl, you're looking at someone who's been lied to, cheated on, deceived, abused, you name it. I've been there, and I ain't going back. I'm working on the only relationships that I know are not going to disappoint me, and that's the one I have with God and the one I have with myself."

Weslee was silenced again by Sherry's openness. And wisdom? She didn't know. Sherry was pretty. *Prettier than me*, Weslee thought. She wore her hair in long, tiny braids, and her running gear outlined her near-perfect athletic body. *So, why doesn't she have a man, and how did she get mixed up in all that mess she's talking about? Sounds to me like she's been hurt, and she's taking comfort—no, hiding—in church.* Weslee pitied her in a way. *She really ought to get herself out there and not give up so soon.* There were good men out there. *I found one*, Weslee thought.

Sherry started singing again.

Weslee laughed. Then she joined in. There were people around them.

"Hey, that's a great song," a guy said as he passed them.

"Yeah, good for you that you can still sing at mile twenty-four and a half," an older man said as he huffed and puffed his way by.

"We're making excellent time," Weslee said, looking at her watch. She was still hurting. Her legs didn't feel like rubber anymore. They felt like lead. But her heart felt light. Sherry was smiling.

"I prayed," she said.

"What?" Weslee asked.

"I prayed for us," Sherry said again.

I'm not going there, Weslee decided.

They stopped talking after they saw the marker for mile twenty-five.

They upped their pace. Weslee's heart was pounding, and her legs were numb. She knew Sherry was feeling the same way. She looked at her watch again. She was going to make it with time to spare. They had a half mile left, and it had been three hours and twenty minutes since she left the start line. She wanted to leap into the air and whoop in victory. But she knew she didn't have the energy.

She looked over at her side, but Sherry wasn't there. She looked back, and Sherry had fallen a few paces behind.

"Sherry, you OK?" Sherry looked terrible.

"I don't know. My legs feel like they're about to give out." Sherry looked as if she would stop any minute. Her face was covered in sweat, and she was running slower and slower with each step.

Weslee slowed. "Don't stop, Sherry. We're almost there."

"No, go on without me. You have to make your time."

"No, I've got plenty of time to spare."

They were running so slowly that some walkers passed them.

Weslee fished out her Gatorade from her sports belt. She gave Sherry the bottle.

"Remember the song, Sherry?" Weslee said as Sherry sipped from the bottle.

Sherry nodded. But she still insisted that she was going to walk.

"OK, my turn to pray for us," Weslee said. And she couldn't believe it as she said those words. *Anything to get us across the finish line*, she thought.

She grabbed Sherry's hand as they continued their walk-limp-run. "God, I'm praying for my friend here, Sherry. She's tired, and she's gotta get across this finish line. So I'm asking you to give her a little strength to make it the rest of the way. Ummm. Thanks. Amen."

She looked at Sherry. Sherry smiled. Then she laughed.

"That was pretty good," Sherry said.

They both laughed. Weslee hadn't really prayed in a while. Her religion was probably the first thing she had lost when she left home to go to college. After seventeen years of being under her parents' strict rules, she couldn't wait to be free—and Evanston had been her promised land.

They continued the walk-limp-run for what seemed like an eternity. Then the crowds on the sidelines got thicker and more vocal. The cheering got louder, and they could hear the loud, cheesy techno music, and an announcer calling out names.

"We're there! We're there!" Weslee suddenly forgot about the pain—hers and Sherry's.

"Yes!" Sherry yelled out.

Then Sherry started running hard. Weslee was taken aback. Then she started running, too. The finish line was in plain view.

"Weslee Dunster of Boston, Sherry Charles of Dorchester," the announcer said as they crossed the finish line together.

They jumped up and down, screaming, and embraced like old friends.

"You did it, girl," Sherry said to Weslee.

"No, you did it," Weslee told her.

She had made her time. Eight minutes to spare, and a new friend in the bargain.

Later, driving back to Boston in the rented Cavalier, Weslee used her cell phone to call home. First she told her sister about the Sherry experience. They both decided that Sherry sounded like a Jesus freak and was probably a little crazy. Weslee wanted to talk more about it but promised Terry she would call from home; it would be cheaper to talk on the land line.

Then Weslee realized she had forgotten to get Sherry's number after they had limped off to separate cars.

Darn, she thought. *Guess I'll just have to go to that church next Sunday.*

Chapter
11

That night, Weslee felt as if she would never walk again. Her lower body felt as if someone had yanked out both her legs and banged them over and over again against a brick wall and then shoved them back into the sockets of her pelvis. She had limped her way out of the car into the apartment building and after a long shower had taken to her bed.

She kept the phone near the bed so that she wouldn't have to move in case it rang. She had left Duncan a message on his cell, telling him her finish time. She had hoped he would be so excited for her that he would call right back.

I just hope he hasn't gone into one of his moods, she thought.

She had called her sister again as soon as she had gotten home from the race. Even before she made it to the shower.

"You're crazy," was what Terry had said to her after congratulating her. "I don't know what would possess you to do that to yourself," she had said jokingly.

It was Sunday, so her parents were having dinner over at Terry's house. Her mother had talked to her quickly. She was too preoccupied with her two grandkids, Kasey and Mark, to bother with Weslee.

Weslee didn't mind. She, too, couldn't help but be captivated by the three-year-old twins when she was around them.

Her father, however, was so proud. He wanted her to send him her medal so he could show it to his friends at his lodge.

"So you get to run the Boston Marathon next," he had said, the pride evident in his voice. "You know, I always knew you were going to do big things. I always wanted to have a boy, but when we first took you home from the hospital, I said that's it for me. This one's gonna make me proud."

"And what about me, Dad?" she heard Terry say in the background.

Weslee had laughed. Her father always said things like that to her. It made her so happy just to make him proud. He believed in hard work and achieving. Whenever she or Terry had complained about anything while they were growing up, he had given them a lecture about how he moved to this country in 1963 with a degree in accounting, leaving a government job and his well-off parents behind to drive a taxi on the South Side and sleep at the YMCA for four years before he got a break, working as a mail-room clerk for LaSalle Bank and then working his way up from there to the accounting department. It hadn't been easy for him; why should it be easy for them?

That's why she and Terry never griped too much about homework, studying, sports, going to church every Sunday, Wednesday, and Friday, getting into Northwestern. They just did it. They used to daydream out loud to each other about leaving home and leaving Chicago. Weslee would dream about moving to New York and becoming a stockbroker or an investment banker, making a ton of money, going to fancy parties, marrying a rich, handsome man and living in a big house in the suburbs. Terry's dream was always to move to Milwaukee with Troy Brumant, the boy next door, and have plenty of kids. Terry's dream had come true right out of college.

"So, how's that fine, rich man of yours?" Terry asked.

"He's fine. He's with his family today. I haven't heard from him yet."

Weslee didn't want to betray how badly she felt about that fact.

"Girl, this is a big day for you. Why isn't he there rubbing your feet?"

Trust Terry to make the obvious so painfully obvious.

"Well, he's got his family thing. They don't get along that well, so I don't think he wants to tick them off." She heard herself and didn't like the way she was sounding.

"Nice of you to make excuses for a grown man," Terry said.

"I'm sure he's coming. He's probably just tied up now."

"Hmm. What time is it?"

"It's eight forty-five," Weslee answered.

"Well, I need to go put the kids to bed. They're up too late as it is. But you know your mother, she'll keep 'em up all night if she has to."

"Fine. I'll see you guys in a couple weeks. Tell Mom I'll bake the pie."

When Weslee hung up the phone, she looked at the clock on her lonely bedroom wall. It was almost nine. Duncan hadn't called. She called his cell again. It went straight to voice mail. She reached for another Tylenol. *At least if these things don't get rid of the pain, they should put me to sleep*, she thought.

Two hours later, she was still awake. She was reading a textbook—half reading it and half looking at the phone.

It never rang.

He did call the very next morning, full of apologies. His family gathering had gotten loud and rowdy, and he just couldn't get away. She was still disappointed, but she didn't want to seem spoiled so she took his excuse lightly, telling him the details of the race.

In typical Duncan fashion, he wanted to make it up to her. This time it was a weekend trip to the Berkshires—another place she had read about but had never been. She was so excited.

Chapter
12

Weslee packed, or prepacked. It was only Wednesday. But she wanted to be sure that she was bringing all the right things on her weekend trip with Duncan. She packed some hiking gear, a nice dress, just in case, and a couple of sexy underthings. She would definitely need those.

Lana sat on her living room couch, her spiky-heeled boots on Weslee's coffee table.

"Wes, I wish you'd come out dancing with us tonight," she said, flipping the channels on the television.

"No way. I'm not going into any more smoky, stinky clubs. I don't know how you do it, Lana."

"You're no fun anymore. Since Duncan started paying a little attention to you . . ."

"What?" Weslee said coming out of the room, a sweater dangling from her hand.

"Well, you never want to do anything fun anymore," Lana said, not taking her eyes away from the TV screen.

Weslee sighed. What she wanted to say was: *I never wanted to go to those clubs. I just have an excuse not to go now.*

"It's not just Duncan," Weslee said. "I've got to get this place cleaned up, plus finish up that Statistics project before Thanksgiving break. I really don't have time—"

Lana raised a hand. "I've heard it before, OK?"

The phone rang. It was Sherry.

Weslee felt Lana's eyes on her as she agreed to have coffee with the other woman.

"Who's Sherry?" she asked, her eyes narrowing as Weslee hung up the phone.

"It's the girl I met at the marathon. Remember I told you about her?"

"Oh, the Jesus freak?"

"She really isn't, you know," Weslee said. "She's devout, but she's totally normal."

"And she's a journalist?"

"Yup."

Lana sniffed. "I don't trust journalists."

Weslee laughed. "Lana, really, it's not like you're Carly Fiorina or Donna Dubinsky."

Lana looked at her blankly.

How could she not recognize the names of two of the highest-profile women in American business? Weslee sighed.

"Where's she from?"

"Why?"

"I just wanna know. Is she fat?"

"No, she's not fat. She's an athlete. And she's West Indian."

"So, she's ugly?"

"Lana, why do you have to be so shallow? It's so childish."

Lana laughed. "OK, Ms. Mature Adult. I'm gonna go now. I'm meeting the rest of the girls at the Rack."

Weslee felt relieved that she would not be meeting the rest of the group from their class at the raucous bar-dance club-pool hall. The place was one of the city's biggest meat markets. The one time she went, she had vowed never to go again. Women were wandering around half-naked as men stared and some even groped at them. Weslee had never been so disgusted.

"Too bad you won't get to see us dancing on the table."
Lana winked as she closed the door behind her.

Weslee continued to pack for her trip to the Berkshires
with Duncan. It was still hard for her to believe she and
Duncan were spending so much time together. He made
her feel like a princess. She was falling hard, and it had gotten to the point where she couldn't stop herself anymore.

With Lana gone from her apartment, she suddenly felt
more hopeful and freer to revel in all the feelings that she
had for Duncan. Weslee knew that a little familial jealousy
was involved, so she tried not to take offense when Lana
would roll her eyes every time Duncan's name came up.

But now she really wanted to talk to somebody else
about this man who was turning her world upside down.
She called Sherry.

An hour later she was in Sherry's car, driving to a part of
the city she had never seen before.

"Wow, so this is Dorchester?"

Sherry laughed. "You say it like it's another country."

More like another city, she thought. The old houses close
together, the faces of color all over the neighborhood, and
the small storefronts reminded her of some neighborhoods
in South Side Chicago. This was nothing like the sanitized
version of the city that she got from her perch on Commonwealth Avenue.

"Yes, this is the real Boston. I couldn't live anywhere
else," Sherry said.

Sherry Charles was one of those people who loved being
deep inside the city, with its noise, crime, litter, and everything else. Her family had been part of the 1980s wave of
Jamaicans, Bajans, Grenadians, and other Islanders who had
left economically declining Caribbean countries for the promise of a job, a home, and an education in Ronald Reagan's
America. Many of them had found those things were not so
easy to come by. Some had returned to their homelands,

discouraged that it took more than just one menial job to get from point A to point B in this promised land. Others stayed, grudgingly putting aside their college educations from back home, to take on cleaning jobs, retail work, construction, and trades to feed their families. They worked hard. So hard that the Americans derided their work ethic: All West Indians have eight jobs, had been the running joke. But they kept on working. Now they made up more than a third of the city's black population, owning most of the houses in the inner city and building a growing middle class right in the heart of Boston.

They stopped into a café in a crowded square teeming with young Cape Verdean mothers, schoolchildren, idle teenagers, and men and women running errands.

"This is Uphams Corner," Sherry announced as she pulled her Toyota into a parking space on the street.

"Wow. This looks a bit like Ninety-fifth Street."

"Uh-uh," Sherry said. "I've been to Ninety-fifth Street—it's much nicer."

They both laughed.

One of the newspapers Sherry had worked for was the *Chicago Sun-Times*. She had been a crime reporter, and as she told Weslee, "I saw under the underbelly of that city."

The tiny restaurant could not have fit in Boston's Back Bay. The staff was too friendly and familiar with the patrons and with each other. They hurled jokes back and forth from the kitchen and traded insults jokingly as they served the customers. Weslee, for a minute, tried to picture Lana in a place like this, and she had to smile at the image. She could hear the boom boom boom of the cars driving by on Columbia Road—just like the South Side. Weslee felt right at home.

They decided on coffee and bread pudding with rum sauce.

Weslee laughed a lot. Loudly and easily. Sherry was

funny, outspoken, self-effacing, and honest to a fault. She reminded Weslee of her old friend Ann Marie when they were both young and carefree and laughed at everything and everybody, sometimes for no reason at all but to laugh.

"So, you met this man at a party on Oak Bluffs?" she asked Weslee curiously. "That Vineyard crowd has a lot of issues. Be careful."

"What do you mean? Like class issues?"

Sherry nodded, sipping her coffee. "Not all of them, mind you. I did a story on that a few years ago, and some of those people are just weird. They'd say the most innocuous thing and then they'd be like, 'I don't want my name in the paper. My friends would just ostracize me.' They're just plain strange, some of them."

"Well, Duncan's really not like that. I mean, at first I thought he was, you know, into the 'Who's your family, and where did you go to school thing.' But we're so close. I think if he had a problem with me not being from money, things wouldn't have gone this far."

"I'm sure you're right," Sherry said. "Have you met anyone in his family yet?"

"Well, I know Lana. But I knew her before I met him."

She nodded. "He sounds like a real catch, girl. Lucky you." Sherry said this with no guile whatsoever.

"I know. I really am lucky." Weslee hesitated. "You know what, Sherry? I was thinking that maybe I should ask him to come home with me for Thanksgiving, you know, to meet my parents."

Sherry pursed her lips. "Wes, you probably should let him take the lead on that one. From the little I know about men, I think they like to be in control of the pacing of things. If you ask, it might freak him out."

It was what Weslee already knew, but she was disappointed anyway.

They talked for hours about Sherry's family. She had

three brothers, all married. Her mother had died of cancer a few years before, and her father had remarried, but they were still close. Her entire family lived within ten minutes of each other.

"You are nothing like Lana," Weslee found herself saying after two hours had passed and there had not been a single disagreement or put-down that left Weslee cringing.

"I have to meet this Lana you're always talking about. She sounds like a real character."

"Oh, she is. And you'll get to meet her soon," Weslee said.

"Uh-oh. That sounded like a warning." Sherry grinned.

"It was."

For the first time since she'd landed in Boston, Weslee felt at home in her skin. She was wearing her new Kors sweater, but Sherry did not even seem to notice it, nor had she complimented her on it. Lana had let out a high-pitched squeal the first time Weslee had worn the gray wooly thing to class. Sherry was also oblivious to the new knee-high brown Costume National boots and the new Tiffany necklace with the intertwined hearts. But once Weslee had gotten over the shock of this sartorial snub she began to relax. This was like the old days, she thought, when she could be her old self who didn't care too much about appearances. And she was having a good old girl-friend time.

"Man, I haven't been in the hood in a while. This is like homecoming!" Weslee laughed, looking outside the café window.

"You and Lana have never come down here before?" Sherry was incredulous.

"I don't think Lana even knows this place exists."

Sherry shook her head and took another sip of coffee thoughtfully, and Weslee wondered whether she was being judged. But she brushed the thought away.

As they rose to leave, it occurred to Welsee that not once had Sherry complained about anything in the tiny eatery. With Lana it was always something: the food was too cold or too hot; the silverware was dirty; the service too slow; the napkins too worn. It had gotten to the point where Weslee herself was beginning to notice those things in restaurants, too. But her increasingly critical eye had not picked up on any of those slips at this little hole-in-the-wall. Maybe she'd been too busy making a real friend.

Chapter
13

The semester was winding down toward the Thanksgiving holiday, and everyone was restless. People were comparing airline deals as they made plans to go home for the holiday. Weslee tried to concentrate as the Information Systems professor explained system query language, but it was difficult to stay focused.

For one thing, she was exhausted. Her schedule at HealthyLife was taking its toll. She still hadn't told Duncan that she had taken a part-time job. The great thing about being a trainer was that she found she was in better shape for her early morning runs. But she was still tired most of the time. It was all becoming too much. There was dinner tomorrow evening with Lana and Sherry, their first meeting, and she felt as nervous as if she were bringing a man home to meet her parents. Then there was the trip with Duncan on the weekend.

She was trying to change the way she thought about Duncan—the permanent, together-forever way. She knew it was soon, and Sherry had warned her that she should slow down a bit, but he was making it so hard. She looked down at her cell phone on her desk. On the display screen was the SMS message he had sent her just minutes ago. "I'm in a meeting, but I'm seeing you naked. Help!" the message said. She had wanted to laugh out loud in class when she read it. That was Duncan. He e-mailed and called all day long through his busy day.

Her cell phone buzzed again. It was another message from him. "Hey, can I come over for dinner tonight? I'll pick something up."

"Ms. Dunster." The professor was talking to her. "Maybe you could give us a brief summary of what we just discussed?"

Weslee's heart dropped, but thankfully she had done the reading. Based on her flimsy memories of the textbook, she bluffed her way through what she knew about SQL for about three minutes, trying to sound as confident and authoritative as she could. Mercifully, the professor didn't throw her out of the class for her halfhearted efforts. She noticed Lana smirking at her from across the room, and she rolled her eyes in response.

It all paid off that night. Duncan came over with Chinese from P.F. Chang's and a bottle of wine at exactly 8:00 P.M.

"I can't wait for the weekend," she said as they ate at her tiny dining room table.

"I'm glad you're excited. You're going to love Williamstown. We're supposed to get snow this weekend, so it's going to be real beautiful."

"Snow. Oh, that sounds so romantic!" She was ecstatic. Maybe they'd just spend the whole weekend inside the inn, looking out on snow-covered hills and mountains.

Then his cell phone rang. He looked at the display screen and turned off the phone.

"You can take it, I don't mind."

"Nah, it's not important."

"You sure?"

"I said it's not important," Duncan blurted testily.

Weslee didn't say anything. This had happened before.

They would be together and his phone would ring and he would just go off into a world of his own, and there was nothing she could do to bring him back. Now the mood at the table had suddenly changed. He grew silent and ate moodily. The first time it happened she had tried to coax him out of it, he had raised his voice to her, telling her to let it be. So she wouldn't try this time. She'd just ride it out. She ate silently, too.

She put the dishes away but kept one eye on him. He went straight for her computer. She noticed that he pulled up his Hotmail account and began to type furiously. Must be work-related, she thought. The only thing that got him all tied up in knots was work. She decided to stay out of his way until his mood passed.

Chapter
14

Calypso music played softly under the chatter of the Sunday night diners at Rhythm & Spice restaurant in Cambridge. The restaurant was one of a tiny handful of real Caribbean eateries in the city. It drew a diverse crowd ranging from MIT professors to local fly girls and boys hoping to grind to the beat of reggae late into the night after a healthy helping of redfish and rice and beans or spicy jerk chicken.

Weslee and Sherry sipped ginger ale and caught up with each other about their past weeks as they waited for Lana to arrive.

"I can't wait for you to meet her," Weslee said, looking at the entrance of the dimly lit restaurant. As usual, Lana was running at least twenty minutes behind.

Sherry looked at her watch. "Well, if the waitress comes back one more time, I'm ordering."

Weslee rolled her eyes. "She'll be here."

And there she was.

"Weslee, sweetie, I'm so sorry I'm late." Lana swiftly removed her expensive-looking tan leather jacket and took the empty seat next to Weslee. She held out her hand to Sherry. "I've heard so much about you."

Sherry smiled and extended her hand.

"Well, this place is different," Lana said, looking around the restaurant. "I don't think I've ever been to a Caribbean restaurant before. Well, not in the States anyway. I mean, I've been to restaurants in the Caribbean." She laughed nervously and looked at Sherry even more nervously. Sherry had stopped smiling.

Weslee couldn't put her finger on it, but something very strange was going on between Lana and Sherry.

To Weslee's relief, the waitress came.

"What do you suggest, Sherry?" Lana asked a little too politely and maybe a bit condescendingly.

Sherry took a deep breath. "Hon, the menu's in English."

Lana cleared her throat loudly, and Weslee could see a quick glint of anger flash across her eyes.

"Well, I'm going to get the jerk chicken." Weslee tried to sound as normal as possible, as if the tension at the table wasn't so thick it threatened to suck up all the air in the restaurant.

"I think . . . I'll just go for the rice and beans and vegetables," Sherry said.

"Are you a vegetarian?" Lana asked, forcing a smile, after she had ordered the jerk chicken.

"No, I just don't eat a lot of meat." Sherry was still not being her usual friendly self.

"Oh, that's right, you're a health-nut runner, too, just like Weslee. By the way, I just love your accent."

Sherry tensed, and Weslee raced to do triage. "I told Lana how we were just dying in that Bay State race, girl." Weslee laughed, but it didn't sound real.

There was no stopping Sherry. "My accent? I was just about to comment on yours. I really can't place it at all."

"Oh, really?" Lana layered on the honey with a twist of sarcasm. "Well, I was born in Massachusetts—on the Vineyard, actually. But I was raised in Rye, New York. I have a lot of family who've lived in Boston all their lives, though."

Sherry nodded.

"What about you? You're from Jamaica, right?"

"Mmm-hmmm." Sherry sipped her water.

"When did you come to this country?"

"My parents came when I was eight."

"Oh, what do they do?"

"My mother was a nurses' assistant; she passed a couple of years ago. My father's an orderly at Mass. General."

"Oh." It was Lana's turn to sip her water and avert her eyes.

"What do your folks do?"

"Um, my mother doesn't really work. She has these groups that she does things with. You know."

Sherry raised her eyebrows. Of course, she knew.

"My father's retired from his family's business."

Sherry nodded.

"So, what's it like working for the newspaper?" Lana's forced interest was almost palpable.

"It's OK. It's a job just like any other."

"Your parents must be so proud of you. You know, the fact that you did so well for a first-generation immigrant. . . ."

Sherry cleared her throat so loudly that diners at the adjacent table glanced over.

Weslee winced. This was not going well. It was as if Sherry and Lana were locked in a boxing ring, circling each other, waiting for each other to say the wrong thing. Sherry especially.

Lana took the hint and sipped her water.

"So, what do you plan to do after business school?" Sherry asked.

"I don't know yet. Maybe travel. Maybe go on vacation to Jamaica." Lana laughed.

"It must be nice to have those options."

"Well, you're not doing too badly yourself. You're working for one of the best newspapers in the country. How did you end up there? Where did you go to college?"

Sherry cocked her head to the side.

Weslee looked at Sherry desperately. Please don't go off on her, her eyes begged.

"I went to Wellesley College; I got my master's at BU."

"Oh, I have a lot of friends who went to Wellesley," Lana said brightly.

"I'm sure you do." Sherry looked around the restaurant. For the waiter? The exit? A weapon?

"Do you know Peony Smalls?"

Sherry yawned rudely. "I knew of her. Listen, I don't think I have anything much in common with any of the people you knew, OK?"

"Well, excuse me. I was just trying to make conversation." Lana sounded genuinely hurt.

"That's OK. Let's just talk about something else." Sherry tapped her forefinger on the table and leaned back in her chair.

Weslee struggled to find something to say that would break the iceberg that was quickly solidifying at the table.

Too late.

"What is your problem?" Lana tried in vain to get Sherry to meet her eyes.

"My problem? What's the deal with you asking me to recite my resume for you? And then assuming my family's a bunch of poor immigrants when you don't even know me." Sherry made no attempt to conceal her anger.

Weslee could see that Lana was taken aback.

"I didn't mean . . . I was just trying to make conversation."

"Conversation?" Sherry laughed derisively. "That's how you make conversation? How about seen any interesting movies lately? Or maybe nice weather we're having. That's making conversation!"

Lana shook her head and laughed uneasily. "I'm having a hard time understanding where this attitude is coming from. Don't take your issues out on me."

Weslee couldn't take it any longer. "You guys," she moaned. They ignored her.

"My attitude is coming from your being late, not calling to let us know whether or not you would be here, and talking down to me. That's the beginning of where my attitude is coming from!" Sherry said, and other diners again looked over at their table.

"You guys, please."

"Sweetheart," Lana said, her voice laced with bile, "you need to stop being so sensitive, I'm not . . ."

"OK, that's it." Sherry stood up. She started to put on her coat.

"Sherry, what are you doing?" Weslee pleaded, standing herself.

"I'm not sitting here with this silly girl. I have better things to do with my time. I'll call you later."

Weslee stood with her mouth open as Sherry picked up her pocketbook and walked out of the restaurant. She almost bumped into the waitress, who was bringing their food.

Weslee turned to look at Lana, who sat at the table looking unperturbed.

Weslee sat down, at a loss for words.

"No offense, Wes, but this is why I do not hang out with foreigners. They come here to this country and they act like you have to treat them special." Lana shook her head.

"Where's your other diner?" the waitress asked in a Haitian Creole-influenced accent.

"She had to leave. Could you wrap up her food please?" Weslee decided she'd stop by Sherry's on the way home. She couldn't decide what to say to Lana, who was digging into her food with gusto, as if nothing had happened. "What was it about her that made you act like that?" Weslee asked finally.

"Act like what? She started it. Don't you start with me, too."

"Well, it just seemed that you were being fake and patronizing." Weslee tried to be as gentle as she could.

"Honey, I'm always fake and patronizing, aren't I?" Lana didn't look up from her food.

Weslee didn't know what to say.

They ate in silence. She was relieved when the check came.

"I think I'll take a cab home," Weslee said at the end of the meal.

She didn't go home. She told the driver Sherry's address.

"I don't know what came over her," Weslee said a few minutes later at Sherry's house. "She can be difficult, but it's never this bad. I'm really sorry."

Sherry shook her head as she devoured her rice and beans and vegetables at the table in her spacious kitchen.

"You yourself have said that this girl can be rude and self-ish, Weslee. Don't apologize for her behavior."

"I wish you would have tried harder . . ."

"I wish I did, too. I know God wasn't pleased with me tonight," Sherry said, shrugging. "But girls like her just make me ill."

"But how could you just lump her in with other people? You only know what I've told you about her. If you got to know her . . ."

"Trust me, Weslee. I know her. I went to a high school where I was one of five black kids. The other four were all like her—striving, snobby, showy, and materialistic. I fit in with the white kids more than I fit in with them. Besides, they always made a point of reminding me that I wasn't really black since I was West Indian. Even at Wellesley, it was the same thing. One girl told me to my face that people like me—people of African descent from other countries—were

stealing from African-Americans because we were just
coasting by on the benefits of the civil rights movement
that they had worked hard for." Sherry laughed bitterly but
didn't look up from her plate.

"But Lana's not like that," Weslee pleaded. "She knows
my folks are from the Islands, and that's hardly ever come
up."

"She is like that, Wes. I'm sorry; she is. They all are. And
you know it, too. That's why you're always apologizing for
her. It's OK that she's your friend. But I can't hang out with
her. It's not just the ethnic thing. I really don't like her personality. And frankly, I don't know why you put up with it."

Weslee sighed. "I'm sorry."

"No need to be sorry. You were just trying to be nice, get
everyone together. In principle, it was a great idea."

Weslee sat next to Sherry, concentrating on the carvings
on the mahogany dining room table. The words echoed in
her head: *I don't know why you put up with it.* But it wasn't
that simple. Lana had brought something out in her that
she hadn't known existed. When she lay in bed at night, she
couldn't wait for the next day to wear another fabulous outfit, another pair of buttery-soft shoes to touch and smell, to
sleep on fine linen, to live her life in a plush cocoon of
seventy-five-dollar moisturizers and forty-dollar lipsticks.
Lana had shown her that. How to love herself in a new way,
with no shame or regret. Sure, it was nice to just let her hair
down and kick back in her Nikes with Sherry, but there was
the other side, too, that needed those nice things. She
couldn't just give up one for the other.

Chapter
15

An otherwise balmy November in Massachusetts was failing to keep up the act. The weather had reverted back to its true colors: gray and ugly. The city of Boston didn't take it well. Every so often people allowed themselves to be fooled by the occasional temperature spikes, and they would mock Mother Nature with their shorts and flip-flops and impromptu games of Frisbee by the Charles River. But then reality would return in full force and they would be just shocked. Shocked. How could it be this cold and snowy? In November!

So the snow came down quickly in big, fat, wet, sticky flakes. They pelted pedestrians fleeing to stores, bus-stop shelters, and subway stations. They stuck to icy sidewalks and forced drivers to turn on windshield wipers to furious speeds to get a better view of the traffic ahead crawling out of the city that Friday afternoon.

Duncan had rented a BMW X5 for their long journey out to the Berkshires, and he was still getting used to the car. "I miss my Z," he kept saying.

"You're such a baby when it comes to that car," Weslee teased. "Do you want me to drive?"

"You? Drive? I want to get there before the New Year."

"Very funny, Duncan. Remember I'm from Chicago. This weather is a picnic for me."

They had tried to beat rush-hour traffic, but then so had everyone else. It would be a slow crawl for the next fifty or so miles. Weslee didn't mind, though. She felt warm and safe in the car with Duncan. She sipped her Starbucks Venti decaf and listened to the weather report on the radio. Ten inches of snow were expected in Boston by tomorrow, double that for Western Massachusetts. Once they got there, she knew it would be perfect.

Three-and-a-half hours later they walked into the Williams Inn. The lobby was quiet except for the staff. The smell of New England clam chowder from the lobby restaurant mixed with the aroma of pine from the huge trees around the inn. A fireplace blazed in a corner. Huge glass windows showed the quaint, snow-covered town buildings and parts of gothic Williams College. It was a storybook New England setting, and Weslee had never seen anything so romantic. She took off the shearling coat that had cost her way, way too much as Duncan checked in at the desk.

They got on the elevator with an elderly couple. The woman eyed Duncan's arm wrapped around Weslee's waist. "Are you newlyweds?" she asked, smiling.

Weslee was embarrassed. Didn't the woman notice that there was no ring on her finger? She hid her left hand just in case the elderly woman chanced a closer look. She didn't want those words, unrealistic as they were, to be taken away from her.

"Not yet," said Duncan, ever the skillful charmer, tightening his arm around Weslee's waist. Her heart leapt at those words. Was he implying something? It's what she had been dreaming of every day for weeks. This "not yet" told her all she needed to know. They were thinking the same thing! *I'm not crazy,* she smiled to herself. *He's feeling the same thing, too. Oh my goodness! My life is going to be so perfect with this man!*

Later at dinner she thanked him for protecting her honor. "How do you know that's what I was doing? I could have meant what I said," he replied.

"Duncan, don't say those things, OK? They make me want . . ." She didn't want to say it for fear of jinxing it.

"Want what?"

"Never mind." She wasn't ready to say what was on her mind.

"Weslee, I think I love you. I know what you're trying to say, that it's too soon. But I can't help the way I feel about you. I want what you want, too. I want us to be together. All the time."

Weslee felt her eyes welling up. How could he just know what she was thinking all the time? "Duncan, I've dreamed of hearing you say those words. I love you. You're what I've always wanted."

She'd planned the whole episode, down to the garter belt she would wear. It would be slow, romantic, and tender; she'd even brought a few scented candles that would set the mood. But no sooner had they walked out of the restaurant than his lips were on her neck, then her ears, then her lips. She felt his hands on her thighs in the elevator up to their room. They'd barely made it inside, and her dress was halfway down her shoulders. "Baby, wait," she protested. "Can't," he mumbled as they stumbled into the room. She could barely think as his lips moved down her body, lingering on her stomach and then below her waist. It was as if she'd entered another dimension, one that claimed all her inhibitions and common sense. She'd never made love that way and not felt ashamed before. With Duncan, she'd felt free to do and say those things she'd only fantasized about in her deepest, darkest dreams. He wanted her to be loud and vulgar, to be aggressive, to not be the perfect lady. It was scary and exciting at the same time. The thought of protection only came to mind long after her third orgasm, and by then it was too late. But she wouldn't give it too much thought. She was on a cloud.

Late into the night she was still awake listening to his light snoring and counting his heartbeats every minute. This was finally it. This would be the man with whom she would spend the rest of her nights. She felt complete, that something that had long been missing in her had finally been found.

The sun woke her up the next morning. It glinted off the covering of snow on the ground outside and shone in slits through the heavy burgundy floor-to-ceiling damask drapes. It was already nine-thirty.

As she brushed her teeth, she decided she would get room service. The phone rang before she could pick it up to dial.

"Hello, Susan?" a male voice said on the other end.

"I think you have the wrong room," Weslee said and hung up the phone quickly. She dialed room service and ordered a huge breakfast. Duncan woke up while she was on the phone.

"Who's calling so early?" He yawned.

"Wrong number." She leaned over to kiss him, and he pulled her back into the bed. She tried in vain to get away from him. "Wait, honey. I'm still talking to the room-service people."

"I can't wait," he said as he wrestled off her short satin La Perla nightgown.

She quickly finished off the order before turning her attention to him.

Twenty minutes later, his cell phone rang. "Wow," he said. "I didn't even know I could get a signal out here."

It was the office. From the look on his face, she could tell it was something serious. "Yes, I did give you the right number. Well, you must have dialed wrong." He frowned.

Room service was at the door. She grabbed a tip from her purse, wrapped herself in her robe, and went to the door. She could hear Duncan talking to his firm.

"So, when do you need me to go there? Are you serious? This Monday? What about Cox? Fine. Fine."

She could tell he was upset. He was sitting up in bed, rubbing his hairy chest and frowning.

"What's wrong?" She kneeled on the bed and ran her index finger up and down his arm.

"It's this client, Jackson. He's probably going to be indicted for fraud and embezzlement. I've got to go to London on Monday to look at things."

"Oh. For how long?"

"I don't know. A week, maybe."

She was disappointed, but she didn't want to let it show. She didn't want him to retreat into one of his moods this weekend.

"Well, that's not too long, honey." She burrowed her head in his chest, and he smoothed her hair.

"Yeah. Now's just a bad time. I don't like dealing with the London office. Everything's just a big hassle over there."

"Didn't you work there before?" He had mentioned something about that once.

"Yes, for a year after law school. But that was six years ago. It's changed."

"But at least you have friends there."

He sighed. Obviously, he didn't want to talk about it anymore. "Listen, we should probably leave early on Sunday so I can pack and get some work done before I leave Monday morning."

Again, she tried to keep her mood bright and upbeat despite her disappointment. "Sure, I understand, honey. Let's have some breakfast."

She chattered on and on during breakfast although she could see him starting to slip away. She somehow managed to persuade him to go sightseeing in the snow. And as the day wore on, his mood improved.

They spent the morning trudging through the snow, visiting little shops and admiring the Williams College campus. Then they drove up to nearby Bennington, Vermont.

Weslee, despite her promise to herself to become frugal, shopped with happy abandon at a long strip of designer outlet stores. Duncan, amused, tried to slow her down; he laughed at her as the bags began to pile up. "You're as bad as Lana." He shook his head. "But at least you're spending your own money and not your folks'." This statement only gave her pause for a brief second. *My own money. My retirement money. Oh well*, she thought. *I'm still young. I have plenty of time to rebuild my savings. It's just money*, she told herself as another store caught her eye.

They stopped in Armani and she bought herself a nondescript pair of black tuxedo pants that cost a week's salary for her or a year's worth of food for a family in a Third World country. But that thought only fleeted through her mind like Marion Jones doing the 100-meter dash. Duncan's teasing only seemed to push her deeper into the frenzy. She couldn't resist a midsize Fendi pouch that would probably go well with a dusty pink cashmere sweater by Luxe she'd recently picked up on Bluefly.com. She bought him three ties. He bought her chocolates at Godiva. Then later that night he gave her a tiny black Donna Karan dress. She couldn't for the life of her figure out when or how he had bought it over the afternoon and managed to hide it from her. He never ceased to amaze her. She was happy as she packed her booty into the car even though the trip had been cut short. She'd spent another two hundred fifty dollars on cosmetics at Chanel, and she couldn't wait to get home to try on all the new colors—the lipsticks, eye shadow, blushes. It would all make up for the fact that she couldn't have Duncan with her the rest of the day.

Weslee hummed along with Jill Scott as they drove back to Boston that clear Sunday afternoon. Her choice. Duncan hated R&B music. Seal was about as much as he could stand.

Differing musical tastes aside, the weekend had been just perfect. It confirmed for Weslee everything she needed to know about this relationship. Duncan was the man for her. He had told her and shown her that he loved her and wanted to be with her. It was not all in her head.

She looked at him and fondled his right ear, her favorite. She was so happy. Even though he was preoccupied and moody now because of his trip to London, she was certain that once he came back, it would be a new start. She was officially his woman. He was her man.

She couldn't wait for her Thanksgiving trip to Chicago the following weekend. She felt safe. It was OK to tell her parents now. Maybe she could even convince him to come home with her for Christmas. She leaned back into the soft leather of the SAV and daydreamed.

Chapter
16

Christmas was in the air, and Lana was out of control. On two consecutive days, she showed up to class drunk. Weslee could smell it on her breath, and she heard other classmates whispering and tittering about it. Over the course of the semester Lana had destroyed any credibility she had with any of the professors. They had ceased to be dazzled by her outsized personality and charm. Never mind that she was always turning in assignments late and generally making a fool of herself in class. She had alienated most of her friends by leaving them in the lurch on group projects. Weslee was the only friend she had left.

Weslee decided that she had to do something. But it was so hard to even talk to Lana. Being around Sherry had reminded her what real friendship felt like, and it was hard to go back to Lana's cattiness, self-absorption, and selfishness.

They had both gone to visit their families at Thanksgiving, and while Weslee had come back excited and kind of sad at leaving her folks, Lana seemed preoccupied and a little depressed. Her mood was the only reason that Weslee had agreed to go with her to yet another party just one day after returning from Chicago.

It was some professional party host's version of a post-Thanksgiving celebration; Weslee decided then that she'd never go to any of those parties again.

They had started off on the wrong foot. Lana took one look at her and decided that she had to change. Weslee had already worn her outfit before to some other event.

"Unlike you, Lana, I'm living off my savings, and I'm not about to put myself further into debt just to impress other people." Weslee was embarrassed but angry at the same time. The few days she had spent in Chicago had meant less money coming from HealthyLife Spa. She couldn't afford to throw away her money on Prada and Dolce & Gabbana the way Lana did.

"Fine. But everyone's going to know you wore this before," Lana had said, flipping her hair again as she headed for the door.

"Everyone who? I don't know any of those people; they're your friends."

"Exactly, Weslee. And who I'm with says a lot about me," Lana had hissed.

"Whatever," Weslee had replied. "I won't go, then."

But Lana had apologized halfheartedly; Weslee ended up going unwillingly.

The party had been loud and raucous. It was another event thrown by Dwayne Short, the self-appointed buppie host of Boston. Weslee had met him a few times and actually liked him. He was a nice enough guy. Sometimes she looked at him while his parties were in full swing and she could just tell that he wanted to be somewhere else. Maybe somewhere quiet, where he didn't have to pretend to be the life of the party to all these young, disillusioned people who were so dependent on him to provide the right situation, the right setting to meet that perfect guy or girl, get that perfect cocktail, get that perfect hookup. He was working the room, cigar in hand, being charming, handsome. Fabulous. But his eyes just looked so tired and empty when he had greeted her. She totally understood. She felt the same way.

Lana, of course, was having a great time. Every other song was her favorite song. All the men wanted to dance with her or get her phone number. She was in her element—the center of attention. Women were throwing dagger looks at her. Boyfriends stared longingly.

Weslee's feet ached. She missed Duncan and hoped he wasn't too busy in London to miss her, too. The music was loud, the smoke stifling, and the smell of alcohol made her nauseated.

Lana had gotten upset with her again. Had told her that she was ruining her good time. Then she left with a guy she had just met, leaving Weslee to cab it home again.

Weslee had gotten home tired and upset. Lana was turning into someone she couldn't stand to be around anymore.

The next day Sherry gave her a pep talk as they ran together along the Charles. "Face it, Weslee. The woman is difficult to be around. You either have to suck it up and accept her for who she is, or you're going to have to let her go. If there's something about her that you feel that you really can't live without, then, good, keep her around. But don't feel that you owe it to her to be her friend. She can find other friends. I have a feeling she picked you over the other girls in your class because you're the only one who will put up with her crap."

As usual, Weslee defended Lana. "Not really. The other girls like to party with her. But she says they're too phony."

"*She* thought *they* were phony?"

A cold blast of wind had ended that conversation as they picked up the pace, trying to reach the end of the run in the wintry weather.

Weslee felt more grounded the closer she got to Sherry. She felt that she could really be herself around her. Sherry was like a sister to her. They both liked acid jazz and reggae music; they both loved to cook, to run, to read. Weslee had returned to New Covenant Church, and she really liked it there, not just because it reminded her of home, but because it made her feel so warm and happy. She had met some of Sherry's friends, and not a single one of them had asked what her father did for a living. Weslee was finally beginning to feel at home in Boston. And Duncan was just the icing on the cake.

When she returned from Chicago, Duncan had been in a murderous mood. She had done her best to be supportive and understanding. He was still bogged down in that embezzlement case with the European client. He had gone to London twice in the last month, for Thanksgiving and then again last weekend. Apparently, the client there required a lot of his time.

But once he got back, things had started to get a little better. The day he returned, it had snowed. They went cross-country skiing at a golf course in Weston that was used as a ski trail in the winter. He brought her back a beautiful Burberry scarf. She had squealed when she opened the Harrods box that night.

She was trying not to notice that most of their time together now was late at night. He hardly ever took her out anymore. Weslee attributed this to the stress of the holidays and the case in London. Their last outing had been the trip to Williamstown. Against her better judgment she had allowed him to start sleeping over a few nights a week. His apartment was only a few minutes away from hers in the South End, but he would come over late, and then one thing would lead to another and he would end up staying. At first, she had decided she was going to hold out, but she couldn't resist him. Once they had made love that first time on the kitchen floor in his apartment, she knew she could never say no to him again. It wasn't that she regretted it.

Not really. She knew he was the one. It was only a matter of time before he made it official. She could feel it. Yes, it had only been two months, but theirs was a different kind of relationship. They knew each other inside out, she thought. Things would change after it all settled down.

She had talked to Sherry about the situation, and her advice was to guard her heart. But that was such a typical Sherry thing to say.

When Weslee had told Lana how close she and Duncan had become, Lana had seemed shocked. Lana's reaction had shocked Weslee. "Don't tell me about it," Lana had said. "I don't want to hear anything more about it."

Weslee had guessed that it was Lana's old spoiled rich girl mean-spiritedness exhibiting itself. *She probably thinks that I'm not good enough for him,* Weslee had thought. She decided to confide solely in Sherry instead.

But now things had gotten to a breaking point with Lana and she really had to do something to fix or end the friendship. And it was going to happen tonight.

The drinking, the abusive attitude—they had to stop. Weslee had tried to talk to her many times but without success. Weslee's constant worry was that Lana would take whatever she would say the wrong way. They had had several skirmishes lately, and Weslee could feel that they were getting ready for the big showdown.

Lana called the afternoon after the disastrous party. "Weslee, I'm getting sick and tired of your crap," she had said. "You really embarrassed me last night. Why didn't you dance with Craig?"

"I didn't feel like dancing, it was one hundred degrees in there," Weslee had said. *And why would I want to dance with that drunken idiot?* she thought.

"I don't know if I can take you to anything anymore. You're going to ruin my reputation." Her New England–Valley Girl accent was shrill and biting.

"Fine, Lana. I don't know if I want to go to anything anymore, myself," Weslee had replied. Lana hung up on her.

Weslee worried that she would never hear from her again. That had been three days ago.

Now it was Friday. She was waiting for Lana to show up. They were supposed to go to a movie. It was a ruse. Weslee wanted to talk, but she thought the only way to get Lana on board was to disguise it as an outing.

So she waited in a hostile December wind at the Loews across from the Boston Common. Lana was late as usual. Weslee waited, tickets in hand. A half hour went by. Then an hour. No Lana. She went in to the ticket booth. They wouldn't give her a refund, so she took the two free passes and headed home. She decided to walk despite the fact that she ached all over from training four clients that morning after a hard run.

But she wanted to think. The walk across the Common and up Beacon Street and then to Commonwealth would give her enough time. She needed to decide what to do about this so-called friendship. Maybe she would ask Duncan for some advice. That is, if he wasn't busy. He was so preoccupied lately.

A half hour later she turned the key in her lock. The TV was on. Duncan had let himself in.

"Hi, babe," she said. She really had wanted to be alone tonight. She had to study for finals. But then, she hadn't talked to Duncan all day. He had been in meetings from morning till night.

"Back from the movies already?"

"She never showed."

He shook his head. "I don't know why you bother with her. I warned you about her."

"I think I just need to clear things up between us. Or I just need to tell her we can't be friends anymore."

"I like the last option better." He gestured for her to join him on the couch. "You smell great."

She kissed him. "I can't stay up with you tonight. I've got to study for my Marketing final."

"Boring. You'll ace that; you don't need to study."

"I wish. I'm not you, Mr. Harvard."

"You're right about that."

She elbowed him in the ribs. "So, are you spending Christmas with your folks?" This wasn't what she really wanted to know. She was half hoping he would ask her to meet his family. Or at least she wanted to know if they were at the point where she could ask him to come home with her for the holidays. She had told her whole family about him already, and she assumed he had told his about her.

He tensed up. "Ummm. I don't know. Depends on Jackson, you know."

Jackson was the client in London.

"I hate Jackson," she whined.

He put his arm around her. "Let's go away for New Year's," he said.

"Really?"

"Yes, really. Anywhere you want. You'll be back from Chicago by then, right?"

"Yes, absolutely. Oh, Duncan. I'm so excited. I'm going to start thinking of someplace. Somewhere really romantic." She snuggled up to him, her Marketing exam way in the back of her mind.

Duncan left early as usual the next morning.

She was so happy. She so badly wanted to go to Vermont. *It must be beautiful there with all the snow,* she thought. They could go to Killington. She hadn't done any real skiing in years, but she was sure she could still handle herself on the slopes. Besides, some skiing might help with her marathon training.

The phone rang as she sat at the small kitchen table eating her Honey Bunches of Oats. It was Lana, all apologetic and sweet about standing her up last night.

Weslee couldn't take it anymore. "Lana, we need to talk. I don't want to do it over the phone, but if you want to keep avoiding me, we're going to have to do it this way."

"Sweetie, I'm in your hood." She was yelling into a cell phone. "I'm right down the street. I'll be right over."

Weslee wanted to study right now. Her first class wasn't until one P.M., and she wanted to use this morning to catch up on the reading she'd slacked off on the night before. But this couldn't wait.

Ten minutes later, Lana breezed into Weslee's apartment. She was all excited, as if nothing had happened and she and Weslee were still the best of friends. Weslee decided to indulge her for a few minutes. It turned into another NC-17–rated conversation about her night with Mark Bronner, her other flame. Weslee tried to tell her that there was no way that playing two guys against each other could be a good thing for her. And that set off the nasty showdown.

"Lana, no matter what you tell yourself, you can't feel good after doing something like that. Those guys are never going to respect you."

Lana's eyes opened wide at first, and then she smirked. "Ms. Weslee, Ms. Perfect," she said in her cattiest, most condescending tone. "You want respect, do you? Well, go ahead and hold out for as long as you want and just hope and pray that my cousin will give you a ring. I just hope you have a lot of patience."

"I'm not holding out so I can get a ring from Duncan." Weslee was trying to keep her cool. "I've just decided that I'm not any man's plaything. I don't sleep with any man I don't love."

"And that's your problem. You don't sleep with any man you don't love. You don't drink; you don't smoke. You're always at church now. You're always putting your hand up in class. You're always kissing the professor's behind. You want to mentor inner-city kids, you're Little Ms. Marathon Runner. Do you see what you are? You're a caricature. No matter what you do, you're never going to be perfect. You're almost thirty years old, and you don't know that yet? Don't try to lecture me. You wish you could be me. You need to start living in the real world."

Weslee stalked off to her room and slammed the door.

I don't have to take this from this spoiled, bratty witch, she thought and then immediately asked God to forgive her for calling Lana a witch.

She paced the floor, seething. *Here she is sitting on my couch, calling me names all snide and nasty. I'm gonna tell her off,* she thought, feeling herself lose it.

She flung the bedroom door open. Lana was just about to leave.

"Listen, you have no right to talk to me like that. You're a self-destructive person, and you've managed to alienate every single person in our class in less than a year. You have no friends left. I'm the only person who'll still talk to you."

"The only person who'll still talk to me?" Lana's voice was brittle with hate, and her face contorted. She lowered her voice to a contemptuous whisper. "Who do you think you are, Weslee? Every thing you've done, every place you've been, every person you've met is because of me. It's because you've attached yourself to me like a little puppy just itching to leech off my friends, my family, and my lifestyle. If it weren't for me, you'd be stuck in this dingy little hole every night, saying your prayers and studying. So don't tell me about self-destructive. You're no better than I am. You're not even in my league. You're just a little nobody who thinks dating my cousin is your ticket to the big time." Lana smiled and flipped her hair. "You really think Duncan gives a damn about your Jamaican ass?" She picked up her purse and walked toward the door. "You'll find out. You're so off his radar, so out of your league!" She smiled her contemptuous smile again, flipped her hair again, and walked out, leaving the door open. "Don't forget who you are, Weslee. No one does."

Weslee's mouth was open. She was dumbfounded, shaking with rage and humiliation as she stared at the open door. She hadn't expected those words to come out of Lana's mouth.

Is this what she's thought of me all this time? I thought we were friends.

Weslee felt the tears coming. She was so angry. A part of her wanted to run after Lana and shove her down the elevator shaft. Another part of her just wanted to cry.

How could Lana say those things? *All this time, she thought I was trying to leech off her and her friends, join their circle and become one of them? I don't even like those people,* she thought.

She called Duncan at his office, but he was too busy to talk. So she called Sherry.

"I'm so hurt, Sherry. Why would she be friends with me if that's what she thought of me the whole time?"

"Wes, don't take it personally. From what you tell me, this girl is in pain. People who do the things she does are hurting. It's not your problem; it's her problem. Listen, you're not the one out there sleeping around and going to class with alcohol on your breath, are you? All you can do is forgive her."

"I can't forgive her after those things she said, Sherry. I'm not that big of a person."

"You have to find it in yourself once you calm down. You have to tell yourself that it wasn't her saying those things. It was something inside of her, the same thing that makes her want to destroy herself with alcohol and dangerous sex. You can be angry, but you can't hold a grudge. It will hurt you as much as it hurts her, probably more."

"I don't know, Sherry. I need to think about this."

"You do that then. And remember, you have the responsibility to be the bigger person."

Weslee was counting down the days until Christmas break. She couldn't wait to just go home and be around family. The last few months already seemed like years, and she was so glad they were over. At least once she returned to Boston in January, things would be different. Different better. Duncan would be finished with this Jackson case. Lana was officially out of her life. Since the big blowup, she had not heard from her nor tried to contact her.

She tried to talk to Duncan about Lana, but he laughed it off again. He just couldn't care less that it was something that bothered her and she needed him to listen.

"You girls, uh, sorry, women," he had said while he got dressed. "You're always arguing and making up. She'll call and apologize, then you guys will go shopping and everything will be OK." He kissed her on the lips and left for work.

"Thanks for being so sensitive about this," she had yelled sarcastically down the hall at him. But he just laughed.

Weslee imagined that she couldn't avoid Lana this week. It was finals week; she would definitely have to face her.

She sighed as she walked into the School of Management building.

She took the elevator to the fifth-floor auditorium. She had studied hard and wasn't in the least bit worried about the Financial Management exam. That was her strong point anyway. Numbers had always been her thing.

She walked into the room and saw that Lana was already there. She was holding court with at least half of the fifty students or so who were in the room.

"Yes, it's going to be the most fabulous Christmas party in history." She laughed, drawing laughter from her subjects, too.

Weslee sat at the other end of the room, but she noticed that Lana was looking at her.

"That's right, everybody is invited."

Weslee rolled her eyes. Last thing in the world she wanted right now was to be invited to one of Lana's parties. She opened her textbook and looked at the pages—not reading, just feigning disinterest in Lana's little performance. Weslee couldn't have been happier when the proctor walked into the room with the tests in hand.

She took the test, relieved that it was not as difficult as she had feared. She was the third to finish. She could feel Lana giving her dagger looks as she walked out of the exam room.

Conflict was not something that Weslee dealt with well. Even as a child, she avoided it by agreeing to do things that she didn't want to, just to avoid a fight. She washed dishes when it was Terry's turn. In elementary school, she sometimes took the blame for things other pupils had done; it was easier than having to defend herself. She had never had a physical fight. She barely ever raised her voice. Anger terrified her—hers and other people's. Therefore this conflict with Lana upset her in a way that she couldn't articulate to herself. She wanted the anger and the shame that she felt at hearing Lana's words to just go away, disappear. So she did her best to forget them. But she couldn't.

That night she tried to talk to Duncan about what was going through her head.

"I thought you were going to stay at your place tonight," Weslee said as he threw his computer bag onto the couch. She was happy that he had decided to come to her place. She needed the comfort. But there would be none of that.

"Don't say anything. I have a headache." He frowned and rubbed his temples.

She went to pour him a glass of the wine he had brought over from his apartment. He always kept his own wine at her apartment since she was not a wine connoisseur. Matter of fact, she didn't know anything about wine except that it made her sleepy. Duncan, however, had tried to teach her. But his lessons had never made much impact and she was perfectly happy with her ignorance. It just wasn't in her to care that there were some really good 1996 vintages coming out of Australia.

He slumped on the couch as she handed him the glass.

"What's wrong?" she finally asked.

"I have to go to London for the holidays."

This was bad news. Well, at least now she was certain that she should not ask him to come home to Chicago with her.

"Christmas?"

"Yeah. This Jackson case is getting out of hand. That guy is a nut. If someone's not there to hold his hand, he's going to end up in jail." He sounded dejected.

"I'm sorry, honey. What are your parents going to say?"

"Well, they'll understand. It's work, you know. Actually, my dad will probably be proud of me." He sighed and pulled off his tie.

She tried to stifle a sigh. She had had it all pictured in her mind, their Christmas together. She had bought three of those Peroli ties that he loved so much. They had cost her a small fortune, but he was well worth it. Now he wouldn't even be here. She looked around at her apartment that she had decorated with Christmas lights. It depressed her. Why was he—no, his work—ruining everything?

Weslee found it hard to understand Duncan's problems with his family. In her eyes, he worked very hard and was very accomplished. But from what he had told her, nothing he ever did was good enough for his parents. His older brothers had all been Rhodes scholars. One of them had already bought and sold three companies and at age forty was retired with a wife and five kids in La Jolla, California.

Another brother worked with Doctors Without Borders and was in a different African country every week healing the sick. At thirty-one, Duncan felt immense pressure to measure up to his parents' expectations. Just being a lawyer at a good law firm didn't quite cut it. Anybody could do that.

So he pushed himself, working long hours hoping at least to make partner before turning thirty-five. Weslee tried to be understanding about his long hours. She had stopped asking him why he didn't just forget about measuring up to his parents' expectations and just do what made him happy. She would never understand. He had made that clear to her more than once.

Chapter
17

Normally, Chicago's O'Hare Airport is one of the worst places on earth. But during the holiday season Weslee thought it the single worst place to be in the universe. Well, maybe except in a hospital bed with some terminal illness, or stuck on I-94 in a snowstorm on the way to O'Hare. But still, the people, the people, the people: all kinds, all shapes and colors, all in a hurry, all in a foul mood. It is the one place where she found it totally acceptable . . . especially in the spirit of the holidays, to hate every other miserable, impatient, tired traveler for being just like you.

People sat tensely at departure gates waiting for boarding to begin. Others milled around, gorging themselves on half-frozen sandwiches and Starbucks coffee drinks: waiting, waiting. *Aargh! When will this end*, she thought.

Weslee glanced up again at the Departure board and prayed for her flight back to Boston to be cancelled. There was no way she wanted to fly in this snow. No way at all.

Yet, she didn't want to stay in Chicago, either. Celebrating Christmas with the family had been great, but she missed Duncan. He had said he missed her, too, when he had called her from London. He was flying home to Boston tomorrow, and they were heading up to Killington, Vermont, for New

Year's Eve weekend. She couldn't wait to see him, though she could wait out this snowstorm.

The need to be with Duncan was overwhelming after being cooped up in the freezing, icy Chicago weather the last week. She had been so excited when he called from London that she made him talk to both her parents on the phone. She could tell that he was embarrassed, but it didn't matter to her. She hoped he would be meeting them soon enough anyway. Weslee tried not to let her feelings get away from her. But why would he go through all this trouble if he wasn't thinking of going all the way with her?

He does love me, she thought. *And I know I want to spend the rest of my life with him.*

She looked up at the Departure board again and then glanced at the overhead TV in the gate waiting area. It was snowing from Chicago all the way to Cape Cod, and it was going to keep on snowing for the rest of the day. She said a prayer. *I need to get over this fear of flying*, she told herself.

She looked around the crowded gate area. *This flight is going to be mobbed*, she thought. There were at least two babies crying already. She wished she could afford a first-class upgrade.

Her cell phone rang.

"Hey, Mom."

Her mother was worried about her flying in the snowy weather.

Thanks, Mom for making this even easier, she thought.

"No, it's gonna be fine," she said, trying to sound confident for her mother's sake. "They won't send a plane out if they know it's dangerous. Come on, Mom. I'll be fine. You're making me nervous."

After a few minutes of going back and forth, Weslee finally got off the phone.

A half hour later, she was in the air and feeling better about the flight. She had brought a book: *Loving the Person*

You Want Him to Love. She couldn't put it down. She was learning so much from it. She knew she had to take a real honest look at who she was before she could expect to find true happiness with her man. That she had to really love and value the person inside of her before she could commit herself to spending her life with someone else. She was so ready, she thought.

An hour into the flight she fell asleep.

The flight attendant nudged her awake to straighten her seat back. They were landing. She was so woozy from her nap that she forgot to be afraid as the plane floated smoothly toward the ground. She looked out the window. It was clear, just a few flurries on the ground.

Weathermen. She rolled her eyes.

She straightened herself up, and ten eventless minutes later they were on the ground. Nice and smooth, not even a bump.

I'm such an idiot, she thought. *I was worried over nothing. Again.*

She had been homesick for her apartment, she realized as she arrived home. She walked through the tiny rooms: the kitchen, living room, bathroom, and bedroom. It occurred to her then: *I'm over Michael.*

She let out a scream. She hadn't even thought of him once in the last few days. Yes, going back to Chicago had stirred some memories. But they didn't hurt. They didn't paralyze her. She was finally over it.

The message light was blinking on her phone. *It must be Duncan telling me his flight information*, she thought. She ran to the phone and pressed the button.

"Hey, babe, it's me. I've got bad news. I can't get away for our trip. I know you're going to be upset. I'm upset, too. This guy is working me to death over here. It's either leave for a few days and go right back or stay and finish this and be home in a week. I promise you I'll make it up to you. I love you."

Her heart sank. She had told everyone. She had even told herself that this could be the beginning of the next phase of their relationship—where he could begin to see her as his future wife. She wanted to die. She had his number at the hotel, but he was hardly ever there when she called. She'd just have to wait till he called her back.

All the anticipation she had felt just melted. She looked around, and her apartment had never looked so dreary. Everything from the couch to the coffee table looked lonely and drab. It was only four P.M., but it was already dark outside. The streets were deserted. With most of the students gone home, Commonwealth Avenue was like a ghost town.

"What am I going to do with myself for New Year's Eve!" she wailed to the empty apartment. *Mom was right. I should have just stayed home.*

She didn't want to think about how angry she was at Duncan and how tired she was of his trips to London. She knew she had to get used to it. He was good at what he did; that's why they gave him all the difficult clients.

The phone rang and she jumped, grabbing it before the first ring ended.

"Hello," she said breathlessly. He had changed his mind.

"Hey, sister Weslee, how was your Christmas?"

Sherry.

"Oh, hey, Sherry."

"What's wrong girl? It's two days before a brand-new year, and you're down in the dumps again?"

Weslee sighed. "It's Duncan. He's stuck in London and he can't make our weekend trip to Killington."

"You were going to Vermont with him this weekend?"

Shoot, Weslee thought. Premarital sex was like smoking crack or first-degree murder in Sherry's book—that would be the Bible.

"Girl, I thought you said you wanted to marry this man."

"Sherry, you don't understand. What we have is more than that. He's not with me because of sex."

"How would you know?"

Weslee decided not to answer that question. She just let the silence build on the other line. Sherry was getting pretty close to crossing the line with her. Her love life was none of Sherry's business.

Sherry broke the silence. "Anyway, I called for a reason. It's funny that you two were going to Killington for the weekend, because our singles group at church is going there on Saturday. Wanna come?"

Weslee thought for a minute. She had heard much about the singles group. She wasn't sure if she could take twenty or thirty Sherry clones, male or female, for a whole day. "Umm. I don't know."

"We're having a New Year's Eve party that night. No booze, but good gospel music, poetry, and even dancing."

"Sherry, I really don't know. I'm really upset over this Duncan thing, so I'll have to get back to you."

"OK, girl, I understand. I'm gonna put your name down just in case. You just let me know. And I'm praying for you, OK?"

Weslee sighed again. "OK, Sherry. Thanks."

She sat in the dark apartment. She refused to turn on the lights or the TV. The darkness suited her mood perfectly. Then the tears started coming. She was so disappointed. She had been so looking forward to this trip, and he just had to cancel.

This would never happen to Sherry, she thought. *What is her secret? She's perfectly happy to hang out with her brothers and sisters and her church friends. She puts all her energy into her volunteer work, not to mention her job at the newspaper. She seems happy. But how can she be happy without a man?* Maybe it was all an act. Sherry did admit that she got lonely sometimes, but she said that she didn't dwell on it. She just tried to live as full a life as possible.

Could I do that? Weslee asked herself. She had never been on her own until the last year or so since Michael had left, and she did not enjoy a single moment of being single. What if Duncan's firm decided to relocate him to London? What would she do then?

Why am I doing this to myself? She stretched out on the couch and picked up the remote. There was nothing worth watching on television.

She looked at the phone. She picked it up.

"Hey, Sherry?"

"Yes, girl."

"Count me in, OK?"

"OK, girl. You're gonna have the time of your life."

Yeah. Whatever, Sherry.

It wouldn't be the time of her life, but she would be surprised.

Chapter
18

Once they had all boarded the bus, it wasn't so bad, Weslee thought. They were a friendly group, and she had to admit that she was having fun. The bus was one of those fancy coach-style luxury boxes. She watched the movie *Brown Sugar* as the bus rumbled up Route 93. She had seen it before, but it was fun watching it with these girls. They were just going on and on about Taye Diggs.

"Nah, he's just too cute, in a little-brother kind of way," one of them said.

"He's not cute. He's straight-up fine," another said.

"He looks small. You know? Small," an older lady said.

"Mmmm, girl, I know what you mean," said another. They all burst out laughing.

Weslee laughed, too. She thought it would be all singing gospel music and praying the whole way up to the ski lodge, but these people knew how to have fun.

Everybody seemed to know and love Sherry. Weslee couldn't help but compare her to Lana. They were so alike in some ways—outgoing, generous, brutally honest, and judgmental—yet somehow Sherry seemed to carry off those qualities without the underlying nastiness that made Lana so hard to take.

I do not miss her, Weslee thought. But she wondered how Lana was handling the holiday season. She imagined that if she and Lana had not fallen out, she would probably be at some fancy society New Year's Eve bash. But it was OK, Weslee surmised. Yes, she could be at some fancy party with rich, influential people, but it would probably have cost her thousands of dollars. She figured that she would have to work for at least six more months to get her finances back to the way they were before she began her spending binge with Lana.

She checked her cell phone. No, Duncan had not called.

She noticed that a few of the men on the bus had thrown glances her way, but they were mostly being cautious, it appeared. They were all talking about the Super Bowl. Some of the women had joined them on the other side of the bus. Weslee didn't care much for football, so she concentrated on the movie.

She listened to their conversation as Taye Diggs's screen marriage to Nicole Ari Parker went down the drain.

The movie was predictable and a little too glossy for her taste. But watching it was better than talking about football.

By the time the credits were rolling up on the screen, the bus was pulling into the ski lodge area. It was mobbed. Families, couples, groups of teenagers, and senior citizens excitedly walked and looked around the beautiful surroundings. They were all acting as if this were heaven—and it could be if a treacherous, snow-covered mountain was your idea of nirvana. They drove up in SUVs, Subarus, Volvos, Hummers, and a few German luxury cars.

Weslee had expected that their black group would stand out, and it sure did. This was Vermont, after all. She remembered Duncan's teasing her when they had driven up to the White Mountains: "You really need to deal with your race hang-ups."

She shrugged off the feeling. No one else in their group seemed to be giving a second thought to the lack of color in the crowd, so why should she?

Sherry was bubbling over as they unlocked the door to their hotel room.

"Girl, I didn't want to say anything on the bus, but Larry said he wants us to be exclusive, whatever that means."

"What? I thought you had only gone out once." Weslee was surprised. Sherry had mentioned this Larry character before. He was divorced and a bit older than Sherry, forty to her thirty. He seemed like a nice guy, a little nerdy, Weslee thought when she met him at the church.

"Yes, but you know how it is. We have these long talks, you know? He really makes me feel special. And he reads the *New Yorker.*" Sherry looked beseechingly into Weslee's eyes as if begging for her approval.

Weslee was touched. She hadn't realized until now how close she and Sherry had become in such a short time—so close that her opinion would actually matter that much. "Well, as long as he doesn't get in the way of your training for the marathon. I can't run that race without you."

Sherry groaned. "Girl, I told you. I'm not sure if I'm doing that thing."

They threw their overnight bags down on the beds.

"So, you gonna hit the slopes with Larry?" Weslee teased.

"Girl, I'm with the group, OK? I'm not here with him." Sherry blushed.

"So you say."

A few minutes later they were outside and in a sea of colorful ski parkas, hats, scarves, and other snow-related gear. There were families, couples, other groups of young professionals like themselves, and lots of young snowboarders looking for a day of thrills and spills. But everybody seemed to be having fun—and they hadn't even gotten on the lifts yet.

Their own group seemed to have splintered off, so Weslee clung to Sherry, Larry, and another sister, Rachel. They joined the line for the lifts.

"Weslee?" She heard a familiar voice behind her and turned around. "William, my goodness!" She was shocked. There he was, looking like Chris Webber in a royal blue ski suit, with a royally beautiful sister next to him. "What a surprise," she said. She felt uncomfortable, as if she had promised him something once and never delivered it.

"What have you been up to?" He smiled that smile of his, and Weslee remembered that night she met him and the couple of hours they had spent at Lana's folks' party. She knew why she felt uncomfortable. How could she have let him go?

"Nothing much, just school and not much else. How about you?" She didn't want to mention Duncan. For some reason, she felt ashamed of the way she had conveniently swept William out of her life and taken up with his friend.

"Well, we got a couple of new contracts, so I'm here celebrating. By the way, this is Megan."

Weslee shook Megan's thin, delicate hand and smiled politely. A tinge of jealousy gnawed at her, but she realized she was being silly. William deserved to be happy.

She quickly introduced Sherry and the others to fill the silence in the air. Then they said their good-byes as she boarded the lift with her group. He stayed behind with Megan. Promised to call her when he got back to Boston. Just to catch up.

"Girl, where do you find those fine men?" Sherry asked as the lift floated across the mountain.

"He's a friend of Duncan's." Well, it wasn't quite that simple, Weslee thought, but it was the easiest way to explain it.

Weslee couldn't get William out of her mind the rest of the day. She had skied until she was sore. But up and down the slopes, all she kept seeing was the look on William's face as he introduced Maria. No, Megan. He looked so happy.

Well, he deserves to be happy, she told herself over and over again, up and down the slopes. *I'm happy; he deserves to be happy.*

Larry and Sherry had disappeared, and she used the time alone to work on her skills. She enjoyed the quasi-solitude. There were people around her, noisy and boisterous people, but she didn't know them and she didn't try to know them. She just did her own thing.

This was such a great idea, she told herself. *I can't believe that I actually wanted to stay in that dark little apartment and feel sorry for myself all weekend long.*

That night, back in the room, Sherry couldn't stop talking about Larry as they prepared for the big New Year's Eve party back at the lodge. Weslee picked up snippets here and there of Sherry's one-sided conversation as her mind wandered to Duncan and how he would be spending this New Year's Eve far away in London.

She checked her cell phone incessantly throughout the night as people around her danced, drank, and kissed. She couldn't get a signal this far up in the mountains, but she checked the phone every ten minutes or so anyway. There was a message waiting. She knew it had to be him. But somehow it just wasn't enough. He wasn't there. So, against her New Year's resolution and her still-shaky commitment to not drink anymore, she had a whiskey sour while at least three couples got engaged right before her eyes.

She had another as she watched Megan and William embrace across the room as the clock counted down to midnight. It was another year, and she was alone.

Sherry and Larry had been making googly eyes at each other all night but not getting too close. Even when the clock struck midnight, they gave each other a chaste little peck on the lips. Was all the walking on eggshells because the other church members had their eyes trained on the couple's every move? Weslee didn't know if she could survive that kind of scrutiny. It seemed that it should be Larry and Sherry's business if they wanted to be affectionate with one another. But the tension around the table was so thick—as if everyone sensed the chemistry between them and wanted to save them from inevitable sin.

She was glad to go back to the room. So much cheer and gaiety was starting to make her feel ill. Now all she had to deal with was Sherry's giddiness. She pretended that she was interested in what Sherry was saying, but she couldn't stop longing for Duncan and wondering about William. *Things must be pretty serious with that woman,* she mused, *if they're up here together on New Year's Eve.*

Maybe it was for the best, Weslee thought, that things hadn't worked out between William and her. Of course it had been for the best. She loved Duncan. He was the man of her dreams. But William could do a little better than that Megan girl, she thought. She just seemed so flaky. Her voice was high, like she was seventeen years old, and her hair, those awful bangs . . .

Weslee got under the covers and murmured her uh-huhs and oh, reallys as Sherry went on and on about Larry. She hated herself for pretending to snore just to get Sherry to shut up.

She couldn't wait for the sun to come up and to be on her way back to Boston.

Chapter
19

It was New Year's Day. Duncan hadn't called. The message on her cell phone had been from Terry, who had stayed up late watching Dick Clark.

"Weswee, it's Tewee," her sister said, using their childhood nicknames. "Just wanted to let you know the twins said Happy New Year. I know you're probably out with that fine Bostonian of yours. Hope you're having a good time. Don't do anything I wouldn't do. Oops, I'm sure it's too late for that."

Normally that message would have made her smile, but now it irritated her. She hated everyone, everything. She cleaned her apartment furiously—dusting, vacuuming, sorting, and alphabetizing. She just wanted everything to be in some kind of order.

Later she lay on the couch, exhausted. He still hadn't called. She began to worry. Worst-case scenarios went through her mind. *Bet Lana knows exactly what he's up to.* But she put that thought out of her mind.

You are so off his radar!

She didn't want to start feeling as if it was over. She knew she was being overly dramatic. Duncan was busy, and she had to learn to deal with that. Michael often missed important days, too. On her twenty-fifth birthday, he had planned a weekend getaway that had fallen through because he just couldn't get away from the hospital. *It goes with the territory,* she thought. With men like Duncan, work always came first. She'd just have to get used to it.

But he could have at least called.

She had talked to her parents. Her mother, for once, wasn't very sympathetic. Weslee did tend to always go for the ambitious, driven type, and then she didn't want to accept what went along with that—that had been the summary of the conversation—no, lecture—from Clara Dunster. Weslee would have to make a choice, her mother had said. Maybe she should try to find herself a man who actually could be there for her all the time.

The phone rang. She looked at it. She didn't want to get her hopes up.

"Hello." She didn't dare hope.

"Hey, babe."

For some reason, tears sprang to her eyes, but she managed to smile. "Duncan, where've you been?" She knew she sounded like a whiny little girl.

"It's been the worst New Year's Eve of my life, Wes. Jackson had this thing at his house, and I did all I could to get away to call you, but I just couldn't."

She was distressed by the sound of his voice. He sounded so tired. "Are you OK? You sound so stressed, honey." She couldn't hide her concern.

"I'm fine. Just a little tired. And I miss you like crazy."

"I miss you, too. When are you coming home?"

"Tuesday. Two more days, then hopefully this will be over. Jackson gives his deposition on Tuesday morning, and I'm flying out Tuesday afternoon."

"I can't wait to see you."

Suddenly everything was OK. They talked as if nothing had happened. He loved her; she loved him. She was so sure of it. He told her funny stories about Jackson's party, about London. He promised that he would take her there as soon as things calmed down.

What was I so worried about? I am so lucky, she thought with a smile an hour later as she hung up the phone.

That Monday she got up early, still sore from skiing.

She felt a little remorse for the end of the holiday season as she walked through the city. Oh, the lights. She would miss the way the trees lit up at night along Huntington Avenue. And the huge Christmas tree at Prudential Center. Oh, and the decorations in the store windows. It was January— dreadful, cold, lonely January.

She walked into HealthyLife Spa, and, as she had expected, it was packed. After a month of gorging themselves on cakes, cookies, turkey, ham, and goodness knows what else, guilt inevitably led people to attempt some form of penance at the gym.

She had only one client today, a new one who was already waiting as Weslee arrived.

Weslee introduced herself as she tried to place the familiar-looking face.

"Hi, there. I know you! I'm Rainee Smalls, Peony's mom."

Peony Smalls. Where had she heard that name before? Oh! Lana's friend from the Vineyard. Weslee cringed.

"Hi, Mrs. Smalls, it's great to see you again. What a coincidence, though."

"It is. And please, it's Rainee. Besides, I haven't been a missus in ten years."

"Oh, I'm sorry," Weslee said instinctively.

"I'm not," Rainee said and laughed loudly. "I've heard so much about this place, I thought I'd give it a try. My New Year's resolution is to lose thirty pounds."

"Wow, that's quite a goal. Well, let me just get some information from you, and we can get started."

Weslee prepared herself for vacuous conversation, name-dropping, gossip, and thinly veiled barbs at her humble beginnings, but there was none of that. Rainee Smalls was talkative, but she wanted to know about Weslee. Why she chose Boston, whether she liked it, where she was living, how she got into personal training, how she managed to balance it all with school and everything.

"My goodness, you're quite a remarkable woman," Rainee said as she gamely perspired through a third set of lat pulldowns.

"I wouldn't say that," Weslee laughed. "I do what I have to do."

"But you seem to have done very well for yourself. When I was your age, I had never held a job even though I had gone to college. I depended on my husband for everything. When he left ten years ago, I was hospitalized for depression for almost a year, that's how lost I was."

Weslee felt uncomfortable at this stranger volunteering all this information to her.

"My two girls, Peony and Blossom, were both away at school. I didn't know what to do. It took me a long time to get my head straight. I'm still getting my head straight." Rainee laughed again. "I just love to see young women like you who have it so together. You know? You're not spending your family's money or waiting for a man to give you an allowance. You know what I mean?"

Weslee nodded. Was that a reference to Lana? she wondered.

Rainee's words made her realize how small a world some people lived in. What Rainee was describing was most of the women she had known at work, at her church in Chicago, at her new church in Boston, the women in her classes, and

Sherry. She wasn't remarkable. What was remarkable was that Rainee thought that she was somehow different because she was living the way most women did in the twenty-first century.

"Whew!" Rainee said as the hour came to an end. "I can already feel those pounds dropping off."

Weslee laughed. "Good. I'll see you next week?"

"Absolutely," the woman said. "I'm going to have to tell all my friends about you."

Weslee hurried for her appointment at Olive's. Sherry had recommended the salon. It was expensive, but it certainly wasn't as pricey as the one she formerly went to on the advice of Lana. And the stylists were certainly more down to earth. She ran a hand through her hair. She badly needed a touch-up. She decided to splurge and get herself a facial and manicure. Rainee had tipped well. She decided she would go shopping for a new outfit, too. *Duncan is probably going to want to go out,* she thought.

She thought of her conversation with Rainee. Not once had she brought up Lana. It was strange, but Weslee was glad to not have to talk about her former friend.

She ran across the street to the salon on Columbus Avenue. She was relieved to find the salon almost empty. Most people were recovering from the holidays, she figured. Her stylist, Heather, had gotten lucky. She showed the other stylists her engagement ring. Weslee did her best to ooh and ahhh along with the other women. She was happy for Heather, who had been with her partner for over ten years, and they had two children, so the ring was long overdue.

Yet Weslee couldn't help but feel a little envy. *When is it going to be my turn,* she pouted inside.

"Girl, so what did you and that fine man of yours do for the holidays?" Heather asked.

"Oh, he was stuck in London on business. But he'll be

back tomorrow." Weslee tried to sound as optimistic and upbeat as she possibly could.

Heather frowned. "Well, I hope you at least went out and partied."

"Oh, sure. I went up to Killington with a few friends. We had a great time."

"Hmmm. I'm not a skier, but I hear it's nice up there," Heather said.

Two hours later, Weslee left the salon and walked up Columbus Avenue in the frigid afternoon air, her hair bouncy and fragrant. She was glad she was wearing the new coat her mother had gotten her for Christmas. It wasn't anything she would buy for herself, especially now that she was still trying to repair her decimated savings. It was a navy blue full-length wool coat with a fur collar. Terry had called it an old-lady coat. But it sure was warm, and it would look sophisticated with the high-heeled Via Spiga boots she had found on sale at Marshall Field's on the Magnificent Mile.

Even though she had officially sworn off her short-lived fashionista phase, she found that she couldn't go back to her old clothes. They didn't excite her anymore. The Gap white shirts and black pants that had taken her so many places now looked drab and boring. She found herself picking up fashion magazines in the checkout line at the grocery store. Her family had commented on her fully made-up face when she had come home on Thanksgiving.

"Boston must be treating you really well," her father had said, raising his eyebrows.

"It's that new boyfriend of hers," Terry had teased.

Weslee knew that it was that, and it was Lana, crazy Lana, too. Despite all her flaws, she had forced Weslee to look at herself in another way. And Weslee couldn't lie; she felt more confident, more beautiful in her new clothes, in her bright red lipstick, in her suede boots. But she didn't miss Lana.

The streets were fairly deserted. That was fine with her. She hoped Saks would be pretty empty, too. That way she could take her time and rifle through the sale rack and find something that hadn't been wrinkled by too much handling. She knew Duncan had something really special planned. She wasn't sure what, but whatever it was, she wanted him to melt when he saw her.

She turned onto Clarendon, and there was William.

"Are you stalking me?" William flashed his Chiclet smile.

"No, are *you* stalking me?" Weslee was surprised. Well, he did live around here somewhere, she remembered. But William was the last person she had expected to run into.

"What's up, FloJo?" He had called her that a couple of times. She wasn't sure if she liked it.

"I just came from the beauty salon. I'm going shopping now."

"I see. Is this one of those pampering days you women talk about?"

"You got it." She wanted to ask about Megan. "What are you up to?" On the way to see her, no doubt.

"I was working at home, but then I got this craving for grits, so I'm heading down to Mike's."

"Oooh. I love that place," Weslee said. Mike's Diner was the greasy spoon of the South End that drew everyone from local street thugs, upscale gay couples, and social-climbing single women to politicians, doctors, and everything in between. It was the place to go when you wanted to get an entire week's worth of calories in one huge, delicious breakfast surrounded by hip and not-so-hip people.

"Wanna come?"

She hesitated.

"Come on," he urged. "A quick bite to eat won't mess up your hair."

She smiled. "I guess not."

The restaurant was crowded all the way from the counter

to the very back of the small dining area, but they managed to get a small table near the window overlooking Washington Street after just a short wait.

Weslee drank coffee as she waited for her South Ender breakfast, a corned-beef hash omelette with home fries and wheat toast. William drank orange juice and waited on his grits, sausages, and pancakes.

After they had caught up with their work and school lives, Weslee could feel the tension in the conversation. So she said the first thing that came into her head.

"So, how's Megan?" *Ugh.*

"Megan? Oh, she's fine. She flew back to New York today." *Oh, long distance. Hmmm.*

"Do you guys get to see each other often? With the distance and all." *Double ugh.* She felt like she wasn't making the right impression. She wanted to sound nonchalant, but she worried that she sounded as if she was leading an interrogation.

"Well . . . Yeah. We're both pretty busy, so it works out."

She had made him uncomfortable. "I understand. Duncan's pretty busy, too. He's coming back from London tomorrow."

He looked at her with a question in his eyes. "You're still seeing him?"

"Yes. Why?" How could he not know?

He was silent for a minute. "Oh, I just thought . . ."

"What?"

"Nothing."

Weslee began to feel a little irritated. "What did you think, William?"

The food came.

"Listen, I don't want to talk about Duncan. How's the running going?"

"It's going well. But *I* want to talk about Duncan. Do you know something I don't?" She didn't quite know why she was getting angry.

"Weslee, I haven't seen the guy in a couple of months. I heard some things, that's all. He's not representing us anymore."

"He's not? He didn't tell me that." *What in the world?*

"No big deal. He couldn't give us the time we needed. It's no big deal. Besides, he was only doing it as a favor to me for a short time."

"I see," Weslee said. "But have you spoken to him lately?"

William raised his eyebrows but didn't say anything. He attacked his grits.

"Is there something going on that you can't tell me?" she asked.

"No, nothing at all," William said, keeping his eyes focused on his plate.

Weslee sighed. She wanted to believe William, yet he was acting so suspiciously, as if he were hiding something.

They ate silently.

"Hey, maybe when things calm down, we could all get together. You know, you and Megan and Duncan and me."

William looked up from his plate. "Weslee, I like you. I liked you the first time I saw you at that party. You're a special person, and that's why I'm going to tell you this. Talk to Duncan. Find out where his head is and what his intentions are before you get hurt."

Weslee lost her appetite. "What do you mean?"

"I'm not going to say any more than what I just told you, Weslee. You need to talk to Duncan."

She looked at him and saw in his eyes that he meant what he said. She would hear nothing else from him. She got up and put on her coat.

"You know where to find me if you need to talk," he said.

She left the restaurant, puzzled. What would be the right thing to do? She wanted to go home and call Duncan right away, but he'd said he would be busy all day and wouldn't be reachable.

William, she fumed. Weslee wanted to kick herself for agreeing to have breakfast with him. Her mood was completely ruined. Instead of strolling happily on the deserted city streets, she walked quickly, her face tight. A dog walker pulled the leash on his dog closer as Weslee approached, but she didn't even see them.

She talked to herself. *How could he?* All the time she thought he was OK with the way things ended with them. He had said he was. But apparently he wasn't, because he was trying to ruin things between her and Duncan. *The nerve of him! Right after I tell him that I want to be friends with him and his bony girlfriend,* she fumed.

With bulldozerlike fury, she cut a wide swath through Saks and Neiman Marcus in a matter of hours. She stopped in the Theory boutique first. Yes, those one-hundred-sixty-dollar T-shirts. She'd need those in eggshell and khaki. And of course the long khaki skirt with the slit up to here. The Andrew Marc calf-suede pants? She couldn't think of anything else worth her three hundred dollars. She loaded dresses, skirts, and blouses over her arm, her eyes scanning the racks for something. Something else to buy. But the anger wouldn't go away. So she went to the jewelry department. Pearls. She would need another set. A multistrand silver necklace with cultured pearls caught her eye. David Yurman! She recognized the name from a *Vogue* ad. Or was it *Women's Wear Daily?* It didn't matter. She bought the nine-hundred-fifty-dollar necklace without blinking, and on a whim asked the salesgirl to include the six-hundred-fifty-dollar bracelet. She then marched off to get shoes, which she could never have enough of. She told the clerk to set aside four pairs of Materia Prima pumps—the same style in black leather, black suede, tan, and pink. They were two hundred forty-five dollars each—

a veritable bargain, she told herself. By then she was almost panting. She didn't know how desperate she appeared to the salespeople who eyed her warily as she darted in and out of the fitting rooms, her arms overflowing. Her single-mindedness didn't allow her to see herself whirling about the store like an addict desperate for the next fix. All she knew was that she was angry and that she wanted. She didn't know what. But she wanted it bad.

She was still stewing when she got home. She threw the shopping bags on the couch and picked up the phone.

"Mom," she said.

"Honey, what's wrong?" her mother asked. Weslee launched into the story of William's unrevealing revelation.

"Don't get upset until you find out the whole truth from Duncan," her mother said. "Don't go getting yourself all crazy over something that may be nothing, child."

"But what if it's something?" Weslee began to think back on all the occasions when Duncan had seemed so dark and moody and quiet. *Maybe he is hiding something.*

Her mother couldn't calm her fears, and she hung up feeling even more frustrated after her mother urged her to "Just come home and decompress for a while."

She sank into the couch.

"Aaargh! Why does everything have to be so hard?!" She looked at the multitudes of shopping bags strewn about the living room floor. The cab driver had gawked as he'd helped her carry them up into her apartment. They'd excited her then, these bags, and the thought that she'd have so many new things to wear into the infinite future. But now the bags on the floor stared up at her like hungry sharks swimming about her feet, and they gave her a sinking feeling. *What in the world did I just do? What is wrong with me?*

Then the doorbell rang. It was almost six-thirty P.M.

"Who is it?" she said into the intercom.

"It's your man." It was Duncan.

"Duncan!" Weslee shrieked. "Oh, my goodness. I'm a mess."

"Who cares? Buzz me up," he said in his hoarse, sexy voice.

She was wearing the same sweater and jeans she had worn all day, and her hair was flat from lying on the couch. "Give me a minute, honey." She gathered up the shopping bags and stuffed the ones that would fit into her already overburdened closet. The others she stuffed under her bed, in the kitchen cabinets, and under the bathroom sink. All the while she kept asking herself why. *I haven't done anything wrong. It's not like I've committed a crime. This is my money that I'm spending.* But still she hid the packages, not wanting Duncan to see this side of her that she herself barely recognized.

She ran to the bathroom to do a rush job on her face and hair before buzzing him up.

"What happened? I thought you couldn't leave until tomorrow," she said as he entered her apartment. Gosh, he looked so handsome, she thought. He was wearing a long wool coat and a navy blue pinstripe suit. Her favorite. He looked tired, and somehow that made him sexier to her—just knowing that he came straight to her from the airport after his long flight.

"Nick said they could take care of the deposition. Jackson's going to be fine. I told them I had to go see my lady." He took her in his arms and kissed her deeply, then began to undress.

She was able to brush aside thoughts of William and her misgivings about Duncan as he led her to the bedroom. She tried to slow him down, but his urgency overwhelmed her. "Babe, I missed you so much," she said breathlessly as he pulled off her sweater. He only groaned in response as he quickly unhooked her bra and pushed her onto the bed. She tried to hide her disappointment as he only pulled her jeans down halfway and quickly moved inside her. *I wasn't even ready*, she complained inwardly. Minutes later, it was over.

Afterward they lay silently. It was night, and the apartment was dark. She was so glad to have him back despite the fact that he was so obviously stressed and tired. His rush to seize her body had just shown how much he missed her, she thought. *This man loves me, would cross the ocean just to make love to me.* This explanation soothed her worries and calmed her disappointment that he had not been his usual loving, giving self. *I'm sure the next time around will be a million times sweeter,* she thought.

"I ran into William today," she said, snuggling even closer to him.

He tensed. "Oh, what's he up to?"

"He's got a new girlfriend. Megan."

"Good for him." Duncan yawned.

"Babe?"

"Mmm-hmmm."

"Is there anything I need to know? About us?"

Duncan tensed again. "Like what?"

"Well, I don't know. Maybe we should just talk about where things are going?"

He was silent for a couple of minutes. Weslee had almost begun to think that he had fallen asleep.

"What's wrong?" he asked.

"Well. I . . . I'm just wondering how you feel about us. You know."

He sighed. "Doesn't the fact that I left London a day early to be with you tell you all you need to know about how I feel about you? About us?"

She felt like an idiot. Why was she doing this to him? Of course she knew how he felt. He was right. She was a fool. *He's told me he loves me,* she thought, *so many times and in so many ways.* She hoped he would just forget she ever asked him anything. She clenched her fists under the cover. She wanted to kill William for putting doubts in her mind. "I know." She tried to move even closer to him, but he didn't respond. "I just missed you so much. I'm sorry."

He sighed and got up. He clicked on the lights in the bathroom and shut the door.

She wanted to die. He was angry. When he became angry, it could last for days. He was so moody. *What have I done?* she thought. She wanted to run into the bathroom and get on her knees and apologize and make everything right again.

"So what exactly did William tell you?" He stood in the doorway of the bathroom. His eyes glowed in the dark of the bedroom.

"Nothing," she lied. She was panicking. She could see the outline of his jaw clenching against the light in the bathroom behind him.

His eyes had turned dark, and his eyebrows knit tightly together in a frown. "Nothing?"

"Duncan, I'm so sorry. I shouldn't have even brought this up." She walked over to him, but he flinched away when she tried to touch him.

"I can't believe you'd ask me a question like that," he said, anger rising in his voice. "All the time we've spent together..." He shook his head. He began to get dressed. "And you go behind my back and discuss me with another man." The tenor of his voice scared Weslee.

"Duncan, I'm so sorry, baby." She was crying now. "I didn't mean to. I just ran into him." She was pleading with him to stay. But he put on his shirt and then his shoes as she stood there helplessly, naked. "Duncan, don't go. I'm sorry."

He slammed the door on his way out of the apartment.

Chapter
20

Duncan was moody the rest of the week; his calls were infrequent and short. And that romantic dinner she'd daydreamed about for weeks had never materialized. She'd forlornly returned the red satin Catherine Malandrino dress to the store. She'd bought it especially for that occasion, and she couldn't stand to have it in her possession anymore. That night he'd left, she had cried herself into a sleepless stupor, resolving never again to bother him with her petty insecurities. She needed to be more confident in his love for her, she decided. Men like Duncan were easily irritated by spineless, nagging women. *Like me*, she'd thought. She needed to be more like Lana. Nonchalant and aloof. *Let him think I don't care much for him, and that will make him want me even more.* Though the dividends from that strategy seemed to be delayed in their payout, she was still holding out hope, willing her fingers not to dial his office number or cell phone three or four times a day. It was agony in its purest form, and she hated herself for being so emotionally off-balance.

She knew he was burying himself in work. He would stay at the office until nine and sometimes ten at night, then come over. They would make love, and then he would go to sleep, waking early the next day to go to his place to change before he went back to the office. He barely spoke to her.

Weslee had stopped trying to get through to him. She knew she had messed up, and she didn't want to make him even angrier than he already was. His coldness was killing her, though. The way he would make love to her was so impersonal. Even when they were at their closest, it felt as if he wasn't there. It was more like she was serving as a stress-reliever, a way he could get physical release. It broke her heart, but she was too afraid to turn away from him. He wouldn't even kiss her good-bye in the mornings.

She hoped, and she prayed, too. She knew this mood would wear itself out. Something would happen, and he would cheer up. He'd be his old self again soon. And they could go back to building their relationship.

The chairs in the fifty-student classroom were new and so comfortable that if a professor was not skilled at keeping his students' attention, they would sink into those swivel chairs and fall asleep. Weslee took notes absently. Return on investment. Return on equity. She wondered why she was enjoying her job at the gym so much more than she enjoyed coming to class. Rainee Smalls had been true to her word. Now Weslee had a steady stream of middle-aged women coming into the gym requesting her services. Some of them had even asked her to do house calls. She had refused because it was against the rules of HealthyLife Spa. Now, as the professor talked about return on investment, she toyed with an idea that had been in the back of her mind for weeks. What if she went solo? What if she quit HealthyLife, let Rainee Smalls and her gossipy friends do her advertising for her? She could make a lot of money. She'd charge them eighty dollars an hour if she had to go to their homes. At that rate, she could afford to bring her car here. Maybe buy a condominium, with lots of windows and off-street parking.

She decided she liked this Financial Analysis class. It was letting her see possibilities. The professor was widely disliked, and that had been one of the reasons she had taken his class. She knew Lana wouldn't be in it. Lana always picked the professors who had the reputation of being easy, agreeable, and easily charmed. Well, Weslee had never gotten by on her charm before, so she decided that she wouldn't try to start now.

She walked out of class with Koji Mako and Haraam Abduraman, now her only friends. "Hey, do you guys want to team up on the project?"

"Oh, yes," Koji said. "We like to work with you. You have good work ethic. You sure you not Japanese?"

The three of them laughed as they parted company.

She walked to the elevator. She had a training client at lunchtime, then another class in the late afternoon.

The click, click of stilettos behind her made her turn back.

It had only been a couple of months since their falling out, so Weslee couldn't figure out why she expected Lana to look any different. Maybe it was because Weslee herself felt that she had changed so much since that first day she met Lana. She was no longer the wide-eyed doormat so starved for company that she would tolerate Lana's selfish antics. As usual, she looked stunning. She had streaked her jet black hair with brownish, reddish highlights, and it warmed her skin, which was now a bit paler.

Weslee swallowed. "Hey, Lana, how are you?" She had been doing her best to avoid Lana since she returned to school a few weeks before. And though it was a small school, she had been successful. So far, they were not in a single class together.

"Wes!" Lana said, her face exploding into a smile as if nothing had happened between them. "Oh my God. You look great! Where have you been? I've been meaning to call, but I think I've lost your number." The words came out quickly and jumbled, as if they had been rehearsed many times.

"I'm doing fine. You look awesome, too," Weslee said kindly. She remembered the numerous times that Lana would smile that same, big, generous, toothy smile to countless people and then tear them apart with her words the minute they walked away. "Well, it was good to see you. Take care," Weslee said, walking toward the stairs.

"Oh. Great to see you, too, Wes. I'll give you a call. We have to get together soon."

Weslee bounded down the stairs. She felt as if she were being chased by something, so strong was the need to get away from Lana's duplicity. It occurred to her that because of their brief, stormy friendship, her life had changed, probably forever. She tried to be pragmatic. It wasn't Lana's fault that she was tens of thousands of dollars in debt to her savings. It certainly wasn't Lana's fault that things with Duncan had gotten so confusing. But she wondered how her life here in Boston would have been different if she'd stayed away from Lana as her instincts had warned. Had the friendship been worth her new, fabulous, head-turning appearance, her relationship with Duncan? She didn't know the answers to those questions. But she lamented the fact that Lana was not a different person. That there had to be this awkwardness between her and another sister. That they could not just be friends and forget all the other stuff. Weslee wondered whether it was her fault. *Maybe Lana's right,* she mused. *I'm just too boring and uptight. No matter what I wear or what I do, I'll never be the kind of girl who can be friends with someone like Lana.* And Weslee still wasn't quite sure whether that was a good or a bad thing.

*   *   *

HealthyLife Spa was slowing down after those first frenzied weeks of the New Year. The slackers were going back to slacking, resolutions safely put away until the following year.

Her client was Marie Bunting, another middle-aged woman that Rainee Smalls had sent her way. "Oh, honey. I wish you could just come out to the house once a week. I hate driving down to Boston. The traffic is just terrible. Just terrible. And we have a home gym that's just going to waste," Marie said.

"Maybe someday I might be able to work something out," Weslee said.

She began to dream again. If only she could get enough of a client base together, she could strike out on her own.

"Marie." Weslee turned to her client as she led her to the StairMaster. "Do you know of any other people who would want training in their homes? I mean, I think I'd like to strike out on my own, but I need to get more clients lined up."

"Oh, honey. Half the women in my book club would sign up. Ooh, and the ladies in my country club, too. You know what? We're having a little tea thing next week; why don't you come along? I talk about you all the time. Rainee will be there, too."

"Really? You mean that?" Weslee asked, her eyes wide.

This could be what she needed.

Later that night, she could barely contain herself. She couldn't wait to tell Duncan about her idea and how well things were going with her new clients at HealthyLife. She cooked a big meal: a sirloin steak, garlic mashed potatoes, salad, the works. She made a maple-syrup pecan pie. It wasn't gourmet, but she knew he would enjoy it.

She pulled the new lingerie from the La Perla bag and headed for the bathtub. Before Lana, she'd thought Victoria's

Secret the holy grail of underwear. Now, thanks to Lana, she knew she had been way off the mark. She looked at the silky baby blue-and-white lace edged teddy on the satin hanger. She'd bought it that day she'd had breakfast with William. That day . . . She tried to put it out of her mind: the uncertainty and rage she'd felt when she didn't know what to think about Duncan. She'd never forgive William for putting those doubts in her mind. She closed her eyes. Things were better now with Duncan. They would get past this. Tonight would be a new beginning.

She'd laid new satin sheets on the bed and had lit some scented candles to get the detergent smell out of the air. He'd said he'd come by at seven—and he wanted to talk. She smiled. She could feel it; he was going to apologize for the way he'd been acting, and they would make up and everything would go back to normal.

I can't wait, she thought as she threw her head back on the pillow at the head of the tub. *After tonight, everything's going to be OK.*

Weslee took one last look at the table before she went to put on her dress. She took the salad out of the fridge. Everything looked so perfect with the new china she had bought at Bloomingdale's on another minispree after she'd become infatuated with a home spread in *Town & Country.* Then she'd thought that her apartment needed a makeover because Duncan must have been so underwhelmed by her Crate & Barrel taste. Her cute furnishings, she'd decided, just didn't cut it. Target wasn't hitting the mark, and she needed to go way beyond Bed, Bath & Beyond. But she regretted it now, and the china had been on her list of things to return, but she just couldn't part with it. She told herself that it could someday become a family heirloom. And that somehow made it worth keeping.

She wasn't too sure about the centerpiece. Arranging flowers had never been her strong suit. *He probably won't no-*

tice, she silently hoped. Again doubt flushed through her as she thought back to the pretty, confident, and well put-together girls that Lana had introduced her to at her parents' place on the Vineyard. *Bet those girls know all about arranging centerpieces.* She sighed. *Duncan loves me for me, and that's all that matters.*

The sirloin was still in the oven. She could smell it. But as good as it smelled, a part of her wished she had had the guts to try the French recipe she had seen in *Bon Appetit.* That might have really impressed him, shown him how worldly she could be. She decided not to worry. Duncan loved her cooking.

At five minutes past seven, she heard his key in the lock. She had to restrain herself from running to the door. Instead, she waited as she heard him enter the living room

"What smells so good?" he called out.

She walked out of the bedroom slowly, wearing her long, chocolate brown Parallel slip dress with the deep vee in the front and back, that moved with her long, slim body. It had the desired effect. He stopped cold in his tracks.

"Whoa. What's the occasion?" He approached her with a sexy leer.

"Do we need one?"

He pulled her into his arms.

"I made dinner." She tried to wriggle away.

"Nuh-uh. We'll eat after." He was nuzzling her neck.

She couldn't say no. But the encounter was strained again as she found herself yearning for his kisses all over her body, his slow and gentle touch, the way he asked her what she wanted, the way he waited for her to climax first. He hadn't done those things in what seemed like forever, and Weslee was beginning to wonder whether those "good" days had all been in her imagination. What was happening to him? Where did all the sweetness go? *Tonight was sup-*

posed to be a new beginning, she thought as he moved quickly and mechanically on top of her. She just wanted it to be over.

Later, as they lay in each other's arms, Weslee struggled to maintain a cheery disposition, but her disappointment fought back. Things had kind of gone in the reverse of the order that she had planned. But it was OK. They could go backward.

"Babe, we should go eat now." She nudged him.

He yawned. "OK."

She set the food before him, and he attacked it as if he hadn't eaten in days.

She loved it when he ate like that. She was so glad she had honed her cooking skills in college. More than anything she had accomplished, it was a talent she was especially proud of.

She sat across from him and ate her salad. "Oh, honey, didn't you have something you wanted to talk to me about?" She looked at him.

He looked up from his plate and then quickly looked down and kept eating. "Let's talk about it later."

She felt a pang inside. He was going back to London. She could feel it. He couldn't even look at her. *At least tonight wasn't a total bust*, she thought as she picked at her garlic mashed potatoes.

They ate in silence until his cell phone rang. He looked at the display and turned it off.

"You're not going to take it?"

"Nah. I think it's a wrong number."

"Duncan, I'm really sorry about what happened the other day. I didn't mean to accuse . . . rush you. I don't know what came over me."

He looked at her for a few long seconds. What came next was sudden and painful and hit like the crack of a baseball bat hitting a ball.

"Wes." He sighed and leaned back in his chair. "I can't do this anymore."

"What?"

"This. This thing. You. You and me. It's just too much. I just have too much going on now. It's just all too much. I can't breathe."

"Duncan . . ." She looked at him incredulously. "What are you saying?"

He didn't answer. He didn't have to. She stared at him, waiting for him to explain, clarify, put it in plain English.

"I'm sorry," he said, a final look in his eyes.

Her hand covered her mouth as she sprinted off to her bedroom and slammed the door.

He didn't leave just then. Ten minutes later he knocked on the door. He knocked for two or three minutes. He didn't hear anything when he put his ear to the door. He knocked again. She didn't answer, so he walked out of her life.

Once she was sure he'd left for good, she walked out of the bedroom slowly. She felt numb. There was something, she assumed it was a knot of tears, stuck in her throat, but she couldn't get it to rise. So she gulped and stood in the middle of her dining room. She looked around. It hadn't been enough. None of it. Not the clothes, not the weekly spa treatments, not learning the names of all that awful sushi that he liked, not drinking those bitter wines, not the new sheets, curtains . . . It didn't change the one thing that needed changing. Herself. *I'm still the kind of girl that gets dumped*, she thought. *Michael, and now Duncan.* She sat on the sofa, and the tears began to spill out of her eyes. She cried silently at first, and then the sobs sent tremors through her body until she lay on the floor, exhausted. *What is it about me?*

An hour later, she sat up and clenched her teeth. Her eyes felt leaden and painfully irritated. *Can't sit here and cry. Can't.* She walked slowly to the closet in the bedroom. There were price tags sticking out of blouses, dresses, pants, scarves, belts that had yet to be worn. She moved closer, smelled the leather, the newness of expensive fabric, and it repulsed her. She began to gather them in piles. Piles for Saks. Piles for Neiman Marcus. Piles for Max Mara. One small pile for Escada. Another for Versace. They would all go back. When she finished, she surveyed the room and took stock. Her heart and seventeen thousand three hundred and fifty-five dollars' worth of clothes and shoes lay on the floor.

She undressed and put on her old worn-out track suit, laced up her Sauconys. She had to get out of that overdone, overpriced, sweet-smelling, creamy, cloying, and deceptively comfortable life that had brought her so much pain. She hit the pavement and ran into the night, not stopping until she had exhausted all the feeling from her mind and body.

Chapter
21

Weslee was glad she had brought what she called her second bible with her to Boston. She never thought she'd need it again once she knew for sure that she was over Michael and in love with Duncan.

Heal Your Heartache had gotten her through those interminable sleepless nights spent crying into her pillow after Michael left. It had kept her from calling him and begging him to take her back. It kept her from doing the crazy, desperate stuff that people do when they joined the ranks of the jilted.

It had been a whole week since Duncan had broken things off. He had called once to find out if she was OK. She had heard his voice on the answering machine but refused to pick up the phone. Part of the healing process was acceptance and no contact with the source of the pain. Acceptance was far down the road, but she was taking a shortcut. She really didn't want to know the real reason why Duncan "couldn't breathe." What she wanted was to feel better. Hearing his voice just turned the knife in the wound.

The day after he had left, she actually went into a liquor store and bought a bottle of whiskey. She poured it into a glass but gagged on the first swallow. It was still sitting on the kitchen counter, almost full.

Sherry had come over and tried to drag her out to movies. That didn't help. She had gone to class bravely, trained her clients at the gym, her thoughts about going out on her own now way in the back of her mind. She apologized to Marie as the opportunity for her to start building her client base came and went. Weslee only did what she had to do. She didn't have the energy or the will to start anything new.

She imagined things. That Lana knew about the breakup and was intentionally baiting her. She ran into her more often now, Lana always in the company of two or three other women. They would whisper things and laugh. Weslee thought, *For sure they are laughing at me.*

On her one hysterical night, she had called home sobbing into the phone. Her father couldn't calm her down. Her mother, worried, had offered to come to Boston. Her sister had told her to come home. She accepted neither offer. She also refused the advice that she should see a shrink or at least get a prescription for antidepressants. She would ride this out.

The first Friday night after the breakup came. And she supposed that she could have gone out dancing or to a movie with Sherry. But that was not the game plan she had in mind.

It's OK to do crossword puzzles on a Friday night, she told herself.

The phone rang. And Weslee let it. It was Sherry.

"Girl, I'm worried about you. You need to get out of that little hole you're in. Weslee? Weslee? Your family loves you, your other friends love you, and I love you, OK?" Weslee heard Sherry sighing on the machine. "Listen, hon. This guy did you a favor, a big one. You can do so much better than that selfish, arrogant . . . Oh Lord. Let me stop before I say something I'll have to ask forgiveness for. Weslee? You OK? Call me if you need to talk."

Weslee almost laughed out loud at Sherry's persistence. But she just couldn't take another pep talk. She had had enough.

The pain of losing Duncan was so unbearable that Weslee felt numb. She had cried for three nights straight and then nothing.

All she felt now was this hollowness inside and somehow strangely detached from herself. It was like she was watching herself go through the breakup and the aftermath. She kept waiting to find out what her next move would be. She kept waiting to break down again or to start screaming. Or to start acting crazy. But so far those things hadn't happened. But she was waiting.

She kept reading self-help books. She'd spent one hundred fifty dollars at Barnes & Noble the day after the breakup. She'd prayed, too. Read the Bible. Listened to sad, sad music. She lit candles. Took comfort anywhere she could find it inside the safety of her own dark little space.

She threw away his pictures, his toothbrush, the Palm Pilot he kept losing in the cushions of her couch. Then she took them all out of the wastebasket and put them in a shopping bag with the two or three shirts he had left in her closet and put the bag by the door.

She didn't expect him to come back. She had thought—no, known—that Michael would come running back. He hadn't. Why would Duncan? They had only been together a few months. But then why did this hurt as much as losing her soulmate of more than five years?

So the days and weeks went by. She went to class. Took exams. Went for long runs in the snow, in the cold. Tried to smile as clients told her their weight-loss stories; tried to concentrate on helping them lose weight. She never heard from him. After about a month, she stopped hoping. She started to try to get used to the emptiness of her apartment, stopped telling herself that maybe he would come to get his stuff.

She went to church and hung out with Sherry and her friends. It was OK. She read, worked, studied, and ran. She took comfort where she could find it.

Chapter
22

One of the characteristics of March in New England was its deceptiveness. It wasn't quite spring, but it knew how to put on airs to make itself seem that way. So this Sunday, it was in the high fifties, and the sun shone brightly. Some of the skeletal trees even sported a few buds. But none of that meant that the snowstorm on its way down from Canada would turn around after it hit Maine. No, just give it a day or so. Then cold reality would hit.

Weslee went through the motions. She smiled and shook hands with Sherry's friends in the church parking lot. They all called her sister. But even with all this love from these folks, she still felt an ache deep down in her heart. They were all so happy with their saved and sanctified selves. But no one could understand what she was going through.

"I'm going to the Shattuck this afternoon, wanna come?"

"What's the Shattuck?" Weslee asked as Sherry eased out of the crowded parking lot and onto Blue Hill Avenue.

"It's a hospital. My mother used to work there before she passed on."

"Why are you going there?"

Sherry glanced at her and shook her head. "To visit some

sick folks. You know? Sick people who have no one to care for or visit them."

"Oh." Weslee felt ashamed for not knowing. She felt ashamed for the next question that she did not ask—why do you guys have to be such do-gooders?

"So, you'll come?"

"Um. I don't know. I should catch up on some reading."

"Weslee." Sherry's voice took on its most motherly timbre. "You know, if you took just a few minutes to focus on someone else but yourself, you'd be surprised at how small your problems will seem."

Weslee did not answer. She didn't have an answer for a comment like that. For one thing, her problems did not seem small to her. But why argue with Sherry? She was still on fire from the sermon.

"Well, maybe for a little while."

"Good. Excellent. Let's go eat." Sherry turned up the volume on her CD player and sang along with gospel singer Freda Battle.

Minutes later they entered Bob the Chef's soul-food restaurant. It was the only black-owned real "sit-down" restaurant in Boston that wasn't in the hood. It was probably the only restaurant in the city that gave Boston street credibility with black folks who were visiting from other parts of the country. But then, even with its finger-licking-good menu and fierce jazz brunch, buffet-style, on Sundays, the clientele was a solid 75 percent white. *Well, what was one to do? Boston is what it is*, Weslee thought.

They were lucky enough to get a table close to the jazz band.

"That drummer's kinda cute," Sherry mouthed to Weslee over the Latin jazz music.

Weslee rolled her eyes. She hadn't noticed. She filled her plate with greens and scrambled eggs and a couple of pancakes, and Sherry did the same.

"We're so good, aren't we?" Sherry wrinkled her nose at their timid choices as other patrons piled chicken wings, macaroni and cheese, and other artery-clogging, delicious fare on their plates.

"We'd better be good. The race is in a few weeks." Weslee went from being excited to feeling dread at the upcoming marathon. She had trained so hard, fifty miles a week over the last five months, but now she just felt tired. Was it all the running, or Duncan? She wasn't sure. All she knew was that the enthusiasm she had felt for running her first Boston Marathon was ebbing daily.

"Oooh," Sherry groaned. "I'd love some of that macaroni and cheese and some of those wings."

"Go ahead. I'm not stopping you."

They walked back to their table with their food.

"You're going to really enjoy talking with those people. I know it sounds depressing, but you'd be surprised. Some of them have some really interesting stories to tell."

Weslee nodded absently as Sherry went on about Shattuck Hospital and its unfortunate patients who had no one to visit them. Sure, Sherry went there out of her Christian guilt. But Weslee knew the reporter in Sherry would be also looking out for a heart-rending story that could get her byline on the front page of her newspaper. But you couldn't hate her for that.

The entrance to the restaurant was crowded, but out of the corner of her eye Weslee noticed William and Megan walk in. She focused on her plate. She hoped that he wouldn't see her. She hadn't talked to him since that day he had warned her about Duncan. She wasn't ready to face him yet. Especially not with perfect Megan at his side. "Let's hurry so we can go. I can't wait."

"Really?" Sherry's face lit up. "OK, I don't really have to finish all of this."

As they exited the restaurant, she could feel William's eyes on her. She never looked his way. *That jerk*, she thought. Her instinct told her to go back there and give him a piece of her mind for ruining her relationship with Duncan. But she decided that it wouldn't do any good. She didn't trust herself to not break down in tears and make a scene. But she definitely would not say hello. As far as she was concerned, he didn't exist. At least that's what she wanted him to think. She walked out quickly and didn't look back.

Lemuel Shattuck Hospital felt and smelled old. It wasn't like the spit-shined, disinfected Northwestern Medical Center where Weslee's own mother had worked for twenty years. Patients sat near the entrance in wheelchairs, looking out onto the glorious oaks that held court over Franklin Park, site of the revitalized city zoo and one of the best public golf courses in the country.

It was such a huge and wonderful contrast: the old, gloomy state hospital—with its drug addicts and terminally ill and abandoned—looking out onto the sunny, open, pristine park with its happy tennis players, joggers, and families playing on an idyllic almost-spring Sunday afternoon.

"Where are we going?" Weslee asked. The smell of sickness tugged at her barely digested brunch.

"Ten. The last floor." Sherry looked at her and narrowed her eyes. "Are you OK?"

"I'm fine."

"You'll get used to the smell."

Weslee didn't want to say that she didn't plan to come back.

Surprisingly, the ward didn't smell as bad as the lobby. It wasn't the smell; it was the sounds: several TVs blared different stations. Some patients were watching baseball spring training, others whatever the networks were showing.

"Hi, Sherry," a heavyset Caribbean woman dressed in nurses' whites called out from the nurses' station.

"Hi, Miriam," Sherry answered.

"How you doing, child? You looking nice today, eh. You comin' from church?"

Weslee recognized the Bajan accent.

"This is Weslee." Sherry gestured, and Weslee held out her hand.

Miriam crushed her in a bear hug. "It's nice to meet you, Weslee. Where you from? I can tell you from the Islands from that face."

"Yeah. My dad is from Barbados," Weslee said, shy at Miriam's too-too familiarity.

"Barbados! Ah! Me, too. What part?"

"Um. Nice to see you, Miriam," Sherry said, taking Weslee's elbow. "We're going in to see Holly."

"Oh, good. She's feeling a little down today. She'll be glad to have the company."

Weslee followed Sherry into a tiny single room. The walls were bare, but there were four vases of flowers, plastic ones, near the door, two on the table on the right of the bed and one on the left.

"Hi, Holly," Sherry said softly and beckoned Weslee closer to the bedside of the skinniest woman Weslee had ever seen that wasn't on a runway.

"Sherry, nice to see you." The woman's voice was strong and dignified; she sounded very educated and as if she had been very beautiful once and knew it. "Who's this?" She looked at Weslee and smiled. But to Weslee it was just skin sliding over bones to reveal yellowing, rotting teeth receding into prominent gums. Her thinning hair was pulled off her face in what Weslee guessed was a ponytail in the back. Weslee held out her hand, but Holly didn't try to shake it.

"Having a bad day, huh?" Sherry asked.

Holly coughed hollowly. "Not as bad as last night. Just a little weak today." She closed her eyes.

"Listen, Holly. I'm going to let you and Weslee get to know one another. I'm gonna go say hi to Cecil."

Weslee's mouth opened to say no, and she grabbed Sherry's arm in protest. Sherry glared at Weslee, shook her arm off, and walked out of the room.

Weslee wanted to flee. Holly's eyes were still closed. Was she asleep? She was just a sack of skin and bones under the white Massachusetts Department of Health blanket. Her TV was on CNN. There were pictures on her table. A daughter, maybe, smiled broadly from one of the pictures. The daughter was petite and pretty; she had short hair dyed chestnut brown and cut close to her head. It illuminated her caramel skin and huge cocoa-colored eyes. She had big, white, beautiful teeth.

"Like that?" Holly's eyes were open again.

"She's pretty. Is that your daughter?"

Holly laughed and then began to cough.

"Do you want me to get someone?" Weslee looked at her worriedly.

But Holly waved off Weslee's concern. "I'm fine." She cleared her throat. "That's me."

"Who?" Weslee asked blankly.

"In the picture." Holly's face looked victorious at the look on Weslee's face. "Five years ago."

"I'm sorry." Weslee shook her head.

"Don't be sorry. I'm not sorry I looked that good."

They both laughed. Holly coughed only twice this time.

Weslee wanted to ask what had happened. She had an idea, but she didn't want to assume. She certainly didn't want to offend Holly.

"I don't have any kids, girl. I'm only thirty-two."

Against her will, Weslee's face betrayed her shock.

"Please don't say you're sorry," Holly said. She closed her eyes, and Weslee didn't say anything.

"Are you OK?" Weslee grew more worried after a minute went by and Holly still hadn't opened her eyes.

The woman nodded.

Weslee was about to call the nurse when Holly opened her eyes again.

"I get this pain sometimes," she said. "It's not too bad today, but last night, girl, you could hear me hollering all the way down the hall."

"Holly. How . . . What?"

"I have AIDS."

Weslee consciously did not say that she was sorry. She certainly felt sorry. She wanted to hug Holly. She wanted to cry. And she wanted to leave this place now.

"I'm basically dying. Don't look like that, hon. I'm all taken care of. I got things settled with God." Holly smiled confidently, showing off what had been her killer smile.

"I don't know what to say," Weslee whispered.

"That's OK. Most people don't. I'm glad you came with Sherry, though. I don't really have any family to speak of. Before I came here I was homeless."

"What happened? You looked so happy in the picture." Weslee realized too late how accusing and naïve her question sounded.

Holly closed her eyes and went out for another minute or so. Weslee watched the news, waiting for her to come back.

"My husband. He was the perfect man, girl. He gave me everything—a big house in Milton, nice cars, vacations, diamonds, a few dozen mistresses on the side, and AIDS."

Weslee put her hand over her mouth. Her heart broke as she heard Holly tell the story of her knight in shining armor who turned out to be her angel of death.

Holly Nieves had been working her way through Northeastern University's law school when she met her husband-to-be, a fellow law student. They had fallen in love immediately and married after just a few months. The marriage was perfect for all of four months, then the cheating began. Consumed by her new job as an associate at a small law firm, Holly ignored her husband's philandering and focused on her career.

They put up quite a front for his family and their friends. They both were smart and successful and bought the toys to show for all their hard work.

"He would always tell everyone that nothing was too good for his Holly." She smiled bitterly. "And I guess I put up with his cheating because he kept buying me things. I even stopped asking questions when he would stay out all night, when girls would call my house asking for him, cursing me out."

It went on for four years before he began to get really sick and couldn't hide it from Holly anymore. He lived one year before she herself began to suffer from sudden shingles attacks. His family paid for his burial and quickly forgot about her.

She quit her job when the shame and the sickness became too much. The house was foreclosed on, the cars repossessed; she had sold what she could to survive for the three years that she couldn't work.

Now there was no health insurance left, and her law firm colleagues had long ago forgotten about her. Her in-laws pretended she didn't exist. So here she was alone, fighting the cancer that AIDS had spliced through her body, and dying.

"Why didn't you go back to your family?" Weslee asked.

"My grandmother raised me. She died when I was twenty-three, a year before I got married. I don't know where my mother is." Holly reached for the remote and switched the channel to *E!*.

"*True Hollywood Story*'s coming on next. That's my show," she said.

"Really? Mine, too," Weslee said.

"You remind me of me a bit," Holly said, clearing her throat again.

"Yeah? How?"

"You're just so sweet and naïve."

"Naïve?" Weslee laughed, but she wasn't sure if she liked being called naïve by a total stranger.

"No offense."

"I'm not offended," Weslee lied. "But why would you say that?"

"Just from looking at you. I just get you." She smiled again, maybe to show Weslee that she was not trying to be mean. "That's a dangerous way to live. Living for love. You meet the wrong kind of man, then he'll take full advantage of that, sweetie. Love is not anything like you think it is. I had the fireworks and the knight in shining armor, and this is where it got me." Holly looked squarely at Weslee.

Weslee nodded. "I know what you mean. I just went through this breakup, and I . . ."

Holly closed her eyes. Weslee let her drift off in her painful world. The nurse came in a few minutes later. "Let her sleep," she told Weslee.

As Sherry pulled onto Columbia Road, she looked at Weslee. "You're quiet. How did it go?"

"I just can't stop thinking about Holly. She's so smart, so young, so . . ."

"Yeah. It's sad, but that's how life is sometimes. She's a strong woman, though."

Weslee felt tears pricking at her eyes. "I just feel so bad knowing that she's going to die. I mean, she could be a friend of mine, or a co-worker."

"Weslee, don't get like that." Sherry patted her on the thigh. "Holly is fine. I know it doesn't seem that way to you, but she is. She's in pain now, but when she dies, all of her pain will be over. She's going to heaven. What happened to her, no one will ever understand why. It's just God and his way of working things. He has a plan for everybody's life, and that includes pain and suffering as well as happiness and success. She was happy once; she'll be happy again forever when she crosses over to the other side."

"I just don't . . ."

"Don't try to understand," Sherry said firmly. "It's not for us to understand."

For Weslee, Holly's illness wasn't the same as just reading the statistics and feeling mild concern yet detachment from them. This was a person in the flesh who had AIDS, and it was too visible, too real. *How can Sherry be so matter-of-fact about this*, she wondered.

"Is this the first time you've seen a . . . a sick person?" Sherry asked as if reading her mind.

"In real life. Yes. I can't believe it . . . AIDS . . . really does that to people."

Sherry sighed. "Yes, that's what it does to people."

Weslee caught the mild exasperation in Sherry's voice.

"Sometimes I feel like the most naïve person in the world, Sherry. Know what I mean? And Holly said it, too. She said I was naïve."

"Mmm-hmmm." Sherry raised one eyebrow. "I wouldn't call it being naïve. I'd say you choose to see what you want to see. Not that it's a totally bad thing. It's probably your built-in defense mechanism."

Weslee thought about this for a moment. "It's just that up till recently I haven't had any reason to meet people like Holly. My world was just work, family, and Michael, and then Duncan. . . ."

"You chose it that way, girl. Same way I chose one day to walk into that hospital to volunteer. That's how I ended up knowing people like Holly. I didn't meet her on the street

or in a club. She's just another sister like you and me."
Sherry paused. "You don't have to see the ugliness in this
world if you don't want to, Weslee. You can just close your
eyes to it and pretend your little world is perfect. But me, I
want to see the good, the bad, and the ugly. It's a big world
out there, much bigger than you and me. And Duncan."
Sherry glanced at Weslee. "And I want a front-row seat to
all of it."

The message was not lost on Weslee. She'd been blind to
everything but her own here and now for a long time. That
route had been smooth and trouble free for the most part.
Much like she imagined Holly thought her own life had
been, married to a man who loved and spoiled her, until the
deadly betrayal. That ugliness stuck to Weslee's skin like a
leech for the remainder of the day, and it wouldn't leave
her. The thought of Holly lying in that bed, so emaciated
and helpless—at age thirty-two. Sherry had a point. She'd
been closing her eyes to the ugliness right in front of her for
way too long. There had to be some good to come out this,
she thought. There had to be.

Chapter
23

The weather was surprising everyone. Spring was managing to sustain itself before April proper. The air was cool and hospitable to living things human and nonhuman. Brave women wore sandals to work, and some men dared to leave their spring raincoats at home. The city was beginning to come out of its thaw. Piles of hardened, dirty snow melted, leaving long lines of water weaving across sidewalks and into storm drains. People were friendlier. The streets seemed cleaner. A feeling of well-being was in the air.

As for Weslee, it wasn't that she was more hopeful. It was that she was feeling less hopeless. She was beginning to put some distance between her and that woman who had fallen headfirst and fast for that dashing, complicated man who had, it seemed, vanished from her life as suddenly as he had appeared in it.

Spring break came and went. Lana had proclaimed loudly, within earshot of Weslee, that she was headed off to St. Bart's for the week. Weslee did the math in her head. Boy, was she glad that she didn't have a five-thousand-dollar vacation to brag about. Instead, she had taken the week to get her last training run in for the marathon and to work full time at HealthyLife. Duncan was still in her thoughts, but she was sleeping normally again, tired from her full days. She was busy, and it felt good.

Since that Sunday at the hospital, she couldn't seem to get Holly out of her mind. She visited her—just once more, she had told herself. Then it turned into once every week. Some days were harder than others. She saw Holly at her worst, when the pain made her angry and spiteful and abusive. But Weslee would stand there and let Holly scream at her to leave her alone and would then hold her while she wept and apologized. On other days, when all Holly felt was weak, they would sit and talk and watch movies. Weslee had made yet another friend.

"Girl, I think we must have been sisters in another life," Holly would say when they would find out that they one other thing in common. Holly, too, loved to cook and had run track in high school. She was full of advice on her good days.

"Wes, why don't you change your hair a bit?" she had said once. "I think you'd look good with it shorter. It's just hanging there now."

"But I thought long hair was in," Weslee had protested.

"Nuh-uh. You need to show off your pretty face more."

Weslee laughed. It was the first time anyone had called her pretty in a long, long time.

She smiled again as she entered HealthyLife. She expected it to be an easy day. She had only one client: her regular, Rainee Smalls. Then she would head off to her late class and then meet Sherry for dinner.

Rainee seemed to be in a strange mood. She was not her usual talkative self.

"Is everything OK?" Weslee asked.

Rainee sighed. "Weslee, what is going on between you and Lana?"

Weslee cleared her throat. The two of them had seldom

talked about Lana. Weslee assumed that Rainee thought that they were still friends.

"Um. We just had a disagreement. We're very different, you know? We just aren't real close anymore. That's all."

Rainee sighed again. "You're sure that's all?"

Weslee paused. "Yes. Why. Is there more?"

Rainee spoke as if she were choosing her words with extreme caution. "Well, it seems that she is very upset with you, from what my daughter tells me. She is saying a lot of things that, frankly, I find really hard to believe."

Weslee's eyes narrowed, and she stopped demonstrating the bicep curl that she wanted Rainee to perform. "Things like what?"

Rainee looked uncomfortable. "I'm not going to get into it. It's really childish. And you don't have to worry. Lana has a reputation among all of us. Her parents really spoiled her. You know she's their only one."

But Weslee would not be deterred. "What kinds of things is she saying about me?"

Rainee sighed. "Honey, it doesn't matter. Your work and your honesty speak for themselves. Actually, I really don't want to talk about this anymore. But I thought you knew what was going on."

Weslee decided not to push further. Rainee was her best client. Because of her, she had seven other high-tipping clients who were begging for her services. She gritted her teeth. Why couldn't Lana just leave her alone? What could Lana possibly be saying about her?

She wanted to leave at that instant and march over to Lana's place and confront her. But what good would that do? She didn't want to face that terrifying rage that was so constantly near Lana's surface. A part of her suspected that this was Lana's goal: to get a rise out of her and to spark another showdown. *Well, I won't give her the satisfaction*, Weslee thought.

7

Weslee was beginning to see what was so obvious to the other people who'd known Lana for a long time. The girl was desperately insecure and angry at the world, yet she was able to hide this with her perfect looks, beautiful clothes, and other material trappings. Those things made her seem attractive, fun, and worth knowing . . . until you got a little closer. Weslee was grim as she remembered her initial misgivings about Lana. Those same misgivings she'd ignored to give Lana the benefit of the doubt and to try to be a friend to her despite all of the veiled insults and subtle putdowns.

Now she's trying to ruin my reputation. Weslee sighed. *Why did I ever get mixed up with that girl? Was my common sense taking a sick day?* She stopped herself. She wouldn't take the blame for this. So she'd made an error in judgment. But the problem was fixing itself. She was moving on. Same way she was moving on from Duncan. *Let Lana talk all she wants,* Weslee thought. *I'm not looking back.*

Chapter

24

It was the day before the marathon, a sunny April Sunday, and Weslee was jumpy and nervous. She wanted to do something to clear her mind. Sherry suggested golf. Weslee had always wanted to take a lesson but had never got around to it.

The Franklin Park golf course in Dorchester was nearly in Sherry's backyard, so off they went after church.

"Now, Sherry, you have to be patient with me, OK? My hand-eye coordination is terrible," Weslee fretted.

"You don't need hand-eye coordination. Where did you hear that?"

Sherry was bubbling over. She and Larry were definitely an item now, and every other word out of her mouth was Larry. Weslee tried to contain her jealousy. She missed Duncan so much now. She had gotten over the anger she had felt initially. Now she just felt lonely. She so wanted to be wholeheartedly happy for Sherry, but her heart just wasn't big enough.

"The last time Larry and I came here, I showed him a thing or two. I'm so glad that man is not a sore loser, 'cause I can't lose, girl. I can't," Sherry bragged as they approached the clubhouse.

Weslee knew nothing about golf courses, but this one seemed pretty nice. She was surprised at how beautiful the park itself was. And to think that it was in the middle of the hood! There was a two-and-a-half mile running trail around the golf course that she knew she had to try running sometime, plus the Franklin Park Zoo was just across the street. It was one of the most beautiful parts of Boston she had seen yet. And it was in the hood. She just felt so proud of that fact.

The old men in the clubhouse treated Sherry as if she was a regular. A regular daughter or granddaughter. She called them by their names as they teased her about her handicap.

"These guys are the best. They're all retired, you know. They just come here every day to hang out. What a life, huh?"

"I bet," Weslee answered. They made their way over to the driving range; Weslee dragging a bag of rented clubs, Sherry with her own set.

"OK, how do we start?" Weslee asked.

"How do we start? Girl, you got a lot of things to learn." Sherry laughed.

"Well, that's why I'm here now, OK?" Weslee looked dismayed.

Sherry touched her shoulder. "I'm just playing with you. At least you're not home thinking about Duncan."

Well, not really.

"Yes, Sherry. At least I'm not home thinking about him. And tomorrow, I'm running the Boston Marathon, and I won't be thinking about him then, either."

"Well, all right then. Let's hit some balls."

A couple of hours later, the sun was setting. Weslee, exhausted by her pathetic and unsuccessful attempts at golf, put up her hands in surrender.

"Sherry, I wanna quit, this isn't working," she said.

"Fine. Fine. I'm tired of your complaining. Why don't you go on to the hospital and I'll meet you there."

Weslee, relieved, walked back to the clubhouse and surrendered her clubs. Then she walked the mile from the clubhouse to the hospital, taking in all the wild, bright colors that the orange sun had laid out across the sky. She hoped Holly had been having a good day. She hadn't been doing too well lately.

She waved hello to the volunteers at the front desk and took the elevator to Holly's ward.

"Weslee, child." Miriam waddled from behind the nurses' station as she saw Weslee approaching.

Weslee could tell from the look on her face what had happened.

"She die last night, child. She die," Miriam said, dropping her head as Weslee began to sob.

"Don't cry, child. Don't cry. She's in a better place." Miriam pulled Weslee close and patted her back as Weslee continued to sob.

"Where is she?" Weslee asked when she could take a breath from the grief that overwhelmed her being.

"They took her away. She's downstairs. Don't go see her by yourself. Wait for your friend."

Weslee nodded and sat at the nurses' station as Miriam went to fetch her water.

She could hear Sherry's footsteps coming up the hall.

"What's wrong?" Sherry said as she looked at Weslee's tear-stained face.

"Holly died last night."

Sherry bit her lip and tried to hold back her tears. "How are you?" she asked.

Weslee shook her head and began to sob again.

Sherry walked around the desk and held her. "I'm sorry, Weslee. I shouldn't have let you meet her now, with everything you were going through. I didn't think she would go this soon. This is my fault."

Weslee looked at Sherry through her tears. "What are you talking about? I'm not sorry I met her. I just . . . She was just so right about me. I'm so naïve. I actually thought that if I went to see her, if I spent more time with her, that maybe she would live longer. I thought I could make a difference for her. I wanted . . ."

"Weslee, you did make a difference for her. She had *nobody* before we came. Before you came. You were the last friend she had in the world," Sherry said.

Weslee nodded. Miriam handed her a glass of water.

"It's OK, child. She used to look for you all the time. She was really happy that you had started to come and see her," Miriam said. "She was a good child. A good child." Miriam sighed.

Later, Weslee stood whimpering outside the morgue as Sherry sprang into action. Her fingers moved swiftly and efficiently as she called the funeral home that had handled her mother's funeral.

"What are you doing?" Weslee mouthed as Sherry spoke into the cell phone.

"I'm not gonna let the state just bury her out there with the rest of the nobodies. Holly had friends, OK? She's gonna go out with a little dignity." Sherry was pushing more numbers, this time calling a florist.

Weslee could only watch in amazement. "What can I do to help? I have some money. I can make calls, too," Weslee said.

"OK. Call the church and ask for Pastor Bob, and then call Fairview Cemetery."

I can't believe I'm actually planning a funeral, Weslee thought as she made the calls. But all the planning and activity made her feel better. It chipped away at the cement block that had been sitting heavily on her heart since she'd heard about Holly's death.

"Know what, Sherry?" she asked as they took a break from their tasks. "I'll pay for it. I feel . . . I need to. Know what I mean?"

Sherry looked at her intently. "Wes, are you sure?"

"I'm absolutely sure," Weslee said firmly. "I'm doing this more for me than I am for Holly." She thought that it was the best investment in herself she could make after the months of throwing away her money on the frivolous and ephemeral. Holly had given her something that was much more valuable and that would outlast the most classic fashions.

Sherry nodded. "I'm glad you can see that."

Chapter

25

The ring of the phone assaulted Weslee's aching head. She grabbed it before the second ring. She looked at the clock—it was already ten P.M. She had run to her bed the minute she got home from the hospital. She really didn't want to talk to anyone in the world, but she picked up the phone anyway.

It was Koji.

"Koji, don't tell me I forgot to turn in my part of the project," Weslee groaned at the sound of the Japanese student's voice on the other end.

"Weslee, did you hear about Lana?"

"No, what about Lana?"

"She had a really bad accident early this morning. She's in the hospital. Brigham and Women's Hospital."

The fog in Weslee's head suddenly cleared up. She threw on a pair of jeans, a sweater, and a baseball cap and rushed out the door.

Luckily she didn't have to wait long for a trolley. She hadn't bothered to ask Koji what had happened. There was no need to explain why and how Lana had ended up driving her Mercedes into a tree at three A.M. on a Sunday morning.

Eleanor was asleep in a chair at Lana's bedside, and the

resemblance between mother and daughter forced Weslee to stop and look at the two for a few seconds.

Lana looked normal, as if she were sleeping and not heavily sedated after six hours of surgery. According to the nurse, most of her injuries had been internal, except for a broken leg.

Eleanor stirred just as Weslee was deciding to leave.

"Weslee," Lana's mother said groggily.

"Hi, Eleanor."

They hugged and Eleanor held Weslee tightly.

"I almost lost her. I almost lost my little girl." She was crying.

"Eleanor, I'm so sorry."

"Do you know what happened? Why weren't you with her?"

"Eleanor, I don't know. I'm sorry."

Eleanor was sobbing now. "We tried so hard, you know. She was in rehab two, three times, a few years ago. She was doing so well. She didn't have a single drink over the holidays. . . ."

Weslee didn't know what to say. Lana had never told her that she had been in rehabilitation or had been treated for alcohol abuse. And obviously Eleanor did not know that Lana had been drinking a lot, a whole lot, over the last year. Lana had fooled the people who were closest to her.

"Eleanor, at least she's safe. The nurse out front said she's going to be OK." Weslee wasn't sure that her words were of any use.

Eleanor sat in the chair again, wringing a tissue in her hands.

Weslee tried to find the right words. She remained silent.

"Her father's so angry with her for lying to us again." Eleanor resumed her weeping. "She's going to pull through. She has to. Then I'm taking her back to New York to stay with me. I thought she could be on her own, but I was so wrong." Eleanor sniffed, then blew her nose.

Weslee put her arm on Eleanor's shaking shoulders.

"You know, you were the first best friend she's ever had. She told me that. That time you came to Oak Bluffs. She said you were the first real girlfriend she ever had. She liked you so much. She said you were so smart. She said you're the only person she's ever known who never makes any mistakes."

The guilt washed over Weslee like a tidal wave. She had been hating Lana so much lately. No one would tell her the extent of the gossip that Lana had been spreading. But she had heard from Marie Bunting and a couple of other clients that Lana had branded her a desperate social climber. Lana had even tried to persuade a couple of her clients not to see her anymore. That news had made Weslee so angry and ashamed, she had told no one, not even Sherry. She had made a vow to herself to never speak to Lana again. But when Koji's call came, her instinct made her come to this hospital room. And now Eleanor was telling her something different.

She thought I was the best girlfriend she's ever had?

The nurse entered the room. They had to leave. Eleanor said she would hang around the hospital until they let her back in the room. Weslee promised to return as soon as Lana was awake.

Weslee decided to walk home from Brigham and Women's Hospital. She pulled her baseball cap far down on her forehead as she walked down Huntington Avenue. She walked slowly, breathing the air deeply.

How could this happen, she asked herself. In one day, Holly had died and Lana was in a hospital bed clinging to life. What was going on? Weslee felt afraid. Death and the threat of it had never touched her life since she lost her grandmother when she was ten years old. She had been so terrified then that her parents had allowed her to stay with a babysitter while they attended the funeral.

Lana would come through, the nurse outside the room had said. It would take her a while to get back to her old self. Her large intestines were badly damaged. But at least she had her life, her hopes, Weslee thought. The tears pricked at her eyes again as she pictured Holly's face in her head, heard her weak voice: "Girl, I'm sure we used to be sisters in another life."

How could all of this happen?

Weslee badly wanted someone to talk to, someone who would comfort her. She pulled out her cell phone and dialed his number.

The phone rang six times and then: "This is William, I'm not home right now, but please . . ."

She couldn't help but think of Duncan. Did he know? Would he visit Lana at the hospital? His arms around her would make her feel less afraid, Weslee thought. She pushed the thought out of her head. Calling him would be the biggest, most fatal step back she could ever take. She quickened her pace.

Weslee had been in her apartment for three hours before Eleanor called her right about midnight. Lana was awake.

Weslee quickly got dressed again and this time called a taxi.

She arrived just as an older man and an elderly woman were making their entrance. The man introduced himself as Lana's father. The woman was Lana's grandmother, Eleanor's mother. Weslee felt strange walking into the room with them. She so obviously didn't belong there.

"Hi, Weslee." Eleanor looked up from her chair beside the bed. She seemed to be in a much lighter mood. "Honey, Weslee's here."

Weslee was nervous as she approached Lana's bed. She wasn't sure what to say, what with the way things were between the two of them. The fact that her family was looking on did not make things any less awkward.

"Hey, girl," Weslee said, trying to be casual. Lana's face was bruised and puffy, and her right leg was in a cast. "You look fabulous."

Lana tried to smile at the joke but winced in pain at the effort.

"We'll let you girls talk," Eleanor said and shooed her husband and mother out of the room.

"How are you feeling?" Weslee knew it was a stupid question.

"I'm hurting all over," Lana said, grimacing.

"I'm sorry."

"For what? It wasn't your fault." Lana wasn't trying, but she was being caustic.

"I'm sorry for the things I said to you the last time. . . ."

Lana held up her hand. "I'm the one . . ." Her eyes began to tear up. "I haven't been half the friend that you've been to me, Weslee." It was the first time Weslee had ever seen Lana come anywhere close to crying, and she was touched.

"No, Lana. Remember, if it weren't for you, I . . . You took me under your wing." Weslee felt her voice cracking up.

"I was just so mean to you. But I couldn't help it. I don't know what comes over me sometimes." Lana was crying.

"Lana, don't upset yourself like this. It's all in the past, OK?" Weslee touched her hand. "It's all in the past," she said again. "Don't upset yourself." She gave Lana a Kleenex.

"I need to tell you something," Lana said, sniffling.

"Whatever it is, it can wait until you get better and you get out of here."

"No, I need to tell you now."

Weslee sighed. She knew she couldn't change Lana's mind; even laid up in a hospital bed, she was still Lana.

"It's Duncan. He's a jerk, Weslee. He's my cousin, but he's a jerk."

Weslee said nothing. Lana would get no argument from her on that one. But Lana's statement was not news to her.

"I should have told you this weeks ago when I found out, but I was so caught up with getting back at you for being right about me." Lana took a deep breath, and the pain was obvious in her expression. She closed her eyes.

"He's engaged," she said after the pain had dulled a little. "He got engaged on New Year's Eve in London to this girl he's been with since college."

Weslee felt a chill go through her body.

Lana looked at her worriedly. "I'm sorry, Weslee. He's a jerk. I should have . . ."

"It's OK," Weslee heard herself say. "We broke up a few weeks ago, anyway."

"So he told you?" Lana asked.

Weslee didn't answer. But she thought, *Well, he kind of did, just not in so many words.*

"I'm so sorry I didn't warn you. But I thought things had ended between them. Then I heard he had started visiting her in London recently, so I thought he had broken it off with you. Then I ran into William the other day, and he told me that he didn't think that you knew the whole truth." Lana was still looking at Weslee with that worried look.

"It's OK. It's OK. I'm a big girl." She wasn't lying. She was trying so hard not to cry.

"Weslee, I'm your friend. It's not OK," Lana said gently but firmly.

Weslee nodded and tried to stifle the feeling of rage that was building in her stomach. It was all too much, she thought. She tried to put all the pieces together. When? How? How could she not have suspected? Then Sherry's words echoed in her head. She'd chosen again to see what she wanted to see. *I am such a freaking idiot!* Weslee thought angrily. *Can I be any more stupid?!* Then a chilling thought wended its way through her brain. Holly! Their experience seemed eerily similar . . . *What if I wasn't the only one he cheated with?* She remembered that one time they hadn't used a condom because things had gotten too hot and heavy; stopping had seemed out of the question. *Oh my God!* She began to hate with a fury she had never felt before.

"Lana, I need to get out of here. I need to go. I'll talk to you later." Weslee bolted out of the hospital and headed home.

Chapter
26

Weslee flung open the door of her apartment and threw the keys and her bag on the floor. All she had had time to do on the way home from the hospital was think. Think about Duncan: the way he lied, said he loved her, spent time at her place. And all along, he knew. Knew he was going to ask this other woman to marry him.

She picked up the almost-full bottle of whiskey that was on her kitchen counter.

"Even told me he'd take me away that weekend. That same damned weekend he got engaged in London!" She spoke to no one in particular and took a swig from the bottle.

"Lying, evil bastard!" she screamed as tears coursed down her face. She paced the floor, taking huge swallows from the bottle. She thought her vision was getting blurry, and her head felt light. But the anger was what she felt the most. It was hot and dark, and it burned under her skin. It was something that she had never allowed herself to feel before, and the feeling of it was scary and liberating at the same time.

She wanted to hurt him so bad. She had tried calling him at his apartment when she had left the hospital, but there was no answer there or on his cell phone. She knew he was probably at his office. What she really wanted to do was go down there and smack him hard in the face in front of all his colleagues. But her common sense told her not to make a scene that would only humiliate her.

She grabbed the phone and dialed the number to his office. He picked up on the first ring.

"You couldn't breathe? You couldn't breathe, but you could get engaged to some bitch?"

"Weslee?"

"How could you lie to me like this? All these months." She was sobbing into the phone. She wanted to scream at him, swear at him.

"Weslee. Calm down."

"No, I won't calm down, you jerk. I believed you when you said you loved me. How could you do this!"

"Weslee, do you want me to come over there?" Duncan spoke calmly and slowly, as if speaking to a child.

"Don't you come anywhere near me!" she yelled into the phone.

"Weslee. Will you just calm down? You're hysterical."

"I'm hysterical? I'm hysterical? You haven't seen hysterical, Duncan!"

She slammed down the phone. She wanted to hurt him. She thought of going to his apartment and smashing his CD collection. Maybe she would break the windows of his car. Call his parents and tell them what he had done. The anger, mixed with the effects of the whiskey, made thoughts of revenge crowd and jumble in her mind until she wanted to scream.

She dialed his number again. "I hate you, Duncan. I hate the day that you were born. I hate you. Do you hear me?"

He didn't answer.

"Do you hear me?"

"Weslee, if you don't calm down I'm going to have to call

your folks, OK? You're scaring me. Why are you doing this to yourself?"

"Doing what to myself? You did this to me!"

"I'm not going to listen to this. Call me when you want to talk about this like an adult."

She heard the dial tone before she could say another word.

She threw the phone across the room. It crashed against the wall.

She sat on the floor and cried herself to sleep.

She woke up, dazed, a few hours later. She looked around the living room. Her head felt swollen. She noticed the phone was on the floor, the receiver off the cradle. The empty bottle of whiskey was not too far away from where it had spilled onto the carpet. She tried to get up from the floor where she had dozed off, but her heavy head wouldn't let her. She lay back down on the floor and looked up at the ceiling.

All those feelings she felt were so familiar: the anguish, the anger, the hopelessness. She had felt them when Michael left. She had felt them again just weeks ago when Duncan left. She had been progressing, moving forward. But now this. She couldn't accept that the last few months had all been a lie. How could she have been so wrong? He must have loved her. After all the time they spent together, all the things they did, all the presents . . . It had to have meant something to him. He couldn't have loved someone else all along. Why would he go through all the trouble? How could she not have even suspected? Were there any signs that she missed? The times he was moody; the last few months, when his lovemaking had gone from tender to formulaic; all those trips he took to London. Were those signs?

How could she have been so stupid? Again. So soon. And Lana knew. William knew. She didn't know. How could she do this to herself again? How was she to get over this? She felt immobilized by all the feelings that were inside of her. Maybe she would just stay on the floor until all the rage and the pain went away. She looked up at the ceiling. She wanted to call on something. On God, maybe, but she couldn't now. She couldn't understand why He would let this happen. Hadn't she suffered enough?

The doorbell rang.

Sherry wouldn't take no for an answer, apparently, because here she was at Weslee's door in full crisis mode.

"Wes, I'm so sorry." Sherry hugged her friend. It had taken her less than an hour to come over after Weslee's desperate call to her.

Weslee just stood there and let Sherry hug her.

It wasn't until hours later that morning, still sobbing as Sherry sat with her, that Weslee realized the marathon had come and gone. She hadn't run.

"We'll run next year," Sherry said as she made scrambled Egg Beaters in the kitchen.

"Maybe I should just get out of Boston. This whole thing, coming here, was probably just a bad idea."

"Oh, please. Think of all you've done in the last few months. All the people you've met. Moi included." Sherry pointed to her chest, smiling. "Besides, this is the greatest city in the world. You're just trying to find your way, that's all. Everybody goes through this eventually."

"Ever think of becoming a shrink, Sherry?" Weslee asked dejectedly.

"I have. But I don't have the patience for simple people who screw up their lives. But you, I could work with you. You just need to toughen up a bit. Stop sitting around on the sidelines of your own life."

Weslee contemplated this. "You know, I've been thinking," she said as Sherry set a plate of eggs before her. "I'm gonna get tested."

"Tested?" Sherry looked confused as she plunked two slices of bread into the toaster.

"Yup. For HIV." The thought hadn't left her mind since that day at the hospital. Her rational mind told her that there was no way in the world that a guy like Duncan could have any sinister disease. But the mental images of an emaciated, coughing Holly wouldn't give her any rest. That could be me, she thought. The fear kept her from sleeping, from concentrating on studying, from breathing it seemed. *I'm not the old me, who only sees what she wants to see*, Weslee told herself. She decided that she wanted the test, dramatic though the decision seemed.

"That's . . . that's wise, I guess," Sherry said, looking at her squarely. "Is that something you've been worrying about?"

"Since I found out about Duncan's . . . er . . . engagement, it's all I've thought about. What if I wasn't the only one he was seeing? What if it hadn't been the first time he's cheated on this girl?"

"Didn't you guys use protection, Wes?" Sherry asked, narrowing her eyes.

Weslee looked down at the table, ashamed. "There was that one time—"

Sherry cut her off, disappointment in her voice. "Well, do what you need to do to put your mind at ease. You shouldn't have to live with that fear on top of everything else." Sherry sat next to her at the tiny dining room table. "You're gonna be fine, Wes." She patted Weslee's hand. "But get the test. It will make you feel better. But you're fine. I believe in prayer, and you'll be fine."

Weslee pushed her eggs around the plate.

"But from what you told me, he's really busy and this girl is overseas, right?" Sherry asked.

Weslee nodded.

"So why would you think he's running around on her *and* you?"

"I don't know. I'm just . . . I'm just . . . I just can't get that image of Holly out of my head. The more I think about it, the more I realize I really didn't know Duncan that well. He was so quiet and moody most of the time . . ." She trailed off, realizing that the same remoteness she had found so sexy was what was causing her the most worry now. "I really couldn't tell you if he was the type to have two women or four women or fifty women." She sighed.

Sherry shook her head. "Girl, take the test then. And I'll say a prayer for you."

Weslee found herself praying, too, that night as she struggled to fall asleep. *I know you'll listen to Sherry's prayers, God,* she thought, *even if you don't answer mine.*

Chapter
27

It felt strange to be around Lana now only because she wasn't the person she was before the accident. Weslee almost felt that she hadn't known Lana at all. Where was the vivacious, perky, loud life of the party that she had met a few months ago? Lana was subdued. Her leg was broken, and her usual feisty spirit seemed to be limping, too. The independent façade she had built so skillfully had crumbled. In the last two weeks she had been forced to depend on others for her most basic needs. And she seemed so humble, pliant, and needy sometimes. It was a welcome change.

Weslee watched her hobble around on her crutches in her apartment. The blender drowned out the noise of the television. It was Saturday—smoothie movie day, Weslee had called it. She had tried to cheer Lana up since her discharge from the hospital, but it had been a difficult task. Lana was sinking further into depression and alcohol withdrawal. It amazed Weslee that neither she nor anyone else had suspected the extent of Lana's problems.

Weslee stopped by Lana's place when she could to give Eleanor or Lana's grandmother a break. They were her full-time caretakers for now. Although the doctor said she could eat solid food, she still struggled to keep anything edible down. Weslee mixed protein shakes, made her oatmeal and fruit smoothies.

"Lana, smoothies are ready," Weslee called out as Lana hobbled her way back to the couch.

"God, I hope it stays down," Lana replied, slowly setting herself down into the couch. "Those pineapple chunks sure didn't."

Weslee resisted the urge to give her another pep talk about thinking positive. It was all she had been doing the last few weeks: trying to raise Lana's spirits, trying to restore her confidence, trying to get her to forgive herself for not being the strong person she thought she was.

"What are we watching?"

"*The Royal Tenenbaums.*" Weslee knew it was one of Lana's favorite movies.

"Could you make more coffee, too?" Lana asked. "I'm sorry. Thanks."

"It's OK. I don't mind being your maid."

"Weslee, you're not. I told you—"

"Lana, relax. I'm just kidding." Weslee handed Lana the smoothie in a tall glass.

"Are you sure?" Lana's face was pained with embarrassment and shame.

"Lana. You are my friend. I want to be here with you and for you."

Lana sniffled.

"Don't get emotional on me, OK? Else I'm going to start asking for the old you to come back."

"I'm sorry. Everything makes me cry these days."

Weslee sat next to her friend and put her arm around her shoulder.

"It's OK. Let's watch the movie."

Weslee watched the previews absently. It was true. She didn't mind being here with Lana. For one thing, it kept her out of the ground zero of misery that her apartment had become. If it wasn't loneliness consuming her, it was Holly and her haunting story of her dream life turned into a fatal nightmare. The funeral had been sparsely attended, mostly hospital staff and one lawyer from her old firm who had seen the obituary that Sherry made sure got in the major newspapers. Weslee had taken the picture of Holly when she was young, vibrant, and beautiful. For some reason it made her feel stronger. Sherry had been right—focusing on other people did make her own problems seem less important. They didn't even seem like problems at all.

She was no fool. She knew that things did not happen overnight. Lana was not suddenly changed for the better. But Holly's death and Lana's accident had made Weslee see that having an imperfect friend was better than being alone. People came in all different sorts of packages, and there was no law that said she had to take the whole package. She could take the parts of it that she liked, that she could stand, and leave the rest. It was that simple. Lana would always be selfish, probably. She was selfish long before Weslee had entered her life. Why would she totally and immediately transform? *Because of how wonderful a person I am*, the old Weslee would have thought. Now she was starting to learn that life didn't work that way.

She teased Lana about the cards that had come in from her friends at the Whaling Museum. "You're a whale buff? That is so pathetic!"

Lana rolled her eyes. "It's just a stupid hobby."

But Weslee had gained a little more respect for Lana. She had never paid much attention to all the books about whales or to the pictures that were scattered over the apartment. A stupid hobby made Lana seem just a bit more human to Weslee.

"Why did you keep all this stuff hidden from me?" Weslee had asked her one night when she dropped yet an-

other bomb by talking about how she would miss scuba div-
ing and all the different Caribbean islands where she had
dived with famous divers.

"I don't know," Lana had shrugged. "Those are just
dorky things about myself."

"No, Lana. Those are the things that make you you. You
don't have to be ashamed of that," Weslee had told her.

Now Weslee looked over at Lana, who was taking small
sips from her glass. "How is it?"

Lana shrugged. "This is so weird. It's Saturday night; we
should be out on dates or out partying. At least you should."

"I'm off the dating scene for now. And after what you've
been through, you probably need this break."

"Ha!" Lana laughed. "If I could walk—or eat—I'd be
out tonight, preferably with a tall, dark hottie."

"Oh, Lana." Weslee sighed. Not a total transformation
yet.

Chapter
28

Sherry held Weslee's hand as she looked away from the needle that was in her right arm. She could feel the thin sharpness of the pain as her own blood snaked its way out of her. She tried not to feel sorry for herself or turn the present into a melodrama. *This only makes sense*, she thought. *I need to do this for my own peace of mind.* She would not blame herself or Duncan or loneliness or stupidity for bringing her to this examining room, this needle, this uncomfortable scene. It was the sensible thing to do, and she would do it with no complaints. But that needle . . .

"Almost there," the nurse said gently.

Weslee sighed. She hated sharp things like needles and matronly nurses with harsh Boston accents and judging eyes. *Almost theah*, the woman had said. She hated anything that had to do with modern health care, waiting rooms, questionnaires, and co-payments. This doctor's office with all its sterility was making her nauseated. She looked at Sherry, who was intently observing the entire scene as if she were in training to become a nurse herself. Sherry's concentration amused Weslee. And she was so glad to not have to do this alone. She would never have considered asking Lana to be here. Somehow that just seemed inappropriate.

Weslee thought Lana would take it as a personal insult—
that she would even consider the possibility of Duncan having HIV. Another part of Weslee was ashamed. Sometimes
she thought she saw pity in Lana's eyes when they talked
about men. Pity that Weslee had not been good enough to
captivate and capture Duncan. Yes, she'd described him as
a jerk, but did Lana really believe that? It seemed that the
men that Lana went after were Duncan clones themselves,
worldly superachievers oozing self-assuredness that over-
flowed into arrogance. Lana probably saw what Weslee was
now beginning to see—she'd been painfully out of her
league all along. And now she was paying the price in fear
and insecurity. Lana would never have gotten so caught up
in the thrall of a man like Duncan that she'd neglect her
own protection. The girl stocked boxes and boxes of Trojans
in her bathroom in plain view of anyone willing to take a
peek. She'd probably have laughed off Weslee's fears and
called her naïve or hilarious in that semipatronizing manner
that was so natural to her that she seemed unaware of it.

"You're done," the nurse said and capped a vial filled
with blood.

"When will I have the results?" Weslee asked.

"It takes about a week. We'll contact you."

Weslee nodded and hopped off the examining table.
"Let's get out of this place," she told Sherry, who had been
mostly silent since they walked into the building.

"Wes, I'm sure you don't have anything," Sherry said.

"I'm not. I'm not sure about anything these days." They
walked out into a blinding bright day on Milk Street, where
the financial district was starting to boil over with hungry
nine-to-fivers burrowing into delis, neat burrito joints, and
other lunch-hour haunts. "I thought Duncan was one thing,
and he wasn't . . . And then Holly had to die like that. I'm
not taking anything for granted, Sherry."

"I know how you feel, but it just feels so strange to be taking this test. It's so drastic," Sherry said.

"Yeah, I know. But I just need to have that piece of paper in my hand telling me that I'm not gonna die because of my stupidity and carelessness."

She was beginning to leave the fear behind as they drove south, away from downtown Boston. She needed to know if her carelessness had put her life in danger. And if it meant getting tested every six months into infinity, she would do it. *It's time to start taking some control of my life,* she thought.

"At least I hope you won't lose any more sleep over it," Sherry cut into her thoughts. "You look like hell."

"I do?" Weslee pulled down the sun-visor mirror over the passenger seat. She did look tired and haggard. She hadn't worn make-up in days. It just hadn't seemed worth the effort. Her days were full of running between classes, Lana's apartment, and worrying about the state of her own physical and mental health. She felt trapped in a cycle of depressive thoughts and activities. Only getting those test results would free her from this. Maybe then she could come around to caring again about inconsequential things like the bags under her eyes or the pimple on her forehead. For now those things just didn't matter much.

"Let's go get a facial tomorrow," Sherry suggested. "I've never had one, and I've always wanted to go to Rosaline's Spa."

Weslee turned to her, surprised. "You want to get a facial?" Sherry was such a vocal opponent of all things self-indulgent that the idea of her doing something as frivolous as getting a facial threw Weslee for a loop.

"You're not the only one who wants to have gorgeous skin," Sherry said defensively, a bit of embarrassment on her face.

"No. No, I didn't mean that," Weslee said. "It's just that with everything on my mind . . ."

"That's exactly why we should go. To get your mind off all this depressing stuff. Besides, you've been Lana's little house slave lately. It's time you treated yourself like a diva again."

Weslee laughed, protesting, "I'm not her house slave. I'm just helping her out until she gets back on her feet." Then she added quickly, as if in her own defense, "She's changing, you know. She's mellowing out."

"Uh-huh." Sherry's tone betrayed her doubt.

Weslee decided to let it go. She did not mind helping Lana at all. The times they spent together now were less frenzied. There was less nastiness, less competitiveness on Lana's part. Maybe it was because she wasn't drinking. But Lana's mellowness made her easier to be around. Weslee had been thinking that there was hope for their friendship.

But maybe Sherry's right, she thought. Her body felt weighted down with worry and fatigue; a facial and a massage would be just what she needed. At least it would temporarily ease some of her stress until the test results came back.

Later that week she still couldn't sleep. She would know in the morning, the nurse had told her the day before. All she could do was stare at the clock as it blinked the minutes away in the dark room. The afternoon at the spa had not helped much. She tried to remember the sensation of the massuse's experienced hands kneading the stress from her upper back and shoulders or the soothing lavender scent that had filled the room, even the sense of peace she'd felt as her face had been cleansed, steamed, and exfoliated. But those memories failed to bring her any closer to sleep.

She hated him. Duncan. She wondered what he was doing at that exact moment, and she was sure that he was not struggling with guilt or wide awake with worry. Not

Duncan, Weslee thought. He was the master of his own uni-verse, and he would lose no sleep over her or anyone else. Maybe her replacement was already lying right next to him in his bed. She would be some foolish girl, easily won over by some cheap token and his false attentiveness. This girl would have to fancy herself some sort of diamond in the rough finally being discovered by the prince she'd deserved her entire life, who'd smooth out her rough edges and turn her into a princess. One look into his eyes and she'd say to herself: no more waiting. Maybe he'd showered her with his charm and made her knees buckle with his intensity and then quickly told her he loved her, too. Maybe, she, too, was planning their future together in her head while he drifted off to Neverland in his mind. Or maybe he was ca-ressing her body right now. The thought made Weslee squeeze her eyes shut; she could not even bear to picture it. Worse, she thought, was it his fiancée who was with him now?

Those thoughts kept her mind occupied until the sun began to creep into her apartment. She left the bed wearily, beaten by insomnia. Today she would have her peace of mind. Sleep would come later.

"People are gonna think we're lesbians," Sherry joked as they sat in the waiting room. "This is the second time we've come here together."

Weslee rolled her eyes. "Why lesbians? Why not sisters? Can you be any more paranoid?" She was in no mood to joke, and Sherry caught the hint.

"OK, Miss Grumpy. I won't talk to you until after we get the results." Sherry picked up a *Cosmopolitan* magazine and read it, snorting every few seconds and exclaiming "Gimme a break!" every two minutes. Weslee crossed and uncrossed her legs a few hundred times, her eyes not leaving the white clock on the white wall.

When the nurse finally called her name, she shot out of the chair like an arrow. Sherry followed dutifully.

She couldn't hear as the nurse explained the test, its accuracies and its inaccuracies and such. She just wanted to know what it said about her.

"See, I told you!" Sherry said triumphantly.

"What?" She hadn't heard what the nurse said; maybe she'd been listening too intently to her own jumbled thoughts.

The nurse handed her a sheet of paper, and she read it. Negative.

"I told you there was nothing to worry about," Sherry said.

She looked at the sheet of paper again. It was true. She was safe. Saved.

She closed her eyes and thought, *Thank you, God. Thank you.* The weight around her heart began to subside, and she felt a new lightness around her shoulders. Sherry hugged her, beaming. "Now will you relax?" Weslee nodded, tears of relief burning her eyes.

"Let's go celebrate," Sherry said.

"Yeah," Weslee said. "Oooh, I think I'll buy myself a new Kate Spade—"

"How is putting yourself into more debt celebrating?" Sherry put her hands on her hips.

Weslee rolled her eyes. "OK, Mom. What do you suggest?"

"Let's go to the museum. We'll have a nice lunch. With dessert."

Weslee chuckled as it struck her again how different Sherry was from Lana, and even herself. The MFA would do for now. But she'd still pick up that red leather bag from Kate Spade at some point when Sherry wasn't looking. Someday, when she didn't have to charge it.

Chapter

29

Days like today convinced Weslee that she had made the exactly right decision by moving to Boston—despite everything that had happened. She looked out the window of her apartment and saw a perfect sky, light blue with puffy, see-through clouds—cumulus, she remembered. She could almost smell the cleanness of the air by pressing her nose up against the glass.

This would be her last run around the Charles before she went home to Chicago for the summer. For some reason, she hated the thought of leaving Boston. But her brain told her that she needed to be physically away from Boston for a while. To get her bearings and properly dispose of everything that had happened to her since that bumpy landing, she had to be away from the source of the pain.

She and Sherry vowed that they would run the marathon next year, come hell or high water. She still felt pangs of disappointment every time she looked at the perfectly broken-in pair of Sauconys she had saved for the race. She refused to wear them again. She had been so ready. But tragedy had a way of putting real life on hold . . .

She smiled unconsciously, remembering the days of

walking this same quarter mile to the Charles, her face freezing, her fingertips and toes numb.

But summer was here, and the sights and sounds of this dazzling Saturday morning were hers to take in slowly, without the cold rushing her on to her goal. There were students strolling along Commonwealth Avenue, darting in and out of coffee shops, parents in town visiting for the weekend and keeping an eye on how their tuition money was being or would be spent, townies busy going about their chores and jobs. Everybody seemed to be in a good mood. That was the thing about Boston. When the sun came out and the air was warm, people actually smiled and showed that they could be polite. But a matter of twenty degrees up or down could drastically change that: murderous heat waves and suicide-inducing blizzards.

This was the last of Boston she would absorb for a while, so she didn't want to focus on her problems. She still had goals even though she had missed the marathon. A change of scenery and people, plus her family would heal her broken heart faster, she surmised. Besides, she was exhausted. Finals, work, and caring for Lana had all taken so much out of her physically. She longed for home and the comfort and familiarity of her family.

She broke into a jog once she reached the trail. *A lot of memories here already*, she thought. *We'll see how I do in round two when I return in the fall.*

Two hours later, sweaty and chafing between her thighs, she burst into the apartment, dying to pee and eager to just feel clean again.

She came out of the shower a half hour later, her hair wrapped in a towel, wearing her favorite blue terry bathrobe. She made a cup of tea and put some graham crackers on a plate and went for the couch. She had waited all day to make this call.

"Hey, William." She hoped she didn't sound as breathless as she was.

"Hey, FloJo."

His voice was so what she needed to hear right now.

"How've you been? Where have you been? I haven't seen you stalking my neighborhood lately."

"Very funny, William. I've been busy." *Busy healing my broken heart*, she wanted to say.

"So, did you run the marathon?" he asked.

She explained to him that she had rushed to be with Lana on that day and so the marathon had been the last thing on her mind.

"Oh, yeah. I hear you've been taking care of her. I guess some things will never change."

They both laughed.

"She's grown up a lot, William. Trust me."

"Whatever you say. She's your friend."

They laughed a lot as the conversation got easier. Twenty minutes later it felt as though their friendship had never lapsed, that Duncan had never happened. But he had, and she couldn't ignore it.

"So, how are you dealing?" he finally asked.

"Dealing?"

"You know what I mean."

"I'm all dealt out. I'm over it." She tried to sound dismissive. She wasn't sure if she should be discussing Duncan with William. She didn't know if she could tell him that some days she spent hours thinking of ways to get him back and on others she spent hours and hours thinking of ways to destroy him. She was over it. She hoped.

"That's good. That's real good. I mean, I know you guys were pretty intense for a while."

"Well, that's all over now." She cleared her throat.

"Listen, I'm sorry about the way things turned out. I

wish I could have done more. But I didn't feel that it was my place."

She sighed. "Have you seen him lately?" she asked. She had vowed never to ask about him, but she broke the pledge.

William cleared his throat. "No. I really haven't, Weslee."

There was an awkward silence.

"So, what's next for you?" William asked.

"I'm outta here."

"Where?"

"Chicago. I'm going home for the summer."

"Are you serious?" he exclaimed.

"Dead serious."

"But what about your personal training thing? Those ladies who lunch can't stop talking about how good you're making them look."

"I'll pick it up again in the fall."

"Why, Weslee? You could make so much dough this summer, especially on the Vineyard. I'm surprised you haven't left that gym and gone out on your own yet. What are they teaching you in that business school?" he joked.

She laughed. "I just need a change of pace, new scenery, different people. Besides, I'm not in business school to learn how to be an entrepreneur."

"Hmm. That first night I met you, you said you've always wanted to start your own business."

"Well, yes, I meant eventually. Maybe doing something in finance."

"But you're happy doing personal training."

"Yes, but finance is what I've spent my whole career focused on."

"So?"

"William!" She was growing tired of the conversation. She didn't want to talk about school or work.

"OK, OK. I won't give you any career advice. All I'm saying is don't ignore an opportunity that's staring you right in the face."

"It will still be there in the fall," Weslee said.

"I hope so. There's a lot of competition out there. I hope you think about this really long and hard before you make a big mistake."

"I know what I'm doing."

"I'm sure you think you do."

Another silence.

"I'd miss you if you left. I mean, you're a great friend for a guy to have around," he said awkwardly.

Just a great friend?

"Well, you could look me up if you're ever anywhere near Chicago this summer."

"Sure. Just promise me you'll think about this some more," he said before they said good-bye.

Chapter
30

It seemed like so long ago that the tiny apartment on Commonwealth Avenue had been filled with boxes waiting to be unpacked. Back then Weslee could never have anticipated that a year later she would have fallen in love again and gotten her heart broken, have a tumultuous friendship with an alcoholic, and lose a friend to AIDS. But, she thought as she waited for the movers to take the boxes away, it had not been all bad. She had made a new best friend, Sherry, a keeper. She had managed to almost salvage her finances without having to drop out of school. And her training clients made her feel that she was the best thing since Billy Blanks. It hadn't been all bad, she thought as she looked at herself in her full-length mirror. Yes, she was wearing a Yohji top and D&G jeans, brands she had never heard of before she came to Boston. She was a different person. Different better.

The doorbell rang, interrupting her thoughts. She buzzed up the woman who would be subletting her apartment for the summer.

"Hi, Beth," Weslee said to the smiling, freckled, dreadlocked woman at the door. Finding Beth Worthy had been a stroke of luck. She was the sister of a friend of a classmate who would be spending the summer in Boston as a law firm intern. She had been highly recommended. Weslee had liked her the first day she saw her. They hugged each other. Weslee was still getting used to Beth's California friendliness.

They made small talk as Weslee took her around the small apartment again, reiterating that she should be extra-careful with the furniture that would be left behind. Weslee prayed that this quiet-looking-and-acting woman did not have a wild streak that would result in any harm to the meager furnishings in the apartment.

Before Beth left, Weslee handed her a card with her parents' address and all the numbers where she could be reached in Chicago. When she handed over the spare set of keys to the apartment, she felt like a parent entrusting a teenager with the keys to a fast car.

"I know you're responsible, so I'm not going to worry," Weslee told the law student, trying not to sound threatening.

"Oh, don't worry, Weslee." Beth smiled.

Alone again, doubt crept up on Weslee as the reality of leaving Boston set in. She did have that view from the living room window of a tiny sliver of the Charles River that she would miss peeking out at in the mornings. And she would miss running by the Charles, eating breakfast at Mike's, going to the MFA, and doing the restaurants with Lana and with Sherry. And of course she would miss her clients. She worried that they would not follow her advice to stay active during the summer. Most had gone to their vacation homes on Cape Cod and the Vineyard, and she suspected that once summer malaise set in, exercise would be the last thing on their minds. She sighed.

She had to say it out loud to convince herself. "I'm doing the right thing. I need to be away from here."

"Hey, your front door's open." It was Sherry.

"Hey, girl. The sublet girl was just here, I must have forgotten."

"Weslee, I'm going to miss you so much." Sherry pouted.

"I'll only be a few hundred miles away. Don't make me feel worse than I already feel, OK?"

Sherry shook her head. "I know why you say you're doing this. But what are you going to do in Chicago all summer long? You don't have a job there. And you're gonna be living with your parents. You're gonna hate it!"

Weslee sighed. She had heard all of this before.

"OK." Sherry raised her arms in surrender. "I'm done talking."

"Where are we going for dinner?" Weslee asked.

"Chez Henri," Sherry replied.

"Ooooh. Cuban sandwich." Weslee licked her lips.

"You always order that. Try something else."

"I don't want anything else. I want a Cuban sandwich," Weslee said in her best Chicano accent.

"Is Lana meeting us?"

"She's supposed to after her AA meeting."

"How is she?" Sherry asked.

"OK. Sherry, are you going to be OK with Lana tonight?"

Sherry put her hands on her hips, cocked her head to the side, and rolled her eyes at Weslee. "Now, girl, you think I'm going to be mean to a sister who's just been through an accident? What kind of person do you think I am?"

"I know. I was just saying, you know."

"No, I don't know, Wes. I really don't know about you sometimes."

"Sorry," Weslee said weakly.

"Sorry I'm late, girls," Lana said as she walked slowly to their table at the crowded restaurant. She had only been off the crutches for three weeks. "Gosh, it is so hard to find a parking space in Harvard Square on a Friday night."

"We're just glad you made it," Sherry said.

Weslee was relieved that there was no measurable tension at the table. She wasn't sure that Lana and Sherry could ever be friends. But this was her going away dinner, so they were obliged to be civil to each other. Maybe someday they could be more than that, she silently hoped.

Weslee felt the nagging doubt about her move creep up on her again as they talked easily about the heat, the humidity, and how it wreaked havoc on their hair and skin. How could she leave her two best friends behind? Who would she hang out with in Chicago? Her sister? Her married friends? She shrugged those questions off as the waiter approached.

"How was the meeting?" Weslee wanted to know. AA had turned out to be Lana's new passion. She wrapped herself up in it the way she used to wrap herself in one of her prized pashminas. Once she got to talking about addiction and recovery, it was hard to stop her.

"It was great. I think I might actually work up the courage to share next time."

"Really? You're ready for that?"

"I'm definitely ready. My therapist says I'm making a lot of progress. Plus, there are so many people in those meetings who are so much more messed up than I am. But I'm not judging." She winked.

Weslee was happy for her. Sherry was still getting used to Lana's issues. For one thing, she didn't really believe that anything but Jesus could cure whatever it was that had made Lana a mess. But Sherry had also learned not to force her opinions on other people.

"Lana, girl, you really need to come to my church," Sherry said. Well, she was trying.

"Maybe I will."

They ate their dinner. Weslee had her Cuban sandwich—the best in New England, she would tell anyone who asked.

"So, guess what, Weslee?" Lana had perked up. "I've got some gossip for you."

Weslee leaned in. "Who, what, where?"

Sherry cleared her throat. Weslee and Lana ignored her.

"A certain ex-boyfriend of yours seems to be having some trouble committing to setting a wedding date with a certain fiancée who is getting more and more impatient with said ex-boyfriend."

Weslee groaned loudly and put her hands over her ears. "Lana!"

"What? I thought that would make you happy." Lana looked embarrassed.

"No, it's OK. I just don't want to hear anything about him. That's all."

"I'm sorry."

Weslee was taken aback by the apology. It was so rare to see Lana contrite about anything. "It's OK. Really. I'm glad you told me. I do feel better. That jerk." She smiled. Then they both laughed.

"He is a jerk," Lana echoed.

Sherry just shook her head at the both of them.

Since that ugly incident on the phone, Weslee had not heard from or seen Duncan, and she didn't want to. After the test results had given her peace of mind, all she wanted was to forget he had ever entered her life, her mind, or her body. She'd vowed to herself that she'd never let any man get her so hooked on his aura that she'd lose her mind like that again. Sherry called it a learning experience, but to Weslee, Duncan had been a huge, life-threatening mistake that she would give anything not to have ever made. But she believed that she was succeeding in moving forward. No need to live in the past, she told herself.

"Anybody getting dessert?" Weslee asked as she eyed the dessert menu.

"Not me," Sherry said.

"Definitely me," Lana piped up. She was making up for living on liquids for two weeks straight after her accident. She was probably the only woman who actually wanted to gain weight, and was doing a good job of steadily eating her way back to a size 4.

"Uh-oh," Weslee said. "Lana, Jeffrey's here."

"Where?" Lana almost jumped out of her chair.

"At the bar." Weslee nodded her head toward where Jeffrey Knight and a friend were sitting. They had not seen Lana.

"Do you want to leave?" she asked Lana.

"No," Lana said, not looking up from the dessert menu.

Sherry and Weslee exchanged glances.

Once she had been released from the hospital Lana had finally opened up to Weslee about her accident.

Jeffrey had found out about her fling with Mark Bronner and had broken things off with her. She had started drinking at home and drank all the way to Jeffrey's place in Cambridge to confront him. His longtime girlfriend had answered the door.

The tree came out of nowhere, Lana had said. She was crying and drinking as she drove down Memorial Drive that early morning. All she remembered was seeing the tree and then waking up in the hospital.

Weslee could tell that Lana wasn't ready to face Jeffrey yet in her fragile emotional state. And she didn't want her to get upset.

"Do you want to leave?" she repeated.

"Leave? Why would I want to do that? I'm having a great time, Weslee. I'm not leaving until I get my chocolate cake." Lana looked up from the menu and smiled.

They gave the waiter their dessert orders.

"Lana, I'm so proud of you." Weslee meant it with all her heart. The old Lana would have gotten up and given Jeffrey a piece of her mind.

Their attention turned to other things as Sherry sipped coffee and envied the other two as they savored their cake.

But Lana kept stealing glances to where Jeffrey was sitting at the bar, until he left. Weslee noticed but did not say anything. She hoped Lana would be OK on her own once she left.

The night air was warm and heavy as they stood outside the restaurant laughing at another of Sherry's jokes.

"I'm gonna miss you guys so much," Weslee said, blinking hard.

"Oh, geez, don't do this!" Sherry wailed. "No tearful good-byes, please!"

"Yeah," Lana piped in. "I've been doing enough crying lately."

Weslee cleared her throat. "I just wanted to tell you guys that I'm so glad I met both of you. It's only been a year, but I feel like you guys have always been a part of my life. I'll really, really miss you this summer." She bit her lip.

Sherry stepped forward and opened her arms, squeezing her in a bear hug. "Aww. Girl!"

Lana looked on, amused. "Wes, why don't you reconsider coming to the Caribbean with my mom and me?"

" 'Cause I can't afford to," Weslee laughed.

"But it's summer! The off-season. Everything's cheaper," Lana protested.

"And I'll really miss the way you keep forgetting that I'm just a poor black girl from the wrong side of the tracks," Weslee joked.

Lana looked embarrassed.

"Relax, girl." Weslee hit Lana playfully on the shoulder. "Relax."

No tears, she told herself later as she lay in bed remembering the night. It had been a long time since she'd been able to allow herself to cherish a friendship. Now she had two. No, this move to Boston had not been a mistake, she thought.

Chapter
31

Coming home felt strange. She did not feel drenched in relief when she saw her father waiting for her at the airport. Instead she felt small, like a child again. He seemed older and tired.

"You look so sophisticated now," Milton Dunster told his daughter as they drove from O'Hare Airport, heading south to Hyde Park.

"Yeah, I had a little makeover, I guess." Weslee smiled.

"It suits you," he said.

They made small talk as the traffic crawled down I-94. Milton Dunster loved talking about politics, and it wasn't too long before he had Weslee headlocked into a conversation about the aftermath of the war in Iraq.

"I'm telling you, they need to send more troops over there and finish the job. All these guys that are walking around Tikrit and Najaf need to be locked up. They're all terrorists."

Weslee was trying not to argue with her father. They shared a lot of views on politics, but he was miles further to the right than she. He knew where she stood on the issues, and one of his biggest joys in life was to get his daughter all riled up about his ultraconservative political stance. It was all harmless fun for him.

"Daddy, how would you like it if, say, Russia invaded Chicago and decided to lock up all the men over age sixteen because they could be terrorists?"

"Well, see, little girl, that could never happen. Russia doesn't have the guts or the capability to invade Chicago, and neither do any of those crumb-snatching little countries that are out there protesting against our attempts to make the world a safer place."

"I knew I should have asked Mom to pick me up," Weslee groaned.

Her father laughed out loud. "See, you can't take it. That's truth, little girl. The truth will get you every time."

She couldn't help but laugh, too.

Weslee and her father had always been close. They were both suckers for details and numbers. He, himself an accountant, had pushed her into studying business and finance. "People are always going to want other people to keep track of their money for them," he would say. When she landed her job as a mutual funds research analyst, he was so proud. "She tells me where to invest my money," he told all his friends at his lodge.

As they pulled up in the driveway of the neat three-bedroom ranch house, Weslee realized how small it was. That had never bothered her before. She mentally made the comparison. It was only half the size of one of Lana's family's summer homes, she realized.

Her mother came running out the front door.

"Look at you! Look at you!" Clara Dunster squealed and hugged her daughter tightly. "You look even more sophisticated than you did at Christmas," she said, standing back to take in the sight of her daughter.

"Mom, you look great, too. You've lost weight."

"Yeah. I've started mall-walking with some of the girls from church."

Mall-walking?

Weslee chatted with her parents, happily basking in their attention. Boston was starting to seem farther and farther away. Once she walked into her old house, she really felt that she was home. All the doubts she had felt about leaving Boston for the summer dissipated. She knew she had done the right thing.

"Well, are you gonna help me with dinner? We've got Terry and them coming in a couple hours," her mother said.

Welsee got busy with her mother in the kitchen as her father settled into his recliner to watch the news in the den.

Dinner was noisy and chaotic. Terry's twins were talking now, and they would not shut up. It did not help that the toys Weslee had brought them made them even more boisterous. Terry could barely get a forkful of food into her mouth without having to turn her attention to one of them.

"Aren't you glad you don't have to deal with all this mess?" Weslee's brother-in-law asked her as Terry chased one of the children away from the stove.

"I sure am," she laughed.

Weslee hadn't felt this happy, this safe, this warm in a long time.

The next morning, Weslee ate a big breakfast, vowing to herself to brave the heat and go for a run by the lakefront in the evening. She obliged her mother's nostalgic request that they go shopping at the Gurnee Mills outlet.

Clara Dunster was happy to have her daughter back in her home. She fussed over her as if she were a little girl again, suggesting things that they did when Weslee was a young girl who spent way too much time with her parents instead of hanging out with girlfriends as other teenagers did.

Weslee had to constantly remind her: "Mom, stop treating me like I'm twelve."

Her father, on the other hand, was more pragmatic. "I'm glad to have you home, but I agree with your friends. You basically left money on the table when you left all those clients behind. I can't believe people will pay you to make them exercise, anyway."

All she wanted was peace, and she knew she wasn't about to get it from her father on that subject. She gladly accepted her mother's invitation to go shopping to get away from his questions.

She ran down the stairs of the Hyde Park home the same way she had all through her childhood.

"Lord, it's hot," her mother said as she turned her key in the ignition of her Ford Taurus station wagon.

"Yeah, I hope this summer's not going to be another killer heat wave," Weslee laughed. "This is the only place in the Western world where when the temperature goes above ninety old people start dropping like flies."

"Wait till you're old, you won't be making jokes like that," her mother scolded.

Her mother drove slowly through their neighborhood, which really hadn't changed much over the years. It was still respectably close enough to the good part of Hyde Park, where the University of Chicago elite lived, its diversity and grit-lite assuaging their liberal guilt, and its charm and academic feel making it still nice enough that their friends from Winnetka would not be afraid to come down for dinner every once in a while.

But once you went far enough east you could see downtown Chicago leaning over sternly, reminding anyone who dared forget that, yes, you did live in the city. And if you went not too far off to the west, the decay and desperation there confirmed that not only did you live in the city, you lived in the inner city.

Weslee tried not to compare the neighborhood with the sprawling home in Rye that she had seen pictures of in Lana's apartment. She was from a different place, that's all. Duncan had said it. *It's no big deal. People just come from different places—none better than the other.*

It still bothered Weslee that she never really was part of her neighborhood when she was growing up. She tried in vain to remember some of the faces she saw as they walked out of their cars and up their walkways. They nodded at her as if she were a stranger. Most of the kids she had grown up with had moved away and were now living on their own in the Loop, in high-rise condo buildings, farther south in the suburbs, and all across the country. The neighborhood was foreign to her. It struck her that she had to be away from Chicago a whole year before she realized how little connection she had to her community.

She had known the other kids on her street, and had played with them, but she'd always felt like an outsider.

By the time she was old enough to be tested, she had been shipped off to the Latin School of Chicago on the Near North Side, alma mater of William Wrigley and Adlai Stevenson. And she hadn't felt like an insider there, either. It was no secret that she was there because she was just a little bit smarter and more fortunate than the average kid in her neighborhood but would never be as smart or even a bit as fortunate as the typical Latin School student.

And that was so obvious. There were the terrible birthday parties she begged her mother to take her to, after which she would always go home angry and hurt that her modest present was met with such disappointment and forced gratitude from the birthday girl or boy. Then all the upper school social events that she eventually stopped going to because of the supremely confident, super-rich A-list crowd and their reign of terror on the weaker girls and boys.

She had just played the whole time. The academics were

not easy, and she had been only a good student in a school full of overachievers. Because of Weslee's always feeling not as smart, not as rich, not as pretty, school didn't become fun until she discovered basketball.

She had played because Terry played, and, she suspected later as an adult, because the school administrators thought it a natural fit for her: "Don't let your height go to waste." She had been a great power forward, and that was what got her to Northwestern on a full athletic scholarship.

She was the only one in her neighborhood that she knew of who went to Northwestern. There had been a boy and a girl in her church who had gotten into the University of Chicago, but they didn't count because they were from Country Club Hills. Her parents had been so proud. They had wanted to throw her a party, but she begged them not to. Who would she have invited? Certainly not her schoolmates from the Latin School; she could never, ever bring them down here. And she had few friends in her own neighborhood. So she had disappeared at seventeen, popping back up every few months to visit her parents. While there she would see other kids she recognized from time to time, and the brief conversations got briefer and briefer, until they turned into hellos, then grunts, then nods.

Now they nodded to her from their cars or windows as she drove by in her mother's Taurus or walked the neighborhood to get some fresh air. No great big bear hugs. No "Girl, where have you been all these years?"

She was the girl who had gone to that school on the North Side and then to Northwestern. "You know, the tall one, with the tall sister with the twins. Oh, I can't remember her name for the life of me," Weslee imagined the neighbors saying.

*   *   *

Four weeks home and she had done everything she wanted to do in Chicago. She had caught up with her friends, acquaintances, old co-workers; babysat her niece and nephew; ran the lakefront path dodging roller-bladers, cyclists, poseurs; shopped on the Magnificent Mile; went to a play at the Lookingglass; had her share of ethnic food in Rogers Park; and did all the other things she thought she couldn't do without.

But she missed Boston terribly. The feeling hit strongest after she spoke with Sherry or Lana. She so wanted to be back there with her new friends. Her mother's fussing stifled her; her father's constant advice, political sermons, and quirky neatness frustrated her. She had to get away.

She contemplated flying up to Boston for a few days, but Sherry had said she was busy working on an investigative report on consumer fraud and would visit Chicago for Weslee's birthday at the end of the month. Lana was headed to the Caribbean with her mother for the rest of July and would spend the remainder of the summer on the Vineyard. To go to Boston would mean that she would be basically on her own.

Ugh. She flipped channels again on the living room television. Her parents were at some potluck dinner at church. It was Saturday night.

She decided to be impulsive. He probably wouldn't even be home, she thought, yet she picked up the phone and dialed.

"William, you're home."

"Hey, Weslee." He sounded genuinely happy to hear her voice. She was relieved at that but kept straining her ears to pick up any sounds of Megan in the background.

"I've been waiting to hear from you," he said.

"Really?"

"I'm going to be in Chicago in a few weeks but didn't have your number to warn you to get out of town first."

She laughed. *He's coming here!!!*

"I've got a two-day meeting in Schaumburg, but that's not too far from where you are, right?"

"No, not at all. I can't wait to see you." She immediately regretted saying those words. It had only been a month.

He didn't say anything, compounding her discomfort. "So, how are things back at mom and dad's?"

"Ugh. It's OK for the most part. They still treat me like I'm twelve."

"Well, you are under their roof."

"Gee, thanks for reminding me."

"No, I'm just saying that they're always going to see you that way as long as you're still upstairs in your little room with all your Barbie dolls."

"William, I don't have any Barbie dolls."

"Not even one?"

She didn't answer. "It's just for the summer," Weslee said, feeling a little shame at living at home. "Once I move back to Boston, I'll be an adult again."

"I'm just kidding. I know how it is. You're lucky. If my business ever went under, my father would not let me back in the house."

"William! Of course he would."

"No, he wouldn't. He told me."

They both laughed. And once again she was able to forget about being lonely, bored, and missing Boston. William always made her feel so . . . so good about herself. That's what it was. She felt good about being herself when she talked with him. The laughter came easily. She didn't feel as if she were somehow unworthy of him the way she sometimes had felt with Duncan.

"So, have you run into the ex yet?" William asked.

Weslee had to think for a minute. *Duncan? Oh, Michael.* She was flattered that he asked.

"Nah. I don't want to, either," she said dismissively, although the reality was that it was inevitable. She was going to a fund-raiser the following week that she knew Michael would be attending.

William laughed. "Can I be blunt? Your personal life is like a movie," he said, still laughing.

"I know," she said wryly. "I don't believe it myself, most times."

"Well, I hope it has a happy ending," he said.

She hurried to change the subject before it turned to Duncan, the last person in the world she wanted to hear about. "So, how's Megan?" Like she really cared.

"She's doing well. She's here, actually; she went out to get groceries."

Weslee's heart sank. "So, she cooks, too?" was all she could muster.

"Yeah, she's actually pretty good."

"Sounds like a keeper to me," Weslee said halfheartedly.

"We'll see. We'll see," William replied.

She couldn't talk to him anymore. She made up some excuse and quickly got off the phone.

"Why did I even call!"

She imagined him waiting in high anticipation in his cozy love nest with the lovely Megan cooking up a lavish dinner. Were the lights down low, too? She didn't even want to think of what they would do after dinner. *Aargh! It doesn't matter,* she told herself. *I'm not jealous. We're just friends. Just plain friends. I should be happy for him. I am happy for him. I am.*

But that image of him with Megan gnawed at her as she tried in vain to find something worth watching on TV. She flipped channels and thought she saw his easy smile and thick shoulders on every single channel. She switched off the power in disgust. *I'm such an idiot,* she thought. *Why did I call!*

Chapter
32

"What do you think? The short dress or the long dress?" Weslee held up the two dresses so her mother could inspect them.

"The long one's dressier," Clara Dunster said, frowning at the spaghetti-strap minidress draped over Weslee's left arm.

"I knew you'd say that. The short one it is, then."

"Why ask me, then?" Her mother rolled her eyes.

"Because you're so predictable, lady." Weslee nudged her on her arm.

"That dress is really short, Weslee Ann." Her mother always used her daughter's full name when she was being critical.

"Oh, Mom."

"Don't 'Oh, Mom' me. You asked my opinion."

"The other one makes me look like an old maid."

"You never know who might be there tonight. A man's not going to want to marry you if you're wearing a minidress."

Weslee laughed. "Mom, I'm not going to this thing to find a husband. I'm going because you begged me to go."

"I'm just saying, you never know."

It was the annual fund-raiser for the hospital where Weslee's mother had worked for twenty years before retiring five years ago. It was also the hospital where Michael was now chief medical resident. Weslee had to wear the minidress. She had been putting in her miles on the lakefront trail all summer, and she looked even sleeker than she had in Boston. She had to show him—and his internist girlfriend.

She suspected her mother knew of her true motives but was remaining silent. She didn't absolutely have to go to the event; her mother had plenty of friends who were willing to accompany her. Her father had a strict policy—no events that required wearing a tuxedo or dancing of any kind—and her mother over the years had adapted by enlisting friends as her escorts.

Clara Dunster broke her silence. "Well, Michael's going to be there with his friend."

"I know that, Mother." Weslee pulled on her black sheer pantyhose.

"And you think that dress is appropriate?"

"Appropriate for Michael?"

Her mother didn't answer.

"Mom, I want to wear the dress. I look good in it, and I don't care what Michael or anyone else thinks."

"OK." Her mother shrugged and walked out of Weslee's room.

Weslee eased into the dress. It was short, and it clung to her like Saran Wrap. She turned this way and that as she observed herself in the mirror: not bad for an about-to-be thirty-year-old. She knew she had surprised her mother with her defiance, but her mother would just have to get used to it. She had surprised herself, too. But she was pleased. She could see herself changing, becoming bolder and braver, and she liked it.

Weslee and Clara Dunster made quite a dramatic entrance into the ballroom of the Drake Hotel on Chicago's

Magnificent Mile. The resemblance between the two tall
and lithe women was striking. They giggled like girlfriends
even though it was obvious that they were mother and
daughter. The younger of the two was simple and elegant
in a short, fitted black dress with black suede sandals that
added nearly three inches to her stately frame. Her hair was
pulled neatly into a bun at the base of her neck, showing off
her diamond stud earrings. The older woman wore her short,
coiffed gray hair proudly and was dressed in a gray satin pantsuit with silver high heels and a stunning diamond necklace.

"Mrs. Dunster," the chairman of the Friends of the Hospital
greeted the two women.

Weslee smiled and nodded patiently while her mother
chatted enthusiastically, drawing more people into a little
circle around her. She made a quick getaway as the conversation grew more lively. She looked for the bar. She was
thirsty and craved a Diet Coke with lemon. She walked
confidently across the ballroom filled with dancing couples.
She held her head high, knowing full well that eyes were on
her.

She ordered her drink, smiling flirtatiously at the bartender, who kidded her for being a teetotaler. "Oh, I'm here
with my mom, so I'm the designated driver," she joked, realizing that her mother would kill her if she had heard the
joke made at her expense.

She sipped her drink and looked around the grand room.
She loved looking at people, especially beautiful black people, and there were many there tonight. They came in all ages,
sizes, shapes, and colors. There were the perennial eighty-
year-old couples who never missed a society party and always took to the dance floor the minute the music started,
doing their thing, arthritis and osteoporosis be damned. There
were also the slightly overweight, overweaved, overly made-
up, underdressed divorcees casing the room, on the perennial hunt for new meat. And then there were the younger,

superskinny, supereducated, super-good-looking, social-climbing girls in their late twenties and thirties on the perennial hunt for a rich husband. It was high drama, and she just wanted to stand there and take it all in for a few minutes.

It was quite a contrast to what Weslee had witnessed on the Vineyard. It wasn't that people in Chicago did not also put on airs, it was just the lack of mean-spiritedness in the crowd that made this party so much more bearable to her. Dark-skinned and lighter-skinned people mixed happily, tension free. There was no color caste system that Weslee could see with her bare eyes. She felt at ease, comfortable.

And then there they were.

Michael looked a little tired and a couple of pounds heavier than when she had seen him last, Weslee noted smugly. She quickly appraised the woman on his arm. She had never seen "her" before, though she had heard her voice on the phone. The petite, slightly pudgy dark-haired woman didn't live up to her voice or to Weslee's worst nightmares of a J.Lo look-alike.

Weslee almost wanted to laugh out loud. She felt so completely over him. She almost wanted to go over to the dance floor and say hello just to show him how fabulous she looked. But she held back. She wanted to enjoy the night. She scanned the room for her mother, and sure enough she was in the middle of another circle of friends.

Weslee felt eyes on her, and she looked in their direction. He was cute and tall enough to dance with, so she smiled at him.

His name was Toby or Joby. She really couldn't hear him above the big band music. His breath was barely tolerable, so she kept her distance. But he was an adequate dancer, and she stayed with him on the dance floor until she felt her make-up starting to run. Then she ran off to the ladies' room.

She missed Lana a bit as she danced with a slightly intoxicated senior citizen. Her biting humor would have made Weslee laugh out loud at this sweet man's moves on the dance floor.

The live band was full of gray-haired men who were having the time of their lives playing old Sinatra and Porter tunes. It was nothing like Lana's parties, which Weslee had to admit were so much more fun than these things. She missed the feeling of anticipation she had felt those nights. That anything could happen, that anybody could come along and change her life. She felt a pang for Duncan, but she shoved it away into the back of her mind and heart.

She looked over at Michael and his fiancée. She had been avoiding them, but she decided to stop hiding. The fiancée walked away, leaving her an opening.

"Hi, Michael." She came up from behind him, so she guessed that was why he seemed so shocked when he turned around and saw her.

"Weslee. My God, is that you?" He slurred his words a bit.

"Yes, it's me. Who else would it be?" She smiled brightly.

"But what are you doing here? I thought you had moved to Boston."

"I'm home for the summer. How are things with you?"

He looked her over.

"How are things with you?" she repeated, trying to get his eyes to meet hers.

"Um. Fine. Great."

"Good. Work's OK?"

"Work's great."

"I'm happy to hear that." She really was. A bit. "Well, it was nice to see you. I'd better . . ."

"Who are you here with?" he asked.

"Uh. My mom and a friend," she lied.

"A friend?" He cocked his head disbelievingly.

"Yes. I really need to get going. It was great to see you." She noticed the fiancée approaching.

"I want you to meet—"

She turned on her heel and left before he could finish. She searched the room for Toby or Joby. She saw him at the bar. Good, she could dance with him. Maybe Michael would think that he was her "friend."

Not that she really cared what he thought of her.

Two weekends later, Weslee and Sherry laughed about a half-drunk Michael left standing at the party while Weslee fled as his fiancée approached.

Sherry was visiting for the weekend to celebrate Weslee's thirtieth birthday.

They had started the day off with breakfast, courtesy of Clara Dunster. After some serious shopping on the Mag Mile, they walked down to Grant Park for the annual jazz festival.

"So you didn't even wait to be introduced to his fiancée?" Sherry asked as they made their way through the crowds in Grant Park.

The lineup at the jazz festival was both big names and local talent. The festival drew crowds from across the city and beyond, even from neighboring states. It was one of the best in the country, and Weslee had missed few of them. Her father had taken her in years past, then she and Michael had gone every year they were together.

This year Weslee couldn't wait to see Liquid Soul, Joshua Redman, and Dianne Reeves. This was one of the things she missed the most about not living in Chicago: great jazz, anytime, anyplace.

"God, there are some good-looking men in this town." Sherry looked around.

"Tell me about it," Weslee said.

"So, how do you feel now?" Sherry asked.

"I feel fine. You know, I thought it was going to be this huge ordeal, that I'd feel some regret or sadness or joy or something. But I felt absolutely nothing. I mean, the guy's gut is sticking out. He was nearly drunk. I don't know what I saw in him."

Sherry raised her eyebrows. "Now this is the same man who almost sent you to a therapist?" she said, putting her hands on her hips.

"I guess I was a different person back then." And she truly believed that.

They listened to the bands and bought CDs, flirted with strangers and tried not to melt in the blazing August sun. When Joshua Redman finally came on, Sherry urged Weslee toward the front of the crowd.

Weslee had seen Joshua once before at the Jazz Showcase with Michael. After that first time, she bought all of his CDs.

Halfway through his set, he stopped to make an announcement.

"Before we go any further, I just wanted to say happy birthday to a friend of mine, Weslee Dunster. Happy birthday, Weslee, from Sherry."

Weslee looked at her friend in total amazement. "How did you do that?"

"Ah, I still had an old press pass from when I worked at the *Sun-Times*, so I used it to get backstage when you went to the bathroom."

"Sherry! You are so scandalous!"

"Happy birthday, girl."

Weslee couldn't have been happier. She hugged her friend as Joshua played the "Birthday Song" on his saxophone. She would never forget turning thirty.

Chapter
33

It was another sticky August in the City of Big Shoulders. The tourists slogged their way up and down Michigan Avenue sipping bottles of designer water. Businessmen slung their jackets over their shoulders and rolled up their shirtsleeves. Children broke open fire hydrants, turning South Side streets into gushing fountains of cool water. The city was crackling with heat, and if the cloudless blue sky was any indication, there was no relief in sight.

Weslee had finally broken down and bought an air conditioner for her bedroom. It was the only way she could sleep. Her parents, having survived decades of Chicago's temperamental temperature swings, stoically sweltered through the nights.

But she couldn't sleep tonight, despite the coolness in her room. She felt restless. The more she thought about it, the more she could see her mistake. It had been too much too soon, and she had gotten caught up in the heady high of romance and Duncan himself. Her first instinct about him had been right. He was selfish and self-absorbed, but he was a charmer, too. And that last part was the one that had gotten her into the emotional black hole she was in now.

She had been trying so hard to just put him away, put the pain away, but it kept coming back.

Her ennui this summer did nothing to ease the pain. Since Sherry left she had felt so useless. She was doing nothing, just sweltering in this big city. She wanted to do something, learn something, go somewhere, any other thing than having him pop back into her mind unannounced and unwanted.

She didn't cry anymore. All she felt was sadness and sometimes anger, and always a deep sense of loss. She was thirty now. No husband, no boyfriend, not even a prospect. She had become a statistic.

The next morning she awoke early and went for her run along the lakefront. It was crowded as usual at seven A.M. with the before-work crowd.

She was a little excited about seeing William, though she knew that his interest was in Megan—the good cook with the high girly-girly voice. Weslee frowned.

Well, she told herself, it wasn't a date: just two friends catching up. She was prepared for it, for him talking about Megan. The jealousy would fade. It was more important to keep him as a friend.

That night she dressed carefully. She didn't want it to seem as if she were going out of her way to look sexy, but at the same time she wanted to look good. She had picked the place: The Red Fish. He had said he wanted Cajun. She wore a plain white linen sheath dress with pink sandals and her favorite pink Kate Spade handbag. Simple yet elegant, she thought. She laughed at her reflection in the mirror, remembering the old Weslee, who just about a year ago probably would have worn khakis and a T-shirt.

She heard the doorbell ring as she applied her lipstick. She didn't hurry. She heard him talking with her father downstairs.

She descended the stairs into the living room. His back was turned to her. She took a deep breath. He was wearing blue—a blue golf shirt and neatly pressed khakis. She loved him in blue. He turned around as she came up behind him, and they both broke into wide smiles on seeing each other.

"Hey, you." She grinned and hugged him chastely.

Her father called out to her mother, who came quickly from the kitchen.

William introduced himself and sat down to chat with her parents.

Ten minutes later, Weslee tore him away from a conversation about soccer with her father that threatened to last forever.

"So, how are you, FloJo?" William asked as he pulled out of the driveway in his rented Toyota Camry.

"I'm all right. Bored, mostly."

He nodded. "You look good."

She smiled and pointed him toward Lake Shore Drive North.

"So, where are we going?"

She gave him the directions to The Red Fish.

The two of them caught up on his increasingly busy schedule with his company, which was growing larger and larger. "I wish you knew how to draft. I'd hire you to work for me," he joked.

"Oh, I'm not joining the work world for another year or so," she said.

"But you're going back to training in the fall, right?"

"Yes. I actually miss doing it. I think about those old women every day. I hope they're taking care of themselves."

He turned to face her for a moment. "See, that's what I don't understand about you."

"What?" she asked, confused.

"You're doing this personal training thing, which you love, and you're making great money, and yet you just leave it behind."

"Well, it wasn't just that. I had to get away from Boston for a while."

"Well, life goes on, Wes," he said after a brief pause. "And you shouldn't miss out on opportunities that are in the present because of something that happened in the past."

At the restaurant, William couldn't stop raving about his sweet potato-stuffed catfish.

"Man, I love this place," he exclaimed. "If I could, I'd marry the chef."

Weslee laughed. "I'm glad you like it. But I think the chef's a man."

She could only finish half of her black beans and rice and blackened chicken; she had stuffed herself on cornbread.

When the waiter came back with the dessert menu, she ordered coffee, and William ordered pecan pie with vanilla ice cream.

"You're going all out tonight," Weslee teased.

"I haven't had a real meal in months. It's been so crazy lately with work. I've been basically eating out of the vending machine in the office."

"That's not good, William. I hope things will calm down soon."

"Not likely. I'm going to be going at this pace until November."

She wondered when she would see him again.

"Will you be going to any of those parties on the Vineyard this summer?" he asked.

"What parties?" She hadn't heard about any parties. The newly sober Lana's social life had ground to a halt, and Weslee certainly wasn't in enough on the circuit to know when or where the next bashes were, much less be invited.

William looked slightly embarrassed. "Well, Eleanor's parties, and the Smalls's. Rainee Smalls."

Weslee cleared her throat. How could she tell him that as much as she liked Rainee and tolerated Eleanor, she did not plan to ever attend any of those events ever again? "I don't know about that crowd. I can only take them about one at a time," she said wryly.

He laughed. "Sometimes I feel the same way. But you have to look at it as networking. I've gotten three or four contracts to design houses from that group over the last two years."

She sighed. "I guess it works for you, then. I just don't like to be made to feel as if I don't belong."

He narrowed his eyes. "Where would you get that idea?"

"Just from the questions people asked me. Listen, I really don't want to talk about this."

"Weslee, it's OK. Just because you met a few jerks there doesn't mean that you should lump them all in the same group. Besides, Rainee Smalls loves you. She's telling her friends all about you. They think you're a miracle worker."

Weslee smiled but wasn't convinced.

"Just take them for what they are. They're just people. If they have hang-ups, it has nothing to do with you. They did the same thing to me in the beginning. And I've known Duncan since our college days together."

That made her feel a bit better.

"But I'm not ashamed of where I come from," William continued. "I'm proud of the way my folks worked hard to raise me and my sisters and put us all through college. There are people who have lived in this country for generations and generations who haven't gotten as far as my parents have come since they left Kingston thirty-four years ago."

William's words touched her and at the same time made

her feel shame at her petty insecurities. Who was she to discount everything her parents—and she herself—had accomplished just because she came face-to-face with people who had more? William was right. Their hang-ups had nothing to do with her.

The sun had just set at eight-thirty, and Weslee did not want the night to end. "When was the last time you rode a Ferris wheel?" she asked as they walked out of the restaurant.

"What?"

"You heard me."

"I don't know. Gee, maybe since tenth grade."

"Wanna go ride tonight?" She was being bold again, and it thrilled her to take control.

He looked puzzled for a spell, then understanding came over his face. "Oh, at the Navy Pier! You know, I've always wanted to do that."

"Well, tonight's your big chance." She was ecstatic that she had actually gotten him excited about something.

As much as Weslee liked the Ferris wheel, she hated the rest of the Navy Pier. To any tourist—especially those with young children—it was a mandatory stop. But to the average Chicago resident, it was hell. The crowded subpar restaurants, the tacky souvenir stores, and the long lines at the Bubba Gump Shrimp Company were enough to drive one crazy. But to Weslee, the giant Ferris wheel made up for all the hassles.

The lights shone brightly way up in the sky, and Weslee couldn't help but get a thrill as she looked up and saw the wheel turning slowly. She squeezed William's arm unconsciously. He teased her for her childlike enthusiasm.

Once they were seated, she was breathless. They both were. He had bought a disposable camera from a souvenir store and began to snap pictures of the night skyline in the distance as they began to rise. "I just love this skyline," he kept saying.

"Isn't this just perfect!" Weslee looked about her and felt the cool summer night air caress her face.

William turned around and took her picture.

She punched him playfully on the arm. "Why didn't you warn me?"

He laughed and snapped another photo of her dismayed face. "I'll make double prints." He nudged her.

"Remember when you were talking to me about Chicago way back last summer?" she asked him.

He didn't look at her. "I remember. That was a while ago."

Yes, before Duncan, she thought.

"It's just so beautiful from here, the city," she said.

He turned to face her, and their eyes met. It was if they couldn't help themselves. He leaned in and kissed her. She hesitated for a second and then kissed him back. It lasted for a couple of minutes before he pulled back, apologizing.

"You don't have to apologize. I wanted it to happen," Weslee said.

She thought she saw him frown, but she wasn't sure.

He turned his attention back to the skyline and started taking pictures again. She felt embarrassed. She wasn't sure what she should say. Maybe he regretted it. Maybe she had made a mistake. She didn't want to lose his friendship. She had to fix this.

"OK. Before we forget this ever happened, can we blame it on the altitude?"

He laughed. "Yes, the altitude." But he still didn't look at her.

She grabbed the camera from him, catching him off guard.

"My turn," she sang as she snapped his picture.

Just like that she lightened the mood. They would try to forget the kiss had happened.

But as soon as he dropped her off around midnight, she couldn't come down off the high that kiss had placed her on. She replayed it in her mind over and over again. It had been totally unexpected, so spontaneous yet so perfect. Close-mouthed yet far from chaste. It had lasted just long enough to let her know that he'd wanted to do it for a while. He'd come close enough that she'd felt his heart racing. *He likes me! He likes me!* She couldn't stop smiling as she lay in her bed looking up at the glow-in-the-dark stars she'd stuck on her ceiling back in seventh grade. *He likes me!*

Chapter
34

Clara and Milton Dunster ate breakfast every morning at six A.M. Milton would leave the house at seven A.M. sharp to head downtown for his job at LaSalle Bank—a job that he couldn't bear to retire from though he could afford to at any time he wanted, frugal as he was. Clara, on the other hand, had been happy to retire at age fifty-five from the hospital. Now she had more time to spend with her grandbabies, her church choir, her friends, her cooking, and on worrying about her two girls.

Weslee pulled out a chair at the table. They looked at her, surprised to see her awake so early.

"Mom, Dad, I'm going back to Boston."

"Honey, why? Was it something we did?" Clara wailed.

"No, no, no. I want to start training again. And I'm really bored here," she said.

After her date with William, she'd felt an energy that was pulling her back to Boston. She was wasting her time in Chicago, she decided. In a month, she would be heading back to school for another grueling year of studying and working at HealthyLife. She couldn't bring herself to spend any more money and take herself on a fabulous vacation as Lana had suggested when they talked on the phone. What she needed to do was earn enough money so that maybe she wouldn't need to return to HealthyLife when classes started again in late September. Sherry had offered her a room in her house so that Weslee wouldn't have to kick poor Beth Worthy out of her apartment prematurely. Weslee had been so excited about her plan that she hadn't slept the night before. She couldn't wait to tell her parents.

"Well, I'm glad you finally came to your senses," Milton Dunster said, putting down his *Chicago Tribune*. "We'll miss you though," he added.

Once her father left for work, Weslee began to pack. She wanted to leave immediately. As she packed, she talked with her sister, Terry, on the phone.

"Girl, what's going on with you? You're always doing crazy stuff these days."

"This is not crazy, Terry. I'm bored out of my skull. Plus, I could be making some serious money this summer."

Terry sighed. "So who's gonna babysit for me free of charge?"

"Sorry. You're gonna have to go back to begging Mom or paying that little girl across the street."

"Man, I'm gonna miss having you around. Why Boston, anyway? It's so far."

"Tewee, you can always come visit."

"I wish I was driving up with you. That sounds like so much fun."

Weslee had decided to bring her Honda with her this time.

"Yeah, right. You and me stuck in a car for sixteen hours? I don't think we'd make it to Toledo!"

Terry laughed. "We don't have to fight if you let me do all the driving."

"Ha!" Weslee said. Terry had always criticized her sister's slow and careful driving.

The next day, Weslee said good-bye to her parents, sister,

niece and nephew, and brother-in-law. It had only been a
few weeks since her return to Chicago, yet saying good-bye
to them again made her feel like a scared teenager going off
to college. She promised to call often from the road and to
be careful. She waved as she pulled her weighted-down
Accord out of the driveway.

*Aaargh. How did my life go from stable and predictable to all
this constant change?* she wondered as the Chicago skyline
faded in her rearview mirror.

Chapter
35

The Boston that Weslee was returning to was not the one she had known. In this Boston, summer didn't mean alfresco dining in trendy neighborhood restaurants, day trips to Nantucket or Block Island, ferry rides from Rowes Wharf to Provincetown, upscale shopping trips, and air-conditioned nightclubs.

In Sherry Charles's Boston, summer meant Saturday afternoon family barbecues at Franklin Park with WILD blasting on eight-foot speakers, kids with Puerto Rican, Jamaican, Ghanaian, Dominican, and Haitian flags waving from their cars as they sped by on narrow streets, speakers booming the summer's hip-hop anthem, young girls in tiny tops and even tinier skirts playing jump rope on side streets, ice cream trucks tinkling with a trail of young children following, and knock-down, drag-out basketball in Washington Park.

Sherry lived in a triple-decker, a three-flat house of the type that had served as Boston's main form of housing for blue-collar city families for hundreds of years. It was where the Jewish and then the Irish lived before they fled the area of the city now populated mostly by people of color, though the Irish maintained their stronghold over South Boston. Many of these houses were built in the early 1900s and managed to maintain their charm and classic New England look over the years. As the real estate boom drove up prices and consequently drove many families out to places like Brockton and Fall River, other newcomers moved in, especially the West Indians, and bought up a lot of the houses in North Dorchester. They would occupy one flat with their families and rent out the other two flats. It was one of the easiest ways to pay the backbreaking mortgages of the city of Boston.

And once the stigma of living in sometimes crime-ridden Dorchester faded, other groups began to get wise to the opportunities. Gay couples and white investors were now snapping up these houses, further driving up the prices. Houses that fetched one hundred forty thousand dollars in 1994 were now tagged at four hundred thousand dollars and up. And the owners were selling, taking the money and buying single-family homes near the affordable parts of suburban Milton and Randolph.

Sherry's house was one of three investment properties owned by her family. They had not sold out totally. Her father, who had made enough money running a grocery store and investing in real estate to never work for anyone else, had just married a Haitian woman and still lived in Dorchester near Codman Square, a burgeoning Haitian enclave. Her brothers and sisters were all living the American dream in quiet suburbs with their spouses and children. Sherry kept the family business going, collecting the rents on her father's three triple-deckers and seeing to tenants' needs, all the while balancing her own life and career.

"Girl, I was so worried about you when I didn't hear from you the last couple of hours," Sherry said as Weslee wearily stepped out of her Honda, her knees sore from the long drive.

"My cell phone died, and then I just couldn't get a signal down here."

Weslee realized with some satisfaction and a little chagrin that Sherry's neighborhood reminded her of certain parts of South Side Chicago. It was nice, but the cars driving by with the booming music would be a problem.

"I have the AC blasting, so hurry up and come inside," Sherry said, grabbing a bag from the car's backseat.

"We can unload the rest of it later," Weslee said breathlessly as she kicked off her slides and sat at Sherry's kitchen table.

"Did you paint again, Sherry?" Weslee looked around. The kitchen was now a misty heather green, not sunny yellow as it had been the last time she visited Sherry's house.

Sherry nodded, a guilty look on her face. "You know me. I saw the paint at Home Depot and I just couldn't resist. Look at the curtains I got to match it at Macy's." She pointed to the curtains.

Weslee shook her head. Sherry was a domestic goddess in addition to all her other talents. She was able to whip up a four-course meal in no time at all and serve it using all the right utensils on a beautifully decorated table.

They made chit-chat and drank lemonade from Ralph Lauren glasses, which Sherry washed immediately after they had finished drinking. Weslee made a mental note to remember her friend's freakish cleanliness.

Weslee couldn't wait to get started seeing her clients again. She decided to start with Rainee Smalls. Her plan was to see her clients strictly in their homes, at least the ones who had home gyms. No need to get HealthyLife Spa involved. That way she could charge them whatever she wanted and not have the spa taking money away from her. It would be a hassle come tax season, but it was worth it, she figured.

"So, are you up for some golf and then dinner with Larry and me later on?" Sherry asked.

Weslee demurred. "I think I'll be pretty tired once I get those boxes out of the car."

Later Sherry left for her golf game, ordering Weslee to take chicken breasts out of the freezer for dinner.

Weslee took it in stride. Sherry could be very bossy and controlling, and Weslee knew that she could not possibly last more than a month living under Sherry's roof. It had only been a few hours since she arrived, but she was beginning to feel like a child. Sherry, in a way, reminded her of her father. Her wood floors were like mirrors. There was not a speck of dust in her multicolored home. Weslee wondered about her seeming knack for acquiring friends with extreme personalities.

She hoped she would not be cramping Sherry's style by staying in her guest bedroom. She knew from Sherry's strict religious beliefs that as close as she Larry had become, they still were not sleeping together. But still.

With Sherry's house to herself, Weslee decided to get started on making phone calls. The first was to Lana at her parents' house on the Vineyard. She was not in, and Weslee was not surprised. *Probably off whale-watching or boy-hunting,* she thought.

She nervously dialed the number to Rainee Smalls's summer home on Oak Bluffs. *What am I doing,* she fretted. *What if those people already found new trainers? What if they're not interested anymore?*

Rainee Smalls was more than pleased to hear from Weslee. "I am so relieved you are back in town. Peony is getting married soon, and I have another huge wedding to attend on Labor Day weekend, and I've gained five pounds! Five pounds! You are just a godsend, Weslee."

Weslee was more than happy to take Rainee Smalls's invitation to visit her home on Oak Bluffs.

Encouraged by Rainee's enthusiasm, Weslee dialed
Marie Bunting, then the rest of them. Some were away for
the summer. Others were happy to hear from her. Still others were caught up in the malaise of summer and said they
would get back to her in the fall. When she was through
with the phone calls, she had made six appointments over
the coming two weeks. That's at least four hundred fifty
dollars, she calculated. It was a good start.

Chapter

36

The blind date had been Sherry's idea. Weslee had never been on one before and did not want to go on this one. But Sherry would not take no for an answer.

Weslee knew the minute he appeared on Sherry's doorstep that he was not the man for her. For one thing, he looked old. He was only thirty-four, but he was just one of those men who aged early and badly.

Sherry had said he was distinguished, a software-analyst friend of Larry's who also happened to attend Sherry's church.

Weslee steeled herself to be bored as he gallantly opened her door on his large Mercedes. He had barely said two words since he introduced himself. As they drove off, he remained silent. Weslee wondered if he had been as disappointed in her looks as she was in his. Oh, well. She decided to make small talk.

"So, Kamar, which part of Nigeria are you from?"

"North," he said and stopped at that.

It was going to be a long night.

The city was hopping on the warm Saturday night, and it made Weslee long for the days of hanging out with Lana on Newbury Street. She chose to remember only the good parts: the people-watching, the food, the excitement, her initiation into the world of fashion.

Sometimes it was amusing to Weslee to remember her vehement opposition to changing from dowdy, penny-pinching Plain Jane to her still frugal yet more fashionable self. Yes, it had hurt seeing her carefully crafted financial plan fall to pieces, but look at how nicely she had recovered. Her savings were now back to a respectable level. She had money coming in again, and she felt and looked so much better now. When Lana was being her worst, it was hard for Weslee to imagine that she could have brought anything good to her life. But Weslee made a mental note to thank Lana for showing her another side of living that she could not have encountered through any other person in the world.

"Where do you want to eat after the show?" Kamar broke into her thoughts.

"Um. I haven't thought about it yet. Do you have any place in mind?"

"How about the Brasserie?"

Weslee's heart lurched. She could never return to the place where she had had her first date and first kiss with Duncan. "No, too pretentious. How about somewhere more low-key?" she ventured quickly.

Kamar suggested Legal Sea Foods. It wouldn't have been Weslee's choice, but she didn't care. As far as she was concerned the night was dead on arrival. At least she would get to see the musical *The Music Man*. She had never seen it before, though she knew most of the songs.

"I've never been to a musical before," Kamar said.

"Oh, really? I'm sure you'll enjoy it," Weslee said, trying to sound upbeat.

She hoped the production would make this night worth something.

* * *

Larry's car was parked outside the house when Kamar dropped off Weslee at eleven-twenty P.M.

She tried to be quiet as she turned the key in the lock, hoping to slip off to her room and not interrupt. To her surprise, they were not in the living room watching DVDs as they usually did. Nor were they in the kitchen playing Scrabble. Weslee went straight to her room, confused. Larry's car was outside, so he was obviously in the house. There was no light under the slit of space between Sherry's bedroom door and the floor.

The truth of what was going on made her feel uncomfortable. She felt like an intruder. There was no way she wanted to be a witness to so personal an aspect of Sherry's life. For some reason she felt betrayed. Sherry had preached to her so many times about abstaining from sex until marriage. Yet here she was sleeping with a man she was not married to.

She undressed quickly and picked up the *Wall Street Journal* she hadn't managed to finish earlier in the day. But it was hard to concentrate on what she was reading.

There was a knock on the door.

"How was your date?" Sherry asked, popping her head in.

Weslee looked past Sherry. "Well, *Music Man* was great, and the chowder at Legals was good. But Kamar, he was just a little too quiet." Weslee was doing her best to sound normal.

"Poor thing. I think he's a little shy. But hey, at least you got to get out."

"Sure."

"Oh, Larry left his car here for the rest of the week. He's gone to Cleveland to visit his family. He didn't want to leave it on his street. They've had problems with car thieves lately."

"Oh!" Weslee said, sounding a bit more relieved than she wanted to.

"So don't go getting any ideas." Sherry winked and walked off to her room.

"What ideas?" Weslee called innocently.

"I know how you think, woman," Sherry called back, laughing.

Weslee exhaled deeply. She couldn't stomach the idea of having another duplicitous friend. Thank God, she thought.

A half hour later, Weslee tried to fall asleep as one of Sherry's neighbors decided to turn up his stereo to full volume just after midnight. She sighed. That never happened in the Hyde Park neighborhood she grew up in. The neighborhood community would tell that person when and where to get off the next morning. And it certainly did not happen in the Loop condo that she and Michael had shared. One month, one month, she kept repeating to herself as she tried in vain to sleep over the booming bass of the reggae music.

Chapter
37

Taking up Rainee Smalls on her invitation to spend a weekend at her Oak Bluffs home had been an easy decision. Weslee was desperate to get away from Sherry's noisy neighborhood, and it would give her a chance to see Lana, who had not been returning her calls lately.

Weslee had just left Marie Bunting's sprawling home in the Chestnut Hill section of Newton and was rewarding herself with a shopping trip to Neiman's. Marie was one of her most divalike clients. "Now, honey, I don't want to look too muscular, so don't make me lift those heavy weights, OK?" It was the same thing every session. Marie hated to sweat, hated to hurt, but wanted to be slim. Weslee told her that unless she gave up food altogether, there was no other plan out there that would help her. So she was exhausted when she pulled out of the woman's home. Richer, but exhausted.

A couple of workout outfits and a bathing suit was all she planned to buy. But the sale racks beckoned over in the dress section, so she answered the call.

"Do you have this in a six?" a tall, stunning woman to her right asked a clerk. The woman looked a bit familiar, Weslee thought. *Hmm. Maybe I saw her in a magazine.*

"Actually, we do. There's one right behind me." The clerk rifled through the overburdened rack and found the size six red dress.

"Perfect," the woman said. "I don't need to try it on. We're in a hurry."

"Great," the clerk said. "Would you like this on your store charge?"

Weslee was trying to mind her own business, but the woman looked so familiar she couldn't stop looking at her.

"Actually, my fiancé's paying," the woman said, looking around the cluttered department.

"Honey," she called out. "Just a minute," she said to the clerk, smiling her perfectly bleached smile.

Weslee's heart almost jumped out of her chest when she saw the man who approached the cash register where the tall woman stood smiling at him.

He looked exactly the same. His skin was golden, the way it was when she had first met him late last summer. His slacks were as neatly pressed, his entire look as put together, his brown eyes still sexy and mysterious.

He turned and looked right at her. She couldn't move.

"Honey, get your card," the woman nudged him.

"Oh, yes," he said.

The sound of his voice tore through her like a tornado. She held onto the edge of the rack. She turned away from the register but did not have the strength to move.

She heard his fiancée thank the clerk.

"Thank you, Ms. Jarrett," the clerk said. "That is such a beautiful engagement ring."

"Oh, thank you. And it's Susan."

They walked past Weslee together. Weslee kept her eyes down, focusing on the clothes rack, but she could feel Duncan's eyes on her as he walked past, his fiancée chattering at his side.

Susan. Susan.

Susan, she now realized, was the one she had seen him with that first night she had laid eyes on him at the party where she had also met William for the first time. Morticia. Susan.

Susan? Someone had mistakenly called her Susan while they were out in the Berkshires. Yes, one of his law firm partners. Even back then, Susan was in the picture? Weslee felt sick.

"Do you need any help finding a size?" the clerk asked politely.

"No. No, thank you," Weslee said feebly.

She didn't dare take the main escalator. She did not want to run into them again. She walked to the handicap elevator, pressing the button for the parking garage. She had to get out of that store.

She clenched her fists as she walked to the Copley Square parking garage. Duncan's very existence on the planet seemed to be too much for her to take. *Why doesn't he just disappear for good?* she asked herself. It seemed that every time she thought she had successfully slain that demon, it reincarnated into some other unwelcome life form. And this time he had to bring company. Until now, the fiancée had been a faceless ghost that she'd tried not to give too much thought to. She'd imagined her pretty but New England bland. But suddenly Susan had to pop up in her tall, golden glory. She was a striking woman, and Weslee found herself wondering why Duncan would cheat on someone like that.

I never even stood a chance, Weslee thought as she mentally placed herself alongside Duncan's fiancée and compared. Susan Jarrett, cold and poised and beautifully aloof. That Susan. The whole time. Weslee bit her lip. All the old feelings came rushing back. The sharp pain she'd felt that night when he'd said he couldn't breathe. Then Lana breaking the news to her about the engagement. And his calm. His smug, smirking calm when she'd called him that day . . .

She stood stock-still in the underground parking lot, shaking with anger. That bastard, she thought. "That sorry bastard!" she yelled out, her voice echoing through the dark, dank, car-filled lot.

Chapter
38

Weslee ran into the house, thankful that Sherry was not yet home from the office. She needed a good, king-size cry, and no one else needed to see her that way.

It lasted a good hour. She just let it all out. She had been holding it inside for months. She had tried and tried to forget him, even managing to persuade herself that she had and was ready to move on. But who was she kidding?

And to see him like this, with his perfect fiancée, who probably never flinched when she was asked what her father did. Weslee pounded the pillow with her fist.

"I'm so stupid!" she said through clenched teeth, her eyes burning.

How could she even think that someone like him could go for a girl like her? She had no pedigree. No exotic beauty to speak of. She was just a regular old black girl from South Side Chicago. Who was she kidding?

She stayed in her room the rest of the night, ignoring Sherry's knocks. She had one thing she could do. It would hurt, she knew. But she wouldn't get any rest until she knew the whole truth, and she knew where to get it.

Lana had seemed mildly perturbed to hear Weslee's distraught voice on the other end when she'd picked up the phone. Weslee could hear conversation in the background, and it briefly occurred to her that Lana might be hosting company. But she didn't care. She had to get the truth, and she begged for it, though Lana was not very good at hiding her decreasing tolerance for the conversation. She even seemed irritated that Weslee was asking her for information. "I don't know why you want to know all this stuff. It's only going to make you feel worse. Why can't you just forget about it, about him, and move on?"

But Weslee persisted.

Lana sighed heavily. "I warned you about him from the beginning," she said calmly.

"Please, Lana," Weslee pleaded. "Just tell me. I need to know so I can just forget it ever happened."

Lana reluctantly answered Weslee's questions. Duncan's fiancée, Susan Jarrett, had moved back to the United States from London recently but was living in New York. She had dated Duncan through college off and on. Both of their families were close enough that everyone expected them to get married. But the relationship had been rocky. Susan, however, had never given up on Duncan, and this time it appeared that they would finally tie the knot. Yes, they had a date, Lana told her. Labor Day weekend.

Weslee's rationale for wanting to know was what people said when they couldn't admit to themselves that they were clinging to shreds of hope: closure. Yes, knowing that Duncan would be married to Susan Jarrett in a month would finally mean it was over between them.

But closure wasn't what she felt once she hung up with Lana. Her mind kept thrusting forward the picture of Susan and Duncan so together, so enaged, in Neiman's, the perfect couple. Lana had pretty much confirmed it for Weslee— Duncan had gotten himself quite a catch. Susan had grown up in Manhattan, in a world of exclusive schools and debutante balls, and was now an investment banker for the world's biggest investment bank. Susan had it all, including Duncan.

Shame and hurt made her close her eyes, her face down in the wet pillow. He had told her he loved her, and she actually thought he had meant it. What in the world could she have been thinking?

"Weslee, are you OK?" Sherry shook Weslee's shoulders, jolting her from her sleep.

"Huh?" Weslee opened her eyes slowly.

"You've been in there since last night, and you weren't answering, so I got worried." Sherry was holding a handful of keys in her hand.

"What time is it?" Weslee rubbed her eyes.

"It's almost nine A.M."

"Saturday?"

"Yes, Saturday."

Weslee got up slowly, the events of the previous day starting to re-register.

"Are you OK?" Sherry asked again, this time looking genuinely concerned.

"I'm fine. It's just a headache."

"I didn't know you—"

Weslee raised a hand and nodded her head and grimaced, hoping Sherry would leave her alone. "I'm fine."

"Are you sure?"

Weslee nodded and headed for the bathroom.

"Hey, let's do something. Something fun." Sherry stood outside the bathroom door.

"Actually, Sherry, I'm not really in the mood."

"Come on. It's Saturday. Let's get out of town. Hey, let's go up to Maine. I'll drive."

Weslee walked out of the bathroom. "I can't, Sherry," she

sighed. "I saw Duncan yesterday. . . . I really don't want to do anything."

"What? Where? Where did you see him?"

Weslee told Sherry how she had bumped into Duncan and his fiancée, not leaving out the addendum from Lana's conversation.

"Oh, Wes," she said, putting her arms around Weslee. "I'm so sorry."

"It's OK," Weslee sniffed. "Know what I really want, though?"

"What?" Sherry asked.

"A big, huge, fattening breakfast."

Sherry raised her eyebrows. Weslee could tell that Sherry was restraining herself from telling Weslee that she should not be eating herself into an even deeper funk.

"Can we go to Mike's Diner for breakfast? That would make me feel better," Weslee said.

Sherry agreed.

"Gosh, I am such a fool, Sherry," Weslee said as they drove to the South End restaurant.

"Stop it," Sherry scolded. "I don't understand why you're being so hard on yourself. The guy is a cad, plain and simple. He knew he had to marry this girl. He should have left you alone or told her that he didn't want to marry her. I don't have to tell you you're better off without him. You already know that."

Weslee nodded. "I know, but it hurts so much. It's just that I thought—"

"I know what you thought and what you're thinking. This was just another love affair gone wrong, girl. It doesn't mean you're not a smart, beautiful, successful woman. Do you hear me, Wes?"

Weslee turned to look at her.

"I know your friend Lana and that whole Vineyard crowd can make you question whether you're worthy to even walk the face of this earth. Trust me, my first year at Wellesley I told everyone my dad was a doctor 'cause I was so ashamed that he hadn't gone to college and had some fancy job. But then some mean-spirited girl, one of Peony's friends, somehow found out and busted me. She told everybody. I was ashamed, but I was happy, too. I never lied again. They still looked down on me, but it didn't bother me, because, you know what? I just didn't care what they thought about me anymore. Girl, I don't live in a fancy neighborhood, and I don't shop at Neiman Marcus, but do you think that's keeping me up at night? I'm doing what makes me happy. I'm living the kind of life I've always wanted to live. And you need to stop feeling you're not as good as or less than, 'cause it's bull. Do you hear me, Weslee? It's bull." Sherry's voice was strong and forceful, the way it changed when she was about to become angry.

Weslee looked out the passenger-side window. Sherry was so right. But it would take her a while before she could truly appreciate those words.

Chapter
39

The divorce had been good to Rainee Smalls. She got the four-bedroom contemporary vacation home near Oak Bluffs Harbor, plus the year-round homestead in Wayland. Yes, she had to work now—she's a part-time English professor at a community college in the city—but she still had done well.

The Oak Bluffs house was not as grand, nor as well cared for, as those of her friends who still had their husbands and their husbands' money, but Rainee knew that her home was welcoming and warm. Its tan and navy blue furnishings suited Rainee's casual attitude. The inside looked more like something out of a Pottery Barn catalog than an *Architectural Digest* spread.

"Just make yourself at home," she said after giving the just-arrived Weslee the tour and showing her to her room. "It has its own bathroom and a view of my little lagoon, my oasis," she said.

Weslee gasped as she looked out of the window to see the tiny little circle of water surrounded by plants in fancy pots and sprouting from the fertile earth.

"Wow. This is beautiful, Rainee," she said.

"I know. I work down there every morning."

They talked at Rainee's kitchen table, drinking decaf coffee in the cool home. Weslee couldn't help but noticing how at ease she felt. It was nothing like the discomfort she had felt the year before at Eleanor's party. Rainee was easy to talk to, warm and open.

Weslee was relieved to hear that Peony, Rainee's daughter, would not be there that weekend. She could not put out of her mind Peony's frosty attitude that first day they met. And from what Sherry had told her of her experiences at school with Peony and her friends, she certainly did not want to see the woman. She wondered how Rainee could be so different from her own daughter.

"This wedding is going to kill me," Rainee said. "I've been so stressed about it. I can't wait to just get that girl married off."

Weslee laughed. "Why? She's on her own in the city, isn't she?"

"Well, yes. But she's not like you, Weslee. Her father's still paying her rent every month. It's like she refuses to grow up. She's more like Lana."

Rainee immediately apologized.

"It's OK. Lana and I patched things up a while ago, Rainee. Right after she had the accident, we had a long talk. All that negative stuff is in the past."

"Is that right? Well, that's wonderful, Weslee. I haven't seen her lately; I hear she's been overseas. But from what Eleanor's telling everyone, she's changed a whole lot."

"Yes, she has. I've only spoken to her a few times in the past month or so. But I'm seeing her today."

After putting Rainee through a rigorous two-hour workout in her basement gym, Weslee was free to go off and explore the island on her own. She opted to visit Lana.

It was a warm afternoon, and she felt it would probably

be better to walk than drive her car around the unfamiliar island. Eleanor's house was about a mile away, according to Rainee.

Weslee walked through the quaint, tiny streets full of tourists, a diverse crowd from young urban professionals to retired couples. She couldn't help but wonder whether Duncan and his fiancée were somewhere on this island. She was hoping against hope that she would not run into him again.

Lana had sounded noncommittal on the phone when Weslee finally got hold of her. "Gosh, I've been so busy lately, Wes," she had said when Weslee expressed concern about Lana's standoffishness. Weslee worried that maybe Lana had relapsed into drinking.

When she finally arrived at Eleanor's house, sweat was pouring down her back and she could feel her white T-shirt sticking to patches of her skin.

She rang the bell and waited. A minute passed, and she rang again. The garage was around back, and she noticed that it was closed. There was no way to tell if anyone was home.

She rang several times, but no one came to the door.

She finally walked away, confused and hurt. She had talked to Lana just the day before and told her that she would be there. What had happened?

The thought that dawned on her as she walked back to Rainee's house, this time ignoring the parade of tourists on Circuit Avenue, was one she did not want to stomach.

Had Lana intentionally snubbed her? How could that be? Hadn't they made up? Hadn't Weslee herself helped nurse her back to health after the accident? There must have been some misunderstanding. Maybe Lana had had to go out suddenly and had forgotten that she had told Weslee that she would be home. There had to be some misunderstanding, Weslee thought.

Chapter
40

Weslee had a choice. She could creep back into Rainee's house and hope that she would not have to explain why she was back so soon from visiting Lana, or she could take in more of the sights. She decided to go for the latter. She walked along the narrow roads of Rainee's neighborhood, absorbing the beautiful, quaint homes with their landscaped yards and fresh-smelling flowers. A few children played in the huge front yard of one of the houses. She smiled at them. They smiled back and one of them waved. She hated herself for thinking that in twenty years they might not be as friendly to people like her. She shrugged it off.

The wind from cars, bicycles, and mopeds whipping past her blew at her skirt. She wished she had her car. She decided to head back to Rainee's house. It was way too warm for a walk. She noticed one particular half-built house farther up the street. Curiosity pulled her to it. It was a very unusual-looking house. The half that had been built was up on stilts and resembled half a circle.

"Like that?" a construction worker on the site said to her.

"Yes. It's really . . . cool looking," she said.

He laughed. "That's how most people describe it," he

said. "The architect who designed it is here. He's out back, I think."

"Oh, that's OK. I was just sightseeing. I really—"

She couldn't finish her sentence. William came from the back of the house, wearing a polo shirt and jeans and construction boots, a clipboard in hand. His eyes met hers, and he stopped short for a few seconds before his face broke into a smile.

"Wes? Is that you?"

"William!"

The construction worker looked from William to Weslee and back again, and then walked to the back of the half-finished house.

"What are you doing here?" they said in unison and laughed.

"I'm visiting Lana. I mean, I'm spending the weekend with Rainee Smalls, and I went to visit Lana, but she's not home."

"Oh. Wow. How come you haven't called?"

She shrugged. She wasn't sure he wanted to hear from her. "I've just been busy. You still haven't told me what you're doing here."

"Oh. That. Yes. This house is one of my problem children." He smiled. It was one of the houses he had designed for a demanding client. "They've changed their minds again about some of the materials; that's why I'm here working on such a beautiful weekend."

Weslee complimented him on the design of the rounded house, and she could see the pride in his face. They made more small talk, and then she began to say good-bye.

"Hey, have dinner with me tonight," he said.

"Um. Uh. OK."

"Can I pick you up at Rainee's?"

"Sure," she said.

She waved good-bye to him and walked away, as if on air, back to Rainee's house, temporarily forgetting about Lana.

"I love this place," Weslee said, looking around the dimly lit shacklike seafood restaurant.

William beamed. "I wasn't sure whether a sophisticated city slicker like you would go for it. But I'm glad you like it."

She laughed.

"You look great, by the way," he said.

She blushed, her pink halter dress accentuating the color on her lips and cheeks.

William talked about his client, a New York businessman who had been holding him hostage for three months with his demands.

"I can't wait for this house to be finished. I'm going off to Jamaica for three weeks, no cell phone, no pager, no Palm."

"Sounds nice," Weslee said, wondering where Megan fell into those plans.

As if reading her mind, he said, "Oh, did I tell you that Megan got a job in California?"

"No. That's great for her," Weslee exclaimed. *Thank God,* she said silently. "So you'll be flying out there a lot, I guess?" She couldn't be any more transparent.

He shook his head. "It really wasn't that serious. We're still friends, though."

The waiter came, giving Weslee a chance to fully absorb William's words. He was single. He was available.

As usual when she was with him, the time flew by quickly. They talked about their families. William remained close to his parents, who lived outside of Boston in the town of Randolph.

"You would like them," he said. "They're just like your folks. So, how's the training business?" he asked as the waiter set his lobster before him and Weslee eyed her halibut hungrily.

"It's going well. I would never have thought that I could make any money at this. I really have Rainee Smalls to thank for that. She's gotten me so many clients, I almost don't have time to see them all."

"Why don't you get yourself organized? You know, Weslee Inc."

Weslee laughed. "This is only a part-time thing to get me through business school. Once I graduate, I'm going back to corporate America."

William leaned back in his chair. "Is that what you want?"

Weslee thought for a few seconds. "Yes. Yes. I want a good, secure profession."

"And that would make you happy?"

"It would make me secure, so yes, happy."

He shrugged and started eating his lobster again.

"OK. What are you getting at, William?" She knew there was something he wanted to say to her.

"I'm not going to give you a lecture. But I will tell you that I was on the fast track at the biggest architectural firm in the country five years ago, and I was bored out of my skull. They thought I could do no wrong, and if I had stayed I'd probably be in some executive office making a lot more than I'm making now, and I wouldn't have as many sleepless nights. But I wouldn't trade what I have now for anything."

"It's not the same thing, William. You've always liked to design homes and buildings and be around construction sites. For me, running, athletics, it's just a hobby, not the way I ever imagined myself making a living."

William sighed. "But that's exactly my point. Know what Mark Twain said? Make your vocation your vacation. This is something you already love to do. Why not get paid for it?

Hell, in a couple of years you'll probably have your own health club."

She laughed uneasily. The more he talked, the more she began to see it. But she was afraid. "It sounds good, William. But this just isn't what I planned for. I just want a job analyzing stock funds for a big investment bank."

"And then what?" He leaned in to her face. "Does that make you excited? Does that make you want to leap out of bed every day?"

"No. But it's secure, and I know it."

He shook his head. "Nothing's secure in life. Not even the things you think you know."

They ate silently for a while, and Weslee tried to process all the thoughts that were going through her head. "Maybe it could work," she said. "I'll have to do some research."

"On what?"

"Well, you know. The costs and stuff like that."

"All you need is some light equipment. And I can help you if you'd allow me to." William smiled.

Weslee ran her hand through her hair. "It just seems so . . . so . . . crazy."

"Wes, it makes perfect sense. Think about it."

"It's just that I've never been a big risk-taker."

"You moved here all by yourself, that was a big risk," he said slowly.

"Yes. But I moved here because of school. I mean, I left Chicago because I wanted to go to business school in the Northeast."

William sighed again. "Weslee, I'm not trying to be your therapist. I'm just trying to let you see that you're capable of much more than you give yourself credit for. That's all. So, when do you go back to Boston?" he asked, quickly changing the subject.

"Monday morning."

"Will I see you at Rainee's party tomorrow night?"

"Wow. She only told me about it this afternoon. But since I'm staying at her house, I'll have no choice but to be there. I'm glad I ran into you today, William." Weslee picked at her lemon meringue pie.

"Me, too." He smiled as he signaled the waiter for the check.

"You like Danilo Perez?" Weslee asked after William had popped the CD into his car stereo.

"I'm going through a Latin, Afro–Cuban jazz period. Work with me, OK?" he joked.

"No! No! I love Danilo Perez. I have everything he's done."

He took his eyes off the road briefly to give her an amused stare. "How come you like jazz and not R&B and hip-hop?"

"Ugh. I can't stand the stuff out there today. I peaked right after Guy broke up." Weslee shrugged. "The last R&B CD I bought was Jill Scott. I still listen to the older stuff, though."

William laughed. "Have I got something for you then," he said and reached into a case of CDs.

Seconds later, they burst out laughing as the sound of Guy's "Piece of My Love" filled the Jeep. Weslee howled as William did his best Aaron Hall imitation, singing "Baby, you can't have all of me, 'cause I'm not totally free . . ."

"You're so insane!" She laughed as tears rolled down her face.

A few minutes later they stood on the front porch of Rainee's house as crickets chirped far off in the dark, dark night.

"Thanks for dinner," Weslee said.

They stood awkwardly, not saying a word but not wanting to walk away.

Weslee, for the first time in her life, took the lead and kissed William softly on the lips. His hands moved up to her face and held it close to his as he kissed her back, gently at first, and then deeper and more urgently, pulling her body close to his.

"William," she whispered when she could catch a breath.

"What?" he whispered back.

"I'm sorry."

He pulled her closer to him.

"For what?"

"For being so stupid."

"No, I was the fool for not snatching you up the first night I laid eyes on you."

He kissed her again, harder and deeper this time, and she felt his insistent desire against her body. She pulled back from him hesitantly and looked at Rainee's house. *We should move this inside,* she wanted to say. Then she weighed what she wanted right now against what was the right thing to do. He took her face in his hands and, as if reading her thoughts, kissed her again. "Let me let you go inside before we get into trouble."

She tossed and turned a half hour later, still flustered and unable to sleep as she grabbed onto the feeling of William's body against hers, his hands stroking her arms, her back, his lips on her neck. She threw the covers off her as the room seemed to grow warmer.

The night with William had seemed magical and yet so easy and natural, like it had happened many times before. Sparks flew and fireworks went off, but it didn't feel as scripted as it had with Duncan. She didn't feel as if she were being tested—on her background, her manners, her clothing, her knowledge of wine and gourmet food. Heck, she never remembered laughing out loud, really loud, with Duncan. This could be real, she thought. The real thing. But she hesitated as a voice in her head put up the caution signs. Was she once again moving too fast? No way, she argued back. There was something deep, a soul connection, with William that first night they'd met. And tonight they'd reconnected. It just felt so right to be with William, so warm and comfortable. And she could see herself inhabiting that cozy place forever. She looked up at the ceiling. If only Duncan hadn't come along, she thought. If only she could just forget about him. Her feelings for the two men were like pieces of a puzzle. She worried that her desire to be with William was just a side effect of a confused heart trying to find a substitute for Duncan. She didn't want to get hurt again. Nor did she want to hurt anyone else.

She couldn't deny what she was feeling. *I hope I'm not being impulsive and foolish with my heart again*, she told herself. But her attempts at injecting common sense into the situation were fruitless. She couldn't stop thinking about the night. About the way she'd floated when he'd kissed her and left her breathless. When he'd left, promising to call her in the morning, it took all of her willpower to not run after him and beg him to stay the night. She had tiptoed in, not wanting to wake Rainee. But Rainee had left a note on the refrigerator saying that she might not be home—she had a date "with a young gentleman."

Now she tossed in the bed, a smile on her face. She would get no sleep tonight, that was for sure. But it wasn't an altogether bad thing. The thoughts keeping her awake were more than welcome to stay.

Chapter
41

Self-promotion is usually not a problem for any entrepreneur worth his business plan, but Weslee was having trouble. It embarrassed her to list her athletic achievements for the pursuit of financial gain. It made her feel as if she was selling out. To what, she couldn't articulate.

She frowned as yet another of Rainee's friends came up to her. "Hi, I hear you're the one who made Rainee look so fabulous. Do you have any cards?"

The party was neither grand nor pretentious, but it was lively and interesting. Rainee's friends formed an eclectic mix, from old-timers who held sway over the island's social scene to graduate students visiting from the city, hippies, journalists, businessmen, professors, and even a professional basketball player. People mixed easily, and Weslee was having a wonderful time. She stole glances at William as he worked his way around the room, no doubt networking as well as partying. She was trying to do the same. Rainee had said that Lana was invited, but so far she had not shown. Weslee had tried in vain to reach Lana. She had left messages on her cell phone, Eleanor's answering service, and even at Lana's apartment in the city, all to no avail.

Weslee sipped her ginger ale and nodded at an older

woman she had met the year before at Eleanor's party. The woman barely smiled back, walking past her to grab the elbow of Charles Huntlin III, a prominent doctor. Weslee smiled as it occurred to her that a year ago such a snub would have torn her up inside. Now she just shrugged it off. She was about to go find William when she heard a familiar laugh.

When had she come in? Weslee wondered. Lana was at the other end of the room, surrounded by three other young women. She looked the same, impeccably dressed, her hair bouncing off her shoulders as she leaned her head back to laugh. Weslee walked over to where she was standing.

"Lana, when did you get here?"

Lana at first looked uncomfortable, then said, "Oh, just a little while ago. How are you?"

"I've been calling and calling. Didn't you get any of my messages?"

The three women turned away and began to talk among themselves.

"Wes, I've just been really busy. I was overseas, and then I came back, and it's just been really hectic," Lana said coldly.

"I know you've been busy. So have I, but you could have at least called back."

Lana sighed. "OK. Maybe I could have. But look at you." She smiled the way she did when she was about to make a cutting remark. "You've certainly come a long way."

"What is that supposed to mean?" Weslee asked, beginning to see the old Lana coming back.

"Well, you're wearing the right clothes, and you're here among all the beautiful people, and you're here all on your own. It's what you've always wanted, right?"

"Excuse me?" Weslee couldn't believe her ears. And all this time she thought Lana had changed.

"Everybody just loves you, Wes," Lana said sardonically.

"Rainee and all her divorcée friends, they all want you to come to their parties. You're quite a hit."

Weslee felt anger and hurt welling up inside her. "Lana," she said, her voice firm and low. "You know what I've just realized?"

Lana looked at her with a question in her eyes.

"You're a sad, sad person. I hope you work out all your problems, and I wish you the best of luck in life. And, yes, I want to thank you for showing me what a real friend should be and shouldn't be. Good-bye."

Weslee walked to the other end of the room where William was standing.

"Let's leave. Let's go to your hotel or something," she said.

"Why, what's wrong?"

"I just need to get away from this place for a while."

William persuaded Weslee to take a walk down the dark, dark streets of the island.

They held hands and walked silently down the quiet road. It was only eleven P.M., but there were few cars on the street. The night was warm and peaceful, with the smell of sea salt in the air. Weslee could see the stars as she stole a look up at the sky.

"I don't understand her," Weslee said remorsefully. "I've never met anyone like her. I've done all I can. It's over."

"I've known Lana for a long time, and she's always been this way, Weslee. It's not you."

"That's the thing, William. I know that now, but for a long time I thought that I could change her if I was more patient. That there was another layer to her that was more . . . more compassionate."

"You can't control other people, Wes. The only person you have control over is yourself," William said as they walked to the harbor. They sat on a bench, holding hands in the dark.

"She's been such a witch to me. Even after I took care of her after the accident . . ." Weslee paused. She did not want Lana to ruin her time with William. It wasn't worth it. She'd wasted enough time already. "Let's talk about something else," she said.

"OK," William said and put an arm around her shoulder. "How about we talk about what you want."

"What I want?"

"Yes. You. What do you want?"

Weslee tried to figure out what he was asking. "From life?"

"From life."

Her heart thudded. She was not prepared for this question.

"I'm glad you're giving it some thought," he joked.

"Well, I want happiness. Like everybody else. I want to be happy. I . . . I want to have a career that fulfills me and a comfortable life. Isn't that what everybody wants?" *Where is he going with this?* she wondered.

"Most people want that," William said. Then, "What about the other part of happiness? The love part."

Oh, I see, she thought. She didn't want to reveal too much to him, but she wanted him to know how she felt. "I want someone I'm comfortable with, someone trustworthy. Someone who makes me feel good about being me all the time, even when I'm sweaty and wearing sneakers." She laughed as he raised an eyebrow. "Oh, and he must worship the ground I walk on."

"Worship?" he asked, turning to her.

"Worship." She smiled.

"That's easy," he said, taking her face in his hands and drawing his lips to hers.

Then she pulled back. "And what about you? What do you want?"

He looked up at the sky. "I want someone who's kind.

And sweet and smart. And beautiful." He turned to face her. "I want someone I know I can always count on no matter what. Someone who I'll never need to lie to because she'll believe in me even when I'm screwing up." He smiled apologetically. "This list could go on for days. As you can tell, I've given it a lot of thought."

She nodded. "I wish I could say the same. I like to think of myself as so even-keeled and pragmatic. But when it comes to relationships, I tend to lose all my common sense and go with my emotions, and that approach just hasn't worked."

"Emotions aren't all bad," he said.

"Yeah. But sometimes they blind you to reality," Weslee said. "But I'm learning. I have learned."

"What have you learned?" he asked.

"I learned that I should always go with my gut." She recalled the first night she'd laid eyes on William and the feelings that he'd stirred inside of her. Again she wanted to kick herself for allowing Duncan to enter her life.

William took her hand in his, and she laid her head on his shoulder.

"I don't want to go back to the city," she said, wanting this moment with William to last for an eternity.

He leaned his head on hers. "Me, neither."

Chapter
42

The change in landscape from Falmouth to Dorchester was not only a result of nature. The two-hour drive made the eye accustomed to well cared for homes with gardens and carefully tended lawns and then landscaped highways with neat green vegetation on either side. Therefore the entrance into the city that began at the top of Route 28 was the visual equivalent of seeing a beautiful woman from afar and then finding that she had disturbingly crooked teeth or crossed eyes when you got up close.

It had been a long drive, and Weslee could not wait to get out of her car, but the distressing sights of city life made her want to head back toward the Vineyard. It was Monday evening, so giant buses clogged the streets, and pedestrians, ignoring the rules of the road, jay-ran in front of frazzled drivers anxious to be home after a long day's travail in the city's innards.

The calm that had settled into Weslee over the weekend dissipated as she maneuvered her way through double-parked cars on Blue Hill Avenue. Oblivious teenagers slowly made their way across the street, ignoring the horns of other motorists and the occasional police car speeding by, lights flashing, on its way to the latest emergency. When she finally made it to Sherry's house, she felt as if she had just been through a raging storm.

"That's Boston's rush hour for you," Sherry said as Weslee put her things away. "I made a huge dinner, Jamaican-style," she added, putting on her Jamaican accent.

Weslee felt a little annoyed. She wished Sherry would let her at least cook or do something to help around the house, but her friend would have none of it. Weslee knew better than to think it was because of Sherry's magnanimity—the woman was a total control freak.

Weslee uncovered the pots on the stove in the kitchen, and saw that Sherry had cooked up a storm: rice and beans, jerk chicken—she had even made a pineapple upside-down cake and ginger beer.

"Sherry, who's going to eat all this food!" Weslee said as she inhaled the aromas over the stove.

"I'll take some of it to Larry's folks." Larry's elderly parents had now become another one of Sherry's labors of love.

Weslee began to set the table, as Sherry always required, in Sherry's mauve dining room. The colors of the house seemed dizzying to her compared with the understated chic of Rainee Smalls's vacation home. But she had to admit, the brightness of it uplifted her mood.

"So, tell me all about the weekend with the black—no, the café au lait—bourgeoisie," Sherry said as they sat down to dinner.

Sherry was silent when Weslee told her about her encounter with William, then indignant when told about Lana's snub.

"I'm sorry, girl. I would have smacked her right across her bony face when she said that," Sherry said. "What does she mean 'You're doing well for yourself.' Humph! You were doing well for yourself long before you even knew she existed."

"I think she thinks that she did me a favor by bringing

me out to the Vineyard that time last year. I mean, yes, she's not totally wrong. If I had never gone out there with her, Rainee Smalls would not have recognized me at HealthyLife that day and I wouldn't have all the clients I have today."

"Weslee, are you serious? The woman was your customer at the spa, OK? She liked your work. Even if she had never seen you before, things still could have turned out the way they did."

Weslee sighed. "True. OK. But I wouldn't have met William or Duncan if it hadn't been for her."

"Why are you trying to give her credit? You need to just let it go. This may hurt your feelings, but she was only friends with you because her life was falling apart. You said it yourself. She's clean and sober now, and she's all into her light-skinned, straight-nosed Jack and Jill friends. I think you just need to let that woman go. She was never your friend."

"I know. I just feel sorry for her in a way, and for myself, too."

"Why?"

"Well, I think if she were a different person, we could have been friends. And I kinda wish I hadn't taken all that crap from her."

Sherry rolled her eyes. "Hey, it happens to all of us. Just don't let it happen again. And, no, she can only be who she is."

"So, what do you think about William?"

Sherry took a forkful of rice in her mouth.

"Well?" Weslee asked.

"Honestly?"

"Yes, honestly, Sherry!"

"Less than a year ago you said you guys were just friends, and you were all hung up on Mr. Perfect. I just don't know if you're sure of what you're doing," Sherry said.

"I know, I thought the same thing. But I always liked

him. I met him first, before I met Duncan, and right away I knew I liked him. But I was just confused by you-know-who."

Sherry's look was skeptical. "Are you sure you're not just doing this on the rebound or to get back at you-know-who?"

"I'm sure. I've thought about it. I think about William all the time."

"And what about him?" Sherry asked. "Isn't he mad at you for picking Duncan over him?"

"No, I don't think so. It didn't quite happen like that. I mean, we had an initial attraction, but he was so busy at the time that we never got together. Then I was with Duncan and he was with that Megan."

"That girl we saw him with in Killington?"

"Yeah."

"Hmmm. She was something," Sherry said, shaking her head.

"Gee, thanks for the vote of confidence." Weslee glared at Sherry.

"No, I'm just saying that she was fine. But you look better than her," Sherry laughed. "Well, I'd just advise you to take it slow. You don't want to go through another heartbreak so soon."

"No. I think this is going to turn out all right, Sherry. I feel so right with him. I'm not nervous and jumpy like I was with Duncan. He just makes me feel so good."

Sherry nodded. "Like I said, give it time."

Chapter

43

Weslee looked out Sherry's living room window to the street, where yet another carful of teenage boys sped past, their car stereo rocking the house. But she smiled this time. She had asked Sherry how she tolerated all the noise. Sherry had said, "After a while you don't even hear it anymore." Weslee still heard it, but it bothered her less and less. She was starting to see why Sherry stayed in this neighborhood even though she could sell her house for five hundred thousand dollars and move to Milton or Randolph, where most of the middle-class blacks and West Indians were beginning to settle. Sherry knew all her neighbors; she still babysat for some of their children's children; she made cookies for the elderly couple next door; she took out the trash for the quadriplegic man two houses up. She yelled at the kids when they dropped burger wrappers and soda cans on the street, and they didn't yell back—they picked up their litter. People knew her, and she knew them. Weslee could see why she would not leave.

It was early evening, and Weslee was glad to have the apartment all to herself. Sherry was covering a story in New York. That gave Weslee a full two days to herself. She only had three clients to see. The August heat was making her customers reluctant to exert themselves. But it really was OK. She sat with her laptop, looking at the spreadsheet of her finances. She would need about three thousand dollars to get her savings back to the level she wanted. Somehow looking at the numbers didn't stress her as much as it had in the past. She was proud of what she had accomplished in the last few months. She thought of Rainee Smalls beaming as person after person told her how great she looked now fifteen pounds lighter. She thought of Marie Bunting flexing her biceps—and smiling. And the other women she worked with getting stronger, happier, and more confident because of the work they had done with her.

Maybe William was right. She could see herself doing this for a living. Watching and writing about mutual funds had never given her this kind of satisfaction. The numbers in her portfolio, she now realized, were empty movable entities. She had lost when the market tanked, then gained a bit, then lost again when she temporarily lost her mind and spent fifty thousand dollars on designer clothes and parties. Now she had her mind back, and she was going to use it.

She began to write an e-mail to the professor of the Entrepreneurship class. She needed some professional advice.

Roy Hargrove's cover of "The Nearness of You" blared on the stereo as Weslee soaked in the bathtub. It was one of her favorite songs. She was sore from running four laps around the 2.5-mile trail in Franklin Park. She was halfway through Paul Theroux's *Mosquito Coast*, which she had started on the ferry to Oak Bluffs weeks ago. Her plan was to read all of Theroux's books before the start of the fall semester. She had one left, *My Other Life*, after *Mosquito*. She could hear her cell phone chiming in the bedroom; probably one of her clients, she thought. They always called at the most inopportune times to change or make appointments. She ignored it.

Twenty minutes later she came out of the tub and contemplated making a huge Greek salad for dinner. As she searched through Sherry's overfull refrigerator, her cell phone rang again.

"Aaargh!" she said as she went to get the phone.

"Hello, Weslee," said the deep, slightly hoarse voice, making her heart leap skyward.

She swallowed.

"Weslee, are you there?" the voice said again.

"Yes, I'm here."

"How are you?" Duncan asked, sounding at ease, as if nothing had happened between the two of them.

"How can I help you, Duncan?" Weslee asked, anger starting to rise in her chest as she remembered the way he misled and lied to her.

He sighed. "I just wanted to know how you were doing. And I wanted to apologize and maybe talk."

"Talk about what?" she hissed.

"About what happened. I feel that I need to explain."

"There's nothing to explain. You're marrying someone else. That's pretty clear to me."

"It's not that simple," he said. She detected the irritation in his voice.

"It's not? Why is that? Is she pregnant? Or is someone holding a gun to your head?"

She could almost see him clenching his teeth. "You don't understand. And there's no need for this sarcasm."

"Don't tell me what there's a need for—"

He interrupted her. "Obviously, you're still angry. I shouldn't have called. Good-bye."

He hung up before she could say anything.

Her plans for her salad upset, Weslee stalked to the

stereo and turned it off. The mood was ruined. How dare he call her and still sound so smug and self-assured? she thought. What made him think that she was interested in his apology or that it could actually make a difference to her?

She called Sherry's hotel room in New York, but Sherry was not in. She called her sister, Terry, who listened sympathetically to her rant.

"Sis, maybe you should have given him a chance to say what he was going to say," Terry said gently.

"And then what, Terry? He'll end up being the good guy? He's just trying to ease his guilty conscience. That's all."

Terry sighed. "Well, you know him better than I do. But if he wants to say he's sorry for what happened, that's not a bad thing."

Weslee was not any more convinced when she ended the conversation with her sister. No one would understand how he had hurt her, made her think that they had something so special. She was so glad he was out finally out of her life, and now he wanted to con his way back in. How dare he?

William was at his parents' home in Randolph, and Weslee was nervous about calling him there, but she just had to hear his voice.

"Hello." A woman's voice with a Jamaican accent answered the phone.

Weslee asked for William.

"Yes. Who's calling, please?"

"It's Weslee Dunster."

"Oh, he told us about you. How are you? I'm his mom."

She didn't know he had mentioned her to his family.

"I'm fine," she said, making small talk with William's mother for a minute before the woman went to get him.

She held, trying to pick up some sense of the loud conversations in the background. Apparently, there was a large family gathering in progress.

"Hey, Weslee." William came to phone sounding jovial.

"Hey, you. Did I interrupt a family thing?"

"No. No. My folks always have people over to the house."

She was so happy to hear his voice, she pulled the phone close to her ear as if willing him to be close to her. The sound of his voice warmed her, and she pulled her knees up to her chest, hugging herself with her arms. She knew she was about to take a risk, but she felt ready.

"William, can you come over?"

He didn't reply immediately, and Weslee's heart began to fall.

"Is everything OK?" he asked.

"Yes. But . . . I just want to see you."

"Uh. OK, sure. Are you sure everything's OK?" He sounded unsure and a little concerned.

"Everything is fine. I just want to see you. I mean, talk to you."

"OK. Give me about forty minutes."

When William walked in the door, Weslee did all she could from telling him right there and then that she was in love with him and wanted to be his. Instead, she offered him a drink.

"Are you sure everything's all right?" He looked at her intently as she settled next to him on the couch.

"I'm fine. I just wanted to tell you thanks." She was losing her nerve.

"Thanks for what?" He sipped from his glass.

"Just for being so understanding about everything. I'm really glad I met you that night."

He began to smile, but she could see confusion in his eyes. "Where's all this coming from?"

"I've had time to think about the mistakes that I've made, and I just don't want you to get the wrong idea of what's going on now."

He put his glass down and faced her. She could feel her

heart pounding. She could tell from his eyes that he knew what she was trying to say but couldn't, and she didn't like the answer his eyes gave hers.

He sighed. "Look, Weslee. I'll be honest with you. I don't think we should move too fast. I know you've been through a lot, and I can't say that I'm sure that you or I are ready for something serious."

"What do you mean?" she said weakly, her heart breaking.

"I just don't think you're ready. You're not really over Duncan yet. And I don't want to confuse things further by pushing things with us. If it's meant to be, it will happen."

"But William, you're wrong. What I feel for you is real. It was real the first time we talked."

"But you chose him, remember?" he said gently.

"I didn't—"

"Listen, Weslee. It's OK. I want you in my life. But I think we just need to take things slow for now." He stood up to leave. "I'll call you tomorrow."

"You're wrong, William." She stood and faced him. Tears pricked at her eyes as he turned away and walked out the door.

He was wrong, wrong, wrong. She was over Duncan, and she was in love with him. How could he not see that? Why was everything going so wrong tonight?

She tried Sherry's hotel room in New York again. No answer. Was there no one in the world who could make her feel better?

Chapter

44

It had been a mistake to think that she could walk the two miles from Copley Square to Downtown Crossing in the soupy ninety-degree weather. She could see the Ritz Residences a few yards away, but it seemed like miles. Bad decision, walking, she thought. Her tank top was sticking to her back, and her gym bag seemed heavier with every step she took. By the time she made it into the building, she could feel sweat trickling down the insides of her legs. The cool air that licked at her face when she walked in the building felt like a reward.

She took the elevator down to the gym, the city's most luxurious and exclusive. It catered only to guests of the Ritz or residents of its million-dollar condominiums. Her client, Younis Pratha, was another of Rainee's friends, a scientist and professor at MIT. When they had made the appointment, Younis couldn't decide whether to hold the session at the sprawling farm she and her husband owned in Carlisle, Massachusetts, or whether she would remain in the city at their two-bedroom condo on the top floor of the Ritz Residences, overlooking the Boston Common. Weslee, her own interests at heart, asked Younis to pick the condo.

It was Weslee's first time in the gym, and it took her

breath away. She thought of William's words just weeks ago. "Maybe someday you'll run your own health club." Weslee sighed. She could definitely see herself running a high-end place like this.

Well-toned women and muscular women exercised on the treadmills, StairMasters, and weight machines. Elegant-looking staff members unobtrusively catered to their every need, from extra towels to bringing them bottles of Perrier. She could smell the relaxing aromatherapy coming from the hallway that led to the spa. Oh, Weslee could definitely see herself running a place like this someday.

It was not hard to spot Younis Pratha. She was wearing a bright orange lycra unitard that revealed too much of her softening body. Weslee could hear her lovely South Indian accent as she spoke to a tall young man. Younis was always very vivacious and flamboyant, from what Weslee had gathered from Rainee.

Weslee was not disappointed. Younis Pratha greeted her warmly, kissing her on both cheeks as she introduced herself. The young man she was talking with walked away, and Weslee immediately began the session.

Younis was energetic, and she moved quickly, allowing Weslee to challenge her.

"Wow, this is fun!" Younis exclaimed. She asked Weslee about herself, her career, and her family as they worked. She was impressed that Weslee would soon be an MBA.

"So I guess you plan to go into business for yourself?" Younis asked. "Something fitness oriented?"

Weslee laughed. "It's an idea that I'm just playing with. I'll probably go straight to an investment bank after graduation."

"That's not too bad. But it's great that you have another option. My husband is a CFO at one of those banks, and I'd hate to have to do what he did to get to where he is now, all those long days and nights, too, at the office. All these years he's wanted to open an Indian restaurant. He's a great cook, by the way." Younis smiled. "But he's been waiting for the right time, to get enough investors, to get the children out of the house. My youngest has been out of the house for five years, and still nothing."

Weslee nodded. It seemed that she was hearing the same drumbeat from everyone.

"Well, I'm not one to tell a smart young lady like you how to run your life. So, anyway, will you be at the big wedding?"

"What big wedding?" Weslee asked.

"The Jarrets' daughter?"

Weslee's heart fell.

"Probably not. I don't know them at all."

"Really? I thought you were good friends with Lana. She's one of the bridesmaids."

Those words hit Weslee like an electric shock. Lana would be a bridesmaid in Duncan's wedding?

"Are you sure?" she asked Younis.

"Yes. Why, did she change her mind?"

"Oh, no. I'm sure she didn't."

"Yes, I saw her last night at Marie Bunting's little dinner party. I was hoping you'd be there so I could meet you."

"Uh...I had a previous engagement," Weslee lied. Truth was, Marie had not invited her.

"Well, Lana seems to be all excited about the wedding. She herself is so in love with Jeffrey Knight. I think they might be next. He's a cutie, isn't he?"

Weslee nodded, trying to smile. She rushed through the rest of the hour while Younis prattled on about this person or the other's dinner party or vacation home. Weslee felt slightly betrayed by Lana. But she couldn't say that she was shocked.

Sherry was home when Weslee dejectedly walked through the door.

"Rough day at work?" Sherry said from her spot on the couch, right near the air-conditioning vent.

"Lana's a bridesmaid."

"A what?"

"She's going to be a bridesmaid in Duncan's wedding."

"Oh, Wes. That really stinks."

Weslee sat heavily in the armchair facing Sherry and smiled. "It's OK. I mean, it's her cousin and all. But it's just occurring to me now that she knew about this the whole time, from the very beginning. She never wanted to hear me talk about him. She knew he had this girl stashed away in London that he was going to marry, but she never said a word to me all that time when I thought we were friends."

Sherry shook her head. "I'm so sorry, Wes. She plays by a different set of rules, that's all. You just have to forgive and forget."

Weslee quickly went to her room. She could tell that Sherry was starting to tire of her endless drama with Lana and now Duncan. She moped, reading absently, on her bed.

Her cell phone rang.

It was William, and as irritable as she already felt, his voice calmed her spirit.

"What are you doing?" he asked.

She recounted the afternoon's events to him.

"Wes, I could have told you that, but I really didn't want to upset you."

"You knew, too!"

"Before you get all upset, listen to me, OK?" William said firmly. "You're taking all of this way too personally. Lana's just a spoiled girl who's never going to grow up. In all the years I've known Duncan and his family, you're the closest thing to a real girlfriend I've ever seen her have. She doesn't know how to treat people like you because every-one else she knows is just like her. I really don't think she meant to hurt your feelings. She just plays by a different set of rules, that's all. You just have to take it or leave it."

What William was saying made sense to her, but she was still angry at him for not telling her what he knew. "I have to ask you an important question," she said.

"Oh, no," he groaned. "Go ahead."

"Are you going to the wedding? And if you're his best man, just hang up right now."

William laughed. "No, I'm not his best man. And I won't go if you don't want me to go," he said.

"What?" Weslee was touched and a little embarrassed for basically forcing William to choose between a longtime friend and her.

"You heard me. If it makes you uncomfortable, I won't go to the wedding."

"William, that is so sweet of you. But I couldn't ask you to do that. Duncan is your friend."

"Hey, why don't you come over here," he said, jolting the conversation onto another lane.

"Where?" Weslee asked, confused.

"To my folks'. They're having a bunch of people over to-night."

"Uh. I'm not sure, William. I planned on staying in tonight. I'm really not in the mood. . . ."

"You don't have to stay long. Just come out for an hour or so."

But what about the other night, she wanted to ask, *when you said we should take things slow?*

"William, don't you think that after the other night—"

"Weslee. Please. Just come out tonight. I want you to meet my family. Just say yes. I'm tired of this back and forth."

She sighed loudly this time so he would hear. "OK, fine. Is this a dressed-up thing?"

"Just relax, OK? You can wear rags if you want to."

She drove to Randolph, trying to process all that had happened during the day. Going to William's house was better than staying home and moping about Duncan's wedding. She was also starting to realize that the thought of Lana being a bridesmaid bothered her even more than Duncan marrying Susan Jarrett. It was as if she had made her peace with him; it was Lana who was still causing her so much disappointment.

The house was crowded. People spilled out from the front door onto the porch in the steamy night. Calypso music blared, and Weslee could smell the curry chicken from the driveway. William met her as she was getting out of her Honda.

"Wow. This is like a real party."

"I told you," William said, taking her hand and leading her past groups of people outside and into the house.

"Ma," he yelled above the loud music.

A petite dark-skinned woman with a short Afro came out of what Weslee guessed was the kitchen. She was holding a can of Sprite.

"William, is this the girl you keep talking about?"

The girl?

"Weslee, this is my mother, Veronica."

Weslee held out her hand. "Hi Mrs.—"

"Call me Veronica," the woman said, going past Weslee's hand and hugging her tightly. She pulled back and held Weslee's waist in her tiny hands. "I've heard so much about you. You're so pretty and tall." Veronica's Jamaican accent was still pronounced even after decades of living in the United States.

"Um. Thank you." She felt so embarrassed. She looked at William. "You have a beautiful home." It was the only thing she could think to say.

"Thank you, dear. Wait here, OK? I'm going to get my husband."

"What have you told them about me?" Weslee asked William.

"Nothing." Playful guilt was written all over his face.

William's father, Daniel, was a bear of a man. He was at least six feet four, and he apparently loved to eat. He was a startling contrast to Veronica's tiny frame.

"How are you?" he said somewhat shyly, shaking Weslee's hand.

Weslee greeted him back, smiling. He was her father, just about fifty pounds heavier.

She began to feel at home as she chatted with Veronica and Daniel about her own parents, the times she had visited the Islands with them, and her life in general. They were some of the most down-to-earth people she had ever met. They reminded her of her parents.

When she finally broke away from William's parents and aunts and uncles, she grabbed a plate of food. She couldn't resist the jerk chicken, pilau, and mini meat patties that were spread out on the table. She figured she'd have to make up for it by running an extra mile or two the next day.

"Hungry?" William came up behind her.

"Yes. I was so busy talking I forgot to eat."

He smiled. "I'm glad you like everybody."

"Well, they're just like my family in so many ways."

"That's why I wanted you to meet them. I felt the same way when I met your folks in Chicago last summer."

She popped a patty in her mouth. "Oh!" she exclaimed. "These are so good!"

"My ma's a pro," he said proudly.

He stole a few bites off her plate, and she pulled it away playfully.

"Let's go for a walk," he said.

The street of tidy Colonial and Tudor homes was otherwise quiet, as most of the neighbors were at the party. He reached for her hand again.

"I'm so glad I came," she said.

"Why?" He stopped and looked at her.

"Because this is a great party," she said. What she really wanted to tell him was that she felt so much better now that she was with him.

"And that's the only reason?" he asked.

She didn't answer.

"Let's talk," he said, starting to walk again. "I'm sorry about the other night. You really caught me off guard."

She didn't say anything. She wasn't sure where he was going.

"Everything's kinda happening at the same time, you know?" he said.

"No, I didn't know," Weslee said, honestly. She had no idea what he meant.

"Well, you know, work and you."

"I didn't mean to add any stress to your life."

"It's OK. I'm just not good at relationships, beginning them especially. I'm much better with work, so that's where most of my focus goes."

Weslee tried to figure out where William was going.

"The other night was just . . ." He ran his hands over his thinning head. "I just wasn't expecting you to say those things. I mean, I was hoping you felt that way deep down, especially after that time on the Ferris wheel in Chicago. But I was never sure."

"What are you saying?" She turned to face him, and again they stopped walking.

"What I said last night is still true."

"So you're afraid that I'd go back to Duncan at the drop of a hat?"

"I'm not saying that. I just don't want to feel like I'm your second choice."

"William, you are my first choice. I was stupid a year ago, and I made a mistake. A mistake I paid dearly for. But I learned. I learned my lesson, and I've grown up, and a big reason for that is because of you. You made me see myself in a whole new way. I know you have your concerns about my intentions or sincerity, but I love you. I'm sure of it. I've waited for you for a long time, and I'm willing to wait as long as it takes for you to feel sure about me."

He looked her in the eye, and she could see his doubts. "Weslee, what would you do if he came back?"

"I would still want you, William. You're the man for me. And I feel strange having to stand here and make a case for myself. I feel like somehow it's not fair. That you should know. But that's OK. I've had to grow up a lot in the last year or so. I know that love is not the fairy tale that I once thought it was. So if I have to beg you, then I will. That's how strongly I feel about you."

He took her other hand in his. "You don't have to beg me. And I'm not trying to put you through the paces. I just want to make sure that you know what you want, because I know I want you. I did from the first day I laid eyes on you. I never had a single doubt. I almost lost a friendship that had been very important to me because I couldn't stand to see Duncan stealing your heart. But you never left my thoughts, Weslee. I felt so guilty about it sometimes, but I just couldn't ever forget the way you looked at me that night we met."

Before William could say another word, Weslee took his face in her hands and kissed him. They closed themselves off to the rest of the world as they stood on the dark, still street.

It seemed like hours passed before a car sliced down the street, flashing its lights on them and bringing them back to reality.

"What do you want to do?" he asked, still holding her close.

She sighed and closed her eyes. "Be with you."

He kissed her. "We're on the street, and my parents have a house full of people."

"I'm aware of that," she giggled.

"But," he said, kissing her to punctuate his sentence, "we could be at my apartment in about a half hour."

She kissed him back. "I'm aware of that, too."

She wanted nothing more than to spend the night in his arms, in his bed; it had been on her mind almost every minute of every day. But she thought back to her past mistakes and desperately wanted things to be different this time. No rushing. No jumping straight into the sack, only to be hurt a few months later after all the smoke from the fireworks cleared. She couldn't afford to mess this up.

"We have plenty of time," she said. "Let's go back to the party."

"Not yet," he said, pulling her to him and kissing her again. "We still have a few minutes before they send out a search party."

"But that'll make it harder for me to resist—"

"I want to wait, too," he interrupted. "As hard as it is."

They burst out laughing at the double entendre.

"We'll have plenty of time to do the nasty," she said.

He narrowed his eyes. "Do the nasty? Did you say do the nasty?"

She laughed, embarrassed. "Oh, you just spoiled the mood!" she protested. "I can't believe you're laughing at my Bell Biv DeVoe slang." She faked a hurt look.

"No, that wasn't BBD. I'm pretty sure it was Teddy Riley who came up with that phrase, circa 1990," he laughed as they walked back to the party holding hands.

She wouldn't have the night end any other way. A man who made her laugh and who loved 1980s and early 1990s R&B was definitely the kind worth holding out for. And she was proud of herself for reining in her impulses. But as her body brushed against his as they walked down the dark street, she began to wonder if she could wait for very long.

* * *

Weslee awoke early the next day. It took a while for her to realize that last night had been real. Yes, she had been with William. Yes, he had told her that he loved her. Yes, everything was all right.

She looked outside. It was another hot and humid day. She could almost see the heaviness coating the atmosphere. But she didn't mind. She felt so calm inside. Not edgy and nervous, just peaceful and content. Last night had been an answered prayer. William had dropped her off early this morning and had told her again that he loved her. It was real, real, real.

She put on coffee. She called home. Her mother answered.

"Hi, honey. What have you been up to lately?"

She wondered where to start. "Um. I was just hanging out with William and his family last night."

"Oh?"

She hadn't told her mother the full story about William. "Yes."

"And?"

"And what? Mom, what do you mean?" Weslee tried to sound innocent.

"Child, I wasn't born yesterday. I saw the way you two were acting when he came here last summer."

"Who was acting?"

"Fine, if you want to keep secrets from your own mother, go ahead."

"OK, fine. Yes. I think I love him. No, I love him. He said he loves me, too."

Her mother laughed on the other end.

"What's so funny?"

"You young people. You meet one guy in Boston, and two weeks later you say you're in love with him. But it takes you a whole year to realize you love this one."

"Mom, I—"

"I'm not criticizing you. I'm just saying that sometimes you don't know what's good for you even when it's staring you right in the face."

"I know," Weslee said humbly. "Will you tell Dad?"

"You know I will. He'll be so happy. You know he just needs to have somebody to talk to about cricket and soccer."

"Well, Mom, I'm not saying we're going to get married or anything." Weslee tried to bring her mother back to reality before she started picking names for her future grandchildren.

"I know. I know. You don't have to tell me that," Clara Dunster said. But Weslee knew the damage had already been done.

"I'm so happy, Mom," she said, grinning like a four-year-old at her birthday party. "I met his folks, and they're so down to earth. His mom's curried chicken is soooo good."

Clara Dunster scoffed. "Better than mine?"

Weslee laughed. "I'm not going there, Mom. But they're just really good people. I felt like I was home when I was at their place last night."

"Well, you already have a home here. Don't forget that," Clara said lightly. "But I'm glad you're happy. See, didn't I tell you a long time ago to find yourself a nice West Indian boy?"

Weslee laughed. "Yeah, right, Ma." She couldn't stop laughing at her mother's self-satisfaction. "I guess you know best after all," she teased.

"You better believe I do," her mother said with all the seriousness in the world.

Weslee stifled her laughter as they said good-bye. *Trust her to take credit for every good thing that happens to me*, Weslee giggled as she hung up the phone.

Later, she sipped her coffee and paged through the *New*

York Times's Sunday Styles section. She had one more call to make.

She had picked a restaurant that wouldn't be overrun with the brunch crowd. She had to have his total attention for what she wanted to say. He was waiting for her at DeMillo's when she arrived. She noticed his skin was even browner than when she had last seen him.

"Hi, Duncan," she said in her strongest voice.

"Weslee." He nodded in a businesslike manner.

The waiter seated them, and she ordered coffee. He asked for water.

She cleared her throat.

"You look great," he said. She was dressed primly in a nondescript blue knee-length tank dress that somehow managed to accentuate her lanky frame.

"Thank you," she said as the waiter swiftly brought their beverages.

"OK, Duncan. I know that you said you wanted to talk, so I'm here to listen."

He looked deeply into her eyes, and for a moment she couldn't turn away.

"I'm a fool," he said. He took a sip of his water and continued. "I'm really sorry that I hurt you. I have no excuse except that I was selfish and cowardly. I wish I had the guts to . . ." He stopped and clenched his jaw.

"To what?" she asked. She could see the pain in his face.

"Nothing. I just wanted you to know that I'm not the heartless jerk you think I am. I have obligations that I can't just ignore."

She nodded. "Obligations to whom?"

He shook his head. "It's hard to explain without sounding like a spineless prick," he said. "But this is how my life is supposed to turn out. Everybody expects things of me, my family . . ." He swallowed. "I know exactly what my future will be if I take this path, Weslee," he said.

"And if you had picked me, you wouldn't have known? That's what it is?" Weslee wanted to laugh. All of a sudden she couldn't remember what she had seen in this man seated across from her. He did sound like a spineless prick.

"It's not that simple. No one would have understood us together."

"No one? Like who?"

He sighed. "I knew you wouldn't understand."

"Oh, I understand, Duncan," she said, picking up her canvas tote and throwing it over her shoulder. "Good-bye. And good luck with Susan."

She couldn't help but release the laughter that had been building inside her in the restaurant. The image of Duncan, in pain and struggling to justify to himself and to her his lack of courage, did not amuse her—it made her relieved that she would never have to look into his eyes again and wonder whether she was worthy. She laughed because she realized that he had never been worthy of her.

Chapter
45

It wasn't the perfect day for a wedding, but Weslee was excited all the same. She loved her dress, and at three hundred dollars, it was almost guilt free. She turned around before the full-length mirror in the bathroom of Rainee's Vineyard home to take one last inventory of her outfit. With Rainee and the rest of the wedding party already at the Van Meers' estate in Edgartown, where Peony's wedding would be held, she had the house all to herself.

She had had her doubts about this wedding. She was going primarily because Rainee had begged her. The older woman had become a friend to Weslee, and it would have been rude to turn down her invitation. Plus, William had told her, it might be a good opportunity to acquire even more clients.

She looked out the window and saw his Jeep pulling up the driveway. She ran down the stairs to meet him.

William whistled as she walked out of the house to meet him.

She did a full turn so he could see the deep vee her dress made in the back. He whistled again, and she smiled. "You like?"

"I love," he said, kissing her as she sat next to him in the SUV.

They arrived right on time, and a few minutes later Weslee could hear the entire wedding party and guests catch their breaths as Peony emerged down the aisle. She did look absolutely regal.

Her hair was pulled up into a bun on top of her head with a few tendrils curling to the side of her face, showing off her tiara veil and pearl-and-diamond button earrings. Her dress was pure white satin, form-fitted with a sweetheart neckline and flaring at midthigh with a long train. "It's a Vera Wang," Rainee had told Weslee. "Thank God her father and his new wife are paying for everything," she had laughed.

Weslee stole a look over at Lana, who sat between her mother, Eleanor, and her boyfriend, Jeffrey Knight. Her face was expressionless as she watched Peony make her way down the aisle to where her husband-to-be, Stewart, was waiting nervously.

The ceremony started, and she could see Rainee pulling out a tissue as the female minister began the exhortation. Rainee had said she was not going to cry.

As the minister pronounced Stewart and Peony man and wife, Weslee couldn't help but steal a glance at William. He squeezed her hand.

Later, at the reception, she found herself running into people who now knew her and asked about her, her business, her life. She had planned to stay close to William throughout the event, but she found herself wandering off on her own to make small talk with acquaintances. She was surprised to discover that Younis Pratha's husband was such a gloomy little man, and she could see why he hadn't opened his dream restaurant. Marie Bunting was haughty and overbearing as usual. Eleanor was polite, and her husband ignored Weslee, but she still smiled at him. She in no way felt at home with this crowd, but at least she did not feel the urge to run under a rock and hide.

She and William joined the line waiting to greet the new bride and groom.

"Having a good time?" he asked, his arm around her waist.

"Absolutely." She grinned.

Peony was radiant as her guests fawned over her.

"Congratulations, Peony. You look absolutely stunning," Weslee said, meaning every word. She shook Stewart's limp, sweaty hand.

"Thank you, Weslee." Peony smiled widely. "Hey, maybe once we get back from Indonesia, we could all get together for lunch, you, me, and my mom," she said, her eyes wide.

"Sure," Weslee said, knowing that this would never come to pass.

As William stopped to talk with another of his best friends from college, she surveyed the room. There were at least five hundred people there. She hoped that she would not run into Duncan—his own wedding was in two weeks—but if she did, she was prepared to ignore him.

She felt a tap on her shoulder.

"Hi, Wes," Lana said, smiling.

"Hey," Weslee said, nervousness creeping up on her.

"How are you?" Lana asked.

"Good, and you?"

"I'm doing well. Hey, do you want to go outside and talk for a bit?"

Weslee hesitated, looking at William, who was so engrossed in his conversation that he did not even notice she was trying to get his attention.

She nodded and followed Lana out the double doors of the great room to a huge patio that looked out onto the harbor way down below.

"I won't be coming back to BU in the fall," Lana stated.

"Oh?" Weslee wasn't surprised; Lana's grades were probably the worst in their entire cohort.

"I'm going to Barcelona for a year. Jeffrey and I are kinda serious, and ScanBank is sending him to their Spanish headquarters for a bit. Besides, I've always preferred being overseas than being in the States."

"Wow," Weslee said. "That's really exciting. I wish you the best of luck." A part of her felt relieved that she would never have to put up with Lana's antics on campus anymore, but another part of her still missed the fun times that they had shared.

"Listen, I know I've done and said some things to you that were . . . But anyway, I can't begin to tell you how sorry I am."

Weslee sighed. She was beginning to feel weary of all the apologies that were coming her way.

Lana continued. "I wish things had been different. I really liked you. I mean, I still like you. But I have a really hard time keeping girlfriends, you know?"

Weslee nodded and smiled gamely. If this was going to be Lana's version of mending things between them, she would accept it and move on. But she didn't want to rehash the past, so she tried to change the subject. "I really like your dress," she said, looking at the pink silken form-fitting sheath with the uneven hemline that Lana was wearing.

"Really? It's vintage. I paid twenty bucks for it at a store in SoHo."

"No way!" Weslee said.

"You better believe it," Lana said. "I have their address somewhere. I can e-mail it to you. I think they have a Web site, too!"

"Oh, could you?" Weslee asked, forgetting the past for a second. In that brief exchange they were like their old selves again, crazy for clothes and willing to talk about it for days and days on end. Weslee found herself smiling guiltily as it occurred to her that those days were behind her and that she and Lana had both changed so much since those wild times over a year ago.

"So, you and Will have a thing going now, I see." Lana's voice was teasing.

Weslee rolled her eyes, smiling, and then shrugged.

"He's good for you, I can tell," she said. "I still can't believe Duncan let you get away from him."

"I really don't want to talk about that, Lana." A small part of her wanted to know whether he was there somewhere among the hundreds of guests, but deep down she knew that it was better that she didn't know. It would only ruin the good time she was having. She wondered if Lana truly meant what she said, that Duncan shouldn't have let her get away. Or was she just trying to be nice? She didn't know the answer to that. *I guess I'll never totally figure her out,* Weslee thought.

"I know," Lana continued. "I'm sorry for bringing it up. But you seem so happy . . . I'm going to have to miss his wedding, but it's better this way. I cannot stand Susan. A lot of people are saying it won't last."

Was this another of Lana's half-truths? "I heard you're one of the bridesmaids," Weslee said. This fact, probably more than any rude comment or snub by Lana, had hurt like hell. The fact that Lana would be in Susan's wedding, knowing what had happened between Duncan and Weslee, had felt like the ultimate betrayal.

"I was, but I quit. She had too many demands. Plus, you should see the dress, Wes. It is awful. It's the ugliest thing I've ever seen in my life. She had some college friend of hers design it." Lana made a face. "So tacky!"

Weslee laughed. Typical Lana. She'd quit the wedding party, but not on principle. In the end it was all about Lana. But Weslee felt a tiny bit of doubt. Maybe Lana had considered her feelings but was too proud to admit it. *Another thing I may never know for sure*, Weslee thought.

They stood out on the patio, talking casually like nothing bad had happened. Lana was full of plans, Weslee realized: to become fluent in Spanish, finish her MBA, and settle down in Barcelona for a few years. "Bumming around" was what she called it. And it all sounded so exciting and glamorous to Weslee. But she wasn't envious, nor did she want to trade places with Lana. She smiled as she caught William approaching from the corner of her eye.

"Oh, I need to get going, too," Lana said as Weslee signaled to William to wait.

"Lana, will you call me to let me know how you're doing?" Weslee asked.

Lana dropped her head slightly, pretending to look in her purse. "Sure, Wes."

Weslee couldn't help herself. She impulsively opened her arms and hugged Lana tightly.

"I'm going to miss you," Lana said, her voice muffled in Weslee's embrace.

"I'll miss you, too," Weslee said and held her at arm's length.

They looked at each other awkwardly.

"I'll see you again." Lana smiled, her eyes wet. "And I'll definitely be in touch."

But Weslee knew better. Her gut told her that this was it, and for some reason that feeling made her want to sob like a baby.

"Bye, Lana," she said. "And thanks for the . . . you know . . . the, uh . . . makeover."

Lana managed a smile, but her lower lip trembled a bit. She raised her right hand and waved, walking away into the crowded dining room.

Minutes later, William and Weslee stood out on the patio and watched as Jeffrey and Lana drove away from the estate.

"You OK?" he asked.

She's gone for good, Weslee thought, biting the inside of her mouth. "I bet I'll never hear from her again," she said. She leaned into William's body as his arms pulled her close.

Chapter
46

Two and three-fifths miles to go, and how Weslee ached. She could feel and hear the crowds on either side of Beacon Street, thousands deep, loud and boisterous on this cool, sunny April morning. But she didn't see them. She looked straight ahead at the back of the head of the runner directly in front of her, a shirtless young man whose thick blond hair was curly and dripping with sweat.

The end was pretty much in sight, but she didn't let up. She would make her time. Two hours and fifty minutes with just about two miles to go. She had done it. She had run the Boston Marathon, and it really wasn't that bad.

OK, it was bad.

"Water ahead. Water ahead."

"Gatorade ahead!"

Volunteers were screaming from the sidelines. It hurt to lift her feet just a bit higher to avoid the tiny paper cups abandoned and strewn on the streets by the front-of-the-pack runners.

But Weslee wouldn't stop. She could feel the finish line.

She stole a glance at her watch. Yes, she would make it in three twenty-two or so if she didn't slow down. So she kept on running hard. Her thighs, shins, ankles, knees—they were all doing something a little bit more violent than just hurting. But her heart rate was steady, and so was her breathing. So she knew that she was OK. It was just pain. That she knew she could handle.

The man's hair kept getting wetter and curlier. Was he increasing his speed? He was her rabbit; she had to keep up with him. Yes, he was running faster. She heaved a huge breath and tried to stay on his back.

Think of something else.

But Weslee really didn't want to lose her focus by thinking too hard, too far. This race, her time, meant too much to her. It had been almost two years in coming, this race. And what was at the finish line was her own little victory.

She knew William was waiting for her. He had promised to personally carry her across the finish line if she couldn't make it. Sherry was waiting, too, camera in hand. She wasn't there yet, but already she felt proud. It had taken her so much to get to this point.

She wouldn't win or break any records. She probably wouldn't even impress many people. But that finish was the line that officially put her in the present she had started creating two years ago and almost hadn't.

Three hours down, twenty-five and a half miles behind her, and boy, did she ache.